THE
HUNTING

Also by Sam Hawksmoor
The Repossession

THE
HUNTING

SAM HAWKSMOOR

*Hodder
Children's
Books*

A division of Hachette Children's Books

First published in Great Britain in 2012
by Hodder Children's Books

1

A Catalogue record for this book is available from the British Library

ISBN: 978 0 340 99709 3

Typeset in Berkeley by Avon DataSet Ltd,
Bidford on Avon, Warwickshire

Printed and bound by CPI Group
(UK) Ltd, Croydon, CR0 4YY

The paper and board used in this paperback by Hodder Children's Books
are natural recyclable products made from wood grown in
sustainable forests. The manufacturing processes conform to the
environmental regulations of the country of origin.

Hodder Children's Books
a division of Hachette Children's Books
338 Euston Road, London NW1 3BH
An Hachette UK company
www.hachette.co.uk

For the YA bloggers from all over that came to the support of Genie and Rian. And thanks to their blogs I discovered a whole host of books I now want to read.

Thanks too to Beverley and Naomi for guiding *The Hunting* through the editorial process at Hodder and Michelle for the brilliant covers. Cheers also to my former students at Portsmouth who kept the faith and will one day be on everyone's iPads and Kindles themselves.

1

Test Subject

Carson Strindberg was in the observation room at the Fortress. The assembled technicians were tense, the atmosphere electric. No one wanted anything to go wrong. Strindberg, the new boss of Fortransco, had a reputation of being hard to please, ruthless with anyone who screwed up. All their jobs were on the line.

The clock said twenty-three hundred hours. A preliminary countdown had already begun. This would be Strindberg's first teleport experience and he was secretly very excited. This was where all the billions had been spent. Everything came down to mere nanoseconds of intense concentrated power.

The test subject was a hitchhiker from Newfoundland brought in by Strindberg himself. The kid had no idea of what was to come. Only that he'd get two thousand dollars cash for just standing very still under bright hot lights. They'd shaved his head, got him wearing a white close-fitting T-shirt and shorts. The way he figured it – he was broke – this would be the easiest

1

two thousand dollars he'd ever make.

The technicians in their spacesuits had to maintain a pristine atmosphere. The only DNA in the teleport chamber would be the hitchhiker's. There could be no shortcuts with Strindberg watching.

Twenty-five seconds flashed on the lab wall in big red numbers.

Strindberg had given him a ride on his way to the airfield. The kid considered it his lucky day when an Aston Martin Virage Volante rag top slowed to a stop beside him. He'd been waiting for a ride for hours and almost given up. He'd always wanted to ride in an Aston and getting picked up by the silver-haired short guy had been the luckiest thing that had happened to him since he'd reached B.C.

'Cool car,' he'd said, putting his knapsack in the small trunk.

'Broke? Need money?' Strindberg had asked as he drove. 'We're looking for young test subjects like you.'

'Test subject?'

'Observation experiment, new sub-atomic enhancement process. Got anything you always wished you could get rid of? That birthmark on your neck, for example. We could erase that, give you a perfect neck.'

The kid instinctively pulled his collar up. It had been

the cause of much strife in his life. Been teased and bullied about it for years.

'We can take care of that, for free,' Strindberg had informed him casually.

'So it's like plastic surgery?' he'd asked, trying not to sound interested.

'But better, faster, non-invasive. Zero pain and comes with full restoration of an unblemished neck. Cost you twenty thousand dollars to get that removed privately – more, probably.'

'Really?' It sounded too good to be true.

'Really. We do a complete DNA map of your body. I mean complete and it's just a blast of sub-atomic particles and you're practically perfect again.'

'Practically?'

'We can take care of blemishes, but we can't fix psychological problems. Been backpacking long? When did you last let your folks know where you are?'

'Haven't logged on since I left St John's. Wanted to take time to think, y'know. I wanted a lot to think about . . . experiences.'

Strindberg had smiled. Perfect. A complete loner. No one to ask questions. He drove to the waiting chopper that would take them to the Fortress.

They had bounced across the field towards the waiting

helicopter, a Sikorsky S-92. The kid was impressed, it was huge and the Fortransco logo on the side was somehow reassuring that they wouldn't stiff him the money. Living on the road had taught him a lot about whom to trust. The waiting crew opened the car doors and were all smiles.

'One Newfie volunteer. Make him comfortable,' Strindberg told the crew. 'What's the weather like at the Fortress?'

'Wet, windy. Not ideal,' the pilot told him.

Strindberg shrugged. 'Well, we have to go. They're waiting for me.' He turned to the kid. 'Coming?'

The kid had seemed impressed. An Aston Martin and a chopper ride all in one day. He'd hesitated a moment and Strindberg smiled, putting an arm around his shoulder to reassure him.

'I think you're going to be impressed by this outfit,' he told him. 'They just had a major breakthrough. I'm going there now to do some reorganization.'

'Can I get paid up front?' the kid had asked.

Strindberg grinned and reeled him in. 'Absolutely. I'm afraid you can't eat until after, but we'll make sure you go away happy. Guarantee it.' He looked at the kid, knew that he was going to do it. He wanted the ride on the chopper. Desperately needed that two thousand dollars.

'Name's Carson Strindberg, by the by. One day soon we're going to be one of the world's biggest cosmetic restructuring companies. That's why we need test subjects. You won't regret it.'

The kid had grinned and practically jumped up on to the chopper.

This really was his lucky day.

Twenty seconds.

And now almost ten hours later, hungry and thirsty, despite the glass of thick orange juice they had just made him swallow, he stood waiting, staring at the men and women in spacesuits as they scanned his body, collating his DNA. Without his hair, the birthmark was huge, from his neck and right across his left shoulder. That too had to be taken into account and mapped so the skin tone that replaced it would be the same as the rest of his body.

The countdown moved to fifteen seconds. He briefly thought of the money paid to him, lying in the locker in the anteroom. He'd head north almost immediately. He wanted to go to Alaska before winter set in – maybe get a job. Anything would do, just as long as he didn't have to go back to St John's.

He focused on the light.

'We want you to relax. Focus on the blue light ahead of you.'

Strindberg watched keenly from the observation room as a technician adjusted the cameras recording the event. 'These are the exact conditions that prevailed when Genie Magee transmitted?'

'Exact, sir, except for the fire. Didn't think we should try to replicate that.'

Strindberg watched the kid and thought how relaxed and trusting he was, totally unsuspecting. Genie Magee had been like this too on her transmission recording. She had looked so relaxed. Or resigned, perhaps.

Five seconds.

The Chief Technician arrived and took the seat next to Strindberg.

'You fond of executions, Chief? Hadn't expected to see you here.'

The Chief attempted a smile. 'This might work this time.'

Strindberg made a note of the Chief's 'might'.

'You're sure this is an exact replication of Genie Magee's transmission test?' Strindberg asked again. He didn't take his eyes off the platform or TV screen showing the empty teleport chamber over in Synchro thirty-five kilometres away.

Two seconds.

The transmission signal went to green for go. The platforms were in synch.

A warning buzzer sounded, signalling a transmission was about to begin.

The kid vanished from the platform. Strindberg was astonished. *It worked*. The damn thing really worked. All those billions hadn't been wasted after all.

Almost instantly the boy reappeared on the Synchro teleport platform. His birthmark was gone. He opened his eyes, blinked – then exactly three point six seconds later spectacularly exploded in a hot flash, casting a black shadow on the curved white wall. Some blood traces trickled down from uncarbonized bits of flesh on the remote camera lens.

Strindberg was momentarily shocked. The Chief held his silence.

'DNA capture ninety-nine point six per cent,' the computer announced dispassionately. 'Subject partially stored on servers 18000 to 19450. Test subject conscious for three point zero zero three seconds.'

Strindberg, recovering, pursed his lips. He was annoyed. He didn't know if they got carbon blowback because the kid was only ninety-nine point six per cent transmitted or what? He needed answers. Clearly this almost worked, but *almost* was completely lethal.

'I want a complete analysis on my desk in an hour. Check the stability algorithms. I want to know what that missing zero point four per cent was and why it hasn't come through. I want solutions, people. Now.'

Strindberg stomped out of the room, glancing briefly at the TV screen showing the carbonized shadow on the Synchro teleport chamber wall. It struck him that it looked a lot like an angel with its wings outstretched.

Even before he left the room the Newfie's effects were being burned, all evidence that he had ever been there erased. He never even existed.

2

The Getaway

'Go. Go. Go,' Rian yelled, frantically paddling against the current. The roar of the river ahead was deafening, made more frightening by the extreme darkness.

The sound of the angry waters being forced into a temporary sluice at one corner of the river was deafening. They could hear but not see, and that scared them even more as it pulled them ever closer.

'Faster, we're not moving quick enough,' Rian shouted, beginning to panic.

'I'm telling you, there's no waterfall on this part of the river,' Renée insisted, paddling just as hard. Huge shadows surrounded them and jostling, bucking trees, some twenty-five metres long or more, nudged the rubber raft as they struggled to make headway.

Moucher barked, sure they were headed to their doom.

They were just moments away from the surging water ahead; if they got trapped they could be crushed and lost for sure.

They could see the shadows of massive trees at weird

angles, all jammed up around them. It was as if a giant had sprinkled a complete forest on to the river and left it to its fate. A perfect log-jam.

'Get ready to jump,' Rian shouted. 'Grab the dog, Genie.'

She already had Moucher in her grip.

'You jump when I tell you,' she commanded into Mouch's ear.

Mouch's eyes were on stalks, terrified. He so desperately wanted to be back on dry land.

The raft crunched against the rocks on the riverbank and Rian jumped out, nearly missing his step and falling.

'Everyone, out now,' he called.

Mouch flew in a perfect leap to safety, propelling Genie to the back of the raft. Renée gathered what little food and water they had and jumped clear. Genie picked herself up at last and followed.

Rian quickly hauled the raft out of the water, pausing only to catch his breath. Only when his vision cleared did he realize just how close to oblivion they had been.

He looked back up the highway towards Spurlake from where they'd escaped. Thought he saw a car, but it was a trick of the light. He didn't want them exposed like this for long. Fortransco would soon work out they'd evaded the roadblocks.

'We have to get the raft up over our heads,' Rian told them.

Renée was nervous. She'd been thinking they were going to get away. Now they'd be on the road – the only road – carrying a raft no less, and with half of Spurlake looking for them.

'We should have gone over the mountain,' she said.

'Snakes, remember?' Genie reminded her.

'Together,' Rian instructed them. 'Up and over.'

The two girls groaned, but it had to be done.

'Heel, Mouch,' Genie told the dog.

'On my mark – one, two, three . . .'

They got the raft up over their heads, cold water dripping down their necks. Flipped it over and nearly got crowned by the paddles Renée was supposed to have stowed away. Rian bent down and got the paddles secured without losing his grip.

'Keep up and stay in step,' he told them as they set off, keeping right to the edge of the road on the riverside.

Genie reflected on why they were fleeing from Spurlake and the evil Fortress all over again. Why couldn't they just forget them, let them go? But she knew, as sure as they faced certain death on this treacherous river, that the possibility of them being allowed to live was pretty remote. Especially now there was a ten-thousand-dollar reward on their heads for their capture. Times were tough; a lot of people would want that cash. Worse, Reverend Schneider was out of police custody and he'd be looking for revenge. What hurt most was the shame she felt that her whole town and all the people in it didn't seem to care about the missing kids. They'd rather believe all the lies Fortransco told about alien abductions – anything rather than believe that thirty-six kids, probably more by now, had all been used in teleportation experiments by the Fortress and most had died in grotesque explosions.

A few people had helped them. Marshall back on the farm, but he'd been beaten and nearly killed for his efforts. And Officer Miller, his son, was probably going to lose his job on the force for all he'd done for them. Then old man Ferry at the gas station, who'd given them the raft to escape downriver to Vancouver once they realized they couldn't get past all the roadblocks.

Thank God for Denis's warning phone call. They'd got out of Spurlake just in time, but it begged the question as to what had happened to Denis, or Cary Harrison or Julia? They'd be hunting down Miho, too, all of them, one by one, grabbing them back to do yet more vile experiments. Herself and Renée were probably the only survivors, the kids who had lived through teleportation and hadn't died. They were valuable. Like Renée said, as important as the first men on the moon. They should be on chat shows – hell, given a parade at least and huge movie deals. Only it was all supposed to be a big secret and no one knew, no one even believed all they'd gone through it. The Fortress didn't want them outside, free to tell tales of their abduction, the horrible crimes committed against children – and worse, no one was even prepared to consider the evidence. Officer Miller had shown the Vancouver investigators the bodies of kids who didn't make it and the half-dog in the freezer, but they weren't buying it. It was incredible to her that people would rather believe in aliens or mass hysteria than the truth, that there was a billion-dollar business in their town making kids vanish into thin air.

Genie stumbled and quickly corrected herself. 'Sorry,' she mumbled. It was hard to keep in step and her shoulders ached.

'Not far now,' Rian shouted from the front, praying the road would stay empty.

Rain began to spatter them again, picking up strength.

The moon peeped from behind the rain-heavy clouds briefly and they could finally see across the river. The log-jam was huge. The biggest Genie had ever seen and it was forcing all the river water to one side as the dam built up. Hundreds, thousands of clear-cut fir trees dumped into the river and sent downstream. They were all supposed to go by road or rail; it was the law to protect salmon and whatever. All were now snagged on a bend in the river. It was part of the landscape in these parts that whole forests got cleared on maturation, but she'd never seen so many in the river at one time. It was choked. She guessed the flood in August must have had something to do with this. Once they were in the river they were hardly likely to fish them out, might as well let them float their way down the Fraser like the old days. She felt sorry for the salmon; how would they get through?

Renée was rubbernecking as well. 'I can't believe this. You sure we want to be in front of this? If the dam breaks we're going to get creamed.'

Rian's arms ached. He was glad he had made the decision; the churning sluice of water that escaped downriver was way too violent for a raft like theirs. They would have been smashed to pieces. This rain was falling like crazy now, beating hard against the road and there would be more of it before the night was done.

'Like the flood all over again,' Genie remarked.

'Don't even think it,' Rian called back. To this day he couldn't believe he and Genie had lived through that, let alone wound up in the exact same place with a pig in tow. 'Keep going. We're going back on to the river about a hundred metres further up. That log-jam won't break without someone forcing it apart. Might have to blow it up.'

'I hope you're right,' Renée said, still not convinced.

'Keep up, Mouch,' Genie called. 'Mouch, where are you?'

Mouch appeared at her side and she wasn't sure but it looked to her as if he'd managed to pull off one sock. 'Mouch? Where's your front left sock? You're supposed to be wearing socks.'

Mouch looked up at her as if she was crazy. It had taken him almost ten whole minutes to get just one sock off. Dogs were not supposed to wear socks. End of story.

They saw the headlights coming towards them. It sounded like a big truck, its noisy engine echoing off the canyon walls.

'We hide?' Genie asked from the rear.

'Move to the edge and crouch,' Rian called out, trying to be heard over the crash of the water beside them. Rian didn't want the driver telling anyone in Spurlake about some people carrying a raft by the side of the road at midnight. Just the kind of stupid thing someone might overhear and realize it was the kids they were looking for.

They crouched, Genie grabbing Mouch to her side. All

four welcomed a moment of rest under the raft as the truck hurtled past, bits of gravel and spray spattering them.

'Up,' Rian instructed.

Renée and Genie followed him up and they began walking again.

It started to rain even harder.

'Oh joy,' Renée exclaimed. 'Couldn't we live somewhere warmer and drier?'

'We're on our way to Mexico, remember.'

'Yeah, but like we could win some sort of prize for the slowest way to cross the border,' Renée replied.

'Getting colder too,' Genie said grinning. 'Come on, girl, we're still ahead. Least you've still got hair to keep you dry.' Genie still resented the Fortress had shaved her head before transmission.

'OK, we're here,' Rian announced. The girls stopped behind him. 'This is the tricky bit. We have to move forward as one and flip the raft on to the river. Got that?'

'Aye-aye, Captain,' Genie replied.

'Yours to command, brother dear,' Renée added.

They stepped off the road and then, keeping it steady, shimmied down the rocks and shale to the water's edge.

'We're going to flip – that's arms up, toss it up away from you and step back. On three. One, two, three.'

It sort of went right. Renée, being taller than Genie, maybe pushed too hard and Genie almost slipped, so didn't push quite enough. The raft almost flipped three hundred and sixty degrees, but Rian caught it in time and it landed right side up with a smack in the water.

'Lucky,' Genie said. 'I thought it was a goner for sure.'

Rian grabbed the raft, worried the current was still running fiercely. 'Get in, guys. Renée, you got the stuff?'

'I got it.'

'Grab Mouch,' Rian told Genie. He could see the dog was backing away. Moucher hated being on water. Didn't mind swimming, just didn't like boats.

'Come here, you little beast. I can't believe you lost a sock already. No walking around; your claws might puncture the bottom, OK?'

Mouch had no plans to walk at all, he was just planning on shaking with fear for the whole way down the river.

Rian jumped in and pushed them off, unpacking the paddles from the straps.

'Finally we are on our way,' he said, looking back at the foaming water behind them. It was too dark to see anything much, but you could hear it loud enough.

'Damn it, I meant to pee,' Renée declared.

'Next stop,' Rian told her. 'You'll have to wait.'

Renée was about to say something sarcastic but thought

better of it. He was doing exactly what they asked him to do, keeping them safe, and she could wait – well, a little while at least.

It began to hail; freezing hard balls of ice pummelled their heads.

'I guess we didn't think to pack an umbrella,' Genie remarked as she tried to calm Mouch, who was trying to burrow under her to get away from the stinging hailstones.

'Just paddle, it'll keep you warm at least,' Rian told her. 'We've got a very long way to go.'

3

Strindberg

Strindberg surveyed the assembled employees of the Fortress, his face impassive. Everyone was severely peeved at him for making them meet up on the roof earlier and, of course, completely humiliated. It was the way he liked it; it made anything he had to say sink in a lot better.

They now stood in the Blue Room – the emergency assembly point, five floors below the surface, the stench of damp human beings giving the air-conditioning a hard time. Strindberg looked at the faces; sheer terror met his eyes. They knew that at least half of them were going to lose their jobs. He raised his hand for their attention.

'I'm going to have some names called. All those called will go directly to the Green Room above here and meet with a Mr Yates.'

An assistant called out a lot of names and those called shuffled out of the room. Were these the ones *with* jobs or those about to be fired? Reverend Schneider looked over those remaining around him and noted with some concern that all the people departed were employees with family. It was just a detail, but significant, he thought.

Everyone remained silent, sitting and standing uncomfortably in their damp clothes waiting for something to happen. Strindberg finally smiled. That was the most disconcerting thing of all, as his teeth seemed to be made of neon white.

'Congratulations. You all still have jobs. For now.'

You could hear quite a few people exhale with relief.

'Let me put this nicely,' Strindberg began. 'Fortransco is a small research centre with a very large cash-burning capacity. Two point one billion dollars to be precise, in the last three years. Two billion spent and, until a few days ago, absolutely zilch to show for thirteen years of active research. Frankly that just isn't good enough.'

No one said anything, they were still waiting to see what 'punishment' he was going to hand out. Strindberg had a reputation for being mean and vindictive.

Strindberg stood slightly on his toes in his two-thousand-dollar Italian leather shoes with raised heels to compensate for his lack of height. 'So, when we learned of your minor miracle, an actual success of nine complete whole-body transmissions, it seemed to be a cause for celebration. Imagine my surprise to discover that you had no idea of how or why the transmissions worked.'

Still no one spoke.

'In fact, were it not for the rapid actions of Reverend Schneider here, you may never have known you'd had a success at all. Nine successful transmissions and not one person here at the Fortress knew about it. Each one of those priceless assets was allowed to run anywhere they pleased, totally unobserved, unrecorded, unmonitored, able to communicate with the authorities, contact the press, expose Fortransco to unwanted scrutiny.

'The most stunning success in scientific history gone – *poof*.'

Everyone stared at the floor. It was true, all of it. Everyone felt truly ashamed – except Reverend Schneider, who felt relieved that he had had the foresight to get word of Genie's reappearance to the Fortress.

'Such carelessness, such disregard for company property will not be overlooked. I have been assured that we will have all nine test subjects back in the Fortress within twenty-four hours. Three are already recovered and our legal department has imposed a gagging order on the parents and all the people who have come into contact with them.

'The cloning division has made some progress in establishing DNA ownership of these test subjects. Fortransco is in the frontline of cell regeneration regulation and we will defend our rights in this area vigorously.

'We have managed to control the local story, so far. The "alien abduction" theory is keeping the supermarket tabloids busy and off our backs.

'This is a billion-dollar organization and had better start acting like one. More specifically, I need child zero. Known to outsiders as Genie, but to us as T309. We have offered a ten-thousand-dollar reward for her capture and also for the capture of another child called Renée.'

Strindberg put his notes down and folded his arms.

'That's it. You have twenty-four hours to work out why the transmission worked and to get the assets back, or *all* of you will be flipping burgers for the rest of your lives. Am I clear? There's a thousand engineers and IT specialists out there who will work for half your pay and be glad of the money. It's your choice.'

4

Water Rats

Renée took her turn with the paddle and Genie swapped places on the raft. The rain and hail had passed over at last; the moon was more often glimpsed between clouds, all of which made it a whole lot easier to see where they were going.

'I can't believe we're back on the river,' Genie moaned, as Rian and Renée paddled. 'I mean, did I ever once study even one book on survival, what to eat, how to suck poison bits out? We just run and never plan anything.'

'We've got potato chips,' Renée reminded her.

Genie ignored her. 'What if it takes weeks to get downriver? It's over a hundred and eighty ks. We're in a raft with no engine, half the river is filled with logs that can crush us at any moment, it's either raining or freezing hail, some bug keeps dive-bombing me and there's rapids ahead . . .'

Rian just smiled. 'You forgot dangerous bears.'

'Thanks, Ri. That helps.' She gave him a mean stare.

Rian steered them into deeper water. 'You're right. We

23

don't know anything about surviving out in the wild. I can't tell the difference between a toadstool and a mushroom. Always meant to learn.'

'I'm hanging on to the chips,' Renée declared.

Genie had very bad memories of floating downriver and this raft felt real easy to tip. Moucher didn't like it one bit, nor the socks they had made him wear. He kept trying to tear off the last three and getting a slap on his paws for his trouble.

Rian knew how worried Genie was. Moonlight gave them a good view ahead and he could see she was anxious about everything.

'Don't panic. Clouds are thinning, we're going to be fine.'

'No talking either,' Renée whispered. 'Voices carry to the shore. Remember I've been out on this river a lot more than you guys have.'

Renée and Rian paddled, keeping the raft steady and moving forward at speed. They didn't need to do much; the current was carrying them at a fair lick at this stage.

Genie sipped water from a bottle. Her job was lookout and she kept a keen eye out for the cops on either side of the riverbank. They were passing Hope now. Greenwood Island would be on her right, she figured. She'd done a school project on the blue herons that nested there.

Streetlights glittered in the small town, virtually nothing moved. It had to be about two a.m. They were well past any roadblocks and far from roads, but soon the river would curve back in and the highway would be right alongside, making them very vulnerable.

They suddenly spun to the left as a surge of water entered from the Coquihalla River. Normally docile, it was unusually swollen after all that rain. Renée nearly lost her balance and the whole raft tilted badly. Moucher whined, Genie clung on and Renée shipped her paddle, suddenly spraying water over them all.

'You know I can't swim much, right?' she said.

Genie looked at her with surprise. 'No.'

'Had an accident when I was twelve. Just can't seem to swim so well any more. Sorry, kinda embarrassing.'

Rian turned to her and whispered, 'Don't worry, we'll save your skinny ass.'

'It ain't as skinny as Genie's.'

'You leave my ass out of this,' Genie said.

'Shh,' Renée warned them. 'Feel that?'

The water seemed to be vibrating around them. There was a distant audible noise like rolling thunder some way off.

The raft drifted into calmer water and they all looked up at the sky. Two helicopters flying in formation, some distance off yet, but clearly audible.

'I can feel it coming,' Genie said, growing anxious. 'Mosquito attack.' She swore and Renée quickly shipped her paddle and put her hands over her ears.

Rian could see a bridge up ahead, a car driving towards it illuminating the huge structure. He hadn't been down the river this far before but knew there weren't many crossings.

'Maybe the bridge will give you some protection?'

Genie hoped so; Renée was already suffering. The Mosquito chopper might be a way off, but it was near enough to give them a powerful sub-sonic blast of pain aimed exactly at their central nervous system. They had been brain-mapped at the Fortress and the technicians knew exactly how to make them scream. Rian was safe; he'd never been caught – yet.

Genie put her hands over her ears; it offered temporary relief at least. Rian desperately tried to get them moving faster towards the bridge, but without Renée paddling the raft kept veering to the left.

The helicopter searchlights seemed to be following the river. Did they know where they were? They'd been only been on the water for a short while and hadn't gone far. One thing was for sure, the Fortress wasn't going to give up. They wanted Genie and Renée real bad.

'Ri,' Genie cried out, unable to stop the noise in her head now.

Moucher began barking but she couldn't hear him. Renée curled up into a ball at the bottom of the raft, emitting a low moan.

Rian closed the distance between them and the bridge as fast as he could. The bridge was huge, stretching over two sections of the river, supported by vast pylons sunk into a middle island. As they approached, Rian grabbed a steel pylon and held on.

Genie and Renée were writhing in pain; unable to think or do anything other than hear the intense buzzing in their ears. Moucher was howling at the choppers as the powerful searchlights penetrated every dark corner of the river.

Rian guided the raft right between the pylons, jumping out and dragging it on to the mud-covered cement. Genie opened her eyes. The choppers were almost on them, but suddenly she felt the noise in her head fade. Renée stirred too, looking up at the bridge overhead as the road blocked the searchlights. The choppers passed directly above them and moved on downriver, lights sweeping from side to side as they searched.

Renée suddenly leaned over the side and retched. Moucher pawed Genie, seeking reassurance that she was all right. Genie rubbed her neck, which was strangely hot and sore, but she knew she was fine. It was like the bridge had pulled a knife out of their heads. Amazing.

Rian suddenly saw blue lights reflected in the water. A cop car had pulled up on the bridge overhead. He put his fingers to his lips to prevent anyone saying anything. He couldn't stop Renée being sick, but at least she could do it as quietly as possible and hope they wouldn't hear it.

You could hear the police radio squawking – and Renée was right, voices carried over water. The cops were out of their vehicle looking at the river, two of them, talking casually to each other.

'You see that?'

'What?'

'Shooting star.'

'No way.'

'Yes way. Right over your head. You missed it, John. I get the wish, not you.'

'I wish you'd shut up.'

'Bright green. Means copper, right. It was full of copper.'

'You're full of something. Get in the car. We have to check Sandbrook. If I were a runaway, I'd head there.'

'It's closed. Closed September the second.'

'And it's empty. A complete vacation resort to hide it. Come on, or ain't you interested in ten grand?'

28

One of them swore and they heard two doors slam before the vehicle took off, crossing the bridge, its headlights illuminating the forest the other side of the river.

Rian looked at Genie and smiled. 'We got to keep moving.'

'You think the river's a good idea?' Renée asked fighting nausea. 'What if the choppers come back?'

Genie gave Mouch a hug. 'We find a bridge fast. At least we know pylons can block the signal.'

Renée shook her head. 'Only one more bridge and that's like miles downstream. We'd have no protection.'

'It's still safer than the road. We're not going to walk to Vancouver, Renée. Come on, give me a hand, we need to get this free.'

'How do we get back at them?' Renée asked, a sense of bitterness overwhelming her. 'I mean, you see these movies about journalists and TV reporters exposing criminals all the time and here's us, we know this is like one of the biggest crimes against kids ever and they're getting away with it. Doesn't that make you mad? We should march into like *The Province*'s office in Vancouver and—'

'And what?' Rian asked. 'You think they'd ever take us seriously? Kids being used for teleportation experiments? No one believed us last time we tried that. The frickin

29

press didn't even turn up. They come when we go missing, but we come back, it's like, oh yeah, alien abduction. We should be so lucky. I fancy our chances better with aliens than the damn Fortress.'

Rian looked over at Renée. 'Don't rock the raft. Keep still.'

'I'm just trying to get comfortable. So what are you guys saying? We just let the Fortress roll over us?'

'We save our asses first. Then think about getting even.'

'We're picking up speed, guys,' Renée observed.

'Hold on,' Genie said, gripping the sides. The water was shallower under them now they were beyond Hope, beneath them treacherous rocks.

The night rushed by. Genie was paddling with Rian now; Renée resting with Mouch, both cuddled up close for comfort, stealing each other's warmth.

Genie had a sudden strange vision that she'd been here before. On this very part of the river in fact, paddle in hand. Only it wasn't her, it was another her she was sensing – and she too was on the water, in a canoe, sitting on a deer pelt in the prow, her husband behind her and a child – *her child* – sleeping beside her. It was the weirdest sensation. She felt a chill sweep over her. She examined the canoe; it was made of wood, carved with salmon motifs and there were some corn cobs by her knees. She looked back at her child sleeping contentedly in a basket and although she couldn't see her husband in the dark, she could feel him and sense his pride.

It was so weird, but also fascinating. This was different to her other trances. Before she had always been in the present, but this was a canoe a hundred or two hundred years earlier. It was exciting and scary being in two worlds at once. She instinctively knew she had been travelling on this river all her life. There were dangers too. Other tribes . . . Her other self was deathly worried about straying into unknown waters. Genie in the present wondered where she had been going.

'Genie? Genie?' Rian was calling her.

Genie realized that she wasn't paddling. Rian was looking at her strangely.

'You OK?'

She swallowed, suddenly dizzy as she was jerked back to reality. 'Er – sure. Just had a weird moment, that's all.'

As Genie resumed paddling she had a strong belief that her ancestors were right there with her. Couldn't see them now, but she could feel them, still feel the presence of the canoe and see her baby's little face. The small part of her that was First Nation knew this river and knew it well.

'We have to take the left fork,' Genie said dreamily.

She didn't know how she knew that, but she knew it for sure.

Rian watched her carefully. He knew her well enough to know she was only partially with them at the moment. He was worried she'd do her usual trick and faint or fall, but she kept paddling and seemed to be in a trance. He frowned. He loved this girl so much, but it scared him when she left him like this. Where did she go? What did she see?

Renée watched everything, alarmed as they came away from the main river and entered a deeper narrow channel that skirted around a little island. A deer stood silently watching them from the water's edge. A bird shrieked somewhere to her right.

She kept her silence, listening only to the paddles dipping in and out of the water and the sound of cicadas on the riverbanks and other creatures unused to being disturbed so late at night.

'Wait. We have to wait. Stop, Ri. Stop the raft.' Genie urged.

Rian slowed them down with his paddle and steered them into the shore, grabbing on reeds to anchor them.

In the distance he could suddenly see the choppers circling, their searchlights hunting. He wasn't sure if Renée or Genie could feel them again; neither said anything. He found a small tree growing out of the riverbank and grabbed it, bringing them to a complete halt.

Genie seemed to be watching something, staring intently at someone perhaps, but he couldn't see anything.

'Bear Island,' Genie said suddenly. 'Ferry was right, we have to make Bear Island by sunrise. We will be safe there.'

Renée shuddered. She was deeply afraid of bears.

'Hide now!' Genie whispered urgently, ducking down beside Renée and Mouch. Rian felt a tad stupid but he curled up beside them, in case.

From absolutely nowhere another chopper swept in from just above their heads, searchlights on, focused on the main river the other side of the small island. Rian took Genie's hand and felt how astonishingly warm her hand was, hotter than ever before. Beside them, Renée was shaking with fear, expecting the worst. The chopper circled, the stark light strafing through the island trees. If they hadn't taken this channel they would have been seen for sure. The chopper finally moved on further downriver. The Fortress had concentrated minds around here wonderfully. People clearly wanted that reward.

Genie relaxed. Rian felt her hands go limp and she was back with them again. He sat up. Mouch was shaking with fear.

'It's OK, Mouch. They've gone. We're fine now.'

Renée gave Genie a hug. 'I don't know what you did or what you saw, sweetie, but you saved our asses for sure.'

Genie sat up – a strange feeling of belonging had come over her. She was sure Grandma Munby had been sitting in the raft with them.

'My grandma came,' Genie told them. 'Others too. They'll help us get down the river.'

'Like ghosts?' Renée asked.

'Like spirits,' Genie answered mysteriously. 'Like ancestors.'

Rian pushed off again and began paddling. He didn't care who had come; whoever or whatever, they had saved them and that was fine by him. They could come anytime they wanted as long as they wanted to help.

'How far is Bear Island?' Renée wanted to know.

'We can be there by dawn,' Genie said confidently.

They moved on, all of them scanning the skies, scared the choppers would return.

The first hint of dawn appeared some hours later. They were all exhausted. No one had slept. Rian's arms felt like lead from paddling but Renée and Genie had swapped over at least twice. All of them were desperate for sleep by now. Mouch whined. He was desperately anxious; he needed to pee at the very least.

'God, I need a latté,' Renée sighed. 'Never knew how much I missed them until I got back to Spurlake. Practically drank McBean's dry on the first day.'

Genie laughed. 'Me, I need a smoothie. Is anyone else thirsty?'

'You think we missed the island?' Renée added anxiously. 'I need to . . . y'know.'

'No idea. But I hope it comes up soon; it's going to be light in twenty minutes and we'll be sitting ducks,' Rian declared.

'The water's so smooth. I love this time of the morning,' Genie remarked dreamily. 'Everything is so perfectly still. No wind, nothing. Everything is just waiting to start.'

They drifted on. The light began to grow. Birds began to sing. Rian grew uneasy. They needed sanctuary and fast. The river was wider and shallower here, the left riverbank was high above them, black rock and shale. The highway was up there somewhere, easy for anyone to spot a lone raft drifting along. The railroad line ran along the other side. He was beginning to think that they should think about hitching a ride when it came through, but how often was that? Did freight trains even run any more? He wished he'd paid more attention to stuff.

An eagle shrieked above them suddenly. They looked up. A lone passenger jet was streaking across the sky at thirty thousand feet, a vapour trail in its wake.

'An island,' Genie whispered. 'I see it. God, I hope it's Bear Island.'

Renée stared ahead. She could only see some trees sticking out of the water mid-stream. Dreams of a hot shower and foaming lattés quickly evaporated.

Genie began to paddle, not going directly to the head of the island but around a small bluff. Now they could see a small wisp of smoke. A house, built on stilts, in the middle of the island.

'Bear Island,' Genie said with satisfaction.

Moucher jumped clear out of the raft and ran along the island riverbank barking with joy, stopping only to have that long, desperate pee. Renée wasn't long after him. She hoped no one was peeking out of any window.

Genie turned and smiled at Rian. 'We've got Ferry's letter to deliver.'

Genie walked towards the cottage, noting that it looked pretty run-down if it was a guesthouse. She grew apprehensive as she grew closer and could see where there was a lot of water damage. The rear section of the house was part torn away. The flood must have reached here too. The whole island must have been swamped and was only now recovering. The remains of a bonfire smouldered. Clearly someone had been trying to clear debris. They shouldn't have left a bonfire to smoulder, even if it had been raining.

'I don't think anyone's here right now,' Genie called back to the others.

She climbed the steps anyway and went up to the stoop. It too felt shaky. Clearly a lot of work needed to be done to make this place safe. There was a notice board with wire laced across it and she slipped Ferry's letter under the wire so it would be safe.

They wouldn't be getting any breakfast here, but at least it was a place to shelter and hide out for the day. She tried the door. It was locked. She didn't want to trespass.

She stooped to pick up a notice that had fallen on to the path.

Regret closed following flood – come back next year? Betty Juniper

'I guess there's no bears and no porridge, hot or cold, here,' Genie commented with a shrug. 'It's a shame. Must have been a cute place once.'

Rian met her at the bottom of the stairs with a big grin. He grabbed her hand and took her over to a bush filled with ripe blackberries. The prickly blackberry trails had grown right over some other bushes and although many had shrivelled, there were enough to eat. 'I think this is why the bears like it here. Breakfast.'

Genie grinned and hugged him. She popped a ripe blackberry into her mouth, impressed by the taste. Sweeter than a strawberry. 'They're late. Usually finished by now. My mother wouldn't let me eat them after October the seventh. Even if the bush was full of them. Some stupid superstition.'

'Well, it's September, so eat.'

'We've got pear trees, absolutely laden. And huckleberries for the bears if they visit.'

Suddenly Genie felt a desperate urge; she realized she really needed to go. 'Got to . . . Don't eat all the berries, OK. Leave some for me.' She turned and ran for the bushes, passing Renée coming from the other way.

'I gotta sleep. I'm bushed,' Renée declared as she reached Rian's side. 'The mosquitoes are *huge* around here. I got to find me a net.'

'It's not so bad. As long as the river flows, it keeps the bugs down. We'll sleep up on the stoop; there's an old sofa there. You OK in the raft, Renée?'

She nodded. 'Sure, bugs ain't going to crawl up through that . . . Help me drag it higher. I want to be in the shade.'

'Sure.' He dragged the raft over to a flat space under a shady tree. It was a good spot.

'You never been camping, Renée?'

She shrugged. 'My whole life has been camping. I'm trailer trash, remember?'

Genie returned quietly and washed her hands in the river, rubbing sand between her fingers to make sure they got clean. She looked across the narrow channel to the shoreline.

'There used to be a footbridge to the other side. I guess the flood wiped that out too. I wonder who used to come and stay here.'

Rian looked across at some hooper birds wading in the distance. 'Bird-watchers, people who liked to get away somewhere secret. I hope she gets to fix it up. I kind of like it.'

'You're seriously weird sometimes, Rian. Google should like hire you to give answers. *Ask Rian* – it could be a TV show.'

Rian looked at Renée with raised eyebrows, just checking she was being sarcastic. He shook his head. 'Cool. That's my life sorted. Come on, eat some berries, girl. You need something more than chips in your gut.'

Renée stuck her tongue out but she helped herself to the berries and seemed to enjoy them. 'They're sweet.'

Genie yawned. 'Getting sleepy, Ri. Like now.' She could feel herself falling asleep right by the river.

Rian strode over and scooped her up, taking her across the grass to the stairs. Genie looked at him through sleepy eyes. She smiled. 'You'll never get me up the stairs.'

Rian laughed and set her down. Genie walked slowly up towards the stoop, so looking forward to falling asleep on the sofa.

Mouch was already there, spread out beside it, his little tail wagging when she stepped over him. The socks he'd been wearing lay in tatters beside him. He definitely wasn't a sock-wearing dog.

'Listen carefully,' Rian told the dog. 'Wake me if you hear anything.'

Mouch let his head hit the floor. He needed sleep too.

'It's lumpy,' Genie warned him.

Rian lay beside her and, even as he removed his shoes and turned back to her, she was already fast asleep.

Rian woke first, bumping his head on the arm of the old sofa he was sleeping on. He looked at the sun; it was still high in a cloudless sky. He was thirsty and needed to attend to business. He gently got up, trying not to wake Genie curled up beside him, her lips still crimson from the berries. Moucher was sprawled on the deck in the shade and barely opened one eye to check on what he was doing. Reluctantly he followed as Rian tiptoed down the steps and first headed towards the bushes, then the river.

He drank from a clear pool with a sandy bottom. It tasted sweet and fresh and he hoped it was safe to drink. Who knew what they dumped into the river upstream, but it tasted fine by him and Moucher keenly lapped from an adjoining pool.

He looked back at the stoop momentarily and saw Genie was propped up on one arm, studying him. She smiled. 'You look cute, Ri. Wish I had a camera.'

'Water's good.'

Genie stretched and yawned and then slowly made her way down the steps towards him. 'God, I feel stiff. There was a spring pressing into me just there.' She indicated her left thigh. 'Look, I'm bruised.'

She joined him, cupped her hands and began to drink, laughing at Moucher who was still drinking. 'You ain't getting in that raft until you have got that all out of you, dog.'

She looked at the channel that separated them from the mainland. 'You think we can catch a fish?'

'With bare hands?'

'I guess not. Seen it done on TV though.'

'In spring maybe. Heard there were so many fish here one time, First Nation fisherman were walking across the river on them.'

'Yeah, but they said the same thing about the cod off Newfoundland. Where are the cod now, eh? Where's the salmon?'

'Wrong season maybe.'

Just to prove them wrong a huge fish flashed by, quickly followed by another salmon. They looked at each other and laughed.

'Go fetch,' Genie instructed Moucher, who was probably thinking the same about her. He hadn't been impressed by berries for breakfast.

Genie grabbed Rian's hand and squeezed it. 'Thanks for getting us here. It's peaceful. Reminds me of when we arrived at Marshall's place.'

'You got us here too.'

He pulled her towards him and they kissed. Genie pulled away. 'Uh-uh, I don't think my breath is so good.'

'Genie,' Rian complained. 'We're on the run. None of us are minty fresh. Eat more berries.'

Genie allowed him to hold her tight and they just gently rocked together, kneeling by the water, Moucher trying to snap a fish as another went by.

'Genie? Ri?' Renée called out, breaking the spell, fear in her voice.

They looked at the raft. She'd slept in there with an old mosquito net she'd found spread over her.

'My legs. They're gone,' she whispered in horror. 'I can't see or feel my legs.'

Genie and Rian raced to her side, but they could plainly see her legs. She looked perfectly normal.

Genie took her hand. 'It's just a dream, Renée. Just a dream.'

But Renée looked terrified. She was staring and trying to feel for her legs. 'They're gone. My legs have vanished.'

Rian put his hands on her legs. 'Renée, I'm holding them. Can't you see?'

Renée was staring but didn't seem to see. 'No. They're gone. They're gone.'

'Maybe she really is having a dream?' Genie suggested. 'Renée, wake up. Wake up, you're dreaming,' she shouted.

Renée looked at her with annoyance. 'I *am* awake. My legs have gone. Look, can't you see?'

Mouch barked, excited there was shouting.

Genie took hold of Renée's hands and pulled them down towards her legs. 'Tell me what you can see and feel, Renée. This? This?'

'Can you feel this?' Rian asked. He pinched just above her knee.

'Ow!'

'OK, you're feeling. That was your knee. Can you feel your legs now?'

43

'Your hands are lying on your knees now,' Genie told her. She snatched a look at Rian; they both kind of shrugged at each other. It was too weird.

'I'm going to rip one of your toes off,' Rian told her.

'Noooo.'

'Feel this?' He flicked her little toe.

'OW!'

'Guess what, Renée? You got legs. Two of them, five toes each. Five dirty toes with amber paint. Since when was amber your toe colour?' Genie asked.

'Amber?' Renée sat up. She seemed to be staring at her feet, but it was hard to tell.

'Can you see my hands?' Genie asked.

Renée nodded.

'They're right here, over your –' she pulled her hands away '– feet.'

'I don't get it,' Renée wailed. 'My legs are there?'

'You are all here. Nothing missing,' Rian assured her.

'But . . .'

'No buts. Wiggle your toes.'

It took a while but Renée closed her eyes and concentrated and her toes definitely wiggled.

'You can't see that?' Genie asked.

Renée shook her head, but if she closed her eyes and

44

pinched her legs she could feel them fine. It was just too strange.

'This ever happen before?' Rian asked.

Renée kept her eyes closed. Looked like she was thinking. 'My foot. I lost my foot when I was trapped at the Fortress. I couldn't walk until the server came back on line and . . .'

Rian looked at Genie. 'Saw it on an episode of *House*, I think. Hysterical memory.'

Renée opened her eyes and looked at him. 'Hysterical memory?'

'Don't ask me to like define it, but this is that. There's nothing missing, but your brain is telling you something is. It's remembered the time you lost your foot.'

'All those hours watching *House* didn't go to waste after all, Dr Tulane,' Genie said, trying to keep it light.

Renée closed her eyes. It sort of made sense. With her eyes closed she could feel her legs. Open them and they disappeared.

She suddenly felt overwhelmingly dizzy.

'Don't leave me. Don't go without me. Promise me you won't . . .' And as suddenly as she had woken she was fast asleep again.

Genie made her more comfortable and together they dragged the raft further into the shade of the tree.

'That was so weird,' Genie said. 'You mean it?

45

About hysterical stuff?'

Rian shrugged. 'Made sense to me, but hell, it's just a TV show. It's a first anyway. Who knows what kinda weird stuff can happen to you guys now you've been teleported.'

'Marshall says I should be making notes. Any changes and stuff. We're like live guinea pigs. All kinds of things could happen to us, I guess.'

'For sure. Every day I just look at you and think it's a miracle you're here and you're OK.'

'I'm only OK because you're here, Rian. That's the miracle.'

Rian held her again. They kissed and this time she didn't pull away. He scooped her up and took her back to the sofa on the stoop and they stayed kissing.

Genie raised her head a moment. 'Mouch, keep guard, all right?'

Mouch was hunting fish, or at least thought he was. It required all his canine attention. He tried to snap at them as they swam by then sneezed as his nose filled with water.

Rian was holding her close, stroking her short, spiky stubble.

Rian rubbed her head. 'Your hair is growing. I'm kinda getting used to you being like this.'

Genie frowned. 'Really?'

'I never really knew how beautiful you are. Some people shave their head and it's pretty scary, but you – you're truly beautiful. I never knew I liked your ears before.'

'My Spock ears?' She laughed, embarrassed.

'They're cute. Makes you look at a person in a different way, don't you think?'

Genie nodded. 'I guess.' She was thinking of Cary and Denis and the others. How scared they must be being back in the Fortress. Had they shaved their heads yet? Had they tried to teleport them again? Were they even alive?

'I hate the fact that we've got no rights. I hate the fact that no one is interested in us. It makes me angry.'

'Maybe it's just too fantastic for people to handle?' Rian suggested.

'I mean, all those people in Spurlake who *know* what happened.'

Rian kissed her neck and began to work his way down. 'Maybe they don't. Maybe only a few actually know.'

Genie closed her eyes as his warm lips kissed her stomach. 'You on their side now?'

'No. I'm just saying it's like cows. Every kid wants a hamburger, right? And they pretty much don't ever think about cows, but if you took them to a slaughterhouse and saw the cow having its throat cut and the blood running out and then saw them cut up the cow with a bandsaw, I guarantee a lot of them would stop eating hamburgers.'

Genie frowned, stopping him from kissing her a moment.

'So we're hamburger?'

'No, but we might be the cows, the invisible cows. My guess is a lot of people at the Fortress never see the cows. That's all I'm saying.'

'Deep stuff, Ri.'

Rian smiled, kissing her belly button. 'I'm a geek, remember?'

Genie pulled him up and kissed the top of his head. 'Hold me tight, Ri. I know what Renée is going through. I keep getting that feeling I'm about to disintegrate again.'

Rian held her tight, kissing her neck. She couldn't believe that this was happening now, but it felt right.

Rian rolled up her T-shirt and she leaned forward so he could tug it off. She crushed her lips into his left ear.

Rian felt dizzy, he needed this so much.

Genie closed her eyes. She tensed as he kissed her again. She felt she was on fire. She wanted this moment to last for ever.

Moucher began barking about an hour later. He was standing out of sight somewhere on the other side of the island. Rian shouted for him to be quiet but he didn't.

Rian pulled on his jeans and ran barefoot to where Moucher was barking. He grabbed his mouth and clamped it and told him to be quiet in no uncertain terms. He looked across the river. A breeze had come up, whipping whitecaps into a fine spray.

Two men with guns in a Zodiac inflatable were heading downstream. A train was rolling along on its tracks on the far side of the river, hauling a huge load, and maybe that's why they hadn't heard Moucher. Rian lay flat on the ground, with Mouch beside him, Mouch was scared a little as Rian held him tight.

'You did good, Mouch, but you have to be quiet now,' Rian told him, trying to calm the dog. Mouch relaxed a little.

Rian could see Genie staring from the edge of the house and he signalled for her to get out of sight. She quickly moved back.

Maybe these hunters hadn't been looking for them, but could they take the chance? It was bad news they were ahead of them now, but then again, they wouldn't be setting off until dark.

Rian watched the men go, one tall, one shorter and young – his son maybe – keeping well to the right of the river where the water was deeper.

He waited a few minutes, making sure they were well out of sight. He let Mouch go and the dog bounced around him, happy to be free, anxious to please.

Rian rubbed his head. 'Go find Genie, OK? Go find Genie.' Mouch ran off, pleased to have something to do.

When Rian got back Genie was dressed and squatting beside Renée in the raft. She looked back at him a moment to check he was all right.

'You sure you're feeling OK, Renée?'

'Why wouldn't I be?'

'Your legs? Your legs feel –' she tried to find the right word '– solid?'

'Solid?' She laughed, frowning at Genie. 'Sure they're solid. You don't like my legs? Why? What's going on? Why do you guys look so worried?'

Genie looked up at Rian and shrugged. If she didn't know, she sure as hell wasn't going to remind her.

'What you got there, Ri?' Renée asked.

'Spear.'

'Spear?'

'Going to catch us some supper.'

'Are you now?' Renée laughed.

'And you're going to make a fire and gather up some of the vegetables growing in the garden.'

Renée looked at Genie and shook her head. 'I told you

he's a meat-and-two-veg kind of guy. So boring. Fusion, Ri, go fusion.'

Genie laughed and helped Renée out of the raft.

'Girl,' Renée declared, 'we got to hit the powder room. Then we'll cook this boy his victuals.'

'Victuals?' Genie smiled, that's what her grandma had called her food. She'd forgotten about that.

'I got no idea what victuals are, but they kept mentioning them in some Mark Twain book we had to read in school once. Stuck in my head.'

'*Tom Sawyer*,' Genie asserted. 'I had to read it too. Never thought I'd get to live like pioneers though. You think we'll ever go back to school?'

'Might. Not around here though. Maybe Mexico. If we ever get there. You think we'll ever get there?'

Genie took her hand and led her towards the bushes and the 'powder room'. 'Sure. We're going to get that yacht, sail as far as we want and never look back. Ever. Cabo won't know what's hit it.'

Renée smiled, linking arms. 'I so want to believe that. I really do.'

Rian shook his head and looked at Moucher. 'Girls. Go figure. You going to help me fish, Mouch? Spear fish?'

Moucher didn't quite know whom to go with, but he was hungry. He stayed with the fish.

5

Bringing to Heel

Strindberg wasn't happy – and that meant no one was happy.

Reverend Schneider stood before him sweating slightly, the way he did when he wasn't sure which way the wind was blowing.

Strindberg was sitting at his desk reading a report. He made Schneider stand and Schneider noticed that the office had been stripped of all the pictures of the Cascades the previous CEO had placed on the walls. The office was huge, but now just had the bare minimum of books and a bank of TV monitors on the wall, one for each floor for the Fortress most likely. Strindberg wasn't the most trusting of men. One could be sure he'd be watching everyone all the time.

'You did well for us, Reverend. Brought in some good "volunteers". Set up a nice little entrapment. I hope to hell that you have dismantled that website and destroyed all traces by now. Legally you put us at a big disadvantage. If anyone could link your activities to Fortransco we could be in big trouble. You clear on this? Just because you got compliance signatures from them, it means squat. They were minors.'

'No one was complaining. I was asked to find volunteers and suitable candidates—' Reverend Schneider began, but Strindberg cut him off.

'These were not orphans. No one misses little orphans. Now we have parents involved. Parents who now know their kids were "possibly" incarcerated by us – and that makes us liable. So far we got them running scared, but if they get smart, we will look bad.

'As it is we just want our test subjects back. It's tough explaining to them that the kids who they think are their Jack and Jills are legally ours, but that's how it is. We own them and it represents billions of dollars of research. I don't know what you were thinking, but I looked at your agreement and it specifically requested orphans.'

'It wasn't easy—' Reverend Schneider said, but was again cut off.

'No, not easy. Nothing about this enterprise is easy. That's why I'm here, to make things work. The project needs professionalism, objectivity and focus. It's been too lax about everything. Happy amateurs with too much of other people's money.

'As it is we're going to have to compensate those

Spurlake parents for the "rights" to use their kids – and we are in uncharted waters here, Reverend. How much for a dead kid? Or soul, as you try to spin it. Don't worry, we'll buy them off. After all, these kids ran away, things weren't perfect at home, right? No matter what they say. It'll cost us, but as long as we get them all back, at least we regain our larger investment.'

'And me?' Reverend Schneider asked. It had already cost him plenty to get the website closed down and to purge the links. Make sure nothing tracked back to him. It would be cached of course on a million servers but it was a dead link and at least it wouldn't point towards the Fortress. Any investigations would end in a Crimean IP address, beyond reach.

'You, Reverend? You got a nice little new church out of us, I understand. You got rich. Each soul extracted a pretty price from us.'

'I—'

'It's over, Reverend. You're out. I'm in. The legal department will have some documents for you to sign and if you even breathe the word "Fortress" or divulge any information that went on here, you will lose everything. You understand? Everything. And I guarantee you will be the next "soul" they test in the teleport chamber. You understand?'

Reverend Schneider blinked. He hadn't quite expected this.

'I want to know everything about Genie Magee,' Strindberg said abruptly.

'She's possessed.'

Strindberg looked at him over his glasses and it wasn't a kind look. 'You can talk like that to your country hicks, but I want a straight, intelligible answer, Reverend. No Audrey Rose crap, OK?'

'Genie Magee has a special talent,' Reverend Schneider began again. 'She can see through people.'

Strindberg smiled and pursed his lips.

'I might hire her myself. See through people? What? Are we talking comic strip here? Alphas with special talents?'

Reverend Schneider took a deep breath. He didn't like the sarcastic tone but felt he had to justify himself.

'She has a demon in her soul. She has abilities.'

Strindberg frowned. 'And we used her as a volunteer?'

Schneider decided to keep quiet about his role in her abduction. 'She signed the waiver.'

'I repeat, Reverend, she was a minor. It has no legal standing. What happened? You were there during transmission, I understand.'

'Won't your people tell you?'

'I want to hear from you.'

'There was a fire. They lost all her data and technically she should be dead. She didn't even transmit for a microsecond. Nothing.'

'But she isn't dead.'

'No.'

'And she led a little song and dance against you in your church.'

Schneider looked momentarily embarrassed. 'Yes.'

'And now we are having to pay out a lot of money to lawyers and parents to keep this thing quiet. But she isn't quiet; she's getting ready to cause trouble. Any ideas on where this protégée of yours might be?'

Schneider shrugged. 'All I know is that she stole a truck and ran off with her boyfriend.'

'Now there's a boyfriend?'

'That's where the trouble started.'

Strindberg made a note on the documents before him. 'It usually does,' he commented.

He looked up again at Schneider. 'I want you to make finding that girl your mission, Reverend. If you want to keep your church – keep that nice fat life you've got making people miserable in Spurlake – you get out there and find her and bring her back alive. You understand? That's your job now. Your only job.'

Schneider stood staring at him, expecting more.

Strindberg didn't even look up. 'You can go. And Reverend,' he added, turning to his computer screen, 'don't even think of coming back without her.'

As Schneider left the room he realized that he was now sure of only one thing; Satan walked the earth and was running the Fortress.

Strindberg had no thoughts of Satan or any other character. He was observing the CCTV camera focused on the four kids in the observation quarters. He knew them as numbers but they were Cary, Julia, Randall and Denis. They were dressed in white T-shirts and shorts strapped to monitoring equipment, checking heart, lungs, blood and brainwave functions. A technician was doing tests on their nervous systems, sending extreme signals to each in turn, watching their reactions as they writhed in pain and screamed until she turned the signal off. She made notes as she performed each test.

These were just lab-rat test subjects now. As far as Strindberg was concerned they weren't even human. These were just replicants. And like all lab rats, their feelings were not a matter for his concern.

He switched to another view. A recording of Genie Magee's transmission, slowed to one second per frame. Something had happened that day that made her transmission different to all others. What was it they had missed? Why had it been successful and why didn't they know that? This was why he was here. This was what he'd pledged the investors to find out. Possessed? What did Reverend Schneider say? She can see through people. A useful skill to have indeed. He watched her calm, rather beautiful face as she began to disintegrate. She didn't even flinch. More than ever he wanted to meet this girl.

6

Hunters

They left the moment it got dark. Genie was a tad reluctant to leave the Bear Island sanctuary, but the other two anxious to move on. Renée wasn't too keen to wait for any bears to show up and wanted to get to the city. She said she'd feel safer there. It was easier to hide where there were people around.

The moon hadn't yet risen, the air was chillier than before and the current seemed faster. Their next goal was getting downriver towards Mission and beyond that Vancouver. Renée had a cousin in New Westminster and she figured they could crash there. If they ever got that far.

'Did you know the Fraser River is our longest river?' Rian said as he shifted positions to get more comfortable as he paddled. 'It's one thousand three hundred and seventy-five kilometres long.'

Genie, paddling alongside, looked askance at him. 'And you broke the silence for this amazing fact.'

'Just thinking, that's all.'

'Well then, it's a good job we didn't start back at Mount Robson, huh? See, I used to sit in the same class as you, Rian Tulane, and occasionally I learned the same stuff as you. And anyway, it's only the tenth-longest river in Canada. No biggie.'

Renée was trailing a hand in the river. 'Guys, shut the hell up. Sound carries on water remember.'

Rian concentrated on paddling, keeping them in the deeper water.

Genie watched some trucks go by on the highway running alongside the river again. Truckers heading home to families, maybe. She was wondering if she'd ever lead a normal life again – not that she'd every really led a normal life to start with. She was curious about what her mother was thinking right now. Did she care if she was alive or dead? Had she known Reverend Schneider was recruiting souls for the Fortress? She sighed; thinking about her mother only made her angry and she didn't want to be angry.

The river picked up speed suddenly as they entered a narrow stretch with steeper slopes on either side. The water was incredibly choppy.

'We getting faster?' Renée whispered, her voice betraying her anxiety.

'Hold on,' Rian called. 'Ship your paddle, Genie.

Damn, I can't see anything, but we're . . .' He nearly lost his paddle and the raft spun all the way round as it collided with some rocks mid-stream.

Not seeing where they were going and what dangers lay ahead was unnerving.

'Hold on to Mouch,' Genie called out, scared now as water cascaded over the prow and drenched them.

'There aren't any rapids, are there?' Renée asked, panic in her voice.

'No. Hell, I don't know,' Rian answered, desperately trying to steady them. 'We've diverted from the main channel, I think. Hang on tight.'

A powerful flashlight suddenly flooded the raft. It blinded all three of them. The light moved away wildly as the other raft turned to cope with the rapid-moving river.

'It's them,' someone shouted. 'I know it is. It's them.'

Genie's heart nearly stopped.

'Jesus,' Rian exclaimed. 'Who the hell?'

'Will they shoot?' Renée asked.

'They don't want us dead,' Genie muttered tersely. 'They'll want the reward money.'

Rian took strength from that. The raft was pitching up and down now as it entered the rapids, a surge of water pushing them forward, squeezing them up against fast-moving debris. All he could do to just hold on, likewise for Genie, now holding Mouch tightly, and Renée was lying flat and twisting her hands through the grab handles – just in case.

The powerful searchlight was still seeking them. Rian ducked down beside Genie.

'Start praying.'

'I *am* praying.'

'Good, 'cause I'm crapping myself here,' Renée said. 'Who the hell are they?'

'Bounty hunters. I saw a pair go by earlier.'

Genie and Renée digested this set of facts. Hunters. Hunters meant guns. Big guns. Hunters liked shooting at things.

The river was moving dangerously fast. Genie clung on to Moucher as Renée tried to grab Rian. Suddenly they plunged down into a foaming rush of water, a jagged rock snagged the inflatable and Rian was sent flying.

A shot rang out real close, pinging off a rock. Genie was pitched underwater, churning in the freezing sluice, gasping for breath. Mouch sprang free. Somewhere ahead Renée was screaming as she stayed with the inflatable, rapidly disappearing downriver. And Rian? Where was Rian? Why didn't he come up for air?

'Rian? Rian?' Genie wailed as she surfaced, but there was no sign of him.

She saw the hunter's flashlight approaching and immediately ducked underwater again wondering how long she could hold her breath. All the while she was praying Rian was OK. Please let Ri be OK . . .

'They are right here,' a hunter was saying as he reloaded the shotgun. 'I can almost smell the money.'

Rian was reeling, tasting blood. He'd bashed his head hard and swallowed a ton of water. He surfaced, turning around to get his bearings. He was still moving downriver. A flashlight was sweeping the water looking for them and Rian, head spinning with pain, had to dive under again to avoid them finding him.

But where was Genie? Where was Renée? He surfaced again seconds later to look for them and was immediately struck hard on the head again by fast-moving timber. He instantly lost consciousness. The river was able to do with him what it willed.

Renée tried to untangle herself from the raft. She'd twisted her hand round the straps to keep her in, but now it was on top of her and she couldn't get free. She was being pummelled by rocks and knew if she didn't flip it over real soon she was going to drown.

The hunter with the flashlight turned to his

father and pulled a face.

'Can't find 'em again, Pa.'

His pa swore. 'I told you, Sean, no shooting. They want them alive, you dumb bastard. No shooting.'

'Sorry, Pa. Accident. I swear it. Accident.'

His father attempted to steer the inflatable closer to where the raft was last seen.

'Sweep again. That's my reward money going under and they ain't going to pay up if they drowned.'

Genie and Moucher were sitting shivering like drowned rats on a rock mid-stream, keeping dead quiet in the darkness. The moon was up at last and could be glimpsed through the trees overhead. She realized that somehow they'd taken a run-off channel the main river was flowing normally about fifty metres away. How that had happened she didn't know, but then not one of them had any river craft.

She watched the two hunters in their inflatable sweeping the water with their flashlight. Where was Rian? She was beginning to panic; she had a terribly bad feeling about him. The hunters wouldn't spot her here, nor could they get their craft near. She discovered her fingers were crossed; she'd been saying a prayer for Rian and Renée and their safety.

You could never count on anything, she realized. Ten grand per head motivated a lot of people in these parts. That was for sure.

The flashlight was sweeping close to her again and she grabbed Mouch and squatted down low behind the rock. Mouch shook with fear and the cold, but kept quiet, just as he'd been told to.

Genie heard the inflatable's motor kick in. They were moving off. Either they had given up or were going downstream. Perhaps leaving, in case the gunshot had alerted anyone. But there was little chance of that out here. There was nothing but farmland and trees . . .

Rian hauled himself out of the river and lay gasping on the riverbank, spewing out river water. He was in agony. His head hurt like hell and blood trickled into his mouth. He wanted to yell Genie's name but the hunters might still be in earshot, despite their outboard engine's noise.

He looked downstream for signs of Renée and the raft, but she had disappeared. He hoped like hell she'd managed to flip it over again and stayed put somewhere.

He clutched his head; he felt incredibly dizzy. Shooting pains suddenly overwhelmed him and he had to cough. He felt bad, real bad. He could feel his temperature spiking, a hot flush sweeping over him; his brain was going to boil over. He really needed Genie now. Where was she? He fell back against the mud and sand, groaning loudly as he clutched his head; the world was spinning around him out of control.

Genie pointed to the riverbank. 'We're going to swim. OK, Mouch? Follow me.'

Genie plunged back in, Mouch quickly followed, his doggy-paddle pretty good, he wasn't far behind her at all. Clambering out over rocks, on the other hand, was harder, but eventually Genie got one half-drowned bedraggled hound out of the water and he shook as hard as he could to rid himself of the river.

'Enough already!' Genie exclaimed.

Mouch gave one last shake and then wiped his head on the grass to be sure.

'Rian?' Genie shouted. 'Rian?'

Genie listened. Nothing. She realized that the river made a lot of noise passing over the rocks. He probably couldn't hear. She hoped so. She had images of him lying bleeding someplace and . . .

'Come on. We got some walking to do.'

Mouch was only too happy to walk. Better than being on the river, that was for sure.

* * *

Much further downstream, Renée had detached herself from the raft and watched it sink by the dim glow of moonlight.

She'd surfaced to discover a log-jam had piled up on a bend and although the water was passing really fast underneath through a sluice, the logs and other debris prevented anything from going any further on the surface. The raft was impaled on a jagged tree branch, useless now. With it had died her courage and hopes. She really hoped the others were safe; was she the only survivor? She suddenly realized that a life without either one of them would be just impossible. Totally impossible.

She felt guilty; she should have saved the raft.

7

Miller Crossing

Officer Miller got out of the cab and let it go. He stretched in the sunshine and looked around him. It was seven a.m. The road was quiet, the way he liked it. Hadn't been out here in a while.

This gas station had sure let time pass it by. Everything looked as he remembered Canada looked like when he was a boy. He smiled and entered the office.

Ferry was reading *The Vancouver Sun*. He looked up and nodded when he saw Miller.

'Was beginning to think you wouldn't come.'

'Busy. Lot of people gone sick.'

Ferry nodded. 'All out looking for those kids, I bet. Ten grand per head is a lot these days.'

'I got a report on the radio that some hunters saw them on the river last night, 'bout ten ks upstream from Chilliwack.'

Ferry frowned. 'Hunters?'

'Father and son, thought they'd collect some scalps. Seems the boy accidentally fired and they think the kids drowned. Pretty freak conditions in the run-off down there last night. Normally the Fraser's slow and easy. Any idea where they got the raft?'

'Might do. You think the kids are dead? Want some coffee? I just made fresh.'

Miller nodded and Ferry went to pour him a mug.

'Chopper been out looking this morning but found no trace of them so far.'

Ferry handed over the coffee.

'Sugar and milk on the side over there.' He pointed towards a ledge by the fridge. Then he lifted his till some and pulled out a note from under it. 'From Genie to you and Marshall. Sorry, I read it.'

Miller took it, surprised but glad to get some communication; things were probably pretty bleak for those kids now.

Dear Marshall and Miller,
We made it this far. Couldn't have done without you guys. Ferry's a good guy. If we make it, we'll send a card to the farm. If we don't I want you to know that you both made me and Ri happy. Please save the farm. One day I know I'll want to come back. Maybe as a ghost, but I will come back somehow. I promise.
Love me & Mouch xxx

Miller folded the note and put it into his top pocket.

'Thanks. Marshall will appreciate that.'

'Truck's out back. I gave it some TLC plus an oil and lube and replaced the front brakes. You were on threads.'

'Dad likes that old truck. Won't join the modern world. Wouldn't even trade it in when they were offering cash for clunkers.'

'Don't build 'em like that any more, that's why. You want I send the bill to Marshall?'

'Damage?'

'Six hundred and fifty dollars. That's cost. Brake pads are a bitch to fit. And the respray's for free. Got carried away and I had some matching paint.'

Miller raised an eyebrow, but Ferry was old school. He wouldn't cheat. If that was the price, that was the price. He got out his Visa card. It was turning out to be an expensive month.

'They're heading to Vancouver. If they get as far as Mission, they could hitch,' Ferry said. 'They're pretty good kids.'

Miller handed over his card and Ferry stuck it in the machine.

'Key in your number.'

Miller did so. It would have to be a gift to his dad. He was pretty broke now.

'I'll let you know if we hear anything,' Miller told him.

'The Fortress going to get away with what it's been doing?'

Miller looked away. 'It might. I'm turning in my badge. Working my notice. I'm not a popular guy in town right now.'

'*The Sun* says there's been a lot of UFO hysteria here, but I don't recall one person saying anything about UFOs.'

'Disinformation. It's standard practice. They won't be taking kids from Spurlake any more but . . .'

Ferry understood. 'They'll still be taking kids.'

Miller took his card back and Ferry gave him the receipt, adding, 'I haven't lost faith in Genie and Rian. They look out for each other.'

'His sister's with him too. Renée Cullen. Known her all her life.'

Miller smiled sipping his coffee. 'I see a lot of bad stuff in my job. But y'know, everyone is hard on the kids these days, but they are pretty good, on the whole. Smarter than I was at their age anyway.'

Ferry grinned and handed over the truck keys. 'Don't give up too easy. Things have a way of sorting themselves out. You give my best to your dad and tell him that he still owes me five dollars for the dog food he bought last year.'

Miller was about to dig into his pockets again but Ferry

71

shook his head. 'He has to pay in person. Gas station rules. And bring the beer.'

Miller smiled. He remembered now, Ferry used to play poker with his dad some years before. He took the keys.

'I'll remind him.'

'Don't worry about Genie. I got a good feeling about that girl,' Ferry said. 'She's still alive until we hear otherwise.'

8

Ruby

Genie wanted to cry. She hadn't found Rian. Nor Renée.

It was daylight already and she'd walked along the river and seen nothing, found no one, and she and Moucher were exhausted and, they admitted it, a little scared. She didn't think she could continue without Ri. There didn't seem to be any point. He was her whole life now.

Mouch looked up at her and seemed bewildered. Not to mention hungry.

A chopper flew over moments later, very low and slow, directly over the river. At first she was expecting a Mosquito attack, and panicked, but then she saw the word 'Police' painted on the bottom of it.

Clearly they were still looking for them. She and Mouch ran for cover under the trees and waited it out. She realized that the hunters must have told someone what had happened and they would be able to identify which part of the river they were in now.

She desperately wanted to shout out Rian's name but

that would have been dumb. If only they had a way to talk to each other.

'Where are they, Mouch? Where are they?'

She tried to concentrate. If she could just concentrate. Why couldn't she concentrate?

Mouch's ears suddenly flattened and he cowered slightly. Genie looked at him. He rarely showed any fear. What was going on?

'He's scared of me, that's all. Stroke his head. He'll calm down.' The voice was familiar but where was the person? Genie looked around and saw no one. She put out her hand to Mouch and he crawled closer to her for safety and comfort. Genie felt there was someone sitting right beside her, but she didn't want to turn her head again. How had they gotten so close and not made a single sound?

'You never showed fear last time,' the voice said.

Genie turned. 'Last time?'

Genie found she was looking at Grandma Munby. A younger Grandma than she remembered, and she was dressed eccentrically with feathers in her hair and a calico skirt, moccasins on her feet.

'Am I dreaming now? You were in the raft with us? I thought I saw you.'

Grandma Munby shook her head. 'No, dear. You're

wide awake. Got yourself in a pretty mess I can see.'

Genie nodded. Mouch squirmed beside her. Clearly he could see her too.

'Will it ever end? Will the Fortress get me, Grandma? 'Cause if it's inevitable, let them get me now. I've lost my friends, lost Ri. I can't live without Ri.'

Grandma Munby smiled, stroking Genie's arm with one of her feathers. Genie could feel it; it was as if warm sunlight was covering her. Even Mouch began to relax beside her.

'I'm here to make sure they don't.'

'They got me before. Where were you then?'

'You lived. You found the others. You have power within you, girl. That's what they want. The magic inside you.'

Genie noticed the ruby necklace hanging around her grandma's neck. Her mother had been so upset that it had been missing when she died. Yet here it was.

'This is yours, y'know. I left it to you. Here . . .' She slipped it off her neck and put it over Genie's head. 'Perfect.'

Genie looked down and saw the ruby hanging there. It was impossible for a spirit to give something to the living, wasn't it?

'It's to keep you safe,' Grandma Munby told her, smiling.

'But what about you? What keeps you safe now?'

'Nothing can hurt me now. Nothing.'

'Did you really kill my father?' Genie asked, instantly regretting she'd asked.

Grandma Munby sighed. 'It was an accident. Whatever I did was to protect your mother and you. I never regretted it. Not for a second. You too will do things to protect the ones you love, Genie.'

Genie didn't believe for one moment that this woman had murdered her father. It had to be a mistake.

Grandma Munby looked around her for a moment. A breeze gusted through the trees and sunlight glistened off the water.

'This is a pretty place,' she declared. 'I miss my river. I wish we'd had more time to get to know each other. Your mother and I were enemies almost from the time she was born. Such heartaches . . .'

Genie put a hand out to her grandma. She was as solid as any real person; it was quite a shock. She took her grandma's old hands and held them, wishing with all her heart that she had gotten to know the old woman better. Her mother had done everything to ruin her life so far. Almost as if she had dedicated her life to the task.

Grandma Munby took a deep breath. 'Can't stay long. Rian is waiting for you. He needs you. He's a good boy. I hope he'll stay with you for ever, girl. Others will want him; you'll have to guard him well. Your child will be wayward, but always honourable and he will respect you. He'll have different talents to you. I can't say what just yet. But your gift, like mine, is to help others live a better life.'

Genie didn't understand why she was talking of her child. How could she know? She and Ri had so few intimate moments.

'No, no, I can see what you're thinking; don't worry. Long after you marry. The child to come in the future.'

Genie felt relief, embarrassment and guilt all at once. It was good to know that she and Ri would marry. She hoped that was true.

'There are surprises ahead, my treasure. Not all goes to plan. But you have more than one guardian. Marshall worries, his son frets. No one you meet forgets you. Remember this, the sky isn't your friend and they won't give up easy. But neither will you.'

Genie bit her lip. 'Grandma, I feel guilty running away. My friends are trapped at the Fortress. I know we have to run, but can I help them?'

Grandma Munby just smiled. 'First save yourself. You're still in danger. Men are coming with guns. The situation has changed. They may not care if you live or die.'

Genie's heart skipped a beat.

'Listen, gather your friends. Go east to the old Cariboo and she'll be waiting for you.'

'Who?'

'She who waits. And, Genie, people love you, but never take it for granted. It is the one regret I carry with me – you never knew how much I loved you.'

'Till now.'

'Till now,' Grandma Munby replied with a smile and a sudden sense of realization. She stood with remarkable ease. 'The ruby belonged to your great-grandmother Snowdancer. Duty is the Munby burden and never to be taken lightly.'

Genie looked down and felt it. It was real, hard; the setting silver and the necklace seemed to be made of a curious entwined fabric. It was delicate and she closed her eyes a moment. It was totally impossible, but Grandma Munby really was there.

Moucher barked suddenly and Genie looked at him to hush him. He was standing three metres away from her, looking downriver and wagging his tail.

Genie looked back. Grandma Munby was gone. Perhaps she had never been there. To her immense surprise she discovered she was lying on her back in a pool of sunshine. She'd been fast asleep, dreaming. But such a vivid dream! Great-grandmother Snowdancer. She tried to hang on to that memory – she wondered if it was real. She felt for the ruby, but that too had disappeared. The weird thing was that she could still feel it around her neck. How weird was that? She realized that she was disappointed it was gone.

Moucher was still barking besides her.

'Moucher? I hope it's you?' Renée called out. She was wading up through the river, easier going than the overgrown riverbank.

Genie sat up and watched Renée approaching. She was so happy to see her and scared to ask about Ri. She hauled herself up and went to greet her. They hugged as Moucher tried to get some attention too.

'I was scared I'd never see you again.'

'Likewise.'

'Ri?' Genie asked. 'Any sign of him at all?'

Renée shook her head. 'He's not downriver, for sure. He couldn't have got ahead of me, I was stuck in the raft long after he bailed.'

'He needs help. He has be somewhere, Renée. We have to look for him.'

They both heard the sound of an approaching outboard motor – someone on the main river in a hurry. They ran for the trees and dived into the undergrowth.

Genie glimpsed an inflatable go by with four men

carrying shotguns. They were still looking for them. They just *had* to get away from the river.

Moucher kept his silence. He understood this game now.

'The raft?' Genie whispered into Renée's ear.

'Gone. Man, those guys looked mean. You think they're the same hunters?'

Genie shrugged, but she knew they couldn't risk finding out.

'What do you think Ri would do if he couldn't find us?' Genie asked her, standing up again and trying to get a view both ways of the river.

'Check all the rocks and deep-water pools between here and where we capsized. You think he . . . ?'

Genie shook her head. 'He's alive, I swear it. He would have tried to find us if he could.'

Renée agreed. They were uncannily close. She was a tad jealous of that.

'I'm sticking with you,' Renée stated.

'I'm not leaving without him,' Genie said. 'I can't.'

9

Coma

'The alarm sounded at eight fifty-five, sir.'

The technician looked pensively into the camera above the monitor. Behind him four of the test subjects lay completely still.

'What happened?' Strindberg asked. He could tell by the panic in the man's voice that it was much worse than he had been led to believe.

'They began to exhibit signs of extreme stress and all complained of not being able to see their legs or their arms. Two couldn't feel their torsos at all.'

Strindberg frowned. 'Not feeling? Their legs and arms were in place? Nothing missing?'

'Yes, sir. They were all complete, sir. Nothing missing at all and the electronic monitors indicated their heartbeats and blood circulation were all functioning normally. Heartbeat and blood pressure were rising as the sense of panic grew, however. It's a psychological condition, we believe. Latent memory from the previous transmissions.'

'And then?' Strindberg sensed disaster. Everything at

the Fortress seemed to be run by amateurs.

'At ten-sixteen precisely all four slipped into a coma, sir.'

'Coma? All of them?'

'Yes, sir. All continue to be in a coma. We have them on life-support. It's very deep, sir. Very deep.'

'And the same thing has happened in Spurlake?'

'At the same time, sir. One of the test subjects we had not been able to return is now in the hospital there under intensive care. We have a twenty-four-hour security in place there.'

'Five in a coma? All at the same time?' Strindberg swore. 'Does that mean that the other test subjects we haven't managed to get hold of could also be in a coma? If so, why? I want to know.'

The technician was dreading the question but knew it had been coming.

'Could be the MAT 7 sub-sonic signal we sent out earlier. Level Twelve experimented with a more specific targeting of the Mosquito shut-down and squirted it down a particular frequency. It was supposed to incapacitate the test subjects for perhaps an hour. Enough to make people panic and rush them to hospital. It was Dr Bellingham's concept and the signal went three hundred and sixty degrees in a sixty-kilometre sweep, at the very least.'

'MAT 7? In English please.'

'We sent a powerful Mosquito shut-down signal to the test subjects and squirted it to a sixty-kilometre radius.'

Strindberg sighed. 'So, instead of incapacitated they are in a coma or possibly out there on the river someplace, dead.'

The technician grimaced. 'Yes, very possibly, sir. If they aren't on life-support they will be dead.'

'Did no one think to test this transmission out first?'

The technician shrugged. It wasn't his call.

'So *we* did this. We destroyed our own billion-dollar assets. I can't believe the incompetence in this place.' Strindberg swore again and slammed his desk. 'I want this Dr Bellingham in my office within thirty minutes and he'd better have a plan on how to wake up our test subjects. Thirty minutes, you understand. I will not tolerate these sloppy standards for a moment longer. Get this message out. Get it right or get the hell out.'

'Totally understood, sir.'

The technician switched off the link and turned to the others watching him. 'Soon there won't be anyone left to fire.'

He looked back at the monitor measuring Cary's heartbeat. The kid was barely alive at all. Same for the others. Be kinder to switch them all off.

10

Ri

It had to be past midday already. Renée and Genie still hadn't found Rian. It was impossible. They had gone up and down the river twice, looked in every crevice. His body wasn't there. He wouldn't have walked off without them. He just couldn't have.

They sat on a rock mid-stream on the river bend with a good view up and downstream. Moucher would be listening for trouble and Genie knew that every minute they tarried here those hunters could be back, or anyone else for that matter wanting to claim the reward.

'Dammit, Rian, please give me a clue!' Genie wailed.

Renée felt her stomach groan. She was starving. The only berries they had found were end-of-season blueberries and they were too sour to eat, having been growing in the shade.

'Would he go on without us? I mean, what if he couldn't find us and assumed we'd been taken?' Renée suggested.

Genie shook her head. 'Me, or you, might be missing,

but Moucher too? They wouldn't take a dog. He would have found Mouch.'

'But he isn't looking for us. He just isn't on the river.'

Genie wasn't sure where to go or what to do. Grandma Munby had said go east, but how could she do that without Ri? And which way was east anyway?

'Grandma Munby said he was still here. I believe her.'

Renée nodded. 'Uh-huh. You know you're like crazy, right? You talk to ghosts and see stuff and . . .'

'I know,' Genie agreed. 'Your point is?'

Renée just smiled. 'It's kinda cool. Like knowing a witch. Can you do spells?'

Genie laughed. 'Sure, I'm going to do the "Shut up Renée the annoying girl" spell, right now.'

Renée smiled. 'I say we go back upriver aways. Right to the place we capsized. I know we think we've been there, but I don't think we have.'

Genie accepted that. It was quite logical. She thought she'd retraced her steps but maybe she hadn't.

'OK. Last time.'

'If he ain't there, we have to keep going. After all, Ri knows where we're headed.'

Moucher splashed and swam alongside them, still puzzled they never seemed to stop for food any more, but he didn't see Genie eating either.

A light plane flew over, but that was the only clue that the world was still going on out there. Genie kept a good eye out for those hunters too, but perhaps she'd been wrong; they may have been guys out to kill birds or deer, or whatever they did out here. Leastways, the river was empty of people.

Renée shouted. 'Oh my God. It's his Converse. Red. Genie, see where the toe had green paint on it.'

Renée picked it up and handed it to Genie. It was definitely Rian's. She held on to it, dreading finding other bits of him. Grandma Munby would have told her if he were dead, wouldn't she? She wouldn't let her go looking for a dead boy, would she?

Moucher began to bark. He swam and ran as fast he could suddenly, heading out of the river to the riverbank, scrabbling up and out, frantic to get to wherever he was going.

Renée and Genie exchanged worried glances. They were scared to find out what Mouch had found. What if Ri was dead? What would they do then?

Mouch was suddenly silent. Genie stopped. They could hear it now. Engine. Someone was coming upstream on the main river.

Genie and Renée ran for where Mouch was crouched

in a dip. Rian was lying there, asleep or unconscious; they didn't have time to find out. They lay flat on the sand. Genie grabbed Rian's hand and was relieved to discover he had a pulse.

The inflatable came upriver at speed. Renée was watching. Two men, one tall, the other young, wearing flak jackets, sporting shotguns. Definitely the same two from the night before.

They slowed, took their time looking around. Renée pressed her face into the sand. She prayed this dip was out of their line of sight.

Genie studied Rian's face. There was swelling on one side of his head and abrasions. His hair was caked in dried blood. He must have hit his head hard. Was he sleeping or unconscious?

At last the hunters gunned the engine again and sped off. Neither Genie or Reneé moved. Just in case.

Genie was just about to stand when she heard a shotgun breach open and snap shut. One of them had got off the boat. Renée looked over at her.

'What now?' she mouthed.

Genie inched her way to the lip of the little dip and checked the scene. It was the younger one. Checking the rockpools for bodies. Just as they had been doing.

Moucher began to growl. Genie quickly grabbed

his neck and his attention and shook her head. Reluctantly he obeyed.

Genie slid back. 'Get me a rock?' she whispered.

'Rock?' Renée took a peek and saw the kid walking back down the rapids.

'We have to get rid of this guy,' Genie said tersely.

'He's got a shotgun,' Renée pointed out. 'Just let him get out of sight.'

'No. Ri needs help now.'

Renée shook her head. 'Stay calm. No rock, Genie.'

Genie desperately wanted to help Rian. She had no patience whatsoever.

The kid took his time and was thorough, looking in every crevice for bodies. Clearly he thought they were dead.

Renée was pointing up to the riverbank trees. 'We can drag him there. We got to get away from the river.'

Genie saw what she meant. There was an open space behind the trees and they'd be hidden. She turned her head to see how far the kid had gone. He was standing right above them, his shotgun pointing at her head. He grinned. 'Which one of you is Genie?'

Genie reacted instantly, without thinking.

Later, she remembered a host of flash images. Herself gathering handfuls of sand and throwing it up towards his eyes. The boy yelling with surprise. A shotgun going off very loud and someone screaming in pain. Rian waking with a sudden shout. Moucher biting the kid real hard on his ankle, followed by some frantic running towards the trees. No way was that boy going to run after them with his ankle bitten and, better yet, Genie had retrieved his shotgun from out of the water.

Renée took charge, grabbing Rian's hand, getting them beyond the trees. They ran across a hay-field spotted with crimson fireweed until they couldn't run any more and collapsed in a heap by an old road. Rian was sneezing from the flowers and had a splitting headache. The lump on the side of his head was the size of a doughnut and he had cuts on his cheek, arms and legs. He was pleased to get his shoe back though, even if it was soaking wet.

'How long was I out?'

'Hours. We lost you. Had to backtrack the river twice.'

Rian hugged both of them. 'You guys should have left me. Big risk to stay.'

Genie was looking back across the field, holding on to some wild peppermint, tasting some and savouring the heady scent. 'How long before they give chase? His father will come back for him for sure.'

'You know how to use that thing?' Rian asked Genie as she toted the shotgun.

She shook her head. 'But just as long as they don't have it, I'm happy. First swamp I see it's going in. Everything happened so fast . . .'

Renée was nursing sores from scratches she'd got from the field. She pointed towards some rabbits jumping up to see over the long grass. 'Cute.'

Mouch saw them but was too exhausted to give chase.

'Hares,' Rian remarked rubbing his head. 'Too big to be rabbits. We got a plan? I hope it includes getting some pills for my head.'

'You should be resting. Getting an X-ray maybe,' Genie told him.

Rian took Genie's hand and squeezed it. 'Uh-huh. We have to keep moving.'

But they didn't move, they all lay there exhausted and nervous, feeling guilty about not moving on but reluctant to stir. Rian kept glancing behind him.

'He ain't coming, Ri. Mouch bit him good and his foot will be hurting. I think he shot it,' Genie said. 'We need to keep moving, guys,' she added, standing up in her squishy sneakers.

That's when she heard a car approaching. Moucher barked. Genie stuck out her thumb, only thinking about what she was doing as the car came into view. Hell, it could have been anyone driving. Cops, hunters, Reverend

Schneider. Anyone looking for them. Too late to worry about that now: the vehicle slowed to a stop.

It was a beaten-up Volvo wagon. The heavy-set woman in a brown felt hat didn't drive off when she caught sight of Rian with his bloodied T-shirt and Renée covered in dried mud. She wound down the window and looked at them hard, as if appraising them. She didn't seem alarmed by the sight of the shotgun or the blood.

'I kinda bet you've got a good story to tell,' she said. 'Get in, put the shotgun in the back and make sure the safety is on. I don't like guns. Where you headed?'

'Vancouver,' Genie told her, walking round to the back and opening it up. Mouch got up first and immediately leaped into the back seat. Genie placed the shotgun alongside some stout walking sticks and a box of cat food.

'I'm heading to Mission. Should be easy hitching from there.'

They all piled in. The car stank of something – some kind of herb, sage possibly; pretty overpowering.

'Name's Betty,' she told them as she set off.

'Betty Juniper?' Genie exclaimed. It had to be. 'Ferry's friend?'

The woman was more surprised than they were. She looked at Genie carefully as she climbed in and shut the door.

'You know Ferry? From the gas station?'

'We just dropped a letter off for you from him at Bear Island. Sorry 'bout your place. Must have been real nice before the flood.'

'Well, goodness gracious. You're Genie Magee. I'll be damned. Grandma Munby's little grandchild. I'm blessed. Ain't it just a goddamn small wonderful world.' She checked the mirror, looking at Rian. 'You hit something hard on the rapids back there, huh. I got myself a lump like that when I was a kid. Thought I'd be tough and went upriver to Hell's Gate, serious white-water rafting. Rite of passage.' She laughed. 'Looked pretty much like you do now, got tossed right out and nearly drowned. I'll never do that again, that's for sure. Genie, open the glovebox, take out some pills and pass them to him. There's a bottle of water down about your feet somewhere.'

'Thank you, ma'am,' Rian said. 'I'm sorry about your place too.'

'It's more than a tragedy. Insurance won't pay out. Act of God and all that. I was in tears for a while, but I had good years there. Might get it fixed, might not.'

'You'd need a new bridge too,' Renée chipped in. 'Weren't you lonely there?'

'Lonely? I was booked solid. Had two big gay weddings booked for fall and the birders come all the time. Some days I had to install a turnstile on the bridge.'

Genie laughed. It was an exaggeration, but she could see why people would go there. Some part of it was probably this loud, friendly woman with an infectious smile.

'Well, I'm in no rush and there's a cute little teahouse about ten clicks down the road. We should get you guys cleaned up. I want to know all about Ferry and you. And how's my house look? Bad?'

'Needs fixing up for sure,' Renée informed her. 'Pears are sweet though and we ate some of your salad stuff.'

She laughed. 'Thank God someone did. You guys must have a guardian angel looking after you. You know how many people are looking for you?'

'Yes, ma'am,' Rian said. 'If you're going to stop someplace, we'd appreciate it if it isn't anywhere near the river. We're a little too popular right now.'

Betty nodded, driving faster now, hardly even slowing for bends. 'Don't you worry. Ferry spoke to me only yesterday. He's fretting himself silly back in Spurlake about you. He'll be so happy to hear you're safe.'

Genie looked at her and heard Grandma Munby's voice again. *Go east on the Cariboo road. She'll be waiting for you*. So weird, so completely weird. Yet true.

'And don't fret about getting to Vancouver. I'll make

93

sure someone gets you there. That Fortress has made our lives a misery ever since they built it. This part of B.C. used to be corner of heaven, now it's becoming like hell.'

Rian fell asleep against Renée's shoulders. Genie thought again of her grandma and remembered to say thanks. They were rescued – for now.

11

A Little Light Surgery

Genie thought the Victorian teahouse was like something out of *Mary Poppins*. An old-fashioned clapboard house with two pointy towers at either end and two guys dressed in tweeds serving scones, apple pie and Lady Grey tea in their back garden under a glass roof. There wasn't even a sign outside, yet there were at least four couples sitting at other tables and someone inside buying homemade jam and cakes. There was nothing like this in Spurlake. She loved the old fireplace with marble surround and a hissing log slow-burning in the grate. A fat ginger cat slept in front of it and barely acknowledged visitors.

'It's like Miss Marple,' Renée hissed as she went to find the bathroom. 'I saw it on TV and it's just like this.'

Genie grinned. She had no idea who Miss Marple was but she was glad Renée liked it.

Rian was eating hot scones, trying not to let the butter drip on to his jeans. Betty talked to the owners and swapped guest horror stories. It was a good respite from their ordeals so far.

Genie saw Renée silently signalling her over to join her in the bathroom. Rian saw it too. 'Impossible for a girl to go to the bathroom alone, huh.'

Genie just sighed, crammed down the last of her scone and went to join Renée. She passed an old grandfather clock in the hallway and what looked like a stuffed penguin. She wondered how the hell that got there.

Renée was in the cubicle already.

'You OK?' Genie asked.

'I'm bleeding.'

'You on?'

'No. I'm bleeding. I got pretty cut up on the river and it's not healing.'

'Can I look?'

'Wait.' Genie waited. She heard Renée flush and then opened the door that she hadn't locked anyway.

'My God, Renée. Why didn't you say?'

Genie was looking at a jagged cut right from the back of her thigh to her ass. It was a good fifteen centimetres long and quite deep.

'You didn't notice?'

Renée was looking at her and shrugged. 'The water was cold. My jeans are still wet and I guess the blood sort of soaked into the denim. It didn't hurt until I pulled them down and the scab peeled away with it.'

'Ouch.' Genie sucked in her breath. It would leave a nasty scar unless it was fixed real fast.

'We have to get something, Renée. You can't just leave it. It might get infected.'

'What will get infected?' Betty asked, entering the bathroom. 'We have to go.'

She saw Renée's cut and her face blanched. 'My goodness, girl, we have to get that treated right away. What happened?'

Renée tried to pull up her jeans, but it was sore and they were damp; she was embarrassed.

'Stay there. I'll get Francis. He used to be a nurse. He's got everything here.'

'Nooo,' Renée protested, but to an empty room as Genie and Betty had already left to find Francis.

Five minutes later she was bent over a chair, bright red in the face as Francis, who took her injuries very seriously, sewed her up, ignoring her protests and her ouches. He cleaned it, stitched it, and rubbed an antibiotic cream on it and tut-tutted a lot, but Renée appreciated his care and, much to her surprise, it didn't hurt too much at all.

Francis even found her a pair of jeans, only one size bigger than Renée and, most importantly, dry and warm.

'I have seen some asses in my time,' Francis said in all

seriousness, 'but yours is a pretty derrière, my dear. You should be proud.'

Renée laughed, but accepted the compliment. It was good to know.

'White-water rafting is dangerous,' Francis was saying. 'I mean, look at Rian's head. You are supposed to stay *in* the raft.'

Rian sat on a chair in a guest bedroom as Francis worked his magic. He patiently read the Vancouver paper *The Province*, left by a visitor. Francis had already rubbed some magic anti-swelling cream on to his wounds, which helped reduced the bump, and Betty was fussing over Genie, wanting to buy her a dress in the next town. Good luck to that, he thought. As far as he knew Genie had never actually worn a dress since she was about six. He tried to imagine what she'd look like and just couldn't. He'd only ever seen her in jeans.

Genie had returned from feeding Moucher out in the car and was looking at her head in a mirror. She noticed her hair was starting to grow again but there was something odd about it. If she looked carefully she thought she saw some white hair growing, like a streak across her head. No way. She'd be a freak. She was about to investigate further when Betty distracted her with some task or other.

'Anything in the paper about us?' Renée asked, walking stiffly out of the bathroom, Francis smiling behind her, proud of his handiwork.

Rian shook his head. 'A nuclear bomb could fall on Spurlake and we'd probably still not make the news. Anything outside the city doesn't exist, Renée.'

'Good,' Genie said, returning to the room. 'We don't want anyone to know about us.'

'Bear attacked a Korean man who chopped all the trees down behind his house in the Kootenays,' he read out.

'Bear was probably pissed off. You'd feel the same way if someone chopped your house down,' Genie declared.

Rian suddenly found something.

'Hey. Check this . . .'

High school graduate Miho Tanaka (eighteen) of Spurlake was found dead possibly from suicide at her home Thursday morning. The mailman raised the alarm. According to neighbours, Miho, who previously has been missing since graduation, returned to discover her mother had died of cancer and was deeply depressed by this. She is survived by her father, Ito Tanaka. Spurlake has been plagued by a spate of teen runaways in the past three years, five times the national average, with thirty-six children going missing. Recently eight

99

returned after a long absence, only to disappear again.
No one is able to offer an explanation for this. Rumours
have circulated that these missing teens have been
attracted by a paid offer to participate in a drug trial
locally but no drug company has admitted to running
any trials in the area. This suicide added to the local
tragedy of Spurlake where one hundred and twenty-
eight people recently perished in the floodwaters.
Although there have been recent rumours of UFO
abductions of children, these were dismissed as
'ridiculous' by Spurlake's sheriff's department.

'Miho!' Renée exclaimed. 'She hardly spoke. She was so
shy. Remember how she carved that beautiful angel out of
an apple? She was like so talented.'

'She was the girl who used the phone and nearly got us
discovered. I remember that I wanted to kill her,' Genie
said. 'God, now I feel guilty. I feel so sorry for her.'

Rian shook his head. 'No way suicide, not after what
she's been through. She was upset about her mother,
but she knew she was dying. She was supposed to have
gone to Vancouver to art school, remember? Miller
gave her the bus fare. It was a Mosquito attack. The
Fortress killed her.'

'We don't know that for sure.' Genie said. 'But it does

kinda disprove your claim that the paper doesn't cover Spurlake, Rian Tulane.'

'Yeah, but why weren't they there when we exposed Reverend Schneider and the Fortress?'

'Because teen suicides are sexy. Teens abducted by aliens are just weird. You going to try and explain the Mosquito attack to them? You think they'd believe that?'

'Mosquito?' Betty was saying as she returned to the room.

'It's how they find us,' Rian explained to her. 'They can target Genie and Renée's brainwaves and shut them down. They've been trying to get them ever since they left the Fortress.'

Betty had no idea what he was talking about. She gathered her things.

'We have to go. Did you thank Francis?'

Renée grinned. 'I gave him a hug.'

Betty nodded, satisfied. 'Good, a hug is important. Come on. You're refugees remember, no dawdling.'

They left. Genie's brain was clouded by the news of Miho committing suicide. After all she had been through? She didn't think so.

Betty was herding them into her car. Moucher was all excited to see them again.

They didn't notice the busboy making a phone call,

giving Betty's car registration number. Negotiating a piece of that twenty-thousand-dollar reward for two runaways.

'I'm going to drop you at the Shell station on Mission road. You will wait there for Mr Collins. He grows organic vegetables near Harrison Lake and he's a good friend. He'll drive you in to Vancouver. But he won't be there until about five. So you must wait. You can trust him. I already called. He has no idea why or who, only I have asked him to pick up three friends and a dog.'

Genie smiled at her. 'You're more than generous to us.'

'I am very fond of Ferry and if he likes you, you're OK with me.'

A chopper swooped overhead. Probably got a good eyeball on the make of vehicle and licence plate. Genie and Renée had near apoplexy expecting pain from a Mosquito attack.

'Oh no,' Rian exclaimed, craning his neck to see up in the sky. 'It's them.'

'Them?' Betty asked.

'Fortransco. They found us. Someone must have—'

'Nonsense, those were my friends. They wouldn't call anyone,' Betty told him crossly. 'I trust them completely.'

Nevertheless she sped up. Genie noted she was going pretty fast for these country roads now. 'Besides,' Betty added confidently, 'they can't hurt us as long as they are up there and we're down here.'

On the second swoop shots were fired, a sharp burst from an automatic rifle. A spray of bullets cut across the road and car. Betty was screaming then abruptly slumped forward, a bullet in the back of her neck, blood spurting everywhere. She was instantly dead at the wheel. They didn't have to time to react. The car suddenly swerved left and began to buck and jerk over an empty field as they headed fast towards the cliff edge and the river. Renée was yelling, Rian had bashed his head again and was howling with pain and Genie tried to wrestle with the wheel as the chopper came in for another run. The river was just metres away. She couldn't get Betty off the wheel.

'Bail out! Bail out!' Genie screamed.

A shot slammed into the car again, smashing glass, and Genie felt hot metal slice through the tip of her shoulder. Moucher was howling and they careened into a rock, tipping over, but still moving forward at speed. Even as Genie bailed, the car was going over the edge of the cliff, sliding down towards the river on its roof with everyone still inside.

She watched the chopper bank over the trees, ready to come back in and land.

Genie looked around. She was the only one who'd

bailed. She yelled after the car and ran, jumping down the sandy rock cliffside, falling, bouncing, crashing through undergrowth and rocks and following the vehicle down to the deep-green river spread out below.

The car landed upside down in the water and instantly began to sink. Genie bumped and scraped her way all the way down. She sucked in some air and plunged in after the car, praying that Ri and Renée were still alive.

She tried to see underwater, but the water was murky. She'd have to feel her way.

Her hands found the rear door. Being upside down, it was complicated to open it. Moucher flew upwards past her, searching for air. She finally entered the vehicle; there was still some air at the top but it was filling fast. Renée was struggling with her seatbelt, upside down in the car, Rian trying to free her, desperately trying to get at the last air. It was totally disorientating being upside down.

Genie sucked in some air and signalled for Rian to go, she had it under control. Indeed she got Renée free, but hauling her out was tough and Genie felt her chest about to burst – she had to let some air out and then it all escaped and she was suddenly desperate.

Renée abruptly untangled herself, trying to control her sense of panic. She was a second away from drowning. Genie pulled one last time and at last Renée came free and they both rose to the surface, coughing and gasping for air.

Rian was there waiting as they broke surface, his head bloody once again as the old wound had reopened. Moucher was already on the shore, shaking. Rian wasn't about to make them swim to shore though. 'Get air, go back under, swim over there.' He pointed to trees at the water's edge. 'Get under the trees.' Their low branch overhang shaded the river. 'Now! Before they see you.'

Genie took a huge breath. Renée followed suit, bewildered and shocked by what had happened. All three swam underwater towards the trees.

Moucher was astonished by their actions. He ran, shaking and vexed, alongside the river, going this way and that, not knowing what to do. They had all disappeared.

Air bubbles and debris were still coming up from the sunken car.

Moucher saw men up high on the cliff looking down and yelped. They had guns. Mouch tried to hide behind a rock, but there was nowhere.

The men fired three rounds into the submerged car and waited a moment. More debris floated up. They seemed satisfied. One was trying to get a signal for his cellphone and not succeeding.

Moucher watched them leave and lay there, panic-struck. Genie had gone. He had no idea what to do and whined piteously.

'I'm beginning to hate this bloody river,' Renée whispered as she clung on to one of the lower branches. 'Genie, I'm getting tired of thanking you for saving my ass, as well.'

Genie smiled, her heart rate returning to normal now. She could hear Moucher howling but she dared not call to him yet. Not till she saw that chopper take off.

Rian lay on his back and floated, his arms keeping him steady in the current. He appreciated the cool water on his sore head.

'One thing we know now. They no longer want you back alive,' he said.

Genie had picked up on that herself. It was disappointing. It was the only card she had in her favour before.

'Poor Betty. It's my fault. Should never get anyone involved. She was such a good person too. I feel so bad . . .'

Renée looked at Genie and then looked away because she knew she would cry. That woman had been really nice and so completely the opposite of her own mother. Why couldn't she have had a mother like Betty? Why hadn't Genie? Life just sucked.

They heard the chopper engines begin to whine.

'Stay put. You don't know what they can see from the air. Stay put until they have really gone,' Rian instructed.

Moucher continued to howl – like he was in mourning, and it broke Genie's heart. But she couldn't call him. Not yet.

'We gonna swim to Vancouver from here?' Renée asked. "Cause I got to tell you, I very seriously doubt I can make it.'

Rian just smiled. But Renée was right. Just what to do now? The river wasn't safe. Neither was the road. Just what did they have to do to get to the city and safety?

'I'd kill for a toothbrush right now,' Genie stated out of nowhere.

Rian watched the chopper rise through the cover of the leaves. It flew right over the crash site, just to be sure.

'They won't leave it at that. They'll send someone to get the bodies out before the cops make a fuss,' Rian stated.

'Then let's get out of here,' Genie said, swimming to shore. 'Mouch, Mouch baby, it's OK. I'm here. I'm here.'

Mouch looked at her with astonishment. He had been so sure he'd been abandoned.

'I'm not leaving you,' Genie told him.

He desperately tried to lick her dry as she came ashore.

Renée walked out of the river and looked down at

Genie, trying to discourage Moucher and just sit.

'Wasn't he supposed to go get help from the friendly farmer up the road who'd come and save our asses, and also has a very good-looking son who will like take on the Fortress single-handed and win?'

'That, I believe, will be in the sequel,' Rian told her. 'Right after we teach Mouch to write our names in the dirt.'

'Oh right, we haven't told him how to write. Stupid us.'

Genie hugged her damp dog. 'Lay off him. He's here, he's looking after me as best he can.'

Rian looked up the cliff they'd just come down and then back at Genie. He realized she was bleeding and had cuts and abrasions all over her.

'I can't believe you ran down this cliff – and lived.'

'I can't believe you survived the crash.'

'Volvo,' Rian stated calmly. 'They test them in rivers like this. I knew soon as I saw the car we'd be safe.' He winked at her and Genie couldn't but help smile back.

'What next, Ri?'

Rian pointed south. 'Walk along the riverbank to the bend, then head in towards the road. We can hitch. But we'll never meet up with that guy in Mission by five p.m. That's for sure.'

Renée pulled off her top and wrung the water out of it. She'd given up on modesty. Being dry was her priority now.

'We have to go,' she said. 'I don't want to be anywhere near here if they send someone. They're going to be angry when they don't find our bodies.'

Genie nodded, pulling off her T-shirt with difficulty. Both Renée and Rian winced at her cuts and bruises.

Genie squeezed all the water out of it and pulled it back on.

'That cut on your shoulder? How did . . . ?'

'Bullet,' Genie said matter-of-factly. 'Weirdly, it doesn't hurt as much as my knees. I don't even want to look at my knees.'

Renée inspected Genie's shoulder. 'Wow. Bullet must have just nicked you. Clean though, more like a burn. It's going to leave a scar.'

Rian came over and kissed her shoulder then hugged her. He whispered something in her ear and Genie smiled, hugging him back.

'Let's go, guys,' Renée said. 'No time for sweet nothings.'

They moved off, more determined than ever to survive the Fortress and all it could throw at them. Genie said a little prayer for Betty Juniper as they passed the submerged car. No one that nice should have to die.

12

City Lights

They waited by the Lougheed Highway. Renée despaired of anyone ever stopping. Moucher whined as cars and trucks drove by, and all the time Genie fretted that the Fortress would find them. They were so exposed by the side of the road and everyone eyed them suspiciously. With good reason, she supposed. They looked pretty beat up. It was Renée's turn to stick her thumb out. If they didn't stop for her, then there was no chance at all, Genie reasoned. Men slowed and looked, but maybe because she was a teen, probably because they were scabby and covered in blood stains, they all drove on.

'We're going to have to sleep out here,' Rian said after a while. 'We should try finding a safe place off the highway.'

'We can't give up yet,' Renée protested.

'It'll be dark soon. No one will stop for us in the dark.'

Genie didn't want to admit it, but Ri was right. She didn't like the idea of hitching at night either; no way to tell what kind of crazy person might stop with bad ideas.

'OK. Let's find someplace safe. Ri's right, Renée. Whilst we can still see.'

Reluctantly she agreed and began to follow them as Rian walked back towards the riverbank.

Moments later a truck stopped some twenty metres or so past them. Genie hadn't been sure it was going to stop at all, but it did and they ran after it. Moucher got there first, barking a couple of times to the driver, who threw a biscuit down to him, which he gobbled real fast before Genie could stop him.

Rian and Genie arrived, breathless, Renée taking up the rear. They looked up at the East Indian driver with keen expressions. What he made of them all, covered in scratches, dried blood and messed-up hair was anyone's guess. He just shook his head.

'You crashed your car? You kids look very sad.'

Genie nodded. 'In the river,' she told him. After all, it was true.

'You driving?' he asked Genie, frowning.

Genie pointed at Rian. 'Him. He's the world's worst driver.'

Rian looked at her with astonishment. 'Am not.'

The truck driver laughed, revealing huge brilliant-white teeth.

'I myself have been in the river,' he told them. 'Twice.

111

This is a very tricky road, very tricky. Especially in winter. Climb up in the back. Don't touch the fruit. Keep the dog still.' He looked at Moucher a moment. 'I give you fifty dollars for the dog. That is a very pretty dog you have there.'

'Not for sale.' She grabbed Mouch and picked him up, holding him close. 'Mouch is my guard-dog.'

The driver grinned. 'You getting in?'

Genie looked at Ri and Renée and shrugged. He'd driven into the river twice! Well, it had to be third time lucky or something.

'Thanks,' Rian told him.

'Where you headed?'

'Vancouver.'

'Must be terrific fate,' the driver said with a big grin. 'That is exactly where I am taking these apples.'

'Really?' Renée asked, always suspicious of coincidences.

'Oh yes, really. Best price for organic apples in B.C. Come on, get in, I am already running late.'

They clambered aboard and found themselves in a truck filled with boxed apples, all carefully placed on layers of tissue to protect them. Guranji Farms – Penticton. They were separated from the driver by stacks of boxes. There was just enough room for them to squeeze in at the back.

'Familiar, anyone?' Renée asked, laughing. 'He's come a long way.'

'Can't believe it's an apple truck,' Genie said. 'They look . . .'

'Perfect. Better than Marshall's apples,' Rian declared.

All three of them vividly remembered spending a week picking Marshall's apples back at the farm. Had that really been such a short time ago?

The truck set off with a jerk and they went flying into each other, Moucher sliding all the way down.

'Ow,' Genie complained.

'Wedge yourself between boxes,' Renée suggested. 'Safer.'

'Especially when he drives into the river,' Genie said.

'Hey,' Rian complained. 'How come you said I was driving?'

Genie just grinned. She was happy they were moving again. She felt more confident that they would escape now and it was sheer luck (or Grandma Munby) that had guided this East Indian driver to stop for them, *and* he was going to Vancouver. She really believed they would get there now.

'Checklist,' Rian was saying. 'I've got three hundred and five bucks left. Genie, the keys? Please tell me you've still got the keys to the yacht.'

Genie fished into her ever-damp jeans and her fingers closed over the precious two keys she'd 'borrowed' from Reverend Schneider and sewn into her waistband – Marshall's idea to make sure she didn't lose them.

'Still here.'

'We have to get in, find the yacht and move off real fast,' Rian said. 'The moment anyone sees us, they'll get suspicious and call the cops.'

'Marshall said it was moored either in a place called Stamps Landing or the Granville Island Marina. Trouble is I've got no idea what it looks like.'

'We have a number. Yachts have numbers,' Rian reassured her.

'We have to stop for a latté first,' Renée declared. 'I just can't spend another day without. Please tell me there's a coffee shop there.'

Rian and Genie exchanged glances, then smiled. Renée was impossible.

13

Keys

Reverend Schneider stared at the row of keys in his office and swore. He, like many others, was totally unable to remember which key was which or where he last put them, which is why he had a spare set made up of all of them and hung with names and numbers on their respective hooks. So he was surprised to see his yacht keys were missing. He tried to recall if he had forgotten to replace them. Then he remembered that he didn't bring them back from his last trip, but left them with the marina office. It was safer. But that only accounted for one set. Where was the spare set? It wasn't here, that was for sure.

It wasn't so much he wanted to go sailing but, given the hostility of Strindberg at the Fortress and the threats to take back everything he owned, he wanted to safeguard certain possessions he was particularly fond of. And all this because of Genie Magee. He felt hatred rising for the child and tried to control it. Her mother had no idea where she might be or where she might go. But she had to be found, dead or alive. Everything he had ever worked for depended upon it.

The yacht keys. Why weren't they here? He needed that yacht. No one knew he owned one, as far as he knew. Except Dan Pickard, the cider man he'd bought it off. He wasn't likely to say anything. The man was fairly friendless in Spurlake. The yacht was important now, might be a useful escape route.

He went through the drawers again. The spare set had to be somewhere. He made a note to call the marina people in Vancouver who looked after it for him and occasionally chartered it out for him. He'd have them check how many sets of keys there were there and get the boat ready. In case he had to disappear himself. Just in case.

14

Anchors Aweigh

The store was Korean – small, but seemed to have everything and the vegetables looked really fresh. They stocked up on rice and pasta and stuff that might last.

'You like wholegrain or honey and oats?' Renée asked reaching for a loaf.

'We're not allowed bread, we're girls,' Genie said.

Renée looked at her with raised eyebrows, then realized she was joking.

'What else do we need?' Genie asked.

'Some sauces for the pasta and chips.'

Genie grinned. 'Chips?'

'Chips,' Renée insisted. 'We're going out to sea. I'm not going without potato chips.'

Genie sighed. She looked back at the busy avenue as an immaculate sixties Chevy pick-up slowly drove by, posing. Two young guys walked past, covered in tattoos and holding hands, laughing at something. She realized that everyone was just doing their own thing here. No judgements.

'It's so different to Spurlake.'

Renée smiled and leaned forward so their foreheads touched. 'We're never going back, hon.'

Genie screwed up her face. 'I'll get some water. We'll need water.'

'Twenty-one dollar,' the Korean woman barked. 'Cash only.'

Twenty minutes later they arrived at Stamps Landing on the waterfront.

'So where is it?'

Now they felt really stupid. Here they were, standing with arms laden with groceries, staring at a space on a jetty where a yacht was supposed to be.

Above them people were eating and drinking in Monk McQueen's, a swanky restaurant built out over the water. All around them were yachts of all sizes and across the water even more yachts, but bigger. There was no shortage of boats in Vancouver, that was for sure.

Rian examined the tag on the key again.

'It definitely says Stamps Landing.'

A guy carrying a gas canister was coming towards them.

'You guys look like trouble.'

Renée tried to smile, but all the hope in her had

gone with the boat that was most definitely not where it should be.

'We were going to sail in *Lord's Business*,' Rian pointed out.

The guy shrugged. 'Not tonight you weren't. Saw it being moved a couple of days ago. Try Granville Marina.'

'That's that way?' Genie asked, looking west.

The guy looked at her as if she were crazy. 'You aren't from around here, are you? Yeah, just follow the path by the water and you'll get there. Won't be anyone there though to talk to, not at this time of night.'

They nodded and watched him walk towards his yacht.

'We are so screwed,' Renée declared.

Genie shook her head. 'Come on, let's go to the next place. Must have been taken there for a reason, right? Don't give up, Renée, we've come so far.'

Rian took Genie's hand. 'Gen's right. May have gone there for all kinds of reasons. Get something fixed maybe. We have keys. If it's there at least we got someplace to sleep, right?'

Renée looked at him and sighed. 'I guess.'

Mouch was already off and running. Didn't like standing near water at all.

They walked back towards the ramp.

Genie looked back across the water at the city glittering

like Christmas beyond. Made Spurlake seem like nothing, absolutely nothing at all.

Renée was looking too. 'I can't believe how many people live here. I mean, these apartments all look into each other. Don't these people want privacy? It's kind of creepy, don't you think?'

'That's how people live in cities,' Rian said. 'They like it.'

'Smell that? Someone is grilling fish. Mmm, I'm starving,' Genie said.

They walked away from the smell of good cooking with much regret.

An hour later they finally found the yacht moored in Granville Island harbour. Some of the yachts there could sleep twenty people or more they were so big. Rian hardly even noticed Reverend Schneider's *Lord's Business* it was so small, but never mind, it was in the water and there was no one to stop them when they unlocked the gate to the tiny marina and made their way on board.

'It's smaller than I expected,' Renée said quietly, trying to hide her disappointment.

Rian opened up the cabin and they quickly entered. Moucher stood on the walkway, scared to make the leap.

'On board, Mouch. Now!' Genie ordered.

He wasn't budging, however. He whined and looked at her with a big question on his face. Clearly he wasn't going to jump. Genie had to scoop him up and carry him over. This was one dog that didn't have sea-legs.

'Get used to it,' Renée told him. 'This is your new home.'

Rian checked the instrumentation on deck. The keys fitted fine.

'We're only half full,' he told them annoyed. 'Probably enough to get us out of here to the next fuelling place. Water tank is full, but who knows how fresh it is? Good for showers though.'

'Showers?' Renée squealed. 'We can have showers?'

'Quick showers,' Rian told her. 'I've been on these kind of yachts before. Hot water lasts about five minutes. You will have to wait for the tank to heat up, though.'

The battery, however, was very low. It would have to be charged.

Rian hooked it up, but it meant they couldn't leave straight away and every delay exposed them to risk.

'Great, I can clean my teeth at last,' Genie exclaimed.

He looked down at the girls in the cabin. They were both brushing their teeth and looked happy.

'You realize this is my first ever vacation?' Genie stated looking up at him.

'We're on the run, Gen.'

'Well, we're going out to sea. Feels like a vacation to me.'

'Me too,' Renée chipped in.

Moucher stood nervously on the floor, his legs slightly splayed. He didn't like this one bit. The floor moved. Floors shouldn't move.

'Moucher's unhappy,' Genie declared, giving him a sympathetic look. 'Poor baby.'

'Feed him,' Rian told her. 'He has to be hungry. Better he gets used to it and goes sick here than out there.'

'Eww, don't get sick, little doggie,' Renée cooed. 'Can a dog eat Tums? I found some Tums.'

'Check to see if they are sugar-free, otherwise he'll get the shits,' Rian answered.

'Eww. Sorry, dog, I'm not risking it.'

Rian grinned and continued to check the yacht over. He wanted to know where everything was situated: lifesavers, flares, you name it. You could never be too careful.

'You'll need to flush the water tank,' a voice suddenly announced from behind Rian.

Rian turned, his heart missing a beat. A deeply tanned man was standing on the walkway watching him. He wore a blue sweatshirt and shorts and old scruffy sneakers on the end of hairy legs.

122

'Oh, hi . . . er, really?'

'Yeah. It's been standing for a while. You got the power hooked up?' He looked down at the connection. 'Oh yeah, you have. Turn the pump on, it's the second switch from the left. There. Turn the handle to E and flush it out and we'll get you hooked up to a fresh supply.'

'Thanks.' Rian got the pump on and heard it start to flush out the tanks. The man bent down to hook up the water supply from a recessed connection Rian had failed to notice.

'Where you headed?' the man asked casually. 'You're late getting started. I was working on the next boat when I heard you arrive.'

Rian wondered if he was a stranger or managed the marina, or what. He kept calm, although his palms were sweating now. He hoped the girls would stay calm too.

'Horseshoe Bay. Picking up Reverend Schneider there for a Bible studies weekend,' Rian told him, making sure the guy couldn't read his face. He was sure people could tell when he lied. Genie was the good liar, not him.

'Well, you're in luck. Fixed the compass only yesterday. I guess if he's coming along, then this is a freebie, huh? When will you be back?'

Genie popped up and smiled at the man. He was wearing Lycra shorts one size too small for him and his massive thighs.

'Hi. Monday, I guess. We have to go back to college. You know how to make the shower work?'

The man smiled back, especially when Renée appeared alongside her in her pants and T-shirt. His eyeballs practically fell out, he was so interested.

'You'll have to wait for the tanks to fill, but I think you have to switch a red dial to up in the shower cubicle and then back again when you finish. I just had the whole thing checked out and everything's working. Oh, there's only small sizes in lifejackets. But that shouldn't be a problem. '

He saw Moucher lying flat by Genie's feet and looking most unhappy.

'Make sure the dog wears a lifejacket at all times, OK. They can make sudden jumps and, when at sea, keep him in the cabin.'

'He's not a good sailor,' Renée pointed out with a cute smile.

'Distract him. Here . . .' He jumped on to the next boat and pulled out a rubber chew toy from a box left on the deck. 'Last charter left this. I was going to throw it out.' He jumped back on to the walkway.

Genie took it from him. She tossed it to Mouch, who spurned it.

'Diesel?' Rian asked him. 'Where's the . . . ?'

'We're waiting on delivery. But there's plenty at Horseshoe Bay.'

Rian nodded. That was annoying, but at least they had enough to get going.

'You been out before?' the man asked. 'The Reverend doesn't usually charter this out to inexperienced sailors. He's quite particular.'

'My dad trained me. He goes out fishing a lot,' Rian answered. It was true, but it had been three years previously and he'd done nothing except watch his dad drink and fish out on the lake, but he wasn't going to mention that.

'Well, there's a guide to the rules of the sea in the cabin. Make sure you read it. There's distress flares in the cupboard and the radio must be kept on. You've got all the safety equipment required. Read the checklist. You have to alert the harbourmaster when you're leaving. All right?'

Rian nodded. 'How long does the water take to fill?'

'It'll be flushed in ten, about half an hour to fill, I guess. Give you time to get familiar with the boat. There's no moon, so it's going to be pretty dark out there. So lights on, and watch out for the wakes from the big ships, particularly the ferries. Don't get close, just get out of their way. If you aren't used to it, it can be scary.'

'We have gas to cook with?' Renée asked from inside.

'Lift the top from the counter on your right. See?'

Renée did so and discovered a sink, stove and all kinds of useful things – pots and pans stowed really tight.

'Neat.'

'Keep it that way. A clean boat is a happy one. You got any booze?'

'On a Bible studies cruise?' Rian asked.

The man laughed. 'I guess not.' He turned away. 'You have a safe trip now, OK? Keep your speed to around eight knots or slower and you'll save gas. No need to go anywhere fast. Oh yeah, weather's going to change. So keep close to the coast. You'll be fine in Horseshoe Bay, but they say pressure's dropping quickly. Can get tricky out there sometimes.'

Rian watched him return to another yacht and disappear inside. They had thirty minutes to wait for the water to fill.

'I'm going to cook,' Renée announced.

'Lucky I brought three bottles of water,' Genie said.

Rian looked up at the sky and the few clouds hovering,

and frowned. The weather looked fine to him, but what did he mean by 'get tricky'?

'You think he'll call Schneider?' Genie asked Rian as he joined them in the cabin.

Rian shrugged. 'No. He's busy. But we can't leave suddenly. That would only make him suspicious. We'll be fine, as long we're all smiling and relaxed. Seems Schneider rents the boat out, so he must be used to people arriving like this.'

Renée just smiled. 'I could go make eyes at him. You see the way he was looking at me? Like he hadn't eaten in months.'

Genie laughed. 'Well, I guess he wasn't looking at me. I swear he was going to drool. Gut feeling, Ri. He won't call.'

Rian looked at her and leaned in to kiss her. 'I hope your gut is right.' He turned to look at Renée. 'What we eating?'

'Fusilli primavera. My speciality.'

Moucher barked. Genie was tearing open his box of biscuits.

'And for starters,' Renée added, looking at the dog, 'all vegetable dog biscuits with added vitamins.'

'Mmm, can't wait,' Rian replied.

Neither could Moucher, who practically ripped the food out of Genie's hands.

127

'Eat slow, Mouch. Have some dignity,' Genie told him, but he ignored her.

An hour later they motored out of the marina and under the Burrard Bridge, real slow and casual, just as they were asked to do. Lights on, keeping out of everyone's way. English Bay opened up to them and Genie continued to be entranced. It was such a magical place. She could see people strolling by the shore and everywhere huge towers of apartments. She had no idea how many people lived here but Marshall had been right, it was a good place to hide. She longed to get to know the city better. It seemed ridiculous to just come and go so quickly. So much to see and they were already leaving. She felt a real pang of regret.

The city seemed to grow ever larger as they could see more of it and, behind it, loomed Grouse Mountain with the summit illuminated around the ski slopes.

Container ships were moored out in the bay and Rian was navigating with care. He had a plan to get them away and refuel at Gibsons, rather than Horseshoe Bay, in case anyone went looking for them there. He realized now he should have picked some other place to say they were meeting Reverend Schneider, like New Westminster, or something, someplace where they had absolutely no intention of going to.

He wasn't exactly sure how far they could go on half a tank of fuel, but as long as they kept it slow, at least forty, fifty ks – enough to get some place. The question was, did they head south to Mexico or go north up the Georgia Strait to Alaska? Which was the better hiding place?

They'd been debating that little problem as they ate.

Renée wanted south. Part of Rian wanted that too, but without documentation they'd soon be in trouble with the US Coastguard, whom they knew could board them anytime when they were in US waters. They could try sailing further out in the Pacific, but Rian looked at the map and that still meant sailing across to Vancouver Island and then through the Juan de Fuca Strait to the open waters of the ocean. He wasn't sure he'd be able to do that, considering they'd be out of fuel and they'd actually have to sail the yacht. He'd never sailed anything longer than a five-metre sailboat and this whole yacht thing was something else.

Hiding in the islands was a better bet. They could do odd jobs on Salt Spring or Galiano, change the name of the boat, stay there someplace and make some kind of life for themselves. Hundreds of hippies did it every year and they survived OK. That was the plan so far, aside from buying fuel with their remaining money.

Renée was tapping the barometer and frowning. 'My father always said you had to check the weather before you ever went out on the open water.' The little hand moved at least five degrees towards 'unsettled'. That probably wasn't good.

'You mean my father,' Rian commented.

'Clearly neither of you ever listened,' Genie said, 'since we never checked anything. He said something about the weather changing, didn't he? You even know how to read a barometer?'

Genie was looking at the device stuck on the wall. It dropped another five per cent when she tapped it.

'What does "severe depression" actually mean? We gotta take aspirin or something?'

Renée laughed but Rian wasn't smiling.

'It says that?'

'Yeah.'

Rian looked at the dark sky. Some clouds were building over the coast and the wind had picked up, but he couldn't see anything that looked real bad. He figured that as long as you could see stars it was OK.

'Could be faulty,' he stated, but they could hear the doubt in his voice.

'Severe depression sounds like sinking. You know, whirlpools that suck you down and . . .' Renée suggested, but kind of tailed off when she got a look from Genie that wasn't too friendly.

'I don't think we're going get tidal waves or anything,' Rian said. 'But make sure stuff is put away so it doesn't fly around, get your lifejackets on and maybe we should head closer into shore. Mouch, stop trying to take your jacket off, OK?'

Genie had tied a rope around his middle and threaded his front legs through the lifejacket. He was not happy, but looked cute. The dog gave him a look. He hated this thing they had tied on him.

Genie and Renée came up on deck to put on their lifejackets. The water looked calm, but then again it was dark – what did they know.

'It's probably broken, you're right, Ri.'

'Don't go too close in-shore, there's rocks, right?' Renée said.

'Any rocks would have a buoy on them with a light.' Rian reassured them.

'We got a chart at least? I saw *Pirates of the Caribbean* about ten times and they had charts,' Renée added.

'I don't think they had charts. They had a magical compass that didn't really work,' Rian contradicted her. 'We aren't exactly in pirate waters, Renée, and if I remember, Jack Sparrow had no idea where he was most of the time.'

'Just like us,' Genie chipped in.

'Do we even have a compass?' Renée asked.

Rian pointed at it and the instrument panel.

'We're doing seven knots, bearing north-west five degrees. Well, we should be. I can't quite see in the dark.'

'Great.'

Genie jumped down into the cabin, disturbing Mouch, was still trying to bite off the strap holding on the lifejacket.

'I'm going to make cocoa. Who wants cocoa?'

Rian and Renée both looked at each other and laughed.

'We do,' Renée shouted down. 'Yay, hot cocoa.'

They drank from plastic mugs and watched the sky. The clouds were definitely building. The boat was beginning to heave up and down as the swell grew. Rian figured that Gibsons had to be about an hour and half away. He wanted to sneak in unobserved. It was late now, most likely impossible to get refuelled at this hour.

Mouch clung to the cabin deck like he was glued to it. Renée was looking into her empty mug. She looked up at Genie momentarily.

'You think Cary is cute?'

'Cary? Cary probably being held prisoner by the Fortress, Cary?'

'I was thinking about him, that's all. He's shy but he's kinda cute.'

Genie shrugged. 'He's short-sighted.'

'Not any more, remember? They fixed that.'

'He's weird,' Rian said.

'I wasn't talking to you. Steer, Rian Tulane.'

'Excuse me for having an opinion,' Rian said, altering course some.

'He's bright. He sees life in numbers,' Genie said. 'I'm not sure he's got a sense of humour though.'

'Well, maybe not, but perhaps he never had much to laugh about.'

Genie frowned. 'Weren't you supposed to be thinking about a plan? Like what we're going to do with our lives once we get where we're going?'

'Oh yeah, that's going to be so thrilling,' Renée sighed. 'No high-school certificate, minimum wage – hell, everyone I know is like that and on social security all winter. I was hoping for more.'

Genie took her hand and held it. 'You'll get more. Things will work out. You'll see.'

'Oh sure, we'll become supermodels, fly across the world and spew our dinners up every night. That was my other plan.'

Genie laughed. 'You're beautiful, Renée. Maybe not

that beautiful, but beautiful. You could be an actress. You ever done any acting?'

'Does lying to my ma count?'

'Hell, yeah.'

'Well, in that case, I am Oscar material. But you've got Rian. He's always going to take care of you. Who'll take care of me?'

'Well, me,' Rian said. 'I am your brother, remember.'

'And you, you have to take care of you,' Genie told her. 'That's what Marshall said, you have to take care of number one. Care about yourself and people will care about you.'

'You believe a guy with one leg who lives all alone? You need a better guru.'

'He's not wrong.'

Genie yawned. She climbed up on a bunk bed. 'I have to sleep. God, like I got to sleep now.' She clung to her bunk as if it was going to tip over and felt her head was swimming. It was one thing feeling tired but this was ridiculous.

'Tired,' Genie mumbled and she knew Renée was still talking to her but she heard nothing.

Renée stared, amazed Genie could go out like that. Like someone flipped a switch.

She went up on deck to join Rian.

'She's sleeping.'

Rian nodded. He looked at her and the bruise on her head. 'You OK?'

Renée smiled. 'Yeah.' She looked out over the water and saw virtually nothing – no lights and no ships. It was if they were in the middle of nowhere.

'What's up?'

'Getting colder and the clouds have moved in. Wind's changed direction too. According to the GPS thing we're about an hour and some from Gibsons. Water should be calm but it's getting rougher. It's your fault, you should never have touched the barometer.'

Renée was about to protest when she saw the traces of a smile on his lips. 'That's a sailing joke, right?'

'Did you tie stuff down? It's going to get rough.'

'Pretty much. I can't believe how dark and cold it is now. Like we're in the *Twilight Zone* or something. Look, I can see my breath.' She exhaled and a frosty cloud lay between them.

'This is that moment just before the *Titanic* hit an iceberg, right?' she added.

Rian laughed. 'No icebergs out here, Renée. Worst case scenario we collide with a whale or something.'

'Killer whales are so forgiving, I hear.'

A huge swell rolled under them and the yacht tilted

forty-five degrees. Renée clung to Rian for dear life.

'Get below and hang on. I think it's going to get a lot worse.'

Renée didn't need telling. She jumped down and grabbed the plastic bucket. Someone was going to need it, for sure – namely her.

15

Radspan

Cary shook her awake. 'Genie? Can you hear me? Genie?'

Genie opened her eyes. She was freezing cold. She looked up and there was Cary looking down at her. She could hear others too. She was no longer on the yacht. Was this a dream? Or real? What just happened?

She turned her head and Denis was trying to get a torch to work and swearing at it. She could see that they were in a kind of tunnel, dug out of chalk. It was dark but there was a blue glow from emergency lighting built into the tunnel wall.

'Anyone know where we are?' Cary asked.

Genie shook her head. 'I don't even know how I got here.'

Denis got the torch to work and flashed it up on the walls. They could make out the words: *Radspan – Warning 100,000 volts. Avoid live cables.*

Genie looked at Cary. 'One hundred thousand volts?'

'There's more than that going through here. You seen the rats?'

'Rats?' Genie thought she'd seen enough of rats back on Granville Island.

'Lot of dead ones. They've been chewing the cable linings. One bite and *fritzzzzz*.'

'Nice.'

Denis came over and helped Genie up. 'Hey, your hair's growing. Cool.'

Genie felt her head; it was reassuringly as stiff as a brush.

She looked at Denis and Cary; they both still had their hair, but somehow it didn't look quite convincing.

'Where are we, Denis?' Genie asked him. 'Are you guys OK?'

'This is the service tunnel, I think,' Cary told her. 'It leads to Radspan. It's what they built before Synchro.'

'But what is it?'

'Early particle collider maybe? It runs for kilometres in a huge circle,' Cary said. 'But you brought us here; we didn't move a muscle.'

'I did?' Genie was confused. Last she remembered was being really, really tired on the yacht.

'You didn't say how you guys are. I mean, I heard they caught you, but have they . . . ?' Genie asked, her voice trailing away. She wasn't sure they wanted to talk about it. She squatted down on an old wooden box. Her head was foggy. Her being here right now didn't make any sense. Denis was as small as ever. Cary didn't look so pale any more – and Renée was right, she realized, he was pretty good-looking for a geek.

'You got away then. I called you,' Denis reminded her.

'I know. But how come I'm here now? We made it, Denis. We got down the river, stole Reverend Schneider's yacht and everything. We were getting away, I swear, and now I'm right back here.'

'Maybe you're dreaming,' Cary suggested. 'Is Renée with you? On the yacht, I mean.'

'Yeah. She is.' She suddenly smiled. 'Did you know she has the hots for you?'

Denis laughed and punched Cary on the arm. 'Told you.'

Cary blushed but was secretly very pleased.

'Really,' Genie assured him. 'She likes you a lot.'

'Well, don't tell her what happened. Especially about the hair,' Cary said, grinning.

'Hair? What happened? I was going to ask you about your hair. It kinda moves.'

Denis sat beside her and leaned up against her. 'Bastards grabbed us. Got Julia too. First thing they did was shave our heads. Told us they were going to teleport us again. Jules went hysterical; they strapped her down

139

and later they took her off someplace else. Randall was in another room too. I heard him screaming.'

'But you've got hair now?' Genie pointed out the inconsistency.

Cary pointed at Denis. 'He found this program. It's like Bratz dress-up software. We can have hair, change our clothes, y'know.'

'No it isn't,' Denis protested, clearly embarrassed.

'Is too. Admit it. You found it on a kids' website.'

'Well, I'm not going around bald for anyone,' Denis told her. 'Not even in your dreams, Genie.'

She smiled. This really was like some surreal dream.

'Miho's dead,' Genie told them. 'We saw it in a newspaper. They said it was suicide but I think it was a Mosquito attack.'

Cary looked at Denis and they shrugged. 'You don't get it, do you?'

'What?'

'We're *all* in a coma. Mosquito attack. Like it was a major electro-magnetic pulse. They just wiped us out. Denis and me – we're lying in the cell now. We're on life-support.'

Genie was confused. She reached out and touched Cary. He was as solid as she was.

'I don't get it.'

'You sure you're conscious?' he asked her. 'You sure you're on a boat? They blasted that thing wide. You could be lying in a coma somewhere. I'm not surprised Miho is dead. I'm just amazed you aren't. We aren't real, y'know? This is a construct, like before.'

'Construct?'

'It's like gaming,' Denis explained. 'You created this place, us, we're like avatars or something. It's all in the mind.'

Genie shook her head. 'No. I didn't. This is real. I know it. You being here is real. If I can touch and feel, it's real.'

Cary shook his head. 'We're lying on a slab with our heads shaved in a coma and they're thinking of switching us off. I'm sorry, Genie, but that's the truth.'

Genie looked at them both and part of her knew it was true. Part of her wasn't accepting it either.

'I know we're here for a reason,' she said. 'We need to find out why, that's all.'

'But you *could* be lying in a ditch somewhere. This is just a wish-fulfilment thing,' Cary stated.

Genie slapped him on his hand; she wasn't taking this defeatist attitude. 'I am here. I'm real. This is what I do. I go places. I don't choose it, or know why it happens, but I am here. If I'm here, it's for a reason. Think, Cary.

Radspan. What is it? Where is it?'

Cary was reluctant to try, she could see that. Denis was frowning, he understood what she was saying. He remembered seeing Genie in Synchro before, during the flood and even then it was impossible she was there, but she had been. He never really thought about it much, but he remembered something else, that odd feeling of hope he always got when he saw her. She could do impossible things.

'Listen to her, Cary. She got us out of the Fortress once, maybe she can do it again,' Denis said.

Genie tried to remember stuff. 'Did either of your legs go missing? Your hands maybe? Renée had an episode an—'

Denis rolled his eyes. 'I lost my feet. Cary was screaming about his arms and legs. That's when it started. They kept saying that there wasn't anything wrong, but I know my feet went missing.'

Genie smiled. 'Latent memory syndrome. Renée was the same. They weren't missing, but your brain switched them off, just like when the servers went down before. Rian worked it out.'

Cary was about to disagree, but then nodded.

'That kinda makes sense. Makes a lot of sense.'

'So, help me guys. Why are we here? Think.'

Denis was shining the torch around and it swept past something on the wall. He stood up and shone the beam on the wall again.

'Hey, come and look at this.'

Genie and Cary walked behind him, stepping over the many cables lining the centre of the tunnel.

'I think we found your answer,' Denis said. 'We've discovered something important.'

They were looking at a map of Radspan – it carried a date. 1998. It was like a subway map and a series of stations. The primary station was Synchro and then it fanned out to an unnamed place and then jumped to Whistler and starting making longer leaps as far as Banff and some place near Calgary and right across Canada as far as St John's. The last six stations were labelled 'under construction'.

'Twenty-five. Fifty. One hundred. Two hundred. Four hundred . . .' Cary was saying. 'Each leap doubles up. Radspan. It fans out from Synchro and each time they were going to try and leap further. It's the original teleport concept.'

Cary was excited now. He turned to Genie. 'Look, here's us.'

He traced his fingers over the map to the point just besides Synchro. 'But it doesn't start in Synchro. It starts here – in a tunnel about half a mile under Marshall's farm. I can take a bet that it's where it is. Almost exactly in the middle between the Fortress and Synchro.'

'Like Marshall's farm.'

Denis was looking at the key code at the bottom of the map and trying to make sense of the different colours and squiggles.

'Maybe we teleported up there the first time because there's some kind of conflict. Remember there was something about the magnetic activity.' Cary was thinking aloud. 'You might be the trigger, but there's something in Radspan that pulled us through.'

Genie smiled, shivering now in the cold. She was a tad confused. 'And this means?'

'If we knew how to get on it, work it, maybe we could use it to escape,' Denis said excitedly.

'It's not a literal tunnel, Denis,' Cary told him. 'It's not a train. And I'd like to remind you guys that we're in a coma in the Fortress. I mean, this is cool and all, but unless Genie can break into the Fortress, wake us up *and* steal our bodies, we're not going anywhere.'

'Come on,' Denis said. 'That first station has to be along this track some place.'

Cary and Genie followed him, but Cary was down again. He still thought it was hopeless. They could barely see anything except the torchlight ahead and hear Denis whistling. He was happier at least.

'Does Renée really like me?' Cary asked.

Genie took his arm. 'Yes, very much. She wants you to figure out a way back, Cary. Your brain is working, right? I mean, if you were in a real coma, surely you couldn't even dream you were with me, and if it was a dream – well, Denis wouldn't be in it too, would he?'

'If it was my dream you wouldn't have any clothes on,' Denis called back and laughed.

Genie smiled. 'Gross, Denis. You're Dirty Denis from now on.'

He laughed again.

A light came on, several more, moving on and on right the way along the tunnel until it came to a distance door.

'We just triggered something.' They could all hear a generator starting up.

Cary smiled. 'Good. Means it's still operational.' He turned to Genie and took a deep breath. 'Thanks for coming, Genie. I know you didn't have a choice, but you know how to make a person hope, y'know?'

Genie said nothing. It was she who was having doubts now. Cary was right. If he and the others were in comas, even if they could get them out, how would she ever wake them up? And why was it so darn cold down here?

Denis got to the door first and he looked at the keypad on it and seemed to contemplate it for a few seconds, then punched in four digits.

The door swung open with a hiss as chilled, stale air rushed out to meet them.

'In the nineties they were still using four-digit codes, can you believe it? The only cool thing about being hooked up to the Fortress is you can access codes. I used to do it all the time when I was inside. Can't believe I can still do it.'

Cary slapped Denis on the back. 'That's because you're still hooked up to the Fortress, remember.' He looked at Genie. 'Denis is all numbers. He can see them like shapes or something. I'm jealous.'

Denis winked at Genie as they pushed the door further open.

'It's my only skill. I'm getting better at it. It's cool.'

They entered a huge dome carved out of the chalk and stone. Lights came on automatically overhead and moisture dripped from stalactites forming in the ceiling. Whatever this place had been, it had been neglected and there were signs of water damage everywhere.

Genie realized it was a primitive version of a teleportation chamber. There were rows of old Cray computers and all kinds of wires and tubes, but it was essentially the same thing.

'Wow,' Cary said, walking up to the transmission pad. He felt the smooth curved granite wall. Noted the shadows burned deep into the grain. They had tried teleporting here and failed.

'It doesn't work,' a voice said behind them.

They spun around and there was Julia sitting in a chair watching them. Her hair looked lank, colourless. She was wearing a simple cloth over her and looked so pale, she might as well be dead.

'Julia,' they all cried out in unison.

'I can't stay. I'm pretty far gone. Genie . . . ?'

'Yes?'

'Did you really get away?'

Genie nodded. 'So far. I don't know why I'm here, but I'm here. I'm sorry, Julia.'

'My mother's heart is broken. They dragged me away from her. Daddy's got lawyers and everything, but they told them I wasn't me. I mean, of course I'm me. Daddy's had a breakdown, he actually cried. Made my heart hurt to see it. I can't believe I'm back. Can't believe I'm going to die.'

Genie shook her head. 'You're not going to die. I'm going to find a way, Jules. I have to find a way to get you out.'

Julia shook her head. 'Too late. Can't stay. Not strong enough. Can't stay . . .'

Julia disappeared before their eyes. They stared at the empty chair.

Genie felt sick. This *was* a dream then. She wasn't doing any of them any good.

Cary was looking at the computer systems. He turned to speak to Genie for a moment. 'They tried, but it would have been hopeless. They would never have had enough memory or power. Even with these supercomputers.'

'Why did they abandon it?'

Denis was looking at a video recording on an old TV monitor he'd fired up. It showed a simple furry toy, a rabbit disintegrating. Another scene, another toy burning – another scene showed it exploding; scene after scene, toy after toy destroyed.

'I guess it just didn't work,' Denis declared. 'Built the whole thing and it just didn't work.'

Genie was looking at an old financial magazine with a faded cover left on a chair: '*Premier slashes science research budget in credit squeeze.*'

'I think I know what happened here, guys. They simply ran out of money.'

She turned around. She was suddenly alone. Cary and Denis were gone. The lights abruptly clicked off. She took in a sharp breath. She was underground and it was freezing cold. It was scarily dark. She didn't even know where the door was, didn't even know the code to get out. She suddenly felt very scared and alone.

'Denis?' she shrieked. 'Denis, the code, the code!'

She sat up and banged her head on the bulkhead.

'Ow.'

'Code?' Renée asked. 'What code?'

Genie stared at her in amazement. She'd been dreaming, of course, but it had been so very real. She felt cheated and frozen to the bone.

She suddenly noticed they were violently rolling and Renée had been sick in the bucket. Moucher was whining and the noise of the wind outside was terrifying. How long had she been gone?

'Shiiiiit!' Rian was suddenly yelling up on deck. 'Hold on to something, there's a huge—'

A giant wave came out of nowhere and rolled over the yacht; water poured into the cabin as the whole vessel tipped almost ninety degrees to one side, throwing Renée, Mouch and Genie against the hard cabin wall.

'Close the hatch,' Rian was yelling as Genie tried to get up, water sloshing around her feet. The bucket of sick rolled by; Renée, she noticed, looked green.

Suddenly they were in a major storm and the waves rolling under and cresting over them were enormous.

'Where the hell did that come from?' Renée was complaining.

'Severe depression,' Genie reminded her as more seawater crashed down into the cabin.

Mouch stood up, dripping wet. He barked once and another wave hit the yacht broadsides, a ton of water just poured in and scooped Moucher out with it as the yacht righted itself.

'Mouch!' Genie yelled. She didn't think, not even for a second. She just launched herself after him.

'Genie, no!' Rian yelled after her. Renée screamed. But Moucher and Genie were gone.

Rian urgently throttled down, trying to turn the boat head on to the waves. It was truly scary out here in this squall. The wind howled around them and the rigging was loose, clanging against the mast. Rian had to cling on to the wheel as he searched for the flashlight.

'Renée, the flashlight? We're in some mini-tornado or something. Can you see her?'

Renée had the flashlight and was fighting her way to the hatch. She couldn't believe Genie had gone after the dog. She'd drown for sure.

'Genie?' Rian was yelling against the wind.

Renée was out of the hatch and had it half closed as Rian snatched the flashlight from her and began to sweep the water.

'Genie?' Rian yelled again as the boat rose and fell with the huge swell. The yacht creaked and, as another wave swept over them, Renée nearly went with it too. She wrapped her arms around the mast and began to pray.

'The lifebuoy! Throw it out!' Rian was yelling at her, but she didn't know how to get to it without being thrown overboard herself.

Rian judged his moment between swells and ran for it, got it out and into the water, making sure the lifeline around it was secure to the yacht. Another wave lashed them and he slowly made his way back to the wheel to bring the yacht around again to face the waves head on.

Renée took the flashlight from him and began to sweep for Genie.

'How far does it go?' Rian was asking, not expecting an answer. 'Genie! Genie!' he yelled again, the wind snatching away his words.

Renée thought she heard a shout. She swung round and thought she saw Moucher. It was impossible; he was in front of them, not behind. Something was moving in the water.

'Moucher?' Renée screamed. 'This way! This way!'

Moucher was paddling for all his worth towards them now he had a light to guide him. But where was Genie?

Rian felt the lifeline to the lifebuoy tighten. For one second he glimpsed the automatic light attached to it.

'Genie?' He began to haul it in, amazed, like Renée, that it was in front of them. The current had to be real strong around here.

They both heard the whistle. Genie was communicating at least.

Rian pulled harder. The line suddenly grew heavier.

'She's got him,' Renée announced.

'Close the hatch fully,' Rian told her. 'Let the pumps deal with the water.'

Renée struggled to close it, her feet slipping on the wet deck, but got it closed – just in time as another huge wave washed over them. She held on grimly, cursing the weather and everything she could think of – including Moucher, who was blameless really.

Rian continued reeling in Genie and Moucher, his hands red raw and freezing now.

'We going to sink?' Renée asked.

'No, these boats are built to survive. We haven't gone over yet. Give me a hand.'

Renée grabbed the line and they both pulled. The

boat was in a dip but as they rose again, the flashlight caught Genie and Moucher in the lifebuoy for just a brief moment, just a short distance away.

'Haul!' Rian shouted.

'I *am* hauling.'

Rian grabbed Moucher first, opened the hatch and dropped an exhausted dog down into what looked a lot like a swimming pool. He didn't protest.

Genie offloaded the lifebuoy and made her way up the stern ladder. The flashlight revealed she was bleeding, but she was OK. She couldn't say anything, she was so cold, and dropped down into the cabin without a word. Renée squeezed Rian's arm and followed, firmly closing the hatch after her.

Rian got the engine revved up again and moving. He didn't want it swamped, and a hard-working engine would maybe get them closer to shore and shallower water. He was angry. Angry with Genie, Moucher, his life and everything. He didn't want to speak to anyone right now. He looked at the compass. They were way off course – he wasn't sure where the hell they were – and they were pretty much out of fuel.

He wondered how long the batteries could keep the pumps going and how long it would take for them to clear the cabin of water. It began to rain – heavy, unforgiving rain – and he couldn't see hardly any distance ahead, but he sensed that the sea was growing more calm and the waves, though big, were not so violent.

He throttled down to save fuel and kept a steady course. Land would be on his right, but as for Gibsons? He had no idea. They'd most likely run dry before he found out.

Renée opened the hatch and handed him a plastic cup. 'Drink this.'

He drank whatever it was and nearly spat it out. Brandy. He swallowed, felt his chest implode, but it did the trick, he was instantly warm again, even if only for a little while.

'You could have warned me!' he yelled, but Renée had already disappeared back inside.

Inside the cabin Moucher was lying on a bunk, Genie towelling him off, trying to revive him. He was silent, occasionally retching up seawater. Renée was trying to fix a bandage on Genie's head from the first-aid kit.

'You are so lucky,' Renée told her. 'So lucky. Jumping off like that? What were you thinking?'

Genie looked at her and pulled a face. 'I wasn't thinking. But I got him back. Besides, I was wearing a lifejacket.'

'*We* got him back. If we hadn't thrown the lifebuoy you

and that dog would still be out there, or floating dead. Genie, it was stupid and irresponsible.'

Genie guessed it was true, she had been stupid. But Renée didn't understand her attachment to Moucher. The dog was her talisman. She had to save him. Had to.

'I think I need another sip of brandy and maybe Mouch does too. I think he's in shock.'

'Rian's the one in shock,' Renée told her. 'You are so going to have to apologize to him.'

Genie nodded. She knew she'd put them all at risk. 'I think we're out of the storm now. Ouch. My lip is bleeding. Those lifebuoys are hard, y'know. Nearly knocked my teeth out when you threw it.'

The hatch opened and Rian looked down. 'We're coming through it. The pumps working?'

Renée nodded. 'Draining fast.'

'You OK?' Rian asked Genie. 'You're bleeding.'

'Sorry, Ri. I really am sorry. I wasn't thinking.'

Rian shook his head. 'You're here. Mouch is back. That's all that matters. But if anyone can find me something dry and warm to wear and some more cocoa, I know someone who will be a lot happier.'

He withdrew and Renée shut the hatch tight.

'He forgives pretty easy,' Renée told her.

'He loves me. You're supposed to.'

'I think maybe Mouch needs to apologize to him too,' Renée said with a smile.

Mouch coughed up some more seawater and lay down and began to lick himself. It was a good sign.

'Cocoa. There's still a litre of milk left. Make cocoa. I'll look for something dry for him.'

Renée nodded. 'I saw stuff in a cupboard by the toilet.'

Genie found a fisherman's sweater. It was well oiled and stank. It was about Reverend Schneider's size. It would swamp Rian; nevertheless it would keep him dry.

'I need to get out of these clothes, but there's only this.' She held up an XL-sized T-shirt that said: *The Lord Knows Everything*.

Renée smiled. 'Well, I hope the Lord hasn't told him what we did to his yacht.'

Genie laughed, then winced as her mouth hurt. 'I so hope we never meet him again. I still can't believe I haven't shot him. I know that ain't exactly Christian, but he is truly the most evil man on earth, Renée.'

'The most evil man on earth is the man that owns the Fortress, Genie. That's evil. Remember that.'

A few minutes later they handed a frozen Rian some hot cocoa and he shed his wet clothes for the huge sweater. It was dry and warm and he even smiled.

'I got good news and bad news,' he told them.

'Uh?' Renée asked. 'Bad news first.'

'We're pretty much running on empty.'

'And the good news?'

'I have no idea where we are. Somewhere off the Sunshine Coast, but . . .' He shrugged.

The engine cut out.

Renée was right. Bad news first.

'What now?'

'We drift.' He was looking at the rigging and wondering if he could get the sail unfurled. Be better than drifting out of control.

'Great,' Genie replied. Then she frowned. 'Don't think I'm any crazier than you already do, but I can smell land. Well, forest anyways.'

Renée sniffed the air and shrugged but Rian stood up and faced the wind. 'You're right. Wind's completely changed direction. It's coming off the land. Score one for Genie Magee.'

'Is that good?' Genie asked.

'If I can free the sail we'll be fine. Current is moving towards land, but the wind is blowing against us.' He sipped the cocoa. 'Mmm, good stuff. Hot.'

'Enjoy it, that was the last of the milk,' Renée told him.

Genie was staring at the barometer. 'If anyone ever tells

me they're down, I'm going to tell them wait until they get "severe depression".'

'Stop with the weather stuff, Genie. I'm so not ever going to go sailing again. What happens now, Ri?'

Rian was climbing towards the mast. He could see that he was going to have a job freeing the sail; the lines were a mess and he doubted they'd ever been used. He looked back at Genie and shrugged.

'When we hear a grinding sound it means we've hit land.'

'Well, at least we can't sink then, right?' Renée said.

Genie met Rian's eyes and they smiled at each other. It was fine. He really had forgiven her. She was sure of it.

Genie's eyes were drawn towards the shore. 'Hey, look.'

They looked. Even from here they could see the house was huge, with giant spotlights illuminating it, just so you could see how much money they had. It was – well, un-Canadian. No one needed a house that big, did they?

'We going to drift there?' Renée asked, clearly worried. 'Rich people have guns, Ri. Or attack-dogs. Maybe this ain't a good idea,' she added quietly.

'We land where we land. I guess this is it, guys. I don't think I can get the sail up in time.'

Nothing happened. The yacht sort of drifted slower

and slower. They were out of the current and now it was down to the tide.

'Hey,' Genie called from down in the cabin. 'I found a whole bag of dry clothes under the bunk.'

They were all down there in a second. Mouch watched them trying stuff on from his perch. He couldn't wait to get back on dry land. Couldn't wait to be dry, period.

'It's like someone was planning a seventies party. I got flares and they're my size,' Renée was saying. 'But what is Reverend Schneider doing with them? Sure as hell he doesn't wear flares.'

Genie put up her hand to Renée's mouth. 'Say nothing. I don't want to know. I just want dry clothes.'

Rian found the empty brandy miniature they had shared earlier. 'I could get used to that stuff. Like swallowing a fireball.'

'It's disgusting. I can't believe anyone drinks it. Don't get used to it, Rian Tulane. One lush in our family is enough.'

Rian had to agree. 'I need dry jeans.'

'Here.' Genie handed him a pair of jeans. 'Legs are short, but they are *so* you.'

'God, Mouch, you smell like a dog,' Renée said, sniffing.

Genie went to poor Mouch, all wrapped up in a towel.

'Salty dog, aren't you! Wanted to swim to freedom. Don't blame you at all, dog.'

She kissed him on his salty head. He licked her back.

One minute later they hit the shoreline and fell head first in a heap. Mouch smacked against the bulkhead and howled. He was definitely never going on water again.

'So much for Mexico,' Genie said with a sigh.

'Come on, we're on land. Look on the bright side, Genie. No one knows where we are so they can't find us. Hell, if you still want to go to Mexico we can hitch there.'

They emerged on deck and stared in awe at the grand mansion before them.

'You remember when we had to read *The Great Gatsby* last year?' Genie said quietly.

Rian nodded. Renée didn't, she hadn't been in school for almost two years now, thanks to the Fortress.

'It's like the biggest house I've ever seen. How many people live here? A hundred?'

Rian took Genie's hand. 'If it's like Gatsby, then only one.'

'One?' Renée asked, disbelieving.

'One very rich man. One very rich lonely man, who is I hope fast asleep right now,' Genie said. She ducked back down into the cabin to rescue some food for Mouch. He'd be hungry again soon now he'd puked his guts out.

Rian looked at them, thinking. 'Grab anything that can identify us. All the wet clothes we were wearing, put them in a plastic bag. Mugs we used. Renée, there's bleach in the cupboard. We have to wipe down the surfaces. It won't be perfect, but let's not make it easy for them to trace this to us, OK?'

'CSI will trace us from every bit of spit, vomit and fingerprints we left all over this thing.' Renée stated.

'One, CSI is fiction. Two, the salt air will destroy mostly everything, and three, let's not leave it to chance, OK? We stole this yacht and now we've wrecked it. Reverend Schneider is going to be pretty mad.'

Genie looked at Renée by the flashlight and they both sighed. Rian was right.

'Then we'll knock on the rich man's door and hope he doesn't shoot us.'

'I'm loving the scenario, Ri,' Renée stated. 'You left out the attack-dogs.'

16

Empty Berth

Reverend Schneider got the call at seven thirty a.m. He was making preparations for a breakfast baptism – one of the innovations he'd brought to Spurlake. Naming the child and a breakfast celebration for all the family. So much more user-friendly than the other churches.

The manager at the marina in Vancouver was not making any sense. He'd left management to his nephew and he'd logged out *Lord's Business*, his yacht, the previous evening. The manager was annoyed that Reverend Schneider hadn't informed him, or paid for fixing the compass. There was three hundred and twenty-four dollars owing, which he was going to take out of the last charter fee. In his opinion, letting kids use it for Bible studies wasn't part of the agreement.

'Bible studies?' Schneider queried, astonished. 'Horseshoe Bay? You got a description of the kids?'

'I didn't see them and they aren't on camera. It was dark when they got here, but my nephew tells me they had a dog with them, which is against the rules.'

'A dog? You listen here – I'm holding you responsible. I mean, I'm up here in Spurlake and you're down there. You just gave my yacht away. Why on earth would you give the keys to kids and let them sail away?'

'They had their own keys,' the man replied. 'It's you who needs to think about responsibility.'

Reverend Schneider was stunned. The keys he'd noticed were missing just the day before. But who knew? Who could possibly know he had a yacht? It was his big secret, his hideaway. Kids and dog? He had a sudden sinking feeling that he knew *exactly* who had his yacht. Genie Magee, that's who. This was her revenge. He was sure of it. She was still alive and so, incredibly, was that darn dog. He could have sworn he'd killed it. The hunters hadn't found her body after all. Fortransco had reported a car that had driven off the highway with Genie in it, but they hadn't actually witnessed a dead Genie Magee and they had also mentioned a dog at the scene.

There was no doubt in his mind at all. It was her.

He looked at his watch. The baptism would be over by nine thirty at the latest. Everything else could wait.

'I'll be there by one. Alert the coastguard. That is a stolen yacht.'

17

Fate's Mansion

Rian woke nursing a stiff back. He glanced out of the window. There was a pink sky and the clouds looked like a million sheep. He looked around and discovered Genie had gone. Renée was still sleeping on an inflatable bed she'd found. Rian was pleased they'd found this hideaway. It was an empty storeroom above the garages, some thirty metres or so from the mansion. With attack-dogs in mind, he'd vetoed going anywhere near the main house. No need to wake them up or disturb them. As long as they were up early, they could melt away. The guy would wake up and find a yacht parked on his shoreline, but no damage done and Reverend Schneider would get it back eventually.

He glanced back at Renée but decided to let her sleep a little longer. He wondered where Genie and Moucher were and how long she'd been awake. He went down the stairs, hoping to find a bathroom.

Outside, the first thing Rian noticed was that the yacht had moved. He knew he'd secured it, let out the anchor.

164

It had beached. No way it could have got away.

'Tide came up. He moved it,' Genie said, walking across the lawn with a laden tray in her hands.

Rian spun around. The yacht was sitting snug alongside a small dock; it looked like a gnat next to the seventy-metre wedding-cake monster yacht moored alongside.

'How?' Rian began.

Genie was smiling. She offered him hot coffee and a muffin.

'Come on, breakfast is served. Did you wake Renée? Check out the back of the garage. Blue door. You'll find a studio flat. Hot shower, Ri. Go find the shower.'

Rian looked at her in wonder, grabbed his breakfast, then spun around and headed back into the garage.

Genie called Moucher and he bounded across the lawn and joined her. He was happy. He'd fed on cookies and some chopped liver. He was even happier to be on dry land.

Genie hollered Renée's name and told her to get up, join her in the flat.

She eventually appeared, bleary-eyed and her face creased from where she'd been sleeping. 'I can smell a latté,' she cooed. 'Where did you get these from, girl?'

Genie just smiled. 'Drink, eat, shower and then we got to go.'

'Go?'

'We scored a ride to Gibsons.'

Renée shook her head. 'I go to sleep in the *Titanic* and wake up in fairyland.'

'Not exactly. Shoo – Ri's already in the shower. We have to be quick.'

Renée clutched her latté and muffin and went in search of the shower. 'You're a star, girl,' she yelled over her shoulder.

Half an hour later they all felt one hundred per cent better than they had in days. Renée was studying the studio flat and making notes as she dried her hair.

'It's neat. Only one window though. Who lives here?'

'No one at the moment. Last guy quit. The guy who lives here owns all those cars out there and he likes to have a full-time guy looking after them.'

Rian had already checked out the Cord 812 SC Phaeton and the Jag XK120. He liked the '63 Ferrari best though.

'Who is this guy?'

'Some rich businessman. He commutes. The cook doesn't know where he goes. She doesn't speak much English. Her husband rescued the yacht and he speaks a little. He seemed excited to see me. Don't know why. I think they're North Korean. She said Mr Strindberg was really nice to her and helped her after she escaped.'

'Strindberg?'

'He owns all this and another thousand acres up the Sunshine Coast so no one can build near him.'

Renée was impressed. 'Wonder what it's like to be this rich?'

Rian wished he had more coffee. 'I guess we'll never know.'

'We're going to Gibsons. Caretaker's going there to get some stuff. At least we have options. I don't know what, but we have to think about what we're going to do.'

'We don't have much money left. About a hundred and twenty-five dollars, I think,' Rian said. 'I don't suppose we rescued any of the food we bought?'

'Nah,' Genie said. 'Water ruined most of it.'

She looked at the clock on the wall. 'We need to go. Come on. Wait till you see what the mansion looks like inside. Like a palace.'

Renée stood up and grabbed Genie's hand. They walked out of the flat, past the antique cars and out into the sunshine. Rian and Moucher followed.

'Maybe he's single?' Renée mused. 'Lonely, rich, foolish man ready to fall the charms of a young thing who needs to be taught the wicked ways of the world.'

Rian chuckled. 'I don't know what you've been reading,

Renée, but consider yourself corrupted.'

'Don't worry. I'd let you have one of the cars, Ri. I won't be mean. You can eat cake, Genie. Any day of the week.'

They walked across the perfectly manicured lawn and entered the mansion.

They were told to wait in the gallery, a huge ground-floor space that ran one whole side of the mansion. It had a black-and-white marble floor, many boring photographs of machines and people none of them knew and some valuable art that made little sense.

Genie had a creeping sense of unease now. There was something odd about this gallery. The objects were all too strange. Bent metal, half-destroyed objects. Was this art or debris? She knew something about modern art and knew it could be found objects or even a toilet seat. Anything could be art, apparently. But this room was filled with half-objects, broken things. She stared at something that looked a like a pet cage, only it looked like someone had take a huge bite out of it. There was a collection of distorted human limbs in glass fish tanks filled with formaldehyde; how gross was that? Another held eyes – some misshapen – and then there were bits of animals too. It was seriously sick art.

'Who owns this place?' Renée asked, staring at a collection of insects with limbs missing. 'He is seriously weird.'

Genie was looking at a framed photo. A young boy was standing next to someone who looked a lot like Marshall, but younger. He was holding up a copy of *The Province* with the headline: *Colder than outer space.*

'I know you'll think I'm crazy, but I swear this is a picture of Marshall with his son when he was a kid,' Genie said frowning, looking for the date. 'Marshall sure looked different back then. Look at his hair, it's on his shoulders.'

Renée came over but shrugged. 'Maybe. It's a stretch. I mean, why would that picture be here?'

Genie was slowly making her way along the wall of framed photos. She stopped suddenly.

'Take a look at *this* photo!' Genie exclaimed. 'Really, what kind of creepy guy owns this place? Ri, come and look.'

They gathered around a photo of a younger Reverend Schneider standing with what had to be Mr Yates, Rian's mother's new boyfriend, and a small guy with silver hair and a fancy suit. They had a shovel between them. Rian read it out aloud.

'Blessing and Ground Breaking – Silverlake 1997, Yates, Strindberg and Schneider.'

'I don't believe it,' Rian said. He was growing worried now. What were the chances they'd know anyone in a photograph in this rich man's mansion? He looked around him at the leather chairs, the marble statues and the vast expanse of marble floor. How many houses had their own art gallery anyway? This guy was super-rich and clearly he had a connection to the Fortress. Was this a coincidence they had ended up here? He didn't think so. Mr Yates's voice droned in his head. 'There are no coincidences.' Yet here was a *picture* of him standing with Reverend Schneider, no less.

Mouch was investigating the underside of the Persian rugs when Genie let out a piercing scream.

'What?' Rian was at her side in a trice.

Genie was staring at a life-sized photograph in a metal frame. It was three metres square. A perfect image of herself, taken at the exact moment of disintegration on the teleport transmission platform at the Fortress. Rian felt goosepimples rise.

Genie stared at it, growing intensely dizzy and scared as all the terrible memories came flooding back. All the blood drained out of her face. Rian caught her as her legs gave way.

'No, no, no . . .' she was saying as she continued to stare at herself. She vividly remembered her arms and legs disintegrating, all her atoms flying away like so much sand – the expression on her face was calm curiosity. Her head was completely bald and the whole air around her seemed to shimmer.

How was this even possible? Who had taken the photo? How had it got here? Who exactly was this man that he had this picture of her? Had he bought them? If so, who was selling them?

'Werry good photo,' a voice said behind them in a strong Korean accent. 'My wife, she knew it you, soon as you come.'

'Jesus,' Renée whispered, horrified. 'Is this a trap? We have to get out of here, guys, *now*.'

They had to carry Genie out. She was too distressed. They put her in the back seat of the SUV and piled in after her. Renée held her hand and Moucher rested his head on her legs, sensing something was up.

Rian could hardly think. He hadn't drawn anyone's attention to it, but they had passed other pictures too. A boy screaming in agony, a framed image of freshly bloodied shadows on the transmission walls, and Fortress people. Another one of Reverend Schneider surrounded by weeping women, praying in the street outside a suburban house.

The Korean driver stared impassively at them. He

wasn't sure what was wrong with the girl, but he was happy because he knew who she was. If she was in the gallery, it meant she was famous, as far as he was concerned. His boss would be pleased to know he had treated her well when she came to visit in her yacht.

Genie took in deep breaths. She was physically shaking, felt wave after wave of nausea. She couldn't get that image of herself out her head.

Rian squeezed in beside her. He could see she was white-faced with shock. He gripped her other hand to reassure her.

'I'm sorry,' he told her. 'I wish you hadn't seen that photo.'

'No.' She shook her head. 'I was meant to. It's fate, Ri. Something guided us here. We can't run any more. It's like a message to us. We can't run, we have to face them.' She closed her eyes but all she saw was that damn image of herself disintegrating. She felt hot tears escape. She was crying for the Genie who disappeared that day. She felt a ton of different emotions and her head swam with anger. She gripped Rian's hand and pulled him closer.

'I had a moment, y'know? I was with Cary and Denis, Julia came for a brief time too.'

Renée and Rian exchanged glances. They knew about Genie's 'moments'.

'When? Just now?' Rian asked, confused.

'No, last night, on the yacht, just before the big wave hit us. We were in a dark tunnel. It led to a teleport chamber, but a real old one, like y'know, something they'd built and forgotten about. Denis found a map on the wall.'

Rian frowned. 'When was this?'

Genie shook her head. 'It doesn't matter. I was with them, like before, only different. They're all in a coma, Ri. They're all on life-support. Randall too. I don't know how or why, but I met them. They're really scared. The Fortress shaved their heads like mine. But there was a massive Mosquito attack. It was supposed to catch me and Renée probably, but it made them all flake out.'

'Where is this tunnel?' Rian was sceptical.

'The tunnel doesn't matter. It's dead, the stuff is antique, useless. But I must have been shown it for a reason. I think I was supposed to come up with a plan to get them out.'

Renée squeezed her hand. 'We can barely keep ourselves out of trouble, Genie.'

'We have to find a way to help them. We can't run away any more. That's why I was shown the picture. I'm sure of it.'

'You said a map?' Rian asked, curious.

'Radspan. It's like a diagram of teleport chambers each slightly further apart. But it's no use, Ri; they didn't have enough power back then. We don't even know if they built any of them. It didn't work. Denis watched a video. They tried, but nothing worked. Anyway, even if I could find a way to get them out, they're in comas. You know how to wake someone up who's in a coma?'

Rian thought about it. If the Fortress couldn't wake them there was no way they could. He was intrigued that there was an earlier version of the Fortress though. Radspan was a strange word but half of it sort of made logical sense. Span – a distance.

'But who is this Strindberg?' Renée asked. 'How did he even get hold of a photo of you? What were all those creepy things in his house? Failed experiments?'

Rian looked at her and all three understood at the same moment that that's *exactly* what they had been looking at. It was a museum of Fortress failures. A grisly record of death – those human limbs in the glass tanks had once been *children*. Kids they may even know. It wasn't art at all.

'Better yet, what were the chances we'd even wind up there?' Renée added. 'God, this scares me.'

'It's the Fortress, it's like a damn magnet, keeps pulling us back,' Rian said bitterly.

'There was an old finance magazine in the chamber,' Genie remembered. 'It was the last thing I looked at before the lights went out. Something about the government cutting back on science research. There was a picture of a small man in an expensive suit. Carson Strindberg, financial adviser to the Premier.'

Rian remembered the small man standing next to Reverend Schneider. 'Like five-foot small with silver hair?'

Genie nodded. 'We were in his house, right? He's rich. We know he's rich. But why has he got the photo of me? There were other pictures too, weren't there? It's sick. If you know what's happening to me and the other kids, it's totally sick.'

Renée pointed at the driver trying to listen and put her finger to her lips.

Rain shrugged. 'I don't think he understands much. He's just a caretaker.'

'But he's going to tell his boss we were here,' Renée protested.

'He's probably already done that,' Rian explained. 'We should expect trouble.'

'I never thought of someone actually owning the Fortress,' Genie whispered.

'I guess someone has to,' Rian mused. 'Someone really rich, like Strindberg. If you saw his photo in the teleport chamber, even an old one . . .'

'It means he knows what's going on and, worse, so does the former Premier, Ri. It means they don't give a damn about us. It explains why none of the newspapers came when we tried to expose Reverend Schneider. We're toast.'

'We don't actually know Strindberg owns the Fortress. We're just guessing,' Rian stated, but even he could see the logic of it.

'I don't care who owns it, Ri. But we have to think of a way to get our friends out of there. It's just not fair. I'm not going to be hunted any more. We're going to have to find a way to face them and beat them. *We're* going hunting.'

Renée wasn't sure. Running away sounded like a better plan in her book. Rian stroked Moucher, thinking that he wished he'd steered them towards Mexico after all.

'You get out now,' their driver said as he slowed at the top of the hill overlooking Langdale Landing.

They looked up, saw the Horseshoe Bay ferry steaming out of the port below.

Renée opened the door and helped Genie and Moucher climb out. Rian thanked him and shook the driver's hand. They waved him off as he drove away. He kept smiling at them; wasn't his fault he worked for the devil.

Genie was looking around, feeling more herself now, trying not to think about that gallery of horrors in Strindberg's house. They had been dropped at the top of the hill overlooking town and the harbour. Shops were opening up and people were passing by going to their jobs or shopping. Langdale was a perfectly normal, sunny, small town; it looked cute. There were a few art galleries and some tourist souvenir places selling First Nation carvings and coffee shops, of course. They gravitated towards a coffee shack that promised *All-day breakfasts with bottomless coffee – just $5.95*. A steal.

Genie tied Moucher to a lamppost, promising to bring back something for him to eat. He cocked his head to one side and Genie had to promise him that she'd be back. She sensed he was more worried than he was letting on. She wondered if he was missing Marshall. She'd been selfish taking him with her. She was beginning to think everything she did was selfish.

'Do they do lattés?' Renée whined.

'They do cheap food and we're broke,' Rian told her firmly.

'I don't think I can eat,' Genie said, hanging back; her stomach still churned.

'You have to eat. Soon we may not be able to,' Rian told her.

She reluctantly followed them both inside. Renée's heart sank when she saw the coffee pot standing on a warmer. They ordered eggs over easy, bacon, hash browns and brown toast with stewed coffee. All of them now realized that, given their financial situation, it might be their last full meal.

Rian was making notes on the napkin. He looked at Genie.

'We need some kind of plan.'

'Mexico, let's walk,' Renée suggested. 'I'm all for getting far away from here.'

'Staying alive is our first priority,' Rian declared. 'Helping Cary and the others to escape has to come second.'

Genie sighed, at last realizing the truth of their situation.

'Ri's right. I'm sorry. It's not fair of me. We can't help them. They're in comas; there's nothing we can do for them. I'm being stupid. Hell, it might have been just a dream. Nothing seems real any more. Seeing that photo of me totally threw me. We have to stay free. I can't allow us to take any more stupid risks. At least we know who the enemy is now. Strindberg.'

'You say "Strindberg", honey?'

Genie looked up at the waitress. She was plump, in a candy-striped uniform and looked harassed.

'The guy with the mansion,' Renée commented. 'Can't believe anyone has a house that big.'

'There's a few like that up the Sunshine Coast, but none as mean as that man. But be careful what you say; a lot of people hate him, but he pays a lot of bills around here. Just because you don't like him, you keep it to yourself. Y'hear?'

Genie glanced at her and tried to decide whether this was a friendly warning or what.

The waitress leaned in and whispered in her ear. 'He's got spies. Man in the hat over there works for him.' She indicated an older man in a suit, having coffee and doughnuts. 'He can put a person out of business – like that.' She snapped her fingers. She straightened up and walked away.

Genie discreetly looked at the man she was indicating and then quickly looked away again. She didn't know him. With luck he didn't know her, wasn't looking for her, but she was acutely aware that even here people would be keen for the twenty-grand reward to find her and Renée.

The food arrived and they fell silent as the waitress pushed plates of fried food in front of them, winking at Genie as she did so. Genie sighed. Quite why she had to be brought into some conspiracy she didn't know.

'Can we just agree to stay alive?' Rian asked as he placed his eggs on top of his toast.

Renée stood up. 'Need hot milk. I can't drink this stuff naked.'

Genie looked directly at Rian a moment. 'Can you borrow me a cellphone? Just some absolute total stranger. One call. One text actually.'

Rian looked at her quizzically.

'Text?'

'To Marshall.'

Renée returned with a steaming latté and a big smile on her face.

'Had to kiss his ass, but I got a latté. Did you know there's a music fest over in Gibsons Landing today? Old country rockers stuff, I think. Town's going to be full by this afternoon. The way we're dressed, we'll fit right in. Be pregnant by dawn and divorced by Saturday.'

'What?' Genie and Rian looked at her and laughed.

'Something my ma always used to say, that's all.' She grinned. 'She didn't approve of Blue Grass. Only church music.'

Genie smiled, her mood lifting as she ate.

'I always wanted to go to Africa.'

'I thought it was Mexico.'

Genie shook her head. 'Never really liked Mexico.

Wanted to go to Cape Town and see where the two oceans meet. I heard you can almost see a line in the water.'

Rian shook his head. 'You are one strange girl.'

Renée began to eat. 'I ain't sailing to Africa. I can tell you that flat out. No way.'

Genie and Moucher took a walk whilst Renée and Rian went to 'borrow' a cell. She didn't go far. Waited for the guy who was supposed to be Strindberg's spy and watched him leave and get into a Lexus. He didn't drive off immediately, taking a call on his phone. Genie didn't know why she was watching him, but she wanted to make sure she could recognize him if he came after her. She knew that the moment Strindberg realized she'd been to his house and left Reverend Schneider's yacht there, he'd be sending this guy out to look for her. Know your enemy. It was her mantra now.

Miller got the text when he went to make coffee for himself and Marshall. He'd brought the truck back. Almost felt brand new after Ferry had serviced it. He took the coffee out to where Marshall was sitting under some shade. He was still nursing his injuries from the fire and beating he'd got, but at least his colour had returned.

'You got a text. You expecting one?'

Marshall looked up. He narrowed his eyes and wiped his brow.

'Only one person I know would send me a text and we told her to throw the damn phone away.'

'Well, it's cryptic.'

'What does it say?'

'*Radspan* – with a question mark.'

Marshall was surprised. 'That's it? You know the number?'

'No, but if she's smart she's using someone else's cell.'

Marshall frowned. It had been a while since he'd heard that word. The pig trotted in from the field and snorted.

'Pig must know it's her,' he said, smiling.

'What do you want to do?'

'Send this first. Verify password.'

Miller nodded and inputted the text. 'I guess we don't want to find it's the Fortress on a fishing expedition.'

'I don't think it is, but I want to be sure.'

The cell pinged with an incoming message.

'*Moucher*,' Miller said, looking up with a smile.

Marshall nodded. 'OK, we're going into my office. I'm not talking without noise.'

Miller took his father's arm and they walked slowly back into the house. Marshall was still getting used to his new leg and his burns weren't completely healed.

They went through the kitchen and into the pantry.

Miller swung out the boxes that hid the secret door and they entered his lab. It was still a chaotic mess, but Marshall pretty much knew where everything was. He flipped a switch, and an audible and irritating electric hum was initiated. He pointed to earphones and they both slipped them over their heads.

'Got to do this; they had plenty of time to put in new ears.'

Miller nodded. He didn't want the Fortress listening in either.

Marshall plugged his cell into his earphones and dialled the most recently received number.

Genie answered on the second ring.

'I've been there. In the tunnel. With the others,' she said quickly, not wasting time on chit-chat.

Marshall was surprised. She sounded strained. He understood more than anyone that she had to keep it quick and cryptic.

'Big dome carved out of chalk,' Genie added, to make sure he understood.

'For real?'

'You know . . .'

Marshall knew. The astral plane. Genie's special skill of spirit-walking.

'Frankly, I'm surprised you're still alive.' He heard

barking. Moucher. His heart leaped, which was surprising for a man who always said he didn't care for that dog.

'Mouch says hi. Probably wishes he hadn't come. Had a lot of stuff to deal with on the way.'

'We heard about Betty. That was a real shame her crashing.'

'We didn't crash. We were driven off the road. She was shot through the neck, tell Miller. She was a good person. I'm really sorry about that.'

Marshall's eyebrows were raised. The police report had said she'd been drinking and driven off the road. Nothing about any shooting.

'I keep thinking the tunnel is a message to me,' Genie told him.

'Got to tell you it was a technical dead-end,' Marshall told her.

'The others were there waiting for me. They haven't got much time. Cary thinks they're dying. There was a massive Mosquito attack. I have to work it out somehow. Can you think about it? Got to go. Keep moving.'

Marshall was trying to think fast. 'Can I reach you on this?'

'No. We will call you.'

'Send a message tonight,' Marshall said. 'I'll be ready for your questions then. Are you . . . ?'

'Yes.'

Genie disconnected and Marshall did the same.

Miller looked at him with burning questions on his lips.

Marshall removed his headphones and frowned.

'Betty Juniper was murdered. Shot through the neck. Someone is covering up for the Fortress in your department. Did they fish the vehicle out yet?'

'No, it's unsafe. The cliff is too soft. A police diver went down but he didn't say anything. I mean, they got her body out. Hard to cover up something like that.'

'We're talking about the Fortress, son. Everyone, including the coroner can be bought.' Marshall walked towards the door, picking up a long thin canister on the way and stashing it under his arm. 'I seem to recall you made some coffee.'

Genie gave the phone back to the girl. 'I'm sorry but Dad gets cranky if I don't call, and I lost my phone.'

The girl just smiled. 'Tell me about it. I think my ma tracks me on Google every place I go. I only have to get within five feet of a guy and she calls.'

'It's a Google world, girl.' Genie smiled and rejoined Rian and Renée. Moucher sat by her feet and leaned in on her.

She felt happier for having called him, even if she

didn't have answers right away. A Harley slowly went by with a man and woman dressed in something approaching Elvis outfits. They were smiling and seemed real happy to be here.

'What's the plan, guys?'

Rian presented Renée like a magician's assistant. 'Renée here has a surefire plan to make us a fortune.'

Renée laughed. 'We *are* going to make a fortune, girl. Let me show you this.'

Genie found herself staring at a red inflatable cushion with sparkles on it. Moucher barked and tried to get in on the act.

'Well, you got Moucher sold,' Genie told her. 'But I'm not sure I get it.'

'We just spent our last bucks on buying every last inflatable cushion in town. Ten cents each. Can you believe it? Warehouse closing down, going out of business. We were just walking and there's this auction going on of everything they own and . . .'

'Serious?' Genie asked, her heart sinking. 'All our money?'

'One thousand and forty-two cushions to be precise,' Renée said.

Genie sat down on the sidewalk and suddenly wanted to cry. Sometimes life got too much, y'know.

18

Secrets of the Universe

'Radspan?' Miller asked his dad when they got back outside with their coffees.

Marshall frowned. 'That girl can get right into the Fortress psyche. She's in deeper than I thought. Radspan was Dr Milan's idea. Radial Spanning. Teleportation transmission tests to designated stations. Cost a fortune. No successes.'

'But it caught you by surprise.'

'Radspan was the original concept. Dr Milan developed his ideas back in the sixties when all that we do now was completely impossible.'

'We're talking "I'm from Mars, you're an idiot, Dr Milan".'

Marshall smiled. 'You remember that? You only met him once back in nineteen ninety-one. You were just a kid.'

'He nearly pulled my ears off and called me an idiot. He made an impression.'

Marshall was trying to pull off the lid of the canister. It

came away finally and he up-ended it and pulled out a map, which he unfurled to show Miller.

'Radspan. This is the ninety-six map. There may have been later additions. You are looking at half a billion dollars here. That was real money back then. Strindberg was one of the original investors. Put his dotcom money into it.'

Miller stared at what looked a lot like a subway train map of Canada with stations clearly outlined. Some still marked *Opening 2000*. It was clearly a totally impossible thing. No one needed a tunnel in the prairies.

'What am I looking at, Dad?'

Marshall took a sip of his coffee, watching an eagle gracefully circling above their heads, scraping the tops of the fir trees.

'If you were going to build a railroad, which would you build first – rail or stations?'

'That's one of those chicken and egg questions. But logic says rail, I guess.'

'Not in Milan's world. Take Radspan One. Which I might add is pretty much directly under here somewhere, about half a mile down.'

'No way.'

'See the tunnels on the map there? Goes all the way to Synchro. Miles of cables, enough space to walk upright and drive a small vehicle.'

'That's incredible.'

'Cost a fortune. '

'So Synchro is Radspan Two?'

'No. Synchro station was never built. But others were. There was a problem with the water table along the way. This was around nineteen-ninety, maybe ninety-one. He'd already started on the other tunnel when he had a breakthrough in late ninety-four and he pretty much realized that he didn't need the tunnels or the cables at all. He was trying to emulate CERN, the Swiss collider concept – you know, atom smashing – and needed speed. Speed is all in this business. Hell, the Hadron Collider only got up to a fraction below the speed of light in two thousand and ten, so he was never going to do that with this half-assed thing shaped like a horseshoe. He was using super magnets to bend light. He was trying for supersymmetry well before he would be able to achieve it.'

Miller was impassive. Science had never really interested him, much to his father's disappointment.

'Anyway, I was on the other team working at the Fortress and going in a different direction by now and he was really resentful that funds were being diverted from Radspan to the Fortress. He came to me about heat problems he was having and the cables burning out and I put him on track with carbon fibre, which radically improved his speeds. Miles Thysen developed the magnetic boosters and Milan's tunnels were completed at last. In ninety-six I'd say he was ahead and he'd installed some new super computers from Cray, the technical leaders at that time, and he was already testing inanimate objects. Some near misses too. He wanted to be first. Whoever was going to get there first would get all the Federal funding, y'see.

'He was so sure it was going to work he commissioned Radspan Phase Two. The stations. The ones on the map there.'

'Connected by tunnels?'

Marshall chuckled. 'You think the government would fund underground tunnels clear across Canada? No, son, this is teleportation. His original idea for the tunnels was to get the atoms up to speed so he could smash them and direct the incredible force generated down the pipe to the transmission generators. The energy needed to get that up and running is huge. That's what we have been up against from the beginning. Speed. He commissioned fifteen stations at set intervals close to either hydro or nuclear power sources. All built in total secret and powered up, ready to go at a moment's notice.'

'He was that sure?'

'He was that sure. I saw some of the early trials. He had human test dummies made of Teflon and he must have destroyed hundreds. But each time they got a little further, a little closer. Science isn't like on TV, it isn't magic. It's painful steps – tiny, tiny and very time-consuming steps.'

'And you were doing the same?'

'We were building at the Fortress and I was working on transmission stability. That's my area, remember. He was the only one working on practical application at the time.'

'That's when Thysen disappeared? I remember something.'

'He experimented with a mouse. It was completely against the rules then. Claimed he sent it to Radspan Five.'

'And?'

'The problem with sending a mouse is that there's a lot of mice out there and how do you know for sure it's yours. There're DNA markers but he couldn't find his mouse.

'He disappeared. Never came back. It caused a huge scandal. As Milan said, anyone can make something disappear, including money. The finance people began to get panicky and were critical, calling it the world's biggest mousetrap. Strindberg was smart, he'd sold out his share early, switched allegiance to the Fortress. He was advising the Premier at the time on science matters and told him Radspan was a dead end. The Premier killed the funding.'

'And history repeats itself right now. Only Strindberg's actually in charge.'

'Like having an arsonist in charge of the fire department.'

'So Radspan was forgotten?'

'Shut down overnight and everyone fired. Some of the teams transferred over to the Fortress, but it was considered a total failure and left to rot. The technology was old.'

'So why is Genie thinking about it?'

'Good question. Hell, I'd forgotten all about it. After all it was shut down in ninety-eight, I think. That's like ancient history to us now.'

'OK but—'

'OK nothing. The point is, why is she thinking about it? Why was she there? Her friends are all locked up in the Fortress again.'

'I know one was taken to the hospital when she collapsed and put under Fortransco guard. But if she wants to set them free, what would be the point if they're all, y'know, in a vegetative state?'

Marshall pursed his lips. 'She was quite insistent

on having been in touch with the others. If she did, it means they aren't brain-dead, Max. There's probably a neural connection keeping them alive. Genie can tap into that. Her skills are remarkable. Someone should study her.'

'I should think she's had enough of being studied. Can you help them?'

'What if she could get to them from the inside?' Marshall suggested.

Miller shook his head and laughed. 'You mean like *Hellboy*? She bursts in, machine guns blazing, and then what? She has to teleport each one of them out of there. They are *so* going to let her do that.'

'Remember, up until recently you didn't even believe teleportation would ever be possible. No, son. Genie's smart. All those kids are maintained on around thirty thousand servers or even more. She can't save them, not the ones on life-support. But what if she could transmit their DNA? What if she could find them, then flash forward them to a Radspan station where we could retrieve them? They'd arrive in a safe, secure environment, and from there they could break out.'

Miller blinked. 'But that means there would be two of them!'

'That's the whole point. We're transmitting DNA.

There could be a way out of this if we had the power.'

Miller frowned. 'But what about the kids lying there on life-support?'

Marshall looked away momentarily. 'They're already dead. I'm pretty sure of it. Whatever happened there – short-circuit, something – their bodies shut down. The fact that they all shut down at the same time means that they were trying something specific and it went very wrong.'

'They killed them?'

'Not deliberately. They were probably trying to control them. They wanted them back. Genie was terrified of this thing called Mosquito. I don't know what it is exactly, but it's most likely a short-wave electronic signal that affects specific brainwaves.'

'But you're suggesting we make copies. It's not even cloning. They'd be copies. Would they even be the same kids? What about their memories?'

Marshall looked directly at his son. 'Don't you get it, son? They are already copies. You can't teleport someone without full deconstruction. They are dead the moment they press the button.'

Miller whistled. 'Do they know that? The kids, I mean, Genie an' all?'

'No. You gonna tell them?'

'Not me.'

'It's the reason Fortransco is claiming them as their property. They know they're copies.'

'Copies with the same brains and memories?'

'That's the miracle, son. That's the miracle.'

19

In Pursuit

Reverend Schneider stared at the space that was supposed to be his yacht. He was incensed. He couldn't believe they had let three kids and a damn dog sail away with his hundred-thousand-dollar yacht. Who the hell would believe he did Bible study classes on a yacht? That would be the day. This was his big secret hideaway and now Genie Magee had stolen it. It had to be her, although he had no positive description.

The question was: where the hell had they gone?

They hadn't taken up any fuel, which meant they most likely didn't have any money. He'd drawn a circle on the map for sixty ks, the maximum they'd probably go on half a tank – if they were lucky. (He discounted they would actually get under sail, but all bets were off if they did.) The real question was, did they go north or south?

They had tried hailing them on the radio, but got no answer. Tracking them via GPS was useless unless it was actually switched on.

One thing was sure, there was no report of them

refuelling at Horseshoe Bay. The worst thing about all this was that he didn't want the coastguard involved. He regretted even mentioning it. He didn't want any publicity or police investigation. The yacht was not just a secret from all those who had given generously for the cause of missing children in Spurlake, but the taxman wasn't aware of it either and there was no way he could write that one off on the church. He was grinding his teeth and felt his blood pressure rising. He stood there at the water's edge, looking out beyond the Burrard Bridge and cursed Genie Magee. Again.

Strindberg stood on his dock, looking at the little yacht. It had obviously had some problems, but wasn't seriously damaged. He'd heard there had been a terrific squall last night and he wouldn't have gone out there for anything. Nevertheless he was more than just a little peeved it was moored here.

Furthermore, he couldn't believe that Genie Magee had been in his home. Eaten breakfast there, with friends. It was like she was taunting him. He realized that he had been lucky that the housekeeper had recognized her from the picture in the gallery.

But that wasn't the point. He felt invaded. There was supposed to be twenty-four-hour security. Where were they? They were *so* going to get theirs. This was a violation. Worse, she had been in the gallery. That was private. If word got out, if certain people knew he'd been collecting 'samples', it could be misunderstood. He didn't let anyone into his private space – ever. No one would understand that was a record of scientific achievement. An archive of everything the Fortress did.

He was angry because this was getting out of hand now. How had a simple girl evaded all those people out to find her? At every sighting she had simply disappeared or got away. Wasn't ten thousand dollars per head enough? Did he have to double it? Or do the job himself?

His houseman had driven them to Langdale. They could be anywhere now. Back in Vancouver or . . . He definitely didn't want them in Vancouver.

But how had she known to come to *his* house? How had she known to target him? How did she even know where his house was? What sinister motive did she have? Had she come to kill him? He pursed his lips. Certainly he knew that he'd do that, if their roles were reversed.

What had they seen in his house? They had been in the *gallery*. Clearly they would know exactly what the objects on display were and he knew she'd seen her photograph. Had quite a reaction to it by all accounts. Serve her damn well right. But who were the other kids? Where had the darn dog come from? What was missing?

His BlackBerry bleeped.

'What?'

It was his personal assistant back in Spurlake.

'Sir? You will never guess who the yacht is registered to.'

'Who?'

'Reverend Schneider.'

'You're kidding.'

'No, sir. I have been trying to locate him. Seems he left town today in a hurry.'

'You don't say.'

Strindberg shut the phone off and turned around.

Genie Magee and Schneider working together now? Impossible. But stranger bedfellows had happened before.

He started to walk back towards the house. He'd have to arrange for a new security team. Genie Magee had been there to give him a message. He got it. Next time he'd be ready for her.

She wanted trouble? She'd get it, in spades.

20

Save Your Ass for Rock 'n' Roll

Renée was wearing a cap she'd nicked from a biker and grinning as she sold her cushions. Even Moucher was in on the act, guarding the money and precious pile of cushions as Rian inflated them with a foot pump he'd borrowed and Genie waved people down trying to get their custom.

She couldn't believe just how many obese people in tight black leather you could cram into one town. It was disturbing.

They'd discovered one of the headliners was an Eagles cover band and someone really famous they'd never heard of who'd had two chart toppers about twenty-five years ago.

Rian had an argument with an old bald guy as to the merits of Led Zeppelin versus Nirvana. He'd never really listened to much of either, but nevertheless he liked winding the guy up.

Every ferry arrival spilled out a few hundred more oldsters on Harleys or big mamas wearing inappropriate costumes. They drove old Chevrolets and Buicks cruising towards Gibsons Landing and Dougal Park, where the actual concert was going on. The traffic was way more than tiny Langdale could cope with, but Renée was right, those asses were going to need inflatable cushions on those hard seats in the concert area or on the grass. They were performing a life-saving service here.

Renée had raised the price to four bucks when she realized she was selling them so fast.

Genie sold four to three rockers in a fancy Mini Clubman and their dog, who got just a bit too excited when she saw Moucher.

Moucher gave back as good as he got on the barking stakes.

'Do we know who Jenner Judge is?' Rian asked Genie, as an old guy in a black leather hat stopped to buy a cushion.

'*I'm going to kill my man unless he gets me first,*' Genie sang. 'Come on, you must have heard that one.'

The old guy laughed and sang another line, '*He'd said he'd leave her before I got old, so I helped him out and left her cold.* That's one mean girl, that Jenner Judge.'

'See, Ri? Lyrics are cool.'

Rian shook his head. 'Uh-huh.'

'Neil Young played here last year and Ry Cooder the

year before,' the old guy told them as he wiped the sweat from his hat band. 'But Jenner Judge gets my mojo working, not that I exactly remember where my mojo is.' He laughed. 'Never miss a Gibsons Rockfest. Thanks for the cushion, guys. Real life-saver. See you there.' He left still grinning.

Genie smiled as she turned to Rian. 'My grandmother would pay huge bucks to go see Jenner Judge. I never realized how wicked the words are till now. No wonder she liked her. Grandma Munby had a weird sense of humour.'

'I think I kind of missed out on this genre,' Rian stated as he pumped air into yet more cushions.

'It's more Country Rock than Blue Grass. See the hockey mom in the Amy Winehouse hairdo by the coffee shop?'

'Yeah.'

'No smirking. She bought six cushions. She has five kids and she brought them all. You see her bumper sticker? *Shoot first – divorce later*.'

'Nice. Hockey moms scare me.'

'I didn't know old people even went to rock concerts. Aside from the kids they brought, I don't think there's anyone here under forty.'

'We should come back next year for the jazz festival,'

Renée suggested. 'Hell, we'll need more stock.'

Genie laughed. 'Don't get carried away, girl. This is a one-time emergency thing.'

Renée stuck out her tongue.

'I'm still worried,' Rian said. 'We ain't exactly in hiding. Strindberg will have contacted Reverend Schneider by now and . . .'

Genie shook her head. 'Don't talk about it. I'm still spooked. I can't believe he has my photo on his wall. Sick bastard, gloating over me being transmitted. Seeing that photo there, I think that's the biggest shock I've ever, ever had.'

Rian nodded. It had freaked him out plenty. Seeing Genie in the frame, her arms and part of her head already disintegrating. It was like a still from a horror movie and she'd looked so calm, so utterly vulnerable and beautiful. His heart had nearly broken in half just looking at that picture.

'We got a plan?' Rian asked her. 'Aside from making our fortune and not hiding?'

'We're hiding by not hiding. They wouldn't expect us to still be here, selling stuff out in the open. Renée's right, we have to change our luck. But we do have to make contact with Marshall again.'

'Later,' Rian said. 'They can trace phone calls,

remember; we don't want Marshall to get into trouble again.'

'I still can't get over the one place we ended up was at Strindberg's house. It's like we are doomed. Everything we do takes us in a circle back to the Fortress,' Genie remarked.

Two huge women in kaftans stopped and wiped their brows as they struggled up the hill on foot.

'Inflatable cushions. Save your ass for rock 'n' roll,' Genie shouted out.

One woman laughed, then dug out a twenty note.

'How much, honey? Love the hair. That's a neat skunk streak. You do that yourself?'

Skunk? She had no idea what they were talking about. She just smiled instead.

'Four bucks each. Already inflated – the air is free.'

'We'll take two.'

Genie smiled as she handed the cushions over with change. 'You have a great day now.'

'We will, honey. We sure will.'

Renée returned for more; she looked really happy. She waited for the women to go and then produced a wad of cash and stacks of Loonies.

'We're making a fortune. Give me another twenty.'

Rian pointed to a pile behind him. 'Grab 'em.'

'You done this before, Genie?' Renée asked her, seeing the pile of coins and notes already stashed under Moucher's guardianship.

'No, but I once sold cookies from my front garden. My ma wouldn't let me go anywhere, so I had this great plan to raise money and run away to Playland. I was ten. Sold a lot of cookies. Then she confiscated the money, saying she had to buy flour and sugar and stuff. I didn't speak to her for six weeks after that.'

'Figures,' Renée said. 'At least you know she's always been a bitch. Didn't suddenly turn, like my ma.'

Rian grinned. 'Genie's a sales natural. She only has to smile and they grab them.'

A truck went by, honked the air horn at them and some horny old guy waved. Renée shouted something rude back and he laughed as he drove on.

'Save your asses for rock 'n' roll,' Genie yelled as more people approached.

Renée laughed. 'God kill me if I ever grow an ass as big as any of these.' She gathered up her cushions. 'I'm going to the corner.'

'Only three hundred left,' Rian informed them and they both groaned.

It was later that she suddenly realized why so many people

were commenting on her hair. Genie was in the washroom in the coffee bar after she'd ordered more lattés. She really was a skunk head. She had a pure-white streak now from her forehead right across to the back of her head. Wasn't even straight. She ran her fingers through her short fuzz of hair and realized it was a good fingernail long now on top. The ends were normal enough but that white streak was weird. She prayed she could dye it. Made her look like a freak.

'How'd you get it so white?' a girl asked coming up behind her. 'Really cool at the back.' She was staring at Genie's head like it was on show.

Genie tried to look at the back of her head, nervous now.

'What? I can't see anything.'

'It's like a half-moon. That's what it looks like. You get it done here?'

Genie shook her head. 'Natural.'

'Really? Wow. It's crazy. You're really beautiful, y'know. Saw you selling cushions. We've been watching you from the boutique next door. My boss can't believe how many you sell.' She smiled, suddenly awkward. 'Just came in for coffee. Crazy day. You ever see so many . . .' She tried to think of a politically correct way of saying 'big' people.

206

'Lard asses,' Genie chipped in. 'Not in one place, no.'

The girl laughed. 'Even our XXL jeans don't fit them and they're like humungous.'

Genie looked at the girl. She was dressed in a petite blue cardigan, a red top with bright-blue Diesel jeans. She was probably the same age as her – tiny, with bright-green eyes. Cute.

'You know the big house up the coast aways? White, huge, gets lit up at night?'

'Mr Strindberg's place?'

'Yeah. Him.'

Her expression changed. 'Don't go near him. My cousin, Sara Bryant, went to see him about a job as his assistant and no one ever saw her again. Not the first either. He denied he ever saw her but she sent me a text from inside his house. The police protect him, but no one likes him. He's rich and he drives around in a real fast car, but don't go near. Promise me.'

Genie nodded. 'I'm not his type. Skunk girls ain't sweet enough.'

The girl smiled. 'Yeah, you definitely look too tough for him.'

Genie smiled and headed out of the door. 'I still got three hundred cushions to sell. See you later maybe. Say hi when you finish.'

Genie collected the coffees on the way out. She wondered if that Sara girl was sitting on a Fortress server, or if she was one of those who'd exploded on the Synchro wall. One thing was sure, that girl was never going to see her cousin again.

Renée was waiting for her to come out. The cushions had almost all gone. Rian was making Moucher take a leak. Genie knew something had happened.

Renée took her coffee and showed Genie a leaflet she'd picked up. 'Some private security cops handing these out up by the concert venue.'

Genie looked at the flyer. It was a picture of her with her shaved head.

Have you seen this girl? Genie has been missing since August. Reward offered. Last seen in Gibsons/Langdale area. Parents desperate to find her.

There was a phone number to call. The photo showed her wearing the white cotton vest they made her put on at the Fortress, but almost anyone she had sold a cushion to would know it was her. They owed her nothing; someone would say something and point them in the right direction.

'Damn.'

'We have to go,' Rian stated as he returned with Moucher. 'We made over two thousand bucks. Can you believe that? Renée's a genius.'

'Yes I am, but we still have to go. Can we get you a hat?'

Genie realized that she was a liability. Those security guys would be coming down the hill any moment now. She was looking across the road and there was the girl she'd just been talking to inside the coffee bathroom. She was staring at her from the boutique window. Genie waved.

'Give me a moment. Take Moucher down to the ferry and buy some tickets, OK? I'll see you there.'

'Where are we going?' Renée asked.

'Horseshoe Bay. Then we'll decide. Go. We have to separate right now.'

Genie left her coffee with Renée and ran across the road to the shop. She didn't look back. It was bad luck to look back.

The girl smiled shyly as she entered.

'You got a wig?' Genie asked.

The girl laughed. 'A wig?'

Genie quickly thought up a good lie. 'My ma will kill me if she sees me with my hair like this. She doesn't even know I cut it. I just found out she's coming to get me.'

The girl snatched at look at her employer, biting her lip at little with awkwardness. 'We don't do wigs.'

The woman at the counter frowned. 'I don't hold with

deceiving parents, but if I was your mother and I saw you with skunk hair and wearing those charity clothes, I'd probably disown you too.'

Genie looked at her incredulously. She had no reply to that. It was harsh.

'So, take her upstairs, Gemma, and find her something. I have some wigs. Nothing modern, you understand. For personal use. Find one and you can leave a deposit. Fifty bucks.'

Genie fished fifty bucks out of her jeans then turned to Gemma. 'I'll need a dress and a cardigan. One like you're wearing will suit fine.' It was the tiny blue wool cardigan with cute pearly buttons.

The woman looked at Genie and made an assessment. 'You're in big trouble, aren't you?'

Genie shrugged. 'My ma doesn't like my friends. She said make a choice. I guess I made a choice.'

The woman clucked her tongue. 'There's two nice dresses in the back. You'll look like a princess. How much money you got? I saw you selling cushions – a lot of cushions.'

'We're getting money together for a deposit,' Genie told her. 'No one will rent us anything without six weeks down.'

'Well, you know how to sell, I can tell you that. If you

ever need a job, come back and see me. Meanwhile, I can get you fitted out for cost – two hundred, and that includes shoes. You can't wear those.'

Genie looked down at her worn, still-damp sneakers and concurred. 'Deal.'

The woman smiled. 'Your mother won't recognize you.'

Genie smiled. 'That's the plan.'

Gemma dragged her upstairs with a broad grin on her face.

This would be fun.

21

Church Girl

Even Moucher didn't recognize her. She didn't even smell like Genie.

Rian had been standing by the ferry foot-passenger entrance with Moucher on a string. Renée was lying back against a truck waiting to load. Cars and trucks were already streaming into the ferry.

'Are we going or not?' Genie asked.

Moucher sniffed at her suspiciously. Rian did a double-take. Renée laughed she was so surprised.

'Wow. Super *Hairspray* retro look. I like it.'

Rian checked her hair and the outfit. She looked like some rich kid – perfectly turned out ready for her first important date or church on Sunday. He was quite taken aback. Genie was truly beautiful.

'What do you think?' Genie asked.

'You don't look as though you'd be going out with me.'

'Yeah,' Renée said. 'You look like you're slumming it with us. The shoes. Flatties. Neat. Oh my God, they have to be Italian leather. How much? Do we have any money left at all?'

'The shoes are second-hand, the cardigan came off the girl in the shop and I paid two hundred for the dress. You think that's too much? Oh and fifty deposit on the wig. She wants it back. It's hot under here. How do people wear wigs without passing out?'

Renée took her arm. 'They took real good care of you. You either held them up at gunpoint or they really liked you.'

Genie grinned. 'Yeah, I did good, I think.'

Rian produced the tickets and shepherded them towards the woman checking them off. 'I hope you have a plan for when we get to the other side. It'll be dark by the time we get there and—'

Genie cut him off. 'It's all good.' She picked up Moucher and carried him under her arm. He wasn't keen and struggled a little in her arms.

'Be good now,' Genie scolded him.

They walked towards the ferry. There was a guy in a brown hat handing out flyers by the stairs. He put one in Renée's hands.

'You seen this girl?' he asked, talking a good look at them all. Renée looked at the picture of Genie and pulled a face.

'Do I look like the kind of girl who'd hang out with a punk? Who shaves their head any more? It's so weird.'

They moved on, left the guy slack-jawed and frowning at the flyer.

Genie waited until the ferry had left Gibsons Harbour before telling them her news. They sat around a table and drank tea. Renée didn't rate the coffee.

'Gemma, the girl in the shop, let me use her cell to call Marshall. He said he's working on something. We have to meet him at Radspan Station Three. If we get there late, he's going to be on Level Fourteen.'

Rian looked at her. 'That's it?'

'That's it.'

'Level Fourteen?' Renée asked. 'What is that? Not the Fortress. I'm not going back there for anyone. I have been in Fourteen. It's cold and dark and—'

'Not the Fortress. Radspan Three.'

'We don't have a map, Genie. We have no idea which is Three or where it is,' Rian protested.

Genie closed her eyes and concentrated. She willed herself to read the map on the wall she'd seen in the tunnel. Everything was still vivid in her mind – all she had to do was go there, see it, shine the torch on it, read it . . .

She opened her eyes. Rian was asleep. Renée reading a magazine. Mouch was spread out on the floor fast asleep.

'I . . .'

Renée looked up at her. 'Welcome back. We're docking in ten minutes. I truly have never seen anyone sit so still in all my life, girl.'

'But, I only just closed my eyes for a second.'

'Uh-uh, I don't think so. You've been gone nearly two hours. Ferry had to stop for ages for a school of whales. I thought they were going to ride right over them, but it stopped and everyone ran up on deck to see, but it was getting dark and—'

'I missed the whales?' Genie was quite upset.

Rian woke, saw Genie was back and smiled.

'You find the map?' He was getting used to her going now.

'Yeah.' Genie nodded. Annoyed that something that seemed to her to have only taken five seconds had been two whole hours. 'Whistler. We have to go to Whistler.'

Rian and Renée exchanged glances. 'Whistler?' They both protested.

'I've got to go to the—'

'I'll go with you,' Renée said, standing. 'Ri, take care of Moucher. He probably needs a pee too.'

Rian moved to an upright position and Moucher

was already up, stretching his legs and watching Genie walking away.

'Walkies?' Rian asked.

Moucher looked at him with definite interest, wagging his tail.

'You know they don't like dogs on the ferry,' Genie called back. 'You'll have to be discreet.'

22

Watchmen

Reverend Schneider sat on a huge leather sofa on the enclosed patio and stared out at the sunset shimmering on the water. At the end of his lawn he could see Strindberg's yacht. All seventy metres of it moored at the dock and beside it, his own *Lord's Business*, which looked like a flea next to his host's showboat. He felt uncomfortable as Strindberg stood next to some valuable glass object staring down at him, his boosted heels showing on his leather boots. Strindberg's house was simply excessive, especially for such a small man. Belonged in Vegas, not here on the Sunshine Coast. Had he no shame?

'Like the house? Sweet deal. Bought it for cash just when the economy went belly up in 2008. Famous actor owned it. You might have seen his films. I forget his name. Ended up on TV, had his own series as a washed-up football player. Turned out he hadn't paid his taxes. I paid three million under the going price.'

Schneider didn't know the actor, but was sure

Strindberg had made his teeth meet on the deal.

'He had no taste, but this much waterfront is pretty good on the Sunshine Coast at this price. Always a good lesson that – pay your taxes, Reverend, or someone might snatch it all back.'

'It's impressive,' Schneider said reluctantly.

'Yes, I believe it is,' he smiled.

Schneider hated it when he smiled. Made him feel very uncomfortable. He felt his palms sweating.

'Unlike this situation, Reverend,' Strindberg remarked, bringing his hands together. 'Leaving aside how you milked us dry to build your little church in Spurlake and somehow found something spare to buy yourself a little pleasure craft. I would like some explanations. You talk of coincidences, Schneider. But I ask you again, how did she know about me? How did *you* know to come here? What was her purpose? To kill me, perhaps? I wouldn't blame her, but I'm just surprised she doesn't want to kill you first, considering you're the one who stole her life . . .'

Schneider felt a constriction around his collar and he was sweating everywhere now, he felt so tense. He'd always detested this little man, neither a scientist nor a visionary. Made all his money shorting stocks or by snapping up companies that had gotten into difficulties. Everywhere he went he got richer but thousands were made poorer. Now he had control of Fortransco. Just when it needed a person of vision to run it, they had allowed this cheap sleazeball to seize control. They'd had this amazing breakthrough, success was coming, and yet Strindberg had chosen this very moment to pounce. He probably didn't even believe in eternal life.

'They stole my yacht. It was only half full of fuel. They have no money. I calculated they could get no more than forty or fifty ks under power, if that.'

'Sailing a direct line from the city to here, that's about right,' Strindberg mused. 'So you *are* thinking coincidence.'

'Yes.'

'Do we know who the others are with Genie Magee?'

'One is her boyfriend, Rian Tulane, I am pretty sure of it. Your Mr Yates lives with his mother.'

Strindberg looked momentarily surprised. 'He does? He hadn't mentioned this to me. What other secrets are there? Spurlake is so damn incestuous, it makes me sick.'

'There's a dog too, but I have no idea—' Schneider went on.

'I don't care about the dog. The thing is, Reverend, where are they now? Why do they continually slip through our fingers so easily? Any ideas? What can this girl do to us?'

Schneider shrugged. 'I told you she was clever. She has gifts.'

Strindberg snapped a pen he was holding in half. His face was red with anger, but he held himself in check. '*We* are clever. *We* built the world's most powerful and only teleportation centre. *We* spent over two billion dollars doing this. *We* are clever; she is just a girl, a simple girl from the hicks. I want to know why she was here and what else she did in my house. She's a menace to the whole project and I want her stopped. No one is taking this seriously. But I am going to make them take it seriously. Mark my words well.'

Schneider felt awkward and uncomfortable. 'We've dealt with this. I am sure it was a coincidence.'

'No, we have not,' Strindberg snapped. 'She's dangerous. I am going to stop her antics. She is making fools of all of us. Do we have any leverage with her mother?'

Reverend Schneider shook his head. 'She has disowned her.'

Strindberg looked disappointed.

'I want her found – and fast. I will not let this child interfere with our investment.'

'I thought her body was important for research?'

Strindberg turned on his heels and walked towards the door. 'That was before she came here and tried to kill me. It was clearly her intention. She's dangerous and I want her eliminated.'

Strindberg turned at the door looking at Schneider with utter contempt.

'Get that thing you call a yacht off my dock, Reverend. I don't mind you ripping off the good folks of Spurlake with your little religious nonsense, but when you rip off Fortransco, it's coming out of *my* pocket. Find that girl or, I warn you, you'll lose everything.'

23

Frost

Renée was running out on the deck, her eyes wild with panic as she searched for Rian. Moucher barked and Rian caught her as she nearly ran by.

'What? Where's Genie?'

'She's collapsed in the bathroom. Come on. We have to get her out of there. This ferry's going to dock soon.'

Rian ran after Renée, Moucher at his side, ducking and weaving around passengers getting ready to leave.

There were two women standing by the female toilet doors pulling faces and making remarks.

'Disgusting, shooting up on the ferry. Disgusting.'

Renée barged through them and Rian followed, Moucher left outside, puzzled and trying to stay clear of the women who backed away, scared of him.

'You can't leave your dog off a leash, y'know. Shouldn't let dogs on the ferry.'

An announcement sounded for passengers to go back to their cars and the women walked away still muttering.

Genie was lying on the cold tiled floor unconscious,

her head bleeding from where she'd fallen.

'She was talking to me, laughing about something, and suddenly she just fell down, cracked her head,' Renée stated, feeling guilty she hadn't caught her.

'She didn't eat,' Rian said, cradling her head in his arms. Her wig had come loose, but she was breathing normally at least.

'Come on, help me get her out of here.'

'She going to be OK?'

Rian ignored the question. Together they got her standing and he picked her up in his arms and carried her out. She felt even lighter than before, if that was possible.

He laid her down on a long seat as Renée went to get some water.

Moucher reappeared and lay down beside her, clearly worried, letting escape little concerned whines, and Rian tried to rub her to get her warm. She was so unbelievably cold.

Renée came back with the water and Rian tried to get Genie to drink. It dribbled right back out and he just let her lay there.

'She's really gone this time.'

Renée was worried. 'We're going to have to get off soon. It's docking.'

Rian nodded. 'There was a wheelchair on the next deck

level. See if you can find it. We might be able to wheel her off. It might stop questions.'

Renée ran, the worried lines in her face pronounced. She was praying Genie wasn't heading into a coma.

One of the crew came back with Renée and the wheelchair.

'He had to unlock it. People steal them, can you believe that?'

'What's the problem?' the officer asked, keen to get off shift.

'Epileptic fit,' Rian told him. 'I thought she was over it but . . .'

The officer looked at Genie with some sympathy. 'She looks like Sleeping Beauty. Poor kid. OK, listen, you can wheel her off, but someone has to go with you. Company policy. She fall?'

'Bumped her head. Don't worry, we aren't going to sue. Can you help us off the boat?'

The officer was making a call on his cell. He nodded at Rian.

'Someone is coming. I need you to sign a release form. We have to go by the rules when someone has a fall. If you sign the waiver you realize that you are consenting to no company liability . . . We'll need the wheelchair back. Anyone meeting you?'

'We're catching a local bus.'

'Oh . . . Well . . . She'll bring forms and see to it that you get off safely. I'm sorry. You've got ten minutes before she comes.'

The man left. Problem delegated. He could go home.

Rian watched him go, looked up at Renée and said, 'Get her up. We'll get her out now. I don't want to sign any forms. They'll need ID and stuff.'

Renée was on it. They levered Genie into the wheelchair, grabbed Moucher and followed the stragglers to the exit. The fewer questions asked, the better. Rian was looking at the bottle of water Renée had brought and left lying in Genie's lap.

'Was the water frozen?'

'No. I filled it from the tap in the washroom; the café was closed already. I rinsed it out,' Renée added, in case he thought she'd brought him a dirty bottle.

Rian held it up. 'You didn't put ice in it?'

'No, I told you, I . . .' She looked at the plastic bottle and stared amazed. 'That's impossible.'

They both looked at Genie and she was blue. She was absolutely freezing.

'Oh my God,' Renée squealed. 'She's frosting.'

Nervous that they might be stopped for stealing the wheelchair, they got her down the walkway and away

225

from the ferry. They parked her outside a pizza place where the oven heat positively blasted out through the open window. Renée placed a reluctant Moucher on Genie's lap.

'Do we call an ambulance? I mean, it's impossible that she's frosting, but so many things are impossible,' Rian was saying, just not sure what the hell to do. Renée squeezed his arm, both staring at Genie as she sat in the wheelchair unseeing, barely breathing. Moucher whined. He was freezing on her lap. Didn't like it one bit.

Level Fourteen was ice-cold and empty, a forgotten level filled with long-unused scientific equipment. She turned around and the movement triggered the overhead lights, which slowly flickered on all around her. She walked towards a wide panoramic wall, realizing just how huge this space was. Frost covered everywhere, walls and computer monitors. She slowly moved towards what looked like a map and she brushed away the icy layer covering it.

RADSPAN – Projected Completion 2000.

Synchro One to Cascadia, which was the name given to the station she had been to with the others, and then to Whistler and beyond that to Nelson, then Banff, with others still marked under construction as far as the East Coast.

So was this Radspan Three? She wasn't sure how one could tell one from another.

'You look frozen.'

Genie whipped around and Cary seemed to peel off the wall. He looked dreadful, as if someone had drained all the life out of him.

'Cary?'

He shrugged. 'I know, I look bad. You don't look so good yourself; you're blue. You know it's minus twenty in here, right? You can't stay long dressed like that.'

Genie was shivering.

'I like the wig though. Cute outfit too. You in disguise?'

'Yeah. Someone called Strindberg is looking for me.'

'Strindberg!' Cary whistled.

'You know who he is? His house is huge. We borrowed Reverend Schneider's yacht and somehow ended up at Strindberg's mansion and—'

Cary chuckled. 'Denis hates Strindberg. He's the one who's got us all locked up and on life-support. He's pure evil.'

Genie looked at Cary. 'How's Denis? How's Julia?'

Cary looked at the ceiling; he didn't really want to say. 'None of us are going to make it, Genie. I've barely got the strength to get here. We're all fading fast. Days left, if that. Randall is almost gone. We're going out, one by one.'

'I'm trying to figure something out,' Genie whispered, horrified that she had done nothing for them so far.

Cary nodded. 'That why you are here?'

'Marshall's coming. I think he's got a plan.'

Cary was looking at the equipment. 'It's ancient. Like looking at Stonehenge and hoping it makes sense as a star map.' He looked directly at Genie. 'We may not make it, Genie. Don't get yourself trapped on our account. You helped us once and you don't deserve what's happened to us.'

'Marshall wants me to see something here. I don't know what. I . . .' Her teeth were chattering. 'I can't think, I'm so cold.'

Cary was looking at a computer monitor and he flicked a switch. Genie looked around her; this equipment was still connected. Still working after all this time. Lights started to come on around the room and somewhere a harsh buzzing sounded, which wasn't probably a good sign.

'Is this stuff supposed to be this cold?'

'I think so. Well insulated. You should see the cabling. It's like encased in huge steel pipes outside. Must use a ton of power to get it working.'

'What are you—'

'Transmission records. Someone was using this site for

teleportation tests back in the nineties.' He read out texts from the screen. 'Tests ten to one thousand and six – negative. Following power and memory upgrade May nineteen ninety-seven from Silverlake hydro, transmission data was improved by eighty-nine per cent. The second series of tests began.'

'Begin video playback,' a computer voice sounded.

Genie walked over to Cary's side and watched the video on the computer screen played on one corner. A clock counted down from ten seconds. A very scared white mouse was staked on a transmission platform. Its eyes were blinking with fear. On 'One' it vanished. There was applause off-screen.

A scientist's face appeared on the monitor; he wore a label: *Dr Milan*. He was smiling. 'As you can see from test one thousand one hundred and three the mouse dematerialized successfully, just as it was supposed to. The question remains, has it reappeared in Station Four in Nelson?'

There was a cut.

The same scientist, Dr Milan, appeared. He was no longer smiling. He looked five years older and unshaven, exhausted.

'After the disappointments of trials two thousand and eight to two thousand and thirty-six we again revised and

229

upgraded memory, but experienced further cooling problems. But what before had taken seconds, now would happen in nanoseconds. We know now that unless we can get speeds up to within a fraction of the speed of light, teleportation will simply not be possible. The Swiss team now building the Fortress has promised this and it seems it may be possible in theory, but we know we are very close here now.

'Test two thousand and thirty-seven was a revelation.'

The screen showed a small white dog sitting on the transmission platform – it seemed to sense something was wrong, but couldn't move, it was clearly drugged.

The same countdown procedure was played out and at the end of it the dog vanished. This time however there was no applause.

Cary frowned. 'I can't believe how many thousands of tests they did here. He was a fanatic. I'm skipping forward.'

Dr Milan was back on-screen. He looked a complete wreck and completely desperate. The date on the screen was 12th October 1999.

'We have just learned that Radspan Project has been terminated. Even though we have clearly demonstrated teleportation through four thousand five hundred tests that in principle material transmission can work, Strindberg, with the aid of his government friends, has shut us down.' He looked directly into the camera; his eyes were haunted.

'Strindberg, I hope you see this. You have no right to do this. We are just months away from a breakthrough. Just months. You are throwing away ten years of practical research.'

Dr Milan began to sob. Cary switched it off, embarrassed.

Genie was so cold now she could barely stand. Cary saw that she was going to collapse.

'You should go back, Genie. I can't feel the cold, but you're making yourself ill.'

'But I don't know what I am supposed to discover. I have to help you.'

Cary offered only a withering smile.

'I don't think I'll ever see you again. Please tell Renée to forget me. She's—'

'No!' Genie shouted. 'You can't give up. You can't give up, Cary. There must be a way.'

Cary disappeared. Genie spun around. She hated the way he came and left so abruptly.

She looked around the station. Where was the door? How would they even find the place up above? She saw someone had sprayed a slogan on the wall above it – something about an omelette.

She looked back at the computer. All shut down now. What had happened to Dr Milan? He looked terrified, as if he'd gone utterly crazy. Four thousand five hundred tests. How many mice and dogs had he made disappear? Someone's much-loved pets he'd probably stolen. It was too horrific to contemplate.

A voice was calling her from far away.

'Genie? You have to come back now. Can you hear me?'

Back where? How did they know she was here? Who was that calling? What did they mean by come back?

'Now, Genie. Now, dammit,' the voice shouted.

She heard barking and the station seemed to be fading around her. She felt despair. She hadn't found anything out. Nothing at all, and Cary was dying, they were all dying.

She felt a stinging pain. She took a sudden deep breath.

Genie opened her eyes, there was a heavy weight on her chest and she seemed to be floating; it was dark.

Moucher licked her face then jumped off her.

'I'm freezing,' she gasped.

Rian and Renée were both staring at her wild-eyed. She seemed to be lying down someplace and it was moving. She remembered the ferry.

'I'm so cold.'

Renée exhaled, clearly relieved to hear Genie's voice. She tucked a blanket around Genie and lifted her head.

'Drink this.'

Genie sipped hot coffee and felt it flow down inside her. It was a curious sensation. She could see that Rian was angry with her. She wondered what she'd done wrong.

'I'm sorry,' Genie croaked. 'For whatever I did. I'm sorry.'

'You've got nothing to be sorry for,' Renée told her. 'Ri's just upset, that's all. You were nearly dead. We were both upset. If Mollie here hadn't helped I don't know what we would've done.'

Genie tried to turn her head but it was too stiff. 'Mollie?'

Mollie stood, swaying a little so that Genie could see her.

'You'll be all right now, my girl. Hypothermia is a dangerous thing. I've seen it a few times. Got you wrapped up well. You'll be fine.'

Genie moved a little and heard an odd noise coming from her clothes. She felt under the blanket. Kitchen foil. She was wrapped like a Thanksgiving turkey. So weird.

'Mollie lent us a blanket and wrapped you in foil,' Renée told her. 'You were covered in frost. It was . . .'

'Remarkable,' Mollie declared. 'And on such a warm night.'

'And where are we now?' Genie asked, as Moucher put a paw out to her and sought reassurance that she still loved him. She squeezed his paw.

'Got a ride from Mollie's son.'

'Hello,' he hollered from the front.

'He's got this Winnebago. We're riding in luxury, girl. I got to get myself one of these. It's bigger than my ma's whole house.'

'You'll need a lot of gas money, hon. I almost never move it now, I only moved it 'cause I had to get the roof fixed after the snow last winter.'

Genie was puzzled. 'We're on the road? I thought . . .' She had no memories of leaving the ferry.

'On the way to Whistler. You said Whistler,' Rian informed her. 'Renée said she saw a bear.'

'Did too. It was sitting just watching the road. It looked so sad.'

'Whistler . . .' Genie mumbled. So odd that she had just come from there. She hadn't the heart to tell them it was a dead-end. There was nothing there but freezing cold. Radspan wasn't going to save anyone.

'Can I have another sip?' she asked Renée, pointing to her coffee.

Renée gave her the drink, glad Genie was showing signs of life.

234

'I have a pain,' Genie said, trying to rub it away. 'My ribs.'

Rian looked at her, real concern in his eyes.

'I always get it after travelling,' Genie reassured him. But it hurt, it really hurt. She wondered why.

Rian held her hand and squeezed it.

'You were gone a long time,' he said. 'You nearly turned to ice.'

Genie nodded. She felt like crying. She wished she could control things. She wished that Rian could know just how much she loved him and she chided herself for upsetting him so much.

'Four thousand five hundred,' Genie heard herself say.

'Four thousand five hundred?' Rian asked.

'Radspan. It failed four thousand five hundred times. They were trying to teleport mice and dogs and none of them arrived whole. None.'

Rian digested the information.

'Dr Milan was running it.' She suddenly remembered the sign above the door in the underground lab. 'He had a slogan written on a wall. "You can't make an omelette without breaking legs".'

Renée made an icky sound. 'Gross.'

'Dogs, mice, me, you – it doesn't matter to them. They'll keep trying till it works every time and then they'll change the world,' Rian declared angrily.

'Or we stop them,' Genie said.

'Or we go away someplace really far away, Genie. I don't want to go to this Radspan. I don't think we can save anyone any more.'

Genie understood. He was probably right. Cary would probably agree with him. She shivered. 'Can I have a cookie or something? I feel sick.'

Mollie offered her a selection. 'You're lucky. You seem to recover real fast. I've got no idea what happened to you, girl. Did someone lock you in a freezer?'

Genie smiled. That's exactly what had happened. The worst of it was that she had to go back there.

'I just got a chill, that's all,' Genie told her. 'A little chill.'

Rian sat down on the floor beside her, pushing Moucher to one side. He took Genie's hands and pressed them tight inside his own. 'Stay with us, Genie. I love you, remember? I can't protect you if you aren't here.'

Genie looked at him and those soft, heart-melting eyes and felt guilty.

'I know. I know. I know.'

24

Whistler

Mollie dropped them off on Village Gate Boulevard, making them promise they would go straight to the Hyatt. Renée had assured her that her uncle was coming to fetch them later at the hotel when she told him they had arrived. You could tell Mollie wasn't convinced, but she was happy to see Genie defrosted and some colour returning to her cheeks.

'You guys get into trouble or need a meal, I'm over at the Blackcomb Trailerpark. Can't miss it. Two miles out of town north and Lot Twenty-nine.'

Genie gave her a hug just to reassure her. 'Lot Twenty-nine. I'll remember.'

'And look after that dog. He loves you, girl, and he's looking thin.'

'I don't know how, you fed him like three times.'

Mollie chuckled and shut the door on them. Her son drove off.

'I could live in that,' Renée told them as they watched it disappear back down to Blackcomb Way. 'It's got everything. Even the toilet is cute.'

'I was thinking you were more the mansion type of girl,' Rian teased.

'Oh yeah, right. I so need an art gallery in my home. Bowling alley I could see, but creepy photos and statues – uh-uh.'

Moucher was busy in a ditch getting rid of all that food he'd been given and Genie felt dizzy. Rian wasn't entirely sure how he felt, but one thing he had noticed was how busy this place was, considering it was eleven thirty p.m. Spurlake would be dead at this hour; this place was buzzing.

'I can't believe how awake Whistler is.'

Three brown-bagging girls in micro-skirts tottered by laughing and giggling. Genie stared at their high heels. How did anyone learn to walk in those? In Spurlake someone would probably arrest them for indecency.

'It's a party town,' Renée announced grinning.

'Any idea where to go?'

'Find me a latté, I need coffee,' Renée declared.

'We have to find Marshall,' Genie told her.

Renée pulled a face. 'After coffee.' She looked across a square. 'We could go to Merlin's. I heard it's wild at night. We have to breakfast at Rendezvous on Blackcomb. Oh yeah, we got to ride on the Peak 2 Peak – eleven minutes between the peaks and great views.'

Genie looked at Renée, amazed. 'We're not skiing. Besides there's no snow. You've never been here before, girl, how can you know anything about Whistler?'

Renée looked at Genie with a big broad smile. 'You think I didn't read online magazines whilst I was in the Fortress? I could read anything I wanted. I got it all planned. Believe me, lunch at the Roundhouse is a must. All cool.'

'Everything's going to need money,' Rian said, trying to bring her down to earth. 'We're fugitives, remember? Got to keep a low profile. Guard the cash. Where are we headed? I mean, do you know where we're supposed to meet Marshall?'

'We have to head towards the All Seasons Hotel,' Genie explained.

'You're kidding,' Renée said in surprise. She was impressed. 'It's like the most expensive hotel in North America or something.'

Rian pointed to a huge building dominating the skyline at the end of the road where it met Blackcomb Way. 'You sure?'

Genie nodded.

'They'll never let us in. Not with a dog,' Renée pointed out.

Genie laughed. 'Not going *into* the hotel, dummy. We're going under it.'

'Radspan is under the hotel?'

'Fourteen levels down.'

Rian shook his head, amused. 'Right, how do you do that? You can't just come in and dig a hole – people would notice.'

Genie suddenly realized something she had mentally filed away. 'Strindberg owns it. He owns tons of land here. The photos in the gallery. He was standing outside this hotel.'

'Can't we just go get a burger at Splitz before we go underground?' Renée protested.

Genie was about to consent when suddenly Moucher barked and took off along the road.

'Mouch!' Genie shouted.

'MOUCH!' they all shouted, giving chase.

The dog could run real fast when excited. He ran towards Blackcomb Way as a truck was coming up the road.

Genie had been thinking that it looked remarkably like Marshall's old truck just as Moucher caught up with it at the lights. A door opened and the dog just hopped in.

Genie and the others stopped dead, the issue of Moucher's disloyalty aside. It did occur to her that it might be a trap. If anyone knew they were coming, if they got hold of Marshall's truck.

The truck pulled over. Two vehicles pulled past it, honking their horns. Genie saw a pair of man's legs awkwardly swing out and felt very relieved.

'You should teach this dog discipline,' Marshall said as they approached. He was grinning. 'He's lost weight.'

'We've *all* lost weight,' Genie replied. 'You too.'

Marshall hugged her, looking at Rian and Renée. 'Good to see you, Rian, and I guess you must be Renée.'

'Hi.' She flashed him a broad smile.

'Get in. Two inside, one in the back.'

'We going to the All Seasons?' Genie asked him as he broke away. He looked surprised at her question.

'You think I'm made of money? Got us a room at a cheap motel back some way from here. Come on. We have things to discuss.'

'Is there anywhere to eat there?' Renée asked.

Marshall smiled. 'I don't want you kids visible. We'll order pizza.' He looked at Genie again with a question on his face. 'That a wig?'

'Yeah. Hair doesn't grow that fast.'

'Well, either way, this is good timing. But I want you off the streets. Max got word there is a huge search on for you guys now. Strindberg is claiming you tried to kill him.'

Genie laughed. 'We what?'

'You broke into his place and threatened him. Serious charges.'

'Never even met him,' Renée protested.

'Well, he's got powerful friends and let's say we concentrate on staying invisible for a while.'

They drove to the motel and parked right outside the room on the ground floor.

Moucher was a picture of happiness itself and Marshall, for a guy who claimed he didn't care for the dog, was making quite a fuss over him. Genie watched and felt a little guilty she had taken him away from him and put the dog through so much.

Marshall ordered pizza whilst Renée and Genie took showers and Rian filled him in on all their travels. Marshall listened intently with growing amazement and admiration that they hadn't been caught.

More than half the pizza had gone before they had even described delivering Ferry's letter to the unfortunate Betty Juniper. And Genie had only gotten as far as the hunters when Rian got back from his shower. She had discarded her disguise and was relieved; the wig was a source of irritation all the time.

By one a.m. they got as far as Strindberg's mansion, the shock of seeing her picture in the gallery and Genie meeting up with Cary and Denis. Marshall was picking up on the subtext however and raised his hands.

'So let me get this right. You don't want me to use Radspan. I'm not sure I want to use Radspan, so that's it? We do nothing?'

Genie slumped. She'd been hoping Marshall would have answers but all they'd done so far is to prove to each other that it was going to be impossible to help the others.

'I want to help them, but I really don't know how,' Genie explained.

Marshall drank some green tea he'd brought with him and thought hard about the situation. Moucher lay with his back paws on Genie and front on Marshall, his affections clearly divided.

'What about Level Fourteen? You say you were there?' Marshall asked her, trying to get things clear in his head.

Genie sighed. 'It was freezing.'

'She nearly froze to death,' Renée interjected. 'She had actual frost on her skin, can you believe that?'

'Frost?'

'It was minus twenty, at least,' Genie remarked. 'There was frost covering the computers and the map of Radspan,

243

I remember brushing it aside.' Genie looked at her hand as if the frost was still there.

'What did you learn?' Marshall asked.

'Everything. Dr Milan made videos of all his teleport tests. They're on the computer hard-drives. The whole place looks like he shut the door and never went back. Cary was with me.'

Marshall nodded. 'He recorded his tests?'

Genie nodded. 'Four thousand five hundred. That's when Strindberg shut it down.'

'Four thousand five hundred,' Marshall exclaimed, his eyebrows shooting up. 'Wow. He was a very determined guy, very determined.'

'Were you working on the same thing?' Rian asked him.

Marshall nodded. 'Same idea, but we were coming at it from a different theory with different techniques. To be honest, he was never going to beat the odds. His system was too slow. He never had enough speed or memory. It was never going to work, no matter what he added to it. There's a corollary that the more wires and power you add to a system, the slower it gets – and he was never going to beat the wiring bottlenecks. We know that, but he didn't know, I guess. He was desperate not to have his funding cut off.'

Renée pulled a face. 'All those animals that lost their lives for nothing. It was never going to work?'

Marshall shook his head. 'Never. He could make things disappear, but he hadn't a hope in hell in transmitting all that DNA and reassembling it in the right order. It was way too ambitious considering his equipment.

'When the Fortress transmitted you guys, for example, bits of your DNA would have been on at least thirty – or even fifty – thousand servers at any one time and the clever bit was the stability programme that remembers where it all is and what order it is supposed to be in. That's what Synchro does. Holds all that information until it is ready to spit it out and re-assemble. He didn't have that logic theorem built into Radspan. He was like black-and-white TV; it's good, but it isn't in colour.'

Genie frowned. 'But we didn't arrive in Synchro when we transmitted. So what does that prove?'

Marshall shrugged. 'That they still don't know what they are doing, I'm afraid.'

'So maybe Dr Milan's mice and dogs went someplace too?'

Marshall conceded that. 'But would they be alive?'

'There must be tons of dog bones someplace,' Genie said with real sadness.

'I believe he bred the dogs specifically.'

Genie was appalled. 'He teleported puppies?'

'He should have come over to our programme; he was offered, but he refused. I remember meeting with him. He looked like your perfect mad scientist – staring eyes. You could tell he was obsessed.'

'I still don't get how they built it under a hotel?' Rian muttered.

Marshall yawned and stretched. 'Where better to hide something secret? It was built to help fund Radspan, I guess, but when Strindberg bought in to the holding company he was campaigning to have it closed right from the get-go. I think he had a falling out with Dr Milan.

'They were all based here in Whistler. I was in Spurlake, as you know. We were on Level Six, working on the stability programme. Keeping molecules stable in transmission is hard science. No one liked how much money we were going through either. This is all frontier stuff and sometimes you get things wrong. Radspan was doomed from the outset, only no one could see that at the time. But that's not why I'm here now.'

Genie felt tired. She could barely keep her eyes open now.

'So why are you here?'

Marshall looked at her. 'Because I think I may have thought of a way you can help your friends. You won't like it, but what with them all being in comas, there isn't much of a choice in the matter.'

'You know why they all collapsed?' Rian asked.

Marshall nodded. 'Extreme Mosquito attack most likely shut down their brainwaves. Literally turned them off. It's designed to incapacitate. Apparently, according to my contact, it's something the defence division of Fortransco was working on for the US Government. I met up with someone from Level Six who is still working on it and he said they cranked it up too high and burned out the neurones. Those kids aren't going to come back from that.'

'But Genie has been speaking with them,' Rian protested.

'Genie has been communicating with Cary because he's possibly found a neural pathway back to his DNA stored on the Fortress servers. That's as good an explanation as I can come up with. I don't pretend to understand half of what Genie is capable of, I just respect it. As a scientist, I'm kind of jealous too.'

Genie looked up at Marshall her face set, demanding honesty.

'So you think they're all going to die.'

Marshall shrugged. 'Yeah. I do. I heard one, maybe two died already. I'm sorry. Even if you could get into the

Fortress and rescue them, you'll never wake them, Genie. It's my honest opinion. They are almost certainly dead or going to die, and soon. The life-support system is just for testing purposes.'

Genie felt hot tears rolling down her cheeks.

Renée felt for Genie, but she was angry. 'They could have done the same to us.'

'That was what they were intending. Still intending, I might add.'

'So if we can't save them, if they're going to die, why are we here, Marshall?' Rian asked. 'Why are you here?'

'I have a proposal. As I said, you aren't going to like it. It's going to sound completely insane, but then, everything in this game is completely crazy.'

'What?' Genie asked.

'You want to sleep first? You're barely conscious.'

'Are you stupid? I need to know now. We all do.'

Renée was tired as well, but she couldn't just go to sleep without knowing. Rian looked at Genie and she could tell he agreed.

Marshall rubbed Moucher's flanks and looked away for a moment as he tried to assemble his thoughts.

'This project didn't set out to produce monsters. It just made monsters out of people. We wanted to save the world. One day in the future they'll think we were stupid burning all that fossil fuel to keep warm and so we can all travel by car or SUV someplace. There really is no excuse for owning a Ferrari, but we'd all secretly want one if we could. Some people say that if we hadn't invented the jet engine, global warming may not have happened. If we hadn't genetically modified food we wouldn't be now able to feed seven billion people on this planet. But we did and you could argue we are now paying a big price for it. The world may not be able to sustain us much longer. Some of us, of course, but seven, eight or nine, or even ten billion people? I severely doubt it.

'When I left university I wanted to save the world from itself. Teleportation was a dream, that's all. A small dream shared by a few people. We thought that if we could teleport people to wherever they wanted to go, we'd save the planet. No more airports, no more jet trails, tourism right down to the individual level.'

Marshall smiled, checking to see if they were listening.

'Of course, things never quite work out that way, do they? To get funds for research it was necessary to go to people like Strindberg. I think he was in the ice-cream business one time. How he got control of everything over the years is worth a study on its own. He made a fortune in ninety-eight in the first dotcom boom and got out just in time. Made a second fortune in real estate and got out before that crashed too. Timing is everything, I guess. But he isn't the kind of person who should be running "development". He never liked the Radspan project and it was his idea I think to build the hotel over it 'cause he was one of those people campaigning for the Winter Olympics back in 2000. He never really had faith in teleportation or mass travel and I guess, in the end, he's right. It was never going to work for mass transit; it's just too difficult, too expensive and too dangerous.

'That why Reverend Schneider's "Eternal Life" project got a toehold. Strindberg liked that. The genetic modification programme has been getting a ton of money for research lately.'

'What?' Genie asked, confused.

'Cosmetic surgery.'

'Like Randal getting thinner?'

'My red hair. They took away my red hair.'

'And my moles,' Genie said, with mixed feelings about that.

'Exactly,' Marshall said. 'They're experimenting with every "volunteer" who comes in.' He held up his hands. 'And before you say anything, I know you didn't volunteer. I'm just telling you what they're doing. They didn't take your moles; they altered your melatonin level most likely. You tan really easily now. Did you not notice how brown you are, Genie? They didn't change your hair, Renée; they sequenced your DNA so that it would dilute the bit that made your hair red. It might seem pointless to you, but not to Strindberg. He doesn't care a fig for teleportation, he wants to open a chain of beauty stores where you go in ugly and come out beautiful. People will pay a fortune for that.'

'This is all about cosmetic surgery?' Genie protested. 'You have to be kidding.'

Marshall rubbed his neck. He was tired now. 'I told you it was crazy, right? But in ten years, fifteen max, they might be more common than Starbucks are now. You'll pay to look beautiful if you think you're ugly or have a big nose or have a limp. That's his plan. One-day DNA fix. You'll plan your kids there. Fix your kids there. Got aggressive tendencies? Strindberg can flick a switch and your kid will be all sweetness and light. The potential is amazing and at the same time scary as hell.'

'You really are kidding, right?' Rian asked.

'Genie is the big breakthrough. Randall too, especially him, from what you told me. If you can successfully make an obese kid thin, just think of the billions to be made from a slimming programme that actually works. There would be lines around the block. You have made it all possible. Of course, you have also made it impossible.'

'Huh?'

'Who are you?' he asked Genie.

'Genie Magee. Genie Magee, more tanned, no moles,' she added.

'Big deal. Small change,' Marshall said. 'But what happens when we live in a world where everyone except the poor can afford to be beautiful?'

'It's a better-looking world. Everyone is hot,' Renée said, grinning.

'Maybe,' Marshall answered. 'Or no one is hot 'cause they all look the same. Imagine five million Mila Kunises or Beyoncés, or whomever they want to look like in the future. One hundred million Natalie Portmans.'

'God, I mean, she's beautiful, but we'd all be the same.'

'And maybe you'd change your looks several times. How many times before there's side effects? What happens when things go wrong? You absolutely know things will go wrong.'

'That's a weird world, Marshall,' Rian declared.

Marshall nodded. 'And as I say often, these days, expect the unexpected. The law of unintended consequences. Let's talk about side effects.'

'I'm all side effects,' Genie said. 'I'm possessed, remember.'

Marshall smiled, then yawned. He needed sleep. 'The

short of it is, you can't save your friends, Genie.'

Genie looked at him. It was beginning to sink in. Cary, Denis and all were truly doomed.

'That's what Cary said.'

Marshall looked at her. 'Where did you last see him, exactly?'

'Level Fourteen. It was really cold, I told you. He was excited to explore the system. He got Dr Milan's tests up on the computer, but you were right. By Test four thousand five hundred he was absolutely crazy.' She shuddered, remembering the cold. 'I was hoping that just being there I'd discover something important, but I don't think there's anything there. I don't think you'll find anything useful.'

'Was Cary aware that his body is on life-support?'

Genie nodded. 'He said Denis was real bad and he didn't think the others would survive. I don't really like to talk about it now.'

Marshall pondered the situation a moment. It was interesting that Cary knew he was on life-support, yet could separate himself out and be with Genie in Level Fourteen.

'You don't believe me?' Genie asked, her voice breaking up.

Marshall stood up, gripping the chair for support as

his leg was awkward after sitting so long.

'I'm thinking ten impossible things before breakfast,' Marshall replied, 'or whatever Alice said.'

'"Why, sometimes I've believed as many as six impossible things before breakfast",' Genie corrected him. 'I read *Alice in Wonderland* at least four times before my mother burned it.'

'She burned it?' Marshall queried. '*Alice?*'

'She burned *Twilight, His Dark Materials* and just about anything with monsters or witches or fairies or vampires in them. She got a list from the library and went through my shelf. Reverend Schneider came round and prayed for my soul – again, and I watched them burn in the back yard.'

'I think it's time we slept. Lots to do tomorrow,' Marshall declared. 'Someone take Mouch out for a pee, please.'

'You were going to tell us something.'

'I have to think. I didn't know Cary and the others knew they were on life-support. It alters everything. Puts a different perspective on it at least.'

'You mean if they're simultaneously conscious or unconscious,' Rian stated.

'Exactly. Which is it?'

'You think I dreamed it?' Genie queried. 'Come on, Mouch. Time to pee.'

'No, and that's the problem. Genie, be careful outside. Keep to the shadows.'

Genie nodded. She stepped over Renée, who was asleep on the carpet.

'We're going to take this to the enemy tomorrow, Genie,' Marshall told her.

The air outside was chilly, instantly waking her.

She looked up at the stars as Mouch hunted for a good spot. They were bright and gave her comfort somehow. All those years as a kid staring out of her window at the stars at night. It was a place to go when her mother was bitching and she was always complaining about something she'd done or would do or hadn't done. She'd travelled to distant stars and made plans and cities and lived a virtual life there. She wondered how they were getting on without her now.

Genie blinked. A cop car drove by slowly. She merged into the shadow of the building and held her breath until it had gone.

'Mouch,' she hissed.

He came running, wagging his tail. He was the happy one at least.

25

Run, Rabbit, Run

Mouch saw it first and stood absolutely still for five seconds. It twitched its ears, highly tuned to anything that moved, and then it saw him and was off. Dog versus rabbit – it's an old story and rabbit usually wins. Mouch darted off in pursuit; the rabbit had a good start and shot across the road.

'Mouch, no!' Genie was yelling and gave chase.

Mouch wasn't listening though. He had a rabbit in his sights and was going for it.

The rabbit just missed a vehicle and got clear. Mouch very nearly got squashed and the car slewed to a stop in a cloud of tyre smoke, the angry driver trying to unbuckle to remonstrate with the girl running after her dog.

'Mouch!' Genie yelled again. Vaguely she registered a car had been involved and a driver got out to shout at her. She glanced back and carried on.

'Mouch!' she yelled, angrily now. 'You get back here.'

And then, because that's what brains do when processing two things at once, it played back the image of the man who'd gotten out of the Mercedes Benz and she nearly had a heart attack when she realized who it was. *Reverend Schneider*.

Now she was no longer angry at Mouch. She was running a little faster than the dog, if that was possible. She was stunned. It just wasn't possible, was it?

Mouch looked back and could see that Genie was no longer chasing him, but running away at full pelt from him, down into the ditch at the side of the road, built to take the run-off in spring from all that melting snow.

Mouch set off to follow her, all thoughts of a rabbit forgotten.

Reverend Schneider was swearing and getting back into his vehicle, when he too had a revelation. The girl, that running girl with a dog, no less, that running girl with just a fuzz of hair . . . could it be? Was it possible? Was that his nemesis, the girl who had single-handedly wrecked his entire life?

He got back in, buckled up and spun the car around in a cloud of hot rubber. He wanted a closer look.

He'd been chasing this girl for almost two whole days now. At every stage she had eluded him, but he'd seen the CCTV footage of her and her friends on the ferry. Seen her disguise. It had taken him a while to realize it was her at all. Traced her to the pizza restaurant where she'd gotten a ride to Whistler, seen the wheelchair she'd abandoned at the ferry terminal with a note saying 'thanks'. They'd been appreciative to get it back and most helpful to enable him to find his sick 'daughter' who'd been tricked into some unorthodox spiritual healing for cancer. They'd been very sympathetic. They had difficult children as well and wanted to help. Reverend Schneider knew how to make people help him.

And now, a scrawny skinhead girl and a little dog nearly running right under his car. What were the chances?

He gunned the motor down the road. He could see the top of her head. She was trying to get back to wherever she'd come from.

He speed-dialled a number on his cell.

'Blackcomb Way. If you've got anyone in the area, she's out chasing a dog.'

'I've got your car GPS tracked. Help will be with in you ten minutes. Count on it.'

Schneider registered his surprise that his car was being tracked. Strindberg clearly left nothing to chance. He slowed, keeping her in sight. He could see that she had nowhere to go. He'd cut her off at the start of the hill and then Fortransco could take over. He felt the elation of a hunter. Finally he would be rid of her.

* * *

Renée woke up on the floor. Her neck was sore from lying in an awkward position.

'Where's Genie? Where's Mouch?' she asked.

Rian came out of the bathroom. His heart skipped a beat.

'She's not back yet? She took Mouch out.'

'Oh no . . .' They both realized something was wrong and raced to the door.

'What's going on?' Marshall was asking, but got no reply; he was looking at an open door. He heard their footsteps running away. He frowned. Genie should have been back by now; it had been nearly half an hour.

Genie took a left and ducked down, running hunched into a huge drainage pipe that ran right under the road above. Her heart was pumping wildly. She couldn't believe her bad luck in running into Reverend Schneider, of all people. It just didn't seem possible. Mouch was at her heels now.

'I hope . . . you feel . . . guilty,' she said grabbing air between words.

Mouch didn't look at her; he sensed that he'd done something wrong. Had no idea what – he was supposed to chase rabbits. Marshall made him chase rabbits all the time back home.

Genie ran to the end of the pipe and saw there was a car park to her left and beyond that some condos. She began to run. She needed to make sure that Schneider couldn't get to the others. Didn't matter if he caught her, but she had to save Rian and Renée.

She ran, keeping low between cars. She knew Schneider's Mercedes would be close by somewhere, but he wouldn't be able to drive in here – there was a barrier at the entrance.

It was then she heard it. A chopper. She could feel the invisible fingers of Mosquito clutching at her mind. The bastard had called the Fortress; they were sending in the big guns.

She needed a place to hide, a place where the signal from the chopper couldn't penetrate and shut her down. She was at the far end of the car park now and the condos were before her. It was nearly two a.m. No one was going to be awake, or able to let her in and who's to say the signal wouldn't get her, even if she got inside?

She prayed to Grandma Munby for advice. Which way to go? What to do?

Mouch saw the storm drain first. He stopped right by it. Genie looked at him, he looked at her and who knows if it was Mouch himself or Grandma Munby intervening, but Genie realized it was a brilliant idea.

She dropped down and crawled in, trying not to see the bugs and creepy-crawlies that would be living there. Mouch entered at the same time and somehow squeezed by and got ahead of her. The Mosquito broadcast couldn't effectively penetrate the ground above her – she'd be safe, for a while.

Renée saw the chopper too and knew exactly what it was as her head began buzzing.

'Mosquitoes,' she gasped. 'Get me somewhere safe, Ri. They know we're here.'

Rian took no chances. They were running along Blackcomb Way. Genie had to be somewhere around, but all he could see was a Mercedes stopped some way ahead, its headlights pointing out across a car park and overhead, a chopper making its way to the area. He couldn't work out how they knew they were here. It was impossible.

He saw the storm drains – half filled with stagnant water. They had no choice.

'Follow me,' he yelled.

Renée could see where he was headed. 'You're kidding, right?'

'Crawl in. Never mind the mud and bugs. It will cut off the signal. Get in now, Renée.'

Renée closed her eyes and wriggled in, smearing mud

all over her head and clothes. Overhead the Mosquito was getting stronger and . . .

'You OK?' Rian called.

'You coming in?'

'It's muddy.'

Rian laughed as Renée swore at him.

The chopper flew directly overhead and he was suddenly thinking about night-vision. He had no choice but to crawl right in behind her.

'Eww, yuk,' he complained.

'I have a headache.'

'You can feel Mosquito under here?'

'No, I banged my head on the pipe. There's a lump just—'

'Ow.'

'About there,' Renée told him.

Rian rubbed his head and wished there was room to turn around. It stank down here.

'You can't feel it?'

'I'm OK. The point is, has Genie found anyplace to hide? How did they find us, Ri? You think they've got Marshall's truck bugged?'

That was exactly what Rian was thinking.

'Yeah. Maybe we can't trust him?' Renée remarked.

'He may not know,' he said, remembering when

he'd left the truck by the Fortress. 'They've bugged his truck before.'

Renée conceded that. 'I guess.

'Rian?'

'Yeah?

'I'm scared. I hate this. I really hate this.'

They heard the shot. Heard someone shouting. Heard the chopper's motor change tone. It suddenly sounded sick, real sick.

'I should go look,' Rian said.

'Don't you leave me here, Rian Tulane.'

'Something's going on, Renée.'

'Stay. I can still feel it. Stay. Genie will be lying low. She knows what to do. She'll make her way back. Stay . . . please.'

Moucher suddenly began to move.

'No, Mouch, stay.'

But he was crawling towards the far end of the pipe.

Genie didn't know what was wrong with the dog. He just wasn't obeying anything tonight.

'Mouch. Stop. Come back now, you hear me?'

Mouch moved even quicker towards the far end and Genie felt obliged to follow. What the hell he was up to, she had no idea.

'You'd better have a good reason, dog, 'cause I am so going to beat you after all this. If it wasn't for you, Schneider wouldn't even know I was here.'

Mouch was already out of the pipe and turned around – giving her a sharp little bark to hurry her up.

'You shut up now, dog. We're supposed to be quiet.'

Genie crawled out of the pipe and it was absolutely dark here. She could see the stars above her despite the streetlights blazing over the road sixty metres away. She looked around her. They were in a garden, the homes closest to the road separated by a wall that extended right around one side of the development.

She bent down and gave Mouch a hug. She was safer here, no one could see her and the chopper was nowhere around.

'Got to find a way back to the motel,' she whispered into Mouch's ears.

Genie began walking, looking for a gate – some way to get out of the complex.

Mouch was close to her heels now, not sure of this place. She could hear all kinds of activity on the other side of the wall. Police vehicles. She imagined they'd set up a manhunt for her. She and Mouch were going to have to go down every rat hole in Whistler to escape.

They passed a home where some people were still up

watching TV on a huge wall screen. Lots of explosions and deafening music. She was sure glad she didn't live next door to them. She continued walking. There had to be way out of here.

She heard the familiar *whoop-whoop* of cop cars. Were they coming for her? She had to find out what was happening. She realized that she didn't even know the name of the motel they were staying at. How dumb was that?

Genie found a tree that grew close the wall and, after telling Mouch to sit and not move *on pain of death*, she jumped up, grabbed a branch and shimmied up to get a view.

There was open ground in front of her and in the distance the chopper was straddled across several car lanes. Cop vehicles and fire trucks had surrounded it and she could see they were making quite a fuss. Reverend Schneider was arguing with law-enforcement officers and she could hear, but not make out the words, that tempers were flaring. The chopper must have broken down. That was a real stroke of luck.

Genie dropped down besides Mouch and patted his head. 'We caught a break. Come on. Time to find a way out of here.'

There was a gated exit and security post. Clearly

whoever lived here was rich, but not so rich they had it manned twenty-four hours. They slipped under the gate and, keeping well behind parked vehicles, went the long way back to the motel.

'No rabbits,' she told Mouch, who kept his head down, aware that she was still cross with him.

Renée was still lying on the floor, but this time she was covered in mud. Rian likewise. They looked at Genie and Mouch with total astonishment.

'You a ghost?'

'Huh?'

Marshall was staring at her as well and Genie had no idea what they were doing or why the other two were muddy.

'You're covered in white dust,' Marshall said. 'Looks like lime.'

Genie caught sight of herself in the mirror and received a shock. She and Mouch had been crawling in white stuff. They really did look like ghosts.

'And the mud? I mean, I go outside for five minutes and you guys are like mud wrestlers now?'

'Five minutes!' Rian protested. 'You've been gone two hours. We looked all over for you and then there was a Mosquito attack and don't tell me you—'

Genie took a deep breath. 'Reverend Schneider saw me. Called in the chopper, the bastard. Had to hide in a drain. The chopper seems to have landed on the road. Cops crawling all over them.'

Marshall grinned. 'They had a malfunction.'

Renée smiled. 'He shot at them. Saw it swoop down and he shot at it.'

'Slowed 'em down. You can bet they didn't get clearance to fly this late at night and the cops won't like that they crash-landed on the highway. Woke a few people up around here, I can tell you. Don't worry, I fired from across the road behind a dumpster.'

Genie was impressed. She didn't even know Marshall had a shotgun with him.

'How do you think Reverend Schneider tracked us here?' she asked. 'It's like we can never shake him.'

'My son checked my truck over before I left. No GPS trackers on my vehicle. But if Schneider's here, it means Strindberg will be following. I know we need sleep, but we need to check out early and get down to Level Fourteen before they close off our access.'

'We're still going down there?' Genie asked.

'No choice and, besides, once we are down there, they won't be able to find you.'

'Why?'

'Because I'm one of the few people who still know how to get in. He's fired pretty much everyone else. He won't be looking for you down there. I doubt he remembers it. Just because he shut something down, doesn't mean he knows what it was or did or even where it is. It's just on a spreadsheet someplace and he moved it into a different column.'

'We have to go,' Genie agreed. 'Cops will have to investigate that shooting. You're crazy, Marshall, but thanks. You saved our asses again.'

'It had to be done. I knew the moment I saw the Fortransco logo what it was.'

'I've got to hit clean up,' Renée declared. 'I'm not going anyplace looking like this. '

'Me too,' Genie decided.

Marshall was looking at Moucher. 'Take the dog in there. He's a disgrace.'

Genie paused at the bathroom door.

'It's entirely his fault, y'know. He chased a rabbit, nearly got squashed flat by Schneider's Mercedes.'

Marshall frowned. 'He does like to chase rabbits. But you shouldn't have chased after him. He's a grown boy. He makes a mistake, he'll pay for it and go hungry. Someone will find him and eventually call the number on his tag. *You* make a mistake and all hell breaks loose.'

Genie knew he was right. She had been stupid.

Rian could barely stay awake. He couldn't remember the last time he slept.

'We have to go down there?' he asked. 'It's going to be cold.'

Marshall nodded. 'It's nearly four a.m. We'll leave at six, pick up some coffee from somewhere and head to the hotel. You can sleep some more down there whilst I try to figure stuff out.'

'Freeze to death more likely. You didn't see Genie when she came back from there – she had frost on her skin.'

Marshall frowned again. 'It's not supposed to be so cold down there. I'll see if I can fix that too. We'll need sweaters. You need to get cleaned up too. Can't have you looking like that out there.'

'We need clean clothes.'

'That I can't fix.'

Marshall lay down; he needed some sleep himself. He was worried he was in too deep now – but he'd made a promise to help, and help he would.

'Hey, leave hot water for me,' Rian called out.

The bathroom door opened and a very wet, but clean, Mouch staggered out, slipping on the vinyl flooring. He looked half the size he did when he went in and very put out by the ordeal.

'Don't shake, Mouch, don't you dare shake.'

He shook – spraying water everywhere.

'Damn.'

26

Descent

Genie was surprised to discover McDonald's was real busy at six a.m. She had no idea that people needed breakfast at this hour, nor that clubwear was required – or virtually nothing in the case of some of the girls, who looked either exhausted or zoned out in most cases. What was clear was that no one waiting for their egg McMuffins, except her and Ri, had had any sleep that night. She adjusted Marshall's baseball cap, at least three sizes too big for her head, but any disguise was better than nothing.

Moucher waited patiently outside, glancing in to make sure she didn't forget to get a burger for him.

Marshall sat in his truck reading a newspaper, content to let them queue, whilst Renée slept in the corner, reluctant to start her day so early.

Rian was nuzzling her left ear.

'What?'

'Just feeling affectionate.'

'In Maccy D's?'

He laughed. It was, he realized, not the place to

271

show any kind of feelings. They were surrounded by hungry zombies, none too keen to have to wait for their food either.

'I was scared last night. You were gone two whole hours and, I don't know, all kinds of things raced through my head. Bad stuff, y'know.'

Genie rested her head on his chest a moment. 'Yeah, I know. I was stupid.'

'Hi, can I take your order?'

They looked at the perky girl with acne and gave their orders.

They brought the food out to the others and handed it through the window. Renée awoke and ate without saying a word.

'Oh, this is Mouch's.'

Genie unwrapped the burger and blew on it to cool it. 'We need to get biscuits and stuff. He's eating all the wrong food.'

'I'll put him on a veggie diet when this is over,' Marshall said. 'I think he's probably had enough adventures for a dog's lifetime with you.'

Genie was about to protest but Moucher jumped up, twisted high in the air and snatched the burger and bun out of her hands, hastily running off to a doorway to eat it.

'Maybe teach him some manners too,' Marshall added with a smirk.

Genie stood outside the truck eating, thinking about what Marshall said. She'd been incredibly selfish taking Moucher with her. She was in no position to offer him a stable home. Of course he had to go back to live at the farm. It was his home, he was happy there. She didn't want to admit any of this out loud, but she knew he was right. The worst of it was that she'd like to go back to the farm too. She'd felt safe there, despite all that had happened.

Moucher growled. There was someone trying to grab his food and he backed off with the burger in his mouth.

'Mouch?'

Genie approached the doorway and was surprised to discover a woman was sleeping there, surrounded by cardboard boxes and all her possessions.

'I'm sorry, I'm sorry. My dog didn't know you were there.'

The grey-haired woman with an incredibly lined face looked at her with astonishment.

'Girl – I know you.'

Genie shook her head.

'I'm sorry. Are you hungry? Would you like some breakfast?'

273

Genie couldn't bear to see people sleeping rough; she'd had a taste of this and was scared this would be her future.

'Got a message for you, girl.'

Genie smiled. 'I got half an egg McMuffin.' She offered it to the woman, who snatched it from her with her black talons extending from her withered hands. Genie was scared of her and Mouch was still growling, even though he'd swallowed the burger whole.

The woman ate the McMuffin. Renée was calling for Genie to come away, but the old woman had an eye on Genie and was clearly trying to remember something. Genie turned but found the talons gripped around her shoes.

'Grandma Munby has a message for you,' the old woman said, her voice a furtive whisper now.

'What? What did you say?' Genie couldn't believe it.

She squatted down; the stench of pee was overpowering and she nearly brought her breakfast up. She saw that the woman's eyes were swollen and she had bruises on her neck.

'You need money?' Rian asked, standing behind her now, making sure Genie was OK.

Genie looked up at him. 'She said something about my grandma.'

Rian looked sceptical. 'How could anyone here know

about your grandma? Even you don't know anything about her.'

The woman put out her hand, the nails almost five centimetres or longer, jet-black and sharp. Rian put a five-dollar bill in her hands.

'Eat something,' he told her.

The hand closed over the money and the old woman looked directly at Genie.

'She says, she don't want to see you – yet. The curse must end with her. You must start anew.'

Genie frowned. It didn't make any sense and Rian, she knew, was keen to go.

'Grandma Munby said this?'

The woman shuddered and turned her head away to the door whilst her hand stayed in the air, pointing at something.

'They watch for you. Everywhere. Many eyes. They scared of the Munby girl.'

Genie looked at where she was pointing and there was a CCTV security camera pointed at McDonald's. They were just outside its peripheral vision. But she quickly flipped her hood up over her head, in case. She'd had quite enough of people recognizing her.

The old woman curled up again and turned over, putting her back to them. The audience was over.

Rian hauled Genie up and they walked back to the truck in silence, Moucher at her heels.

'What was that about?' Marshall asked as they climbed back in.

'Some crazy stuff,' Genie replied. 'Can't believe people sleep in doorways out here in Whistler. Where does she go in winter, for God's sake?'

'It's a tough world,' Marshall declared as he started up the engine. 'When all those banks and pensions went bust back in the recession, no one was thinking about the old folks. No one was thinking about the human cost at all.'

Renée gathered up all the packaging and dashed out to the bin and back again. She smiled as she climbed back in. 'Just doing my bit for the planet.'

'If we cared about the planet, we probably wouldn't be eating here at all,' Rian said, raising his eyebrows.

'She said something about the cameras watching me,' Genie remembered.

Marshall nodded. 'She's not crazy. The Fortress is probably hooking into every CCTV camera in the city, probably all over Canada. They can use face-recognition software to track you down. Should've had you wearing my hat and your hood earlier. My fault. They can most likely access the cameras inside there too. The new software can process one thousand faces a minute. They already know you're in Whistler; they just want to know where. The truth is, you probably pass a camera every thirty metres in a normal city. The best you can do is keep moving, don't let them predict your destination and travel at night; the software doesn't work well in the dark.' He snatched a look at her. 'It was lucky for you it was dark last night, huh?'

Rian swore. 'It's like . . .'

Marshall shook his head and backed out of his space to the road.

'It's not like, it *is*. We're moving rapidly towards a police state. Why the hell do you think I live in the country?'

'But it's for our safety, isn't it?' Renée asked.

'When it's for our safety, we're all for it. But what if it isn't? What if really bad people control it? We lived ten thousand years and never needed to know where everyone is all the time. Seems now we do. Are we any safer? Strap in and keep your heads down. We're heading to the enemy. Anyone wants to quit, say so now, because there's no going back.'

No one spoke. The road was quiet. The sky red. 'Red sky in the morning – shepherd's warning,' Genie remembered. Typical.

'What did the crazy lady want?' Renée asked suddenly.

'Money,' Rian answered quickly. He didn't want any

discussion about it. It was too weird.

Genie was still shaken that some random homeless person had known who she was and even that she had a message for her, from her grandma no less. It was just simply impossible, but it had happened. Rian was her witness.

Marshall drove them to the hotel, entered the underground car park and kept on driving, snaking further and further down, six levels in the end. He parked in a far corner beside a caged-off section where all kinds of equipment and extractor ducts could be seen behind some dusty canvas screens.

'Rian, can you see any cameras?' Marshall asked.

'I'm looking.'

They were all searching. It wasn't well lit at this level and there weren't so many vehicles parked. Some SUVs and three old Chryslers that were so dusty they looked they had been left there for years, their tyres deflated.

'None. None visible.'

'One pointed at the elevator,' Renée declared, spotting it on a far wall.

Marshall nodded. 'Good. Well, we shan't be using that elevator. All out. Don't leave anything personal behind. Genie, grab my driver's licence out of the cubby-hole.

Let's not leave anything that can ID us. Rian, take my tool bag, won't you.'

'What about the licence plates?' Rian pointed out as he picked up the heavy canvas sack.

'You see any?'

Rian went around the back – it had gone. He looked at Marshall and smiled. The old guy was smarter than he thought. He noticed the truck had been cleaned up too and resprayed.

'This the same truck?'

'Ferry got carried away. Gave my son a bill for six hundred and fifty dollars. But she runs a lot sweeter. I reckon I can get at least another fifty thousand miles out of it yet.'

Moucher was out, made sure he cocked his leg on all three Chryslers and they assembled by the truck. Marshall went to investigate the wire cage they had parked by.

'Run the checklist,' Genie told Renée.

'Water. Six litres. Two days' supply of cookies. Dog biscuits. Some beef jerky for Marshall, which looks disgusting, and chocolate.'

Rian looked at her and shook his head. 'If we ever have a threat of nuclear war, I won't be sending you out to get the supplies.'

'I put the chips back,' she protested.

Genie grinned. Renée was impossible.

'Over here – and be quick,' Marshall called.

They hauled their stuff to an opening in the cage. At first Genie thought Marshall had cut his way in, but when he closed the wire fence again after her she saw that it was just a snug fit and made to look permanent.

He pulled a grubby tarp off a large three-metre-high section and revealed a door with an electronic lock. Marshall winked at her.

'Security back then wasn't so sophisticated. I came here in ninety-five. Not much has changed so far.' He keyed in a number written on the back of his hand and somewhere inside they heard a click and something roll back. He looked relieved.

'In and be quick. You too, Mouch.'

They entered. The door automatically closed behind them. Their noses immediately picked up on the cold air as they climbed down ten steps to an underground lobby. Lights flickered on around them and they stood there in a florescent glow, Renée amazed at the weird orange rubber flooring. Genie and Rian were checking out the elevator, mindful they had to go to Level Fourteen.

'Don't even try to use the elevator. It hasn't been serviced in over thirteen, fourteen, years. We walk down. All the way.'

Genie quickly realized what this meant for Marshall. 'Your leg?'

'Going down is the easy part. I'll test the elevator later, but I am not about to risk our lives on it now.'

'What stairs?' Renée asked.

Marshall grinned. 'The great thing about Radspan. They used the same design for every station. Behind you, Renée. Push the big R.'

She spun around and now she could see it. A big orange R on the wall. The letters *a d s p a n* were fading beside it. She moved towards what looked like solid wall and pushed. The wall resisted a moment then slid to one side, as if it had been waiting all this time.

'Are there cameras?' Renée asked.

Marshall shook his head as he followed her in and made sure the door closed behind them. 'No cameras. Privacy was something people still prized back in the nineties and, besides, who'd be watching? Only ghosts in this machine.'

He chuckled as he took up the rear and they climbed down the ever-winding stairs, Moucher's claws echoing back as he went ahead, automatically turning on the lights as he came to each floor.

'I can't believe the power has been left on all this time,' Rian commented as they passed the ninth floor. 'I mean, why didn't they turn it all off?'

'It was never shut down permanently. Radspan was mothballed. Maybe some people thought we might need it again. It's just been forgotten, that's all. People running it were all let go and it just sits here, ticking over,' Marshall said, halting at the tenth, his leg giving him grief.

Rian put the canvas sack down a moment, needing to swap over hands. Marshall noted the deep grooves in his skin.

'Sorry, heavy. I know. Lot of stuff in there.'

Rian just smiled. At least he wasn't carrying the water.

'How many levels?' Renée asked.

The lights suddenly went out. It felt like someone had wrapped a blanket over them it was so dark.

'Wave your hands in the air,' Marshall instructed.

They did and the lights flickered back on.

'God, that was scary,' Genie remarked, moving off down the stairs again.

'Sixteen levels per station. I seem to recall this station tapped into the thermals. There's superheated steam under here and that gives a steady stream of free energy. Of course, when they powered up they sucked all the energy from the grid around here as well. If we get it up and running, they'll notice up top.'

'That mean they'll come looking?'

Marshall grinned. 'Nope. They won't have a clue. But I wouldn't want to be in an elevator up there when it happens.'

They finally reached the fourteenth floor and dropped their loads on to the orange floor. Moucher was sniffing the door and there were signs on the wall about no one could enter unless wearing protective thermal suits.

Genie pointed to the sign. Marshall smiled.

He limped over to a plastic panel on the far wall and with a momentary struggle prised it open. There were two thermal suits hanging there.

'Two of us are going to be cold,' he said, annoyed.

Moucher barked.

'Three of us, sorry, Mouch. Least you got fur. I've got my jacket and a hat. You three work something out, OK?'

'How cold will it be?' Renée asked.

'Very,' Marshall told her. He pulled out several pairs of gloves from the recess. 'Enough for all of us. That's a start, at least. Remember you lose heat from the top of your head, so keeping your head covered is the first priority. Genie should wear one of the suits. I'll need her conscious.'

Renée looked at Rian. She took a deep breath and figured it out.

'Give me your sweater and your jeans. I'm going to double up and I can stick this under my T-shirt.' She found an old yellowing newspaper in the recess at the bottom. *The Vancouver Sun*, third November 1996. Someone had cut out the headline.

'Smart girl. You'll probably be the warmest.'

Marshall buttoned up his jacket, flipped up the collar and went to push buttons on the keypad.

'When the door opens we have to move in quickly. So get suited up and someone grab Mouch. He might get scared.'

Genie was the first to be suited and so she grabbed the dog and held the water in the other hand.

Marshall frowned a moment. 'Leave some of the water out here. I don't want it to freeze.'

'I don't get why it has to be so cold in there?' Renée asked.

'We're almost one hundred metres underground right beside superheated water. Think hot springs, lava, the hot inner core of the planet. That explain it a little? Floor Fifteen is a buffer and below that we have the power generators tapping high-pressure steam. They'll still be working powering the hotel above as well as all this.'

Renée nodded. Joy – she had a choice: freeze to death or boil. Nothing was ever simple. Why couldn't they have built this system on a tropical island, or someplace more civilized?

Genie looked at them all. It was like they were going into space or something. She smiled to herself and then suddenly had a thought.

'What's today?'

'The sixth,' Marshall replied.

Genie looked back at Rian, now suited and looking at stupid as she felt. 'It's my birthday.'

'Really?' Rian asked. 'Oh my God, so it is. Genie!'

Marshall keyed in the numbers.

'You can celebrate later. If we survive this.'

Genie waited with mixed emotions. She'd made it to sixteen. Never thought she would, but she had. Renée mouthed 'Happy Birthday' to her and Rian tapped her gloves. Genie didn't mind. She thought back to her last birthday. She'd just met Rian, she'd been floating on air and even though she never had a chance to celebrate, he'd lit a candle on a muffin in the coffee shop for her and made a fuss. This wasn't going to be a happy muffin day.

A speaker suddenly crackled into life.

'Speak password now.'

Marshall frowned. He hadn't expected that.

He looked back at Genie.

'I'm sorry. I have no idea what that might be,' he told her.

Genie knew though. The word just popped into her head. She'd heard Denis's voice loud and clear.

'Ingrid,' she announced.

The door was released and it sounded like the opening of a tomb as cold gas escaped. All of them shuddered a little. Would they ever get out of here and see daylight again?

'Welcome, Dr Milan.'

Marshall looked impressed. 'You can tell me later how you knew that,' he told her. 'Ingrid was Dr Milan's long-suffering wife.'

They entered the underground chamber, Moucher sticking real close to Marshall's feet. It was freezing cold. Bright overhead lights came on, dazzling them. Genie recognized this as a place she'd been to before, but the others walked in to a huge surprise. This was no simple underground floor. The roof was a huge dome covered in frost, the lighting suspended from the ceiling. On the wall was a huge Radspan map with all the stations actual and under construction illuminated by blue lights. The door began to close and all of them looked back, wondering if they'd be able to open it again.

They could feel the air changing and the atmosphere was constricting; all sensed it was harder to breathe down here.

'God! This is where you were, Genie? No wonder you were so cold.' Renée was already shivering.

A female computer voice declared, 'Air purity at ninety-eight per cent.'

Marshall took his bag from Rian and went over to the control system. He took out a dry rag and began to wipe the screens.

'I might be able to raise the temperature. It shouldn't be this cold,' Marshall mumbled as he booted up and tried to make sense of things.

Renée stood shivering. 'God, look at all this stuff. They must have spent millions on electronics.'

'Looks like *Nostromo*, the spaceship in *Alien*,' Rian whispered.

'Don't even say it,' Renée told him. 'I'm scared enough without any monsters leaping out at me.'

'No monsters here,' Marshall muttered. 'Go find the kitchen. At this temperature the coffee will probably be preserved. Dr Milan used to drink a lot of coffee.'

'Yay, latté,' Renée shouted.

'I think the milk might be off by now,' Genie remarked drily.

'Funny,' Renée said, pulling a face.

Genie went to reassure Moucher that they weren't really going to live in a fridge – when she saw them. Cary, Denis and Julia were sitting on a bench at the far end of the chamber. Cary was wearing a yellow padded lifesaver, but the other two their normal one-piece undergarments.

'Er – Ri?'

Rian looked to where Genie was staring. He saw them too but there was something odd about them, aside from the fact that they weren't moving.

Marshall saw them too, but made no comment and left it to Genie.

'I found coffee and powdered milk,' Renée called out from the kitchen area. 'What do you do with powdered milk, exactly?'

'Read the instructions,' Genie told her.

Genie walked towards Cary and the others.

'Cary? Denis? Jules? Can you talk?'

Cary stood up. Genie realized that he looked painfully thin.

'What—' she began.

'Genie, they just took us off life-support. All of us. Randall is dead. For sure.'

Genie abruptly realized she wasn't going to save them. The whole trip had been for nothing. She felt sick to the heart.

'Does that mean . . . ? Does that mean you're all going to die?'

Cary nodded. Genie noticed that Julia was having trouble holding her image steady and Denis was struggling as well.

'What will they do with the bodies?' Genie asked, and then bit her lip. It was a harsh thing to ask.

Cary didn't want to say. 'Do I have to give details?'

'I'm cold,' Julia complained. 'You took so long to get here.'

Genie almost smiled; it was comforting to hear that Julia still knew how to moan.

'Marshall's got some ideas,' she told them.

'Better than being dead?' Denis whispered.

Marshall walked over for a moment, curious to meet them.

'Not entirely. Which one is Cary?'

'Me,' Cary replied.

Marshall nodded. 'You were here before, with Genie, right?'

'Yes, sir.'

'Show me how you got past Dr Milan's security. I can only get the system up, but I'm access denied.'

Cary moved slowly towards him. 'Sorry, we're being maintained on only half the servers they normally use. There's been a major server crash in Synchro after a storm.'

Marshall understood. 'Take your time. We're here to help you and that's our sole mission.'

Cary looked at him with a puzzled expression. 'We're going to die. I don't think we can be helped.'

Marshall shrugged his shoulders. 'It's not what you expect. You might reject my plan, but it may be worth a try. 'Fraid you'll have to trust me. Radspan is technically redundant, but it follows the same principles. I think we can access it. What I need is a direct line to the Fortress and Sychro servers. I need you to tell me the moment they are back online.'

'Yes, sir.'

Cary reached the control workstation and immediately set about opening it up.

Genie went to check on Renée whilst Rian and Moucher joined Julia and Denis.

'You think he can help?' Denis asked.

Rian could see that he wasn't his normal self. He seemed listless. Rian felt sorry for them all. The chances of saving them were very remote now.

'It's a long shot. Genie nearly got cornered by Reverend Schneider last night. He's here in Whistler, can you believe it?'

Denis could, but barely registered any emotion. 'Got no strength. Sorry.'

Rian put a hand out to him and Denis tried to put his hand up as well, the juice was only slight, but Rian could at least feel something.

Marshall called out from the other end of the chamber.

'We're in. Kids, listen up very carefully. We are talking very primitive capacity here, compared to what you guys are stored on. We've got liquid-cooled T3e machines here, which were fast for their day, but: one, they haven't been upgraded, nor can they be. Two, they haven't been serviced. OK, the good news is they haven't been in use either, but kept on a minimum maintenance cycle for all these years and clearly not blown up, but, just like the elevator, you don't know that a rat hasn't got into the system and eaten all the cables. Also, I think your average Apple iMac has probably got more power and memory than one of these today, so keep that in mind. We are talking ancient history in computer terms.'

'What's the good news?' Rian asked.

Marshall was studying the data. 'Thanks to Cary here, I am hooked through to Synchro. I can confirm that they have thirty-two per cent server capacity, but are aiming to be up and running by two p.m. – the latest. There's a huge storm over my farm at the moment.'

'You ever think that the Fortress attracts them?' Genie asked.

291

Marshall was about to dismiss that, but suddenly it made sense. He'd never really thought about it. 'I'd have to compare the weather charts going back to ten years before they built it to give you an answer. Another day perhaps.'

'Yeah, maybe we can save these guys first?' she replied with an encouraging smile.

Marshall took a deep breath.

'Cary, Denis and Julia are here because they are stored on the servers, we know that. Your souls, for want of a better word, live on because no one has dumped the data yet. I don't want to be pessimistic, but that will happen *real* soon; you're taking up memory real estate and that is expensive over there.'

Genie looked at Cary; he was watching Marshall keenly, trying to keep himself together.

'We are talking thousands of megawatts keeping you visible right now. Someone will notice the spike and try to fix the "problem". But essentially, you are light, that is exactly what you are.'

'Light with memories,' Cary added.

'And that's what I'm worried about,' Marshall told him.

'What?' Cary asked.

'I'll come to that, but I can see from the data here that they really did four thousand five hundred test transmissions from here. That's one hell of a lot of tests.'

Cary hung his head. 'I know. They all failed.'

'You want us to use this system to escape the Fortress?' Denis asked, his voice rasping with the effort.

'Yes and no,' Genie told them.

Julia looked at Denis and they both seemed confused now.

Marshall held up his hand. 'This system doesn't have enough memory to transmit a toenail. But with some modifications, we can use it as a booster to an original transmission from the Fortress.'

Cary wasn't sure now either. 'What are you—'

Genie intervened. 'We want you to resend yourselves. But instead of arriving in the forest like before, you are going to redirect yourselves here.'

Marshall pointed to the transmission platform. 'We're going to put those receptors in a semi-circle right on the platform here and there's a direct link to the Fortress via Radspan. It will be safer.'

He walked over to the wall map and pointed out the Whistler station. 'We're here. There's a huge magnetic leyline running through Whistler and there's a confluence of energy right here. Dr Milan knew what he was doing. Leylines are probably the key to this. Birds and animals use them as direction finders; even whales and honeybees can navigate using the earth's magnetic field. It's linked to magnetite, which enables them to sense magnetic changes. I read up on this after you guys materialized. There had to be a logical explanation. Think of Radspan as a man-made leyline, and I have no idea why I didn't think of this earlier, but the first tunnel runs right under my farm. See here? This dot is my farm. I didn't put this dot here, by the by.'

Cary looked at the map and understood. It made sense. They were just using Radspan as an escape tunnel, but transmitting to a different location. They wouldn't be using the Radspan computers, couldn't even if they wanted to.

'But we're almost gone,' Julia wailed. 'My body is dying. I can't move it. I can't find my way from a locked room to the transmission platform and . . .' She started to cry.

'And this is the hard part,' Marshall explained returning to the control panel.

'You're going to die, Julia. You too, Denis; you also, Cary. I can't lie about this. No one can save you. But you can save yourselves.'

'I don't get it,' Denis said. 'If we resend our DNA here, there would be two of us.'

'Not for long,' Marshall told him. 'Not for long.'

Denis suddenly got it. 'Oh.'

Cary walked over to Julia's side to comfort her.

'We're just going to die?' Julia wailed.

'And yet, not,' Rian told her. 'You'd be a new Julia, right here, with us, made of flesh and blood again.'

'But, my memories? Would I remember you? Anything?'

Cary looked over at Marshall, who frowned.

'You might not remember anything prior to being recaptured. It may not be such a bad thing. I really can't say,' he told them.

'Coffee,' Renée announced, walking out from the small kitchen with a tray of steaming cups in her hand. 'No milk; powder stuff is like totally disgusting.'

Genie took a cup from her. It smelled good, even if it was black.

'Jules, it would be like it just happened,' Genie reassured her.

'And us?' She was thinking of the real Julia, dying back in the Fortress.

'There's no us,' Cary told her.

'And if it doesn't work?' Julia asked her lips trembling.

There was a distinct silence for a moment.

'There's no reason why it wouldn't work. We just have to figure out how to resend the data, that's all, and reroute it here.'

'Can we think about it?' Denis asked.

'You *have* to think about it,' Marshall told him. 'You're in a bad situation. I have to get you out of there before they turn you guys off – and here's the truth of the matter. You can't go home. The Fortress would just seize you again. So think on that too.'

Denis was angry now. 'Don't we have rights? What happened to our rights? Why didn't the police protect us, Marshall? Why didn't the newspapers care about us?'

'Because no one believes it,' Rian told him. 'Because you were all dead the moment you met Reverend Schneider. Because you're all copies already, because of many things. If you do this, Denis, you can't go home as long as the Fortress is in control of Spurlake.'

'I'm a copy too,' Genie pointed out, though she had never accepted it.

'If you want a biology lesson,' Marshall told them, 'the human genome is entirely about making copies. That's what babies are, copies of both adults, complete with their flaws and genetic histories. It's really no different.'

Renée pulled a face. She hadn't realized that things had gotten so tense. She took a coffee to Marshall, who accepted it and drank it quickly to get back to work. Renée wanted to say something herself, after all she too was a copy.

'Well, better a copy than dead. Better to breathe and eat real food. I love being alive. I never knew how much till I met Genie and my brother, Rian. It doesn't matter what we are, as long as we are. Right?'

Cary was looking at the map again. 'And if it really doesn't work?'

Genie put a hand out to him, wishing she could give him a hug.

'You'll go out with a big bang. A very big bang.'

Cary looked at her, then Denis, and then suddenly laughed. It was infectious. It was hysteria, but at least they weren't screaming.

Cary turned to Marshall. 'OK. How do we do this?'

Marshall was busy looking at the screen. 'Some of the servers just came back online. You feel any different?'

Cary was about to say no when Julia let out a shout. 'My hair. It just changed colour.'

They all looked at her bright auburn hair. It practically glowed. It suited her. All the more ironic considering the real Julia was lying on a slab in a Fortress lab completely bald.

Marshall's eyebrows were working full time as he tried not to be caught by surprise.

'Good demonstration and it gives me some hope,' he muttered. He suddenly smiled. 'Julia, come here.'

She came over, moving much more fluidly now.

Marshall pointed at the screen and smiled at her. 'Be

brave. What can you see here?'

Julia looked at the screen and saw only a pile of numbers shimmering on the screen.

'Numbers.'

'That's a tiny infinitesimal piece of you.'

'It is?'

'It is. So let me explain this just once. I am not going to ask you to transmit, not like last time, OK? This isn't about you guys standing on a platform and hoping you're not going to be smeared on a back wall in Synchro. We've moved on from that. You, Cary and Denis there have already been digitized. You're right here, or rather on thousands of Fortress and Synchro servers. What I'm proposing is that we find the on switch and send you guys here. That means we have to find your initiating sequence trigger.'

Julia looked at him and drew a blank. She heard the word 'trigger' but that was it.

Cary turned her around. 'Don't panic. That's what I'm here for.'

'And you, Cary, need to travel back down the line to the Fortress and get the Radspan tracking coordinates from Station One. This is going to be like searching for a needle in a haystack, but at least you know what the haystack looks like and, with luck, the needle.'

Genie frowned. 'Is there anything I can do?'

'I want you to go with him. Watch his back; get him out of trouble if anyone catches him there. It's your job to send Cary here after he's sent the others.'

Genie stared at him like he was a crazy man.

'I don't think they study quantum physics in Grade Ten, Marshall. Please tell me – how do I go back down the line?'

'You know all those little episodes you have when you go missing?'

She nodded.

'It's time to focus. Instead of letting it happen to you at random times, you have to control it, use it. You understand me?'

'Cary, look here. This is the start sequence protocol for teleportation. I knew where to look 'cause I wrote some of this code. You have to memorize it. It has to be done right. Can you do that?'

Cary smiled. 'I can just store it on memory. Sometimes it's a lot easier existing like this than being real.' He looked at the pages on the computer for just a microsecond. 'Done.'

Marshall nodded. 'Yeah, impressive. But check for any last-minute updates. They are refining this process all the time, after each transmission.' He was looking at the computer data. 'Poor Dr Milan, working with thirty-two-bit processors. They're on five hundred and eighty now and we still need double that.'

Marshall watched the screen as Cary manipulated it. He realized that he was doing it with his mind.

'Are you using telekinesis?'

'Yeah. Sorry, you forget I'm a machine. All it needs is the right questions.'

'Rian, help me with the receptors. We have to hook them up around the platform in the right sequence. I'm hoping they will act as a focal point like before, up on the farm. Renée, I want you to search for something to wrap these kids in when they arrive. They will be practically naked and very cold.'

Renée nodded.

Cary turned to Genie a moment. 'They will freak back in the Fortress. If we're sending our guys out, it's going to swamp the servers and drain all the juice. What if it blinks out?'

Marshall was looking at a dusty manual left in a corner.

'Send them at thirty-second intervals and – this is most important, Cary – purge them all from the memory before you yourself leave. Belay that. *Don't* purge yourself before you go. You'll have to time delay that task. Leave a coded message that wipes all the server memories. They won't be able to stop it.'

Denis looked up sharply. 'But that means anyone still stored on there will be killed.'

Marshall looked back at Denis. 'Kid, you've seen what happened to the ones who didn't get stored right. It ain't pretty. You guys got lucky. They had it right, but didn't know it. You save who you can – it's harsh, but you can't save someone who isn't really one hundred per cent there. You understand?'

Denis thought about it. It was true. He didn't like it, but it was true. 'When are we going to do this?'

'Shift change. Five o'clock tonight,' Marshall said. 'Something always going wrong at the changeover, so they won't think anything of it and they'll be so busy trying to trace the power surge, they won't realize they are transmitting until it's over.'

'How long is each transmission?' Genie asked.

'Thirty-seven point five seconds,' Cary answered, looking at the data on-screen. 'Any longer and it gets unstable.'

'Who do we save?' Renée asked.

'Whoever you can,' Marshall answered.

'What if they're already dead?'

'Denis already came back once. Right? Let them explain that. Our job is to get them out and get them away. Your job is to find a way to survive after. That will be the really hard part.'

Marshall was looking at the Radspan manual again.

'Cary, Dr Milan made some interesting notes here. When you're inside, the brain activity is coded pale blue; each different element is colour coded now. I heard they'd adopted that. You have to check each person you want to transmit and make sure all the datastream is routed back to that person. There will be a code number for each of them and all their bits. We are talking trillions of bits. It should work, but even if there is one server down at the moment of transmission, you could wind up missing an ear or your hair changes colour or whatever, you follow me?'

Cary nodded. Almost anything could go wrong and probably would. He got it.

'You will be reborn in the reverse sequence that you were deconstructed.'

'I know this isn't the time and place to mention this,' Denis said, 'but did anyone ever see *The Fly*?'

Julia screeched, 'I did not want to hear that, Denis Malone.'

Marshall chuckled. 'Fly DNA is small; your DNA is strong and much bigger. You could chuck in a swan, doesn't necessarily mean you'd grow wings. You'd be a freak, but they maintain a very clean lab, Julia. There won't be any flies there.'

'It's arriving here, with a dog and coffee and—'

'You'll be fine. Hell, you turned up in the forest last time and you didn't get any bugs growing out of your head,' Genie told her.

Cary suddenly blinked out.

'Hey.' Genie spun around looking for him. Denis disappeared before her eyes and then Julia.

Marshall looked at the data on-screen. 'Power's down again. They might be doing repairs after the storm. No need to get scared.'

'I have to go help him?' Genie asked.

'You have to find a quiet corner and do whatever you have to do to go there, Genie. I want you helping Cary. No one can touch you and you'll be safe here.'

'But where will I find him?'

'He'll find you. He always does. I think you have some kind of natural signal. Couldn't explain it, but nevertheless . . .'

He was taking the receptors out of the bag and handing them to Rian. 'We have to wire these into this system. It will alter and boost the magnetic pull. I hope.'

Renée felt kind of spare. 'What do I do?'

Genie took her gloved hand. 'Keep everyone happy

and don't forget to hug Mouch. He's shivering.'

Moucher did look miserable curled up on some magazines in the corner. He looked up at them, then went back to sleep.

'This is all I have to do?' Genie asked, unsure of how to help.

Renée nodded, shivering. 'Don't be scared, OK, and bring Cary back. I'm kinda getting used to him again.'

27

Denis Sets a Trap

Genie was squatting in a corner, desperately trying to concentrate. She had no idea how one deliberately travelled. She wasn't sure what the real word was for what she did. Was it magic? Or what? It had always just happened before; now she was supposed to look for something to trigger it. She fiddled with a metal washer she'd found and discovered that it calmed her. She was staring at Marshall and Rian working on the wiring when suddenly the room shifted. Nothing else, it was more like an electrical fault, that was all. She looked back at Moucher and he was staring at her now, his little quizzical face studying her.

'Anything?' Marshall asked her.

Genie frowned. 'I only just got here.'

Marshall shook his head and smiled. 'Been over ninety minutes already.'

'No way.' Genie was stunned. 'Impossible. I just sat down this second.'

Renée emerged from the kitchen. 'Oh, you're awake.

Tea and cookies? Mouch has already had his.'

Genie was astonished. How the hell? Ninety minutes? Worse, she could no longer remember what it was she was supposed to be doing.

'Is there a washroom?'

'It's tiny and stinks of sulphur, but it works,' Renée told her. 'Come on. You need those cookies, girl, I can tell.'

Genie sat in the tiny toilet carved out of the rock and tried to think. What just happened? She seemed to have blinked and almost two whole hours disappeared. Just like on the ferry. Perhaps she was losing it.

Renée was talking to her through the door. 'I don't think this is going to work, y'know. I mean, they're practically dead. It's probably wrong to bring back people from the dead. Don't you think, Genie?'

Genie was washing her hands. The water was brackish and warm. The walls were warm too. Somewhere deep below this rock was molten lava, if she had that right. Too weird.

She opened the door. Renée smiled at her.

'You look like a ghost. You're really pale.'

'Don't feel so good, that's all.'

'It's not so cold now. Marshall fixed the temperature; it was stuck. Come and look at this.'

Renée seemed really enthusiastic all of a sudden.

'What?'

'Come see.'

Genie followed her to the small room at the side of the chamber. Marshall and Rian were in there watching a TV screen.

'It's Dr Milan,' Rian told her as she curled up beside him.

They were watching videos of Dr Milan preparing his experiments. Each one meticulously recorded and each one a failure.

'You're watching all four thousand five hundred!' Genie asked, appalled.

Marshall glanced back at her as Renée gave her some hot black tea and two cookies.

'Just the last ten. He'd made a lot of progress. I had no idea.'

'But you said he couldn't succeed,' Genie reminded him.

'True, but he was a determined kind of guy and very resourceful.'

'Isn't that a . . .'

They watched as he placed an emaciated Alsatian on the platform and injected it with something; the dog quickly slumped. He placed a tag around its head too and turned to the camera.

'Test four thousand four hundred and ninety-seven. Rufus. Stray dog number fifteen. Transmitting to Station Five.'

Dr Milan walked away to behind the camera. His hair was wild and he looked exhausted.

The light suddenly grew intense and the screen whited out, but the dog completely disappeared. Station Five came on the line over a speaker moment later. The voice sounded excited.

'Dr Milan. We have legs. Repeat. We have four dog legs. *They twitched!*'

Marshall shook his head.

'This was never mentioned. We had no idea he'd got so far.'

'What about the rest of the dog?' Genie asked, unable to look at the screen, the words 'they twitched' reverberating around her brain.

'Didn't make it. But it's impressive the legs got there at all given how little memory he had. I can't believe Strindberg shut him down.'

Genie didn't like to watch this. OK, it was *history*, so it was important, but it was also cruel and disgusting.

She didn't look at the next. She knew how this movie ended.

Marshall advanced the tape to the last test.

'Test four thousand five hundred and one.'

Rian looked at the box to check. 'It says one hundred to four thousand five hundred. Doesn't mention four thousand five hundred and one.'

'Then it's going to be interesting. It'll be the last one they ever did.'

Dr Milan walked on to the platform. He looked absolutely haunted, his hair a total mess. He was barefooted and looked unshaven. A man completely on edge. All of them wondered what he was going to do. There didn't seem to be a dog or cat with him.

'This is for Carson Strindberg. You say I wasted your money? That this will never work? Well, let me show you *this*, Strindberg. *This* is where your money went. Goodbye, Ingrid. This test is for you.'

Dr Milan pressed a button on a remote and let it drop just outside the platform area. He stood and braced himself.

'Oh my God . . . he's going to send *himself*!' Genie exclaimed in horror. This was a suicide.

The light intensified. You could see the beginnings of the transformation, his eyes registering with fascination as he began to disintegrate, something Genie understood well and then – *boom*.

He exploded.

A blackened human shadow formed on the wall and unprocessed flesh slid to the floor in a bloody mush.

Renée screamed. Genie just stared as Rian gripped her hand.

Marshall stood and quietly turned off the video.

'I'm sorry. I should have stopped it the moment he walked out there.'

Genie shook her head. 'He must have known that would happen.'

Marshall nodded. 'Sometimes you hope too much for a change of luck.'

He walked out of the room, ashen. Moucher got up and followed.

They'd been there seven hours. Waiting. Marshall still tinkering with the platform and all the receptors, trying to make sure it was ready – not quite sure if it was going to be of any use or not.

Rian was reading up on the experiments to ward off boredom and Renée watched *The Breakfast Club* on the TV. She'd found a stack of old videos and was fixated now on teen angst.

Genie was feeling guilty. She wasn't sure of her role and she was sure that for some reason she seemed to have lost all her ability to 'travel'. That was the problem with a gift you didn't know how to control. It was either on or off, it seemed.

Moucher came over and sat beside her and she cuddled him.

'I'm sorry, Marshall. I can't seem to do anything. I feel bad.'

Marshall looked up at her from the floor and shook his head.

'It was always going to be a long shot. I only needed you there to help Cary transmit himself. I am sure he's bright enough to get the others here, but sending his own data, that might be tricky. If you can't go, you can't go. No one will blame you, I promise you that.'

She appreciated him saying that, but she knew it wasn't true. If the others came through and Cary didn't, she didn't know how she'd live with herself.

'I worry about their memories,' Genie added. 'They've been through so much, and they won't remember anything, not even us.'

Rian glanced at her. 'Maybe they will. Maybe memory is not just information. It's not genetic, so it isn't being transmitted, and so it must be coming from someplace else.

Marshall stood up, groaning as he tried to straighten his good leg.

'The great mystery of the hippocampus. The brain has a hundred trillion synapses connecting nerve cells to other cells. One of my colleagues was working on the electro-chemical process of perception. You guys have both been teleported and you remember a previous existence. You're living proof it works, but there's no exact code for your memory. Nothing we've written, anyway. I mean, they've mapped your brains, so anything you've ever done is retained, but quite how it comes along with the whole package . . . ?' He grimaced. 'Beats me.'

'Well, that's reassuring,' Genie replied and she pulled Moucher's ears gently and bent down to kiss his head.

She opened her eyes and she was standing in the parking garage above them. She looked down. She was wearing her thermal suit and it would be very visible under the lights. She shrank to the shadows behind an old dusty van.

Two security guys were investigating Marshall's truck, getting excited that it didn't have any licence plates.

Genie was annoyed. She wasn't supposed to be here, she was supposed to be with Cary. How on earth had this happened?

The security guys took a photo of the truck with one of their phones and then headed back up the ramp to the next level.

Genie was about to relax when the elevator door opened and Reverend Schneider came out of it. Genie almost wet herself. There was nowhere to hide and she knew he would be able to see her if he looked in her direction.

He walked over to the truck and inspected it. He was on a phone to someone.

'Looks a lot like one from Spurlake. Only this is smarter. No plates. The one I know has scorch marks and this is too well cared for. I don't think it's the same.' He disconnected and pocketed his phone.

Reverend Schneider was looking at the other cars covered in dust, and was puzzled. He was paying particular attention to the puddles by the three cars, sniffing them. Genie realized this was where Moucher had peed. He looked up, couldn't see any leaks in the roof. He turned to go back to the elevator when he spun around and started to walk towards the van that Genie was hiding behind.

Genie started to panic, praying he wouldn't discover her.

Reverend Schneider stopped and paused a moment. His phone was ringing again.

'Schneider.'

'Where? Does she have a shaved head? Check for a

Fortransco symbol on the back of her neck. We branded her. Only way to know.'

He was turning again. 'I'm coming back up. Be there in five minutes. Do not let her get away. You hear me?'

He swiftly moved towards the elevator.

Genie watched him go and suddenly exhaled, unaware till now that she'd been holding her breath. Branded? She'd been branded? She stood up, wondering what to do next when someone touched her on the shoulder and she screamed.

The old woman was there, the one who'd been in the doorway next to McDonald's.

'You can't escape. You can't win. They're looking for you.'

Genie stared at her with growing horror. Why did this woman haunt her? How did she know where to find her?

The woman smiled, revealing stained yellow teeth.

'There's a hole growing where no hole ought to be. When it comes, it's the end.'

Genie didn't understand. Couldn't understand. She backed up further towards the wall and suddenly felt quite warm. She leaned her face against the rock and it was very warm on her skin.

'My space,' the old woman informed her, settling back with a rug into a crevice in the wall.

Genie suddenly understood how she survived. This was a cosy recess, well hidden, warmed by the natural thermals in the rock. The old woman might be crazy but she knew how to keep warm.

'Shadow-stealers are back. Stay well hidden,' she told Genie.

Car tyres squealed on an upper floor and Genie looked away, wondering what and where she should go. She was confused now. Was she 'travelling' or was this real?

There was a strange noise coming from behind her and she turned to discover the old woman was gone. No rug, no nothing. She'd completely disappeared.

'What's going on?' Genie wailed. 'What's happening to me?'

'Hey, keep it quiet, don't let them know we're here.'

She was suddenly staring at Cary. She was in the Fortress. They were in a control booth beside the platform. Cary looked pleased to see her.

'I was kinda hoping you'd turn up. I've figured it out.'

Genie was dizzy, hardly able to keep up with this moving around. She needed to sit and found a stool to grip on to.

'Do I have a tattoo on my neck?' she asked.

'You mean, like this?' Cary turned and showed her his neck.

The Fortress logo was right there at the base of the neck.

'Yours is tiny. I saw it before. Denis thinks they are using them to track us, but if so, they aren't doing such a good job.'

Genie wasn't so sure.

'Marshall's ready,' she told him, trying to recover her wits.

Cary sighed. 'Julia passed away at noon. There was a power failure. Denis is hanging on.'

Genie looked away fighting tears. Poor Julia – why couldn't she have hung on.

'And you?' Genie asked quietly.

Cary shrugged. 'I don't want to think about it. This idea is crazy enough. Come on, I have to show you what to do.'

'Can I touch stuff? I mean, am I here, for real?'

He thumped her arm. Genie mouthed, 'Ouch!' But he'd made his point.

'Just don't ask me to explain it. That's all.'

Genie took a deep breath. This was exactly where she was supposed to be. She needed to pull herself back together.

'Schneider's in the hotel above Radspan. He ran off to see a girl someone thinks is me. We need to know where he is. If we ever get out of this, I don't want him on our backs any more.'

Cary nodded. 'I'll tell Denis. He doesn't have much strength but he hates Schneider enough to keep tabs on him.'

'That's the other thing. I'm worried about Denis. He's so small. How's he going to survive on his own? He can't go home. He can't go to the farm. We haven't discussed any of this . . . stuff.'

'I'll be back. Stay put and quiet.'

Genie blinked and Cary was gone. She did as she was bid and sat there, silent, scared, confused and going slightly mad.

Cary was back as suddenly as he had left.

'Denis has gone to track Schneider.'

'Thanks.'

'About what happens next – can I ask you something?'

'Sure.' Genie had no idea what he'd say.

Cary looked unsure of himself momentarily. If it wasn't about computers, he tended to get confused.

'It's about Renée.'

Genie looked at him, then slowly smiled.

'I told you, she likes you. She *still* likes you.'

Cary looked very relieved. 'Enough to go with me?'

'We all have to disappear. She'll go with you, Cary. I know it. We need to get this show on the road.'

Cary put his finger to his lips. A technician was walking into the transmission chamber. He did a spot check, ticked a chart on the wall and killed the lights, the whoosh of the electric doors closing behind him as he departed.

Genie and Cary were sitting in the control room, lit only by the glow of instruments on the panel.

'I collected all of us who teleported to the farm. I've got bad news about Miho though. I really do think she committed suicide.'

'No, it was a Mosquito attack,' Genie insisted.

'Her mother died before she got to the hospital and her father was flying to get her to take her to Japan and—'

'Oh my God.' Genie felt terrible. 'She hated her father.'

'I know. But she took her own life before he got there. I know it's true because the technicians were talking about it. Everyone is scared they're going to lose their jobs if they don't figure out how to make the Fortress work. They keep going over the video and transmission data, want to know what was so different about it.'

Genie shrugged. 'I hope they don't find out.'

'So,' Cary asked, 'I need to know. Do we bring Miho back? I'm not good at playing God.'

Genie looked at him and, for the first time she could remember in a very long time, she felt completely overwhelmed, and sobbed. Poor Miho. She'd been so desperate to talk to her mother. She must have felt so alone. To kill herself, after all she had been through. It wasn't right, wasn't right at all.

Cary watched, alarmed. Genie was the strong one. He realized he shouldn't have told her. He was being insensitive and stupid.

Genie looked up suddenly. 'Is she still on the database? Is she still here? Can we save her?'

Cary nodded. 'The moment all the servers are in synch, I'm pushing the button.'

'Talk to her. Tell her Genie needs to know if she wants another chance.'

Cary realized she was right. Only her body was dead, right? She still existed, just like the rest of them, as long as they were on the servers.

'This is what Reverend Schneider was going on about, isn't it? Eternal Life. No one dies. I hadn't really thought about it. No one ever dies, they just renew themselves as things wear out. Jesus, no one will ever need kids again. That is so radical.'

Genie felt dizzy again with the enormity of it.

'Talk to Miho, Cary. I know you can. Maybe she won't have a memory of dying. Just ask her if she wants another chance to live. Tell her that her mother is gone, but she's with us now. She's not alone. That's important. She's not alone.'

Cary vanished. Genie felt sick, but it was just nerves. That, and being back in the Fortress again. She stared at all the computer hardware around her and so wished she could blow it all up. The worst of it all was Cary was right. This was the future. Everyone who could afford it would want a back-up of themselves on the servers. No one would ever need to die again. Or get old.

She wiped the tears from her eyes and waited. If she were Miho, what would she choose? Life? She took a deep breath. Some birthday this was turning out to be.

28

Hitch

Reverend Schneider was annoyed. The girl wasn't even close. She was about thirty, for starters. Didn't these people read the memos? They were looking for a fifteen-year-old kid with a shaved head, with a dog. The other question, why? Why was she here? Where was she going and with whom?

He drove back towards the hotel. His phone beeped. He answered it using his hands-free.

'Schneider.'

'Strindberg. Meet me in the penthouse suite. I'm flying in.'

That was it. The phone disconnected. He'd been summoned.

He overtook a tourist bus and took a right towards the hotel. He didn't like being summoned to see Strindberg. He was close to finding Genie. He knew it. They'd blown it last night. God knows who shot at the chopper, but they weren't going to find out and now the cops were curious as to what Fortransco was doing there without authorization.

All he knew was that God had to be really interested in Genie Magee because she lived a charmed life. He certainly didn't want to make it easy.

Schneider drove down the ramp to the hotel. He slowed at the first sharp bend. Didn't see the pale, barely visible image of Denis Malone jump into the back seat. Didn't notice anything.

Denis smiled. He was there and he wasn't going to let this monster out of his sight now – even if this was the last thing he ever did.

He rode up in the elevator with Reverend Schneider. This was a good game. He felt stronger, realized that some more of the servers had come back online. He'd learned so much since going back into the Fortress machines. He'd been learning to blend, for example. He didn't need to stand next to Reverend Schneider and risk being noticed. He could blend with the elevator. It was a lot like smearing himself over the surface like butter. He liked this idea. He could be anything, anywhere. He didn't have to be Denis, the small kid. He could be the TV you watch, part of the building you live in. This was a good game.

Schneider went all the way up to the thirty-first floor. He was met by a gruff pony-tailed security man called Henry, who closely inspected his pass before letting him off the elevator.

Denis was already inside, staring with wonder at all the TV screens in Strindberg's penthouse suite. He was watching everything: the Fortress, Synchro, Spurlake main street and, Denis quickly realized, he had software hunting for Genie. It was scanning the streets of Whistler, every face, in every shop, or car, or elevator, or washroom, every place that had a CCTV camera – the system was searching for her.

Strindberg came out of another room with a coffee in his hands.

'Where is she, Schneider? This has gone on long enough.'

'She's still here. Somewhere. I got a good description of her at McDonald's this morning. She was there with a dog, talking to some homeless woman.'

Strindberg nodded. 'We have new investors coming onboard. I want her out of the picture before that happens. You have no idea how big this deal is now. She *has* to be found.'

Schneider looked pensive. 'I know this is crazy, but I swear she's been to this building.'

Strindberg immediately frowned.

'I'll put more security on.'

'I'm not sure that will help. Is there any reason she'd come here? I mean, I don't get it. Why Whistler? What's here for her? Why isn't she running away?'

Strindberg looked out across the resort and contemplated that thought.

'She wants me. The moment she arrived at my house it became clear to me that she wants to kill me. If she's been here, it's to scope it out.'

'She's just a girl.'

'She's just a girl who has evaded us on a continuous basis. She's like a loaded gun, Reverend. I want her gone. By any means necessary.'

'The chopper . . .'

'Someone shot at our chopper last night. Did you know that? They discovered the fuel lines had been shot away. You still think she's an innocent little girl?'

'She didn't shoot it down.'

'Someone did. Someone's helping her.'

'Someone?'

'I've made enemies. No one rich can evade that. She's found someone who wants me dead and the Fortress discredited. That's all I can think of.' He had an idea and took out his cell, speed-dialling his PA.

'Jenny, go through all our ex-employees and find a connection to Whistler. Doesn't matter what. Someone is helping Genie Magee and they are sheltering her here.'

He disconnected and looked at Reverend Schneider.

'And you are waiting for what?'

Reverend Schneider wasn't listening. He was watching the TV. It was flashing *Suspect Identified*.

Strindberg noticed it too. 'Horstman Trading Company, Blackcomb Way. She's shopping? Get on it.'

Schneider turned around and headed for the elevator.

'Take Henry with you and be discreet,' Strindberg added.

Reverend Schneider got into the elevator with the security guard, who made ready his weapons. He didn't say a word, didn't even look at him. He had a job to do.

The elevator door closed and Strindberg went back into the other room.

Immediately another screen flashed *Suspect Identified* and another, and another. Genie's face peered out of all the screens. She was everywhere.

Denis smiled and walked towards the elevator. It had been simple to trick the software. It would see only Genie now. Every young girl it ever looked at would seem to be her. She'd be everywhere and nowhere, and they'd never figure out how to fix it.

Denis was beginning to realize that he quite enjoyed technology. The elevator doors opened and he stepped in.

This was going to be fun.

29

Dr Milan's Final Word

Genie was sitting on the floor of the control room, staring at the banks of servers and operating systems. She was wondering how her real body was doing back in Radspan. So weird to be in two places at once again. She wondered if Grandma Munby had always lived with that as well, if it hadn't made her a little bit crazy.

Cary was back. He looked flustered and he looked for her.

'What did Miho say?'

'She's conflicted, but I'm going to try anyway. We have to do it now.'

'Now?'

'I just got word on internal emails that they're going to do another test. They'll be here soon.'

Genie stood up. 'What do I do?'

Cary looked at her and realized that what he had set up was actually quite difficult to manage.

'Your job is to transmit me. But you have to press the buttons in the right sequence. It's complicated.'

'And if I screw up?'

'I explode.'

'No pressure then.'

Cary looked at her and smiled. 'No pressure.'

Denis appeared in the control room suddenly. He looked curiously happy.

'I've changed the code on the entry door. It'll keep them out for about ten minutes.'

Cary nodded.

'All the servers are up. You're ready to go, Cary?' Denis asked him.

'God,' Genie whispered. 'I'm scared.'

Denis was suddenly quite close to her.

'I fixed the security cameras. They won't be able to see you when you leave Radspan.'

'You did?'

Denis smiled. 'I did.' Then he turned to Cary. 'I'm not coming.'

Cary looked at him with astonishment.

'This is our only chance, Denis. You have to come. It'll work. You won't explode. It'll work. It'll be just like before, in the woods.'

'I don't want to be that small kid any more. I don't want to be Denis any more.'

Genie looked at him, confused. 'But you won't be

anything if you don't go. They'll delete all the stuff on the servers and you won't exist at all.'

Denis just smiled. 'I made up my mind. And I'll still be around. I don't have to be stored here. I can be everywhere. Cary understands.'

Cary did understand, but didn't necessarily comprehend.

'You'll never be flesh and blood, Denis. You'll never be real.'

Denis walked back to the end of the control room. Genie noticed he'd changed his hair and was wearing a leather bomber jacket. Denis was changing.

'I'll be there, when you need me. I made up my mind. I don't want to be "real" or shorter than my stupid sister. I'm going to live for ever. You'll see. I'll be turning up in places you never thought of. Being flesh and blood isn't everything, y'know. There's all kinds of possibilities.'

'Denis—' Genie began.

He pointed to the control panel. 'Countdown started. Pay attention. I'm not saying goodbye. But good luck – and thanks for being my friends.'

He disappeared.

Genie felt a lump in her throat. He'd chosen to stay with the machines. That was so . . .

'He started the sequences. I haven't shown you what you have to do yet.'

Genie heard the panic in his voice. 'Show me. Show me now.'

She looked up suddenly. She could see technicians trying to get into the teleport chamber, puzzled their swipe cards weren't working.

'Show me now, Cary.'

Renée was cradling Genie in her arms. She'd begun to moan some time earlier and had seemed to be choking. She held her and stroked her head to calm her.

'What's happening, Marshall?'

Marshall hadn't got a clue, but Rian had. He returned from the kitchen with a warm wet towel and sponged Genie's face and neck.

He looked at Renée. 'It soothes her. She's been gone for ages now. These trips are getting longer.'

'You worried?'

'I worry about what will happen in the future. It's dangerous. Just losing control like this. I know she's trying to help, but I'm scared for her.'

'I wonder where she is?'

'I don't know, but she's tense. Look at her clenched hands. She's really tense right now.'

The speakers by the computer suddenly crackled. All of them looked across the room.

'Dr Milan would like to speak to Marshall Miller,' the computer voice said.

Marshall's hair practically stood on end. Renée and Rian felt goosepimples rise on their arms. It was just a computer voice but it spooked them all.

'Dr Milan would like to speak to Marshall Miller,' it repeated. 'On-screen.'

Marshall and Rian wandered over to the computer control screen. They looked at each other.

'Type in "Hello",' Rian told Marshall.

Marshall did just that.

'Hello, Marshall Miller here.'

Rian looked back at Renée to make sure she was OK.

All of them had seen the video of Dr Milan exploding. This wasn't a guy stored on any servers. This was a dead guy communicating. Altogether different to anything else that had happened.

'Dr Milan on-screen in five, four, three, two seconds . . .' the computer voice told them.

Marshall stood back a little, nervous. He looked at Rian.

Rian shrugged. They watched as one quarter of the screen came to life. This was 'live' streaming from beyond the grave. Totally weird.

'Good afternoon, Marshall. Have I been gone so long? You look so old.'

Marshall was surprised, then noticed the camera at the top of the screen.

'Had an accident, Dr Milan. Prematurely went white.'

Marshall was trying to remember when they had last met. Must have been at least fifteen years. A long time.

'I might say that you don't seem to have changed a bit.'

Dr Milan smiled. 'An illusion, I assure you.'

'Are you a ghost?' Rian asked.

'Who is speaking?'

'Rian Tulane. I am assisting Marshall.'

'Ah yes. I see you now.'

'I need to know that too,' Marshall told him. 'We saw Test four thousand five hundred and one.'

There was a momentary silence.

'It was a last throw of the dice.'

'That I understand, Dr Milan. But it doesn't explain your presence here now.'

'A young man found me – Denis. Test four thousand five hundred and one was a partial success, despite all appearances. He explained to me about the servers in Synchro. I am speaking to you from there.'

'Denis?' Rian asked. 'Our Denis transferred you?'

'Showed me a way out beyond the firewall, I'd prefer to

call it. Your stability programme worked well, Marshall. I was impressed when I saw your design. I am overawed to meet the first successful teleporters. To think they arrived at your farm unaided.'

'They had a little help from an electrical storm,' Marshall informed him. 'All you lacked was power and speed, Dr Milan.'

'Power and speed. It was ever thus.'

'Why are you here now?' Marshall asked, amazed that Dr Milan and Denis seem to have connected.

'To warn you. Shut down the E3. You will have incoming transmissions in . . . eighty-five seconds. The amount of power coming through will melt the cable cores. You must shut down now and prepare for incoming.'

Marshall began the shut-down process.

'It will be hot, the coolant—' Marshall began.

'The fans will operate normally to keep it cool,' Dr Milan cut in. 'Shut down now. Wait! You need to switch to manual operation for the doors.'

Marshall could see the auto-manual light flashing and made the switch. A light came on over the exit door.

'Manual override on,' the computer announced. 'Doors unlocked.'

Marshall paused on the shut-down.

'Goodbye, Dr Milan.'

'I shall cease to exist in ten seconds. Please convey my regrets to my wife, Ingrid,' Dr Milan told them. 'She still lives nearby.'

Marshall shut down. It was a slow set of sequences and as things began to quieten they could hear the automatic rush of the fans keeping the overheated computer cool.

'That was so weird,' Rian declared. 'He's been living in limbo all this time and Denis set him free?'

'Denis is getting about. I'll have to ask him about that when he comes through.'

Moucher began to bark. He'd sensed a change in the atmosphere.

'Grab him,' Marshall told Rian. 'Keep him still.'

With the computer down, the temperature began to rise. All eyes were on the transmission platform.

'I don't understand. If the power is down, how does this work?'

'It's taking power from the grid. Dr Milan is probably right. The sudden surge of grid power on those old cables would most likely overload everything. Renée, cover yourself, and leave Genie. Get the clothes and fresh water ready. They are going to need help the moment they arrive. All of you, shield your eyes. It's going to get immensely bright in here.'

Renée lay Genie's body flat, spread her denim jacket

over her face, making sure she could breathe OK and left a thick book under her head to lift it off the floor. She ran to the transmission area and stood ready beside Rian.

'I'm scared. What if they explode?'

Rian took her arm. He was worried about the same thing.

'Turn away,' Marshall instructed them. 'Close your eyes, cover them and go back ten paces. Do it now.' They both began moving.

Instantly there was a bright, intense burst of light that swamped them, shone right through their hands so they could see the bones. Renée screamed with fright. The heat on their backs was intense and she smelled burning.

Moucher was yelping, trying to hide behind Rian's legs.

And then it went incredibly dark. Worse, the extractor fans had ceased to work.

Strindberg saw all the computer screens blink out. He stood up and looked out across Whistler. The power flickered and blinked out for just a second right across the city and beyond. He was annoyed. He had a meeting in an hour and he didn't want anything to go wrong. He wondered what was going on and only briefly thought of the Fortress and an impending transmission. He checked his watch. 16.44. This had nothing to do with Fortransco then; the next test wasn't due till twenty-one hundred hours. Nevertheless, he was intensely annoyed.

'Can you see anything?' Renée asked. She was almost blind, despite having her eyes closed during the transmission.

'Here, now, quick,' Rian was calling. He couldn't see so well either. He was over by the transmission platform and there was definitely a body lying there. He knew he had to get them off the platform before the next one arrived.

'Who is it?' Renée asked. It was too dark to make anything out and the only light came from the emergency blue light over the door.

'Off the platform now. Just haul him or her off,' Marshall instructed them.

Rian did just that, establishing where their shoulders were and lifting whomever it was off and on to the floor at the far end.

'Get ready for another. Move to the rear of the room. We were way too close before,' Marshall added. He groped his way to the kitchen area and took Moucher in there. He couldn't see anything at all. 'Renée? Rian? Kitchen area. Safest place.'

The light started again.

Rian and Renée jumped into the kitchen and shut the

door. Even so the brightness of the light that shone from the base and sides seemed brighter than the sun and they all had to look away.

Mouch was whining, paws trying to cover his eyes.

As soon as the light began to fade Rian and Renée were out the door to haul the kid off the platform. Their eyes were better adjusted now. They could see it was Miho.

Miho's eyes opened. She looked startled and afraid.

'You'll be fine. You'll be fine,' Rian told her. 'You're safe now. Cover your eyes, Miho.' Reluctantly Miho put her hands over her eyes.

He carried her over and put her beside Julia, the first one to come through. She was still unconscious.

'Kitchen,' Renée shouted. 'Next one incoming.'

The light was just as intense – the smell of burning stronger this time. Marshall sensed something was wrong.

'Stay back,' he told them. 'I'll get this one.'

Rian stayed in the kitchen with Renée and Moucher. He splashed water on his face to try and cool his eyes.

'Who?' Renée was asking.

'Julia and Miho so far,' he told her.

'Rian!' Marshall shouted.

Rian dashed out of the kitchen, the smell of burning intense now.

Marshall had Cary halfway off the platform.

'Cables are burning. The fumes from the plastic will asphyxiate us if we don't get air extracted. When we shut down the computer it turned off the extractors.'

Cary had scorch marks on his back. They put him with the others and quickly covered them as they dashed back to the kitchen.

They remained there for five whole minutes before they realized no one else was coming.

'That's it?' Renée asked. 'That's all we saved?'

'Saving one is good,' Marshall remarked. He was puzzled Denis hadn't come through. Just three.

Renée suddenly remembered Genie.

'Go to them. I need to make sure Genie's OK.'

She burst out of the kitchen only to find Mouch was already with Genie. He was standing right beside her, looking at her very oddly.

'What?' Renée asked him. 'Is she back?'

Moucher rested his head on Genie's shoulder and whined. Renée felt suddenly scared. It wasn't a good sign. Not a good sign at all.

Strindberg stared out across Whistler. The power was out now completely. The whole resort was in darkness. His phones were down. All the power had gone. There was a sub-station fire in the distance. The emergency lighting kicked in, which was a comfort, then spluttered out. Right now he realized, a lot of people would be trapped in elevators across town, including his own building.

He wondered what had caused it. It wasn't cold, it was early evening and there was no excessive power use. It certainly wasn't the weather, it was very mild for the time of year.

Another sub-station fire broke out across town. He began to get worried. Was Whistler under attack from terrorists? If so, who on earth would attack a ski resort? Made no sense at all.

Marshall led them out of the chamber. The air was already unbreatheable. They'd had to carry everyone out to the corridor and shut the door. And now they all faced those steep stairs.

'Do we wait for them to recover?' Rian asked.

'How long did it take before?' Marshall asked Renée.

Renée shrugged. 'I don't know. I was like in suspended animation and then suddenly lying on the forest floor. Once I woke up I was OK pretty quickly. Their legs will be weak though. No way they can climb stairs.'

'Then we'll have to carry them.'

Renée looked at the three girls and Cary. She

understood why Julia and Miho were out of it, but why hadn't Genie recovered?

'I'll carry Miho. But how are you going to carry three of them?'

'In stages,' Marshall told them, thinking of his own bad leg. 'Genie may come back to us soon, with luck.'

'What about the power? We could use the elevator?'

'Believe me, you're going to find Whistler in total darkness. We probably sucked power from the whole of B.C. I can't believe how bright it was.'

'Genie, press now, press now!' Cary shouted as he began to stir.

30

Brownout

It was bad enough that all the power was out right across the city, but the first indication was that the source of the failure pointed directly to the All Seasons Hotel itself.

Strindberg was on his way down by the stairs – and there would be hell to pay.

A Fortransco employee met him coming up the other way on the twentieth floor. He was out of breath and frankly scared of his boss. His hands shakily clutched the flashlight, which illuminated the space around them.

'Where are the emergency lights?' Strindberg demanded to know. 'There's a lot of panicky people in this hotel who are not happy with you guys.'

'We've identified the source of the brownout, sir.'

'Good. What was it? Generators? I can't believe our generators could take out the whole city. Besides, what happened to the thermal generators? They never fail.'

'The spike has blown everything out. It's not just here in Whistler. It's right down to North Vancouver as well.'

Strindberg frowned. 'You're telling me that our

generators failed and it knocked out most of B.C.? That makes no sense.'

'The energy spike was right off-scale; only the Fortress uses that kind of power, sir.'

Strindberg shook his head. 'There is no connector. They were scheduled for a test at twenty-one hundred hours tonight. They shouldn't have been draining power and, besides, you know it's not connected to the grid. This is bull.'

'Fortress experienced a full-strength transmission at sixteen thirty-seven hours, sir. I got them on the satellite phone. The system suddenly booted up and there was a huge burst of energy for nearly seven minutes. There's been an incident. I don't know the details yet.'

'Seven minutes?' Strindberg protested. 'That's crazy, it would burn out circuits, the heat would be—'

'And the power spike was channelled down to something called Radspan.'

'Radspan! Impossible. It was mothballed years ago. If that amount of power was channelled through Radspan it would burn out . . .' He suddenly realized the implication. Radspan was connected to the grid. That had always been its flaw; it could never generate enough power.

That kind of energy burst sustained for a whole seven minutes would overheat cables, there would be fires

burning underground, and if it jumped stations –
absolutely it could bring down the whole power system.

'There's a Radspan station under this hotel,' Strindberg
informed him.

'Sir?'

'There is a mothballed Radspan station under this hotel
and it's connected to the grid. They were right; we are the
source of the power outage. God, get some men down
there. It's probably on fire right now! I knew we should
have dismantled the damn thing.'

'I don't understand, sir. There's a car park under the
hotel. That's it.'

'And below the car park there are sixteen more levels.
The generators are on Sixteen. You'll need a team of fire-
fighters and they will all have to swear to secrecy. You
understand. This won't be a picnic.'

'I don't think I have a team. They're out inspecting
damage. There're fires breaking out all across town.'

'Then get them back, get them back,' Strindberg
shouted. 'We have a fire brewing down below and if it
gets out of hand this whole hotel will go up with it. You
understand? Get the evac plan in action *now*!'

Strindberg wasn't sure what to do. Go down and find
out how bad it was or head out of town. He didn't want to
be here when everything imploded.

'I'm going to go up to my chopper on the roof. I've got good communication links there. I'll get some experienced help for you.'

'Yes, sir.'

'Get moving, man. You've got a fire to put out.' Strindberg turned and started to climb the stairs. It was time to abandon ship.

31

For the Life of Genie Magee

Genie tried to send herself back, wake up in her own body, but nothing happened. She'd opened her eyes and found she was still in the control room and the Fortransco staff had broken through the outer chamber door. She was frozen there, afraid. There was absolutely nowhere to hide and they'd kill her if they found her and knew she'd been sending her friends to Radspan.

She wasn't alone after all, she realized. Denis was still with her, smiling, casual as anything.

'You're still here.'

'Can't leave you to the wolves, can I?'

'You should have transmitted. Denis, this is wrong. We came to save you.'

He smiled. '*I'm* here to save *you*. Watch this.'

'What are you doing?' She realized he was manipulating the computer.

'Doing what we should have done a long time ago.'

'What? We're supposed to dump all the data off the servers. Marshall thinks it will be—'

Denis shook his head. 'There's no one left we can save. They've been making sure of that. The others were lucky to get out. Their core DNA was stored on Level Three servers. They've been upgrading and dumping data. Marshall is right about one thing; we were stored on at least forty thousand servers. But everyone A through to G is already deleted.'

'You sure?'

'Yeah. I promise I'd save them if I could.'

'But that means you . . .'

Denis smiled. 'I am now stored on the nuclear research facility in Nebraska. I looked for the biggest capacity I could find and that's where I am. I'm not going to lose anything, from now on. They can't touch me.'

'You've changed so much.' Genie regarded Denis with awe. He was so confident now.

Denis grinned. 'You started it. I'm learning everything I can. I was so obsessed with getting home and seeing Mom and Dad I never really thought about what I really wanted. When they snatched me back – I discovered I could be anything I wanted.'

Genie watched the Fortransco technicians gather in the transmission chamber. They seemed to stop and gawp as they saw Genie and Denis inside the control room. Denis waved, just to annoy them.

'The door's locked. Don't worry, they can't get in. Just got one more thing to do and then we'll leave,' Denis told her.

Genie looked at the faces of the technicians as they argued about what was the best thing to do. She turned and watched Denis.

'What are you doing now?'

'Sending every test transmission to YouTube and a link to every news-broadcaster I could think of. One of them has to take it seriously this time. I already sent them all of Dr Milan's tests. They are going to look so sick around here when they find out.'

Genie stared at him with astonishment.

'Mine and yours too?'

'All of them. We'll be famous. In my case, dead famous.' He grinned as he glanced over at her. 'Don't worry, I've got a way out of here. They aren't going to get you.'

Genie didn't want to say that she didn't want her transmission on YouTube, but she understood why he wanted to do it.

'Every missing kid, every missing dog or cat,' Denis was saying. 'If this doesn't stop the Fortress, nothing will. People may not care about us kids from Spurlake, but they care a whole lot about their precious pets. You can bet on that. There might be riots.'

A chair slammed against the control window, making Genie jumped out of her skin. The glass didn't even crack.

Denis laughed. 'It's bulletproof glass.' He waved at the technicians. 'Try again, suckers. I've got one more surprise for you.'

Denis pressed a button and suddenly everything came to life. The transmission platform was active; the technicians suddenly realized this. They were in the teleport chamber, they could be transmitted. Some instantly began yelling and screaming to shut it down, but the control room was soundproof. Genie could see the power indicator was rising. It began a countdown to transmission at ten seconds.

'Video cameras on,' Denis said, a smirk on his face. 'This won't be pretty.' He turned to Genie. 'Let's go.'

He moved past her and ducked under a table. 'Come on.'

Genie looked back at the transmission room. Saw a woman pressed against the wall trying to keep out of range, saw two men trying to get back out but the door was locked and, as the countdown reached one second – a man turned to run but he disintegrated before her eyes and vanished into thin air.

'Now, Genie! This place could get real hot in a minute.'

There was a panel in the wall, which led to the airducts. It was wide enough to crawl into. Genie hesitated.

347

'You have to crawl along for two metres and there's another panel. Kick it out and I'll meet you there.'

Genie took a deep breath. Suddenly there was a loud wet slap on the window behind her. She didn't have to look back. Carbon blowback! Someone's DNA was plastered over the control-room glass.

She climbed into the air-duct and quickly moved forward into solid darkness. Her fingers found the outline of another panel and she turned round to kick. Her mind could never quite get a handle on how she was just as solid here as back in Radspan. If she was a ghost, how could she kick anything?

'Kick harder,' Denis called from the other side.

Angrily she kicked again and the metal panel fell with a clang to the ground below. Burning fumes immediately invaded her nostrils.

Denis pulled her out. 'We're in the tunnel that leads to the first Radspan station. The cables have overheated and the plastic's burning. Cover your mouth and nose and follow me close.'

'Thanks . . .' Genie began, but started to cough.

She couldn't see anything. She stumbled after Denis, trying to keep up with him, her throat getting tighter, her eyes stinging. Denis reached back, took Genie's hand. The smoke was overwhelming. She could barely breathe. Her eyes were tightly closed and she stumbled over melting cables towards a door. She didn't understand why she hadn't gone back. She was done. She had sent Cary. She didn't know if Julia had transmitted; the feedback said only ninety-nine point one per cent of her was sent and zero point nine per cent of a person was going to be a lot, wasn't it? They were in a panic, trying to rush it. Cary could only save those he could find – and then there was the shock of Denis saying he didn't want to go. She didn't fully understand it, couldn't persuade him that he'd grow, that in just a couple of years he'd be at his normal height. She still couldn't believe he'd got her out of there.

Denis reached some steps and negotiated with the door lock, seeming to listen to something inside his head for a moment before entering a code.

The door swung open and they both ran in, quickly closing it after them, sealing out the smoke, Genie coughing and gasping for breath. 'God, can't see,' she muttered, spitting out a nasty taste in her mouth. 'My eyes . . . Thanks, Denis. Thanks.' She coughed some more and staggered back against the door, clutching her throat.

There was a single blue light hanging from a wire in the ceiling. There were in a storeroom filled with dusty computer parts. Denis went towards the emergency exit door.

'You have to climb from here. It's sixteen floors,' Denis informed her, turning round. 'Genie? Genie?'

Denis realized that she'd gone. He frowned and sat down, feeling very bad suddenly. He could have gone with her; he could have transmitted before Cary. This was what he wanted, right? So why did he suddenly feel so utterly alone?

'I'll miss you, Genie,' he mumbled sadly, a lump in his throat.

32

Vertigo

They were on the tenth floor and already exhausted and sweating from the exertion. Carrying your own weight up stairs whilst acrid plastic smoke drifts by wasn't easy.

So far only one of the teleporters had fully revived. Miho still seemed confused and Julia limp. Cary was struggling to climb the stairs on his own, but his legs were like jelly and he felt nauseous.

Rian carried Genie up a few steps and then went back for Miho, who could walk now, but not without help. Then repeated the process. All the time his lungs were filling with smoke and he was getting weaker. Renée managed Julia, and Mouch was already at the top barking for them to hurry up.

'Any way we can get Mouch to shut up?' Marshall asked. 'I don't want people to know we're down here.'

'Someone must know we're here, the smoke must be coming out somewhere up there,' Renée said, coughing again. She had one hell of a headache from the fumes.

Suddenly it was as if the sun exploded down below

and they all had to cover their eyes again.

'What?'

'Another transmission,' Marshall answered. He couldn't face going down those stairs. But who had transmitted, how? Cary was supposed to be the last? Had Denis changed his mind?

'I'll go,' Rian said, waiting for his eyes to adjust again.

Marshall grabbed his sleeve. 'No. Stay . . . They won't survive one second down there in those fumes. Nor will you. It's too hot down there now. We have to keep going up. It could turn into a fireball any minute.'

'But—'

'Absolutely not, Rian. It would be stupid. Utterly stupid. Get us all to the surface. That's your job. There's no one to save down there. Believe me.'

Rian could sense the air was growing more choked and polluted by the second. Reluctantly, he had to accept Marshall was right. He went back up the stairs, trying to blot out an image of someone lying on the platform, gasping for air.

On Level Fourteen the platform was red-hot. The air stank and hung heavy with melting plastic fumes. A twisted heap of newly arrived body parts lay on the platform. Something stirred for just a second, something no longer human, something wearing a lab coat. Someone died. No one saw. The air suddenly ignited with a *whoosh*. A flash fire leaped across the whole floor, consuming the oxygen and everything in its path.

Marshall had to rest. His leg was in agony and he was afraid he'd have one of his fits. He was as disappointed as the rest of them that they hadn't saved as many as they hoped. He was worried about their reception upstairs. It wouldn't take long for someone to realize the problem came from Radspan and someone had to remember it was down here.

There was a piercing scream as Miho suddenly collapsed in a heap, taking a huge gulp of air. She was suddenly fully conscious and scared.

Renée was at Miho's side in a flash. 'Miho? What?'

Miho stared at Renée as if she didn't know her and then coughed as the smoke got into her lungs.

'There's a fire down below,' Renée explained to her. 'We're on our way to the surface. You're OK. You're out of the Fortress.'

Miho looked at Renée and then seemed to remember her.

'Renée?'

'Yes, Renée. Cary and Genie got you out.'

Miho suddenly remembered something. 'My mother. My mother died. I was . . . You were . . . We escaped . . . I . . .'

She was confused but she had a distinct memory of dying, of not existing. Yet here she was – again with Renée.

'Got to get you moving,' Renée told her. 'We have to get moving.'

Cary came to join them. He tested Miho's memory. 'Where is Dave's Muffin House?'

Miho frowned, confused by the question, then answered, 'Spurlake.'

Cary smiled. 'Brain still intact. Good. Come on, you've got to use your legs.'

Renée looked at Cary as if he was mad. Dave's Muffin House was the only thing he could think of?

'Oh my God, I'm solid again,' Miho said, realizing with astonishment that she could feel her legs. 'Cary Harrison, right?'

'Right.'

'Oh-oh, I'm going to be sick.' She turned to one side and spewed over the wall.

Renée looked at Cary and he shrugged. 'I feel nauseous too, if it helps.'

'Keep moving,' Rian called from the back. He had Julia

with him now. She was showing no signs of coming round at all and he was worried. Almost as worried as he was about Genie.

'Move on up,' Marshall told them. 'I'm sticking with Genie for a moment.'

Rian had Julia over his shoulder and felt his legs buckling. Only ten floors to go, but the smoke was getting to him now.

Genie twitched. Moucher barked suddenly and was skittering back down the stairs.

'She's coming back to us,' Marshall announced.

Moucher was there at the exact moment Genie jerked back to life, banging her head on the hard wall. Moucher was right there, paw on her arm, staring at her to make sure she was OK.

Genie saw the dog, got a mouthful of smoke fumes and pulled a face. 'Mouch? Denis?'

'He didn't come through,' Marshall told her, standing. 'Welcome back, Genie. We have to move quickly, there's a fire below.'

Genie saw him, put out a hand to him and he pulled her up and gave her a hug.

'I was so scared I wouldn't get back,' Genie whispered quietly.

'Me too. Me too,' he replied.

Genie broke away. 'There's a fire at the Fortress. The cables in Radspan overheated.'

'Same here.'

'Ri?' Genie queried, looking around.

'Up ahead carrying Julia.'

Genie suddenly remembered that Julia had a problem. 'She's only ninety-nine per cent, Marshall. I think . . .'

Marshall understood. 'We will face that if and when she wakes. Come on, up. We have to go. These fumes will kill us.'

'Go on up,' she told Moucher. 'The air's bad.' The dog was only too happy to go back towards the fresh air and ran back up to join Rian.

'Who made it?' Genie asked as she took Marshall's arm – or he took hers; it was hard to tell.

'Miho, Cary, Julia. That's all.'

Genie looked at him. 'I'm sorry. I'm sorry we couldn't save more.'

Marshall urged her up the stairs. 'Saving one is amazing; you helped get three out.'

'Julia just opened her eyes,' Rian called down.

'Genie's back with us, Rian. Keep moving,' Marshall shouted back up. He looked back down the stairs and it seemed to him the smoke was intensifying. 'Don't open the outer door until we're all there,' he added.

To Genie he voiced his real concern. 'We have to get out real fast up there. The moment the door opens it's going to draw the fire up the stairwell – the oxygen and updraught will make it go critical.'

Genie was thinking about the other side of the door.

'Does anyone know we're down here?'

'They'll know Radspan is on fire. Anytime soon someone is going to open that door to find out just how bad it is.'

'I hope it isn't Reverend Schneider,' Genie remarked.

Marshall smiled briefly. 'I rather hope it is, give him a glimpse of the hell he helped create, eh?'

They gathered in the small lobby at the top of the stairs. Rian was covered in sweat, having done almost all the heavy lifting. Cary was out of breath, clutching his chest. Renée and Mouch stood with a blanket over them to cut out the acrid smoke. Julia lay on the floor, awake, but lifeless. Rian caught Genie's hand and squeezed it hard.

Marshall gasped, clearly in desperate pain from the climbing and appreciative that Genie got him there.

He closed the door to the stairs. The smoke was still swirling around them, but at least it cut off the supply.

'We don't know what's on the other side. Might be nothing, might be Fortransco people. If my truck's there,

357

run for it and get in. If it ain't, run, scatter and leave me with Julia. I'll deal with them. There's an all-night café two blocks over. Meet me there. If I don't make it, get the hell out of town. My guess is that it's going to be dark. The power will be out. There will be chaos.' He looked around for Rian. 'Rian?'

'Marshall?'

'If I am detained, find some transportation. I don't care whose. Get these kids gone. I don't know where will be safe. But get over to the islands. There're places to hide and people always need help on a farm.'

'We won't go without you,' Genie reassured him, 'or Julia.'

'I think we need to get going,' Cary urged them.

Renée flung off the blanket. 'I can hear something.' She moved towards the elevator door and put her hands on it, yelping with pain as she jumped back. 'Jesus, it's hot.'

Marshall could smell it now. 'Damn. Rian, open the door. Everyone, get out of here as fast as you can, y'hear me. Fast as you can.'

Rian found the manual lever, swung it over and the door opened. Instantly they could hear the roar of the fire coming up the elevator shaft.

'OUT. OUT. OUT!' Rian was yelling as they all piled through.

Genie grabbed Julia – she was so incredibly light – and stepped through, Marshall right behind her.

But not fast enough. The flames exploded out from under the elevator door – seemed to come right out of the walls – and Marshall stumbled out of the doorway with his jeans on fire.

Renée acted quickly and smothered them with her blanket. They heard barking. Mouch was still in there.

'Mouch!' Genie screamed.

He jumped, yelping loudly, his tail on fire, practically landed on top of her and she rolled him in the canvas on the floor, extinguishing the flames.

'God!' she exclaimed. Mouch whimpered with shock and pain.

'Shut the door!' Marshall shouted, but it was already too hot to touch and they backed away towards the wire cage.

They realized that all was dark behind them, the flames were all the light there was. The underground car park was empty. Completely empty. The truck was gone, so were all the old cars.

Marshall staggered over to the wire fencing and pulled it away so they could get out.

'Run, scatter, meet you-know-where,' he told them. 'I've got Julia.'

Rian grabbed Genie's hand, Renée snatched the other. They had no intention of losing each other now.

'Cary,' Renée shouted. 'With me.'

'We can't leave him,' Genie protested.

'Stick to the plan,' Marshall insisted.

They were in the car park now. They all heard the tyre squeals of a vehicle coming on down at speed.

'Go!'

They ran, hoping they could find cover before the vehicle arrived. Mouch, torn between masters, followed Genie, very concerned about his sore tail.

Marshall put Julia over his shoulder and began to walk.

Julia tried to speak, her eyes focused on the flames spewing out of the underground door. She couldn't seem to say anything, but she knew something bad was going to happen. She tried again. Nothing. She couldn't even scream.

The explosion was so intense behind them Marshall was picked up and thrown ten metres or more. He landed and rolled, realizing with dismay that Julia was no longer in his arms. His leg was gone and he was smouldering, he was so hot.

He looked back down the slope and saw the whole floor was burning as a hot liquid was spreading on the concrete floor.

An arm shot out and someone pulled him to one side as a truck came around the corner and plunged down towards the sixth floor. He looked around for Julia, saw her out of the corner of his eye, very awake now and clearly terrified.

The driver was going too fast. He braked but the floor was covered in burning oil and the truck drove right into the heart of the flames, its horn blaring on impact with a wall.

Marshall and Julia saw two Fortransco uniformed men jump out on fire, screaming, trying to find a way out of the flames.

Marshall found himself being hauled up.

'Come on. I found your truck,' Rian told him. 'Julia, can you walk? Follow me.'

Julia nodded. She seemed to have lost the power of speech, but she knew who Rian was and what was happening and crawled to her feet, bemused and dizzy but able to keep up.

Rian dumped Marshall in the back of his truck with Cary and Moucher. Julia followed and flopped down at Marshall's feet. Genie looked back at them with a worried expression through the window.

'Get back in, Ri, we gotta go. Now!'

Renée swung the door open as Rian jumped in and

Genie accelerated out of there, the fire behind them filling her mirrors.

Marshall regretted abandoning his prosthetic leg. Julia tried to make him more comfortable and Moucher hung on for dear life, ears flat, scared to death. Genie was swinging the truck round the sharp turns as if the devil was after her.

Sparks flew from the base of the truck as she hit the street and, although there was confusion and the whole town was plunged into darkness, she threaded her way through it with skill.

'We should stop and check for tracking devices,' Rian said, remembering what he'd found before.

'There's no power; they can't track anyone right now,' Renée pointed out. 'Watch out, there's people walking.'

'I'm watching, I'm watching.'

'Where are we headed?'

'Vancouver.'

They stared out across Whistler. The whole town was blacked out, punctured by fires that seemed to have broken out in many places.

The traffic was all snarled on one area, but Genie just bumped over the curbs and down on to the opposite lanes and kept on driving.

'Hey,' Rian protested.

'You can't lose a licence you haven't got,' Genie explained.

She made a left. Went right around some people disputing an accident and duking it out in front of their headlights.

'Keep going,' Renée told her, looking back at where they had come from.

Marshall was knocking on the rear window. Rian slid it back.

'Slow down and take a look behind you, kids.'

Genie slowed, but she could see it in her mirrors. The All Seasons Hotel was on fire. Radspan was finally claiming its own. It was huge and would only get bigger. She had done this. They would hate her even more now.

Cary spewed. 'I'm OK, it's just Genie's driving.'

Genie smiled. She moved forward again, but kept to the limit. Instinctively she knew that Fortransco would have enough to worry about without chasing them at this moment.

'Where do you think Reverend Schneider is right now?' Genie asked no one in particular.

'Far away. Far, far away,' Rian told her.

Renée looked out of the tiny rear window at Julia. She was so changed. She looked so tiny and scared, the shaved head looked brutal.

363

'Julia? You feel better yet?'

Cary spoke for her.

'She isn't speaking. I'm sure she knows who we are, but she can't seem to speak.'

Genie knew why too. She was ninety-nine per cent certain why anyway.

'Maybe it's a side effect,' Rian suggested.

Genie looked at him. 'Maybe. But Cary couldn't find one hundred per cent of her.'

Rian and Renée winced. That was not going to be easy to explain to her.

'She's alive, at least,' Genie pointed out. 'A whole lot of kids aren't.'

She drove on. The chaos and darkness disappearing behind them, a virtually empty road ahead.

'Do we have a plan?' Rian asked.

Genie smiled. 'We ever had a plan actually work out yet? I think we're a whole lot better without plans, Rian Tulane.'

Cary leaned in for a moment. 'Marshall says there may be a place to go in Squamish. About twenty minutes up ahead from here.'

'I wanted to get us to Vancouver,' Genie replied.

'He says if the power's out there the chaos will be worse than here. We can overnight in Squamish.'

Genie saw the logic of it. No one would know them. It was probably safe and they could plan the next move. Besides, everyone was exhausted.

'OK.'

In the back of the truck Marshall gripped his stump. It was giving him grief. But they'd got out alive and he never thought they would. When they did the investigation about the fire, Fortransco would have a hell of a lot of explaining to do. It would cost them plenty.

Cary stroked Moucher, who was madly licking his damaged tail. The fur had gone, his skin was blistered in places, but it would recover.

'You think I'll have side effects too?' Cary asked Marshall.

Marshall looked at him carefully, aware that Julia was asleep now.

'You come through one hundred per cent?'

'I guess.'

'Julia was ninety-nine point one, right?'

'Yeah. I'm sorry. I just couldn't find all of her.'

'And that's always going to be the problem, I think. Storage. If you think you're one hundred per cent, you probably are. You're pretty unique, kid, transmitted successfully twice. That's quite something.'

'I'm scared I'll . . . well, we . . . will all have problems later.'

Marshall nodded. 'When we designed this programme, and I was only there at the beginning, remember, we took the view that everyone who ever teleported should be screened. If there were problems, you either didn't send them or you fixed the problem. That's what was decided. You wouldn't want to send someone with a dodgy liver or dicky heart. So chances are, kid, you and the others will all live a lot longer than anyone else, if you get my drift.'

Cary looked at him and understood and felt a lot better about things.

'You think teleportation will catch on?' Cary asked.

Marshall laughed. 'Ask Genie and, for God's sake, tell her to slow down.'

33

Calling Flight 101

Reverend Schneider had known things were going wrong hours earlier. Strindberg hadn't gotten control, and finding Genie Magee was just impossible; she was everywhere, but nowhere. And he knew that this time it wouldn't be kept quiet and they'd be looking for someone to blame.

Which was why he was anxiously looking at his watch and waiting for the next flight out of Vancouver.

He'd seen the sub-stations explode in Whistler, seen the power go out across half of B.C. and he hadn't waited. The airport had its own power source, flights were still coming in and leaving, and he aimed to be on the very next international flight. He didn't even care where, but as luck would have it, it was La Paz, Mexico, and he had friends there.

There was a small bank account down there too. Not much, but enough to get by for a while. The church would have to do without him. Been meaning to give it up anyway; business had dropped off considerably since the kids reappeared and sowed suspicion in the town. Not everyone believed the alien story – certainly not the parents who'd lost their kids twice – and he knew there were stories being told about him about town.

It was time to go. Good timing was everything when things went bad.

'Reverend Schneider?' a voice called out.

He looked up. It was Vince, Fortransco Head of Security.

'Not thinking of going anywhere, are you, Reverend?' The menace in his voice froze Schneider's heart.

Game over.

He began to sweat. Wondered briefly if he could run for it. His flight had just been given a gate.

'Conference,' he told the man. 'Just a few days in Cabo San Lucas.' He began to shake. Vince had been known to crush a man's neck to a pulp in a disagreement. Everyone was afraid of him.

Vince smiled and sat next to him. Reverend Schneider noticed that he too had a small overnight case with him.

'Cuba,' Vince said, tapping his ticket. 'Since they discovered all that oil, they need more security. Good offer, couldn't refuse.'

Reverend Schneider also remembered that there was no extradition from Cuba either. The police wouldn't be able to get him there.

'You speak Spanish?' he asked the man.

'Learning, learning,' he smiled.

Reverend Schneider stood up on shaky legs. 'My flight . . .'

Vince nodded. 'I wouldn't hurry back, if I were you.'

Reverend Schneider turned, his heart beating wildly and sweat trickling down the insides of his shirt. He walked away towards the Departures door. Wondering if the man had been joking and would pounce before he got to Customs. Nothing happened. He daren't look back, but he noted wryly that neither of them had chosen to teleport to their destinations.

Strindberg was at home. The lights were on, the Sunshine Coast wasn't affected by the power meltdown. He'd been shocked at the damage as he'd flown over the resort. Substations on fire, the power surge had fried circuits everywhere and it would take weeks, months to get it all back to normal.

He was burning. He had a grand fireplace, big enough for four big logs at a time. But burning now were papers, documents, photos, any and everything that connected him to Fortress teleport experiments. It was a good fire. An expensive fire.

His cell rang. Probably for the twentieth time in an hour.

He'd heard about the problems at the Fortress. The entire nightshift test transmission team obliterated. A terrible accident. There would have to be an investigation, it would cost yet more money. Fortunately they had signed documents that absolved the company of liabilities in case of human error and this would be human error, most certainly human error.

'Strindberg.'

'Do you have power?' The Night Operations Chief at Synchro asked him.

'Yes. We haven't been affected here.'

'Then I suggest you take a look at YouTube. Type in "The Fortress". The whole thing's gone viral.'

'Viral? YouTube? Isn't that some teen thing – music videos and stuff?'

'Take a look, Mr Strindberg, and then maybe you might want to leave town. I think quite a lot of people are leaving . . .'

'What? What the hell's going on? First Radspan comes back to haunt us, then this accident – what's going on?' Strindberg demanded to know.

'Just so you know, sir, the All Seasons is going to be a total write-off. Everyone was evacuated, as far as we know, but it's burning out. With the power being out and the underground fire – there's no water pressure for the fire department. We will be lucky if it doesn't spread.'

'The whole hotel?' Strindberg couldn't believe it. It was his best money-spinner.

'And you might want to see if your insurance policy mentioned it was built over an unstable power source, sir.'

The Synchro chief hung up. Strindberg stared at the fire. What the hell else could go wrong?

He walked over to his laptop, already online. He searched for: *The Fortress.*

YouTube Videos Being Watched Right Now

He didn't even have to search. There were five listed right at the top with *Genie Magee*, *Cary Harrison*, *Denis Malone*, *Dr Milan* and more *Radspan Test Transmissions.*

He'd get them removed, he'd sue, he'd soon stop this.

His cell rang again. It was Vince, his Head of Security.

'Hi, Mr Strindberg.'

'Have you seen YouTube?' Strindberg exploded. 'Have you seen what someone has put up there'?

'Yes, sir. Have you seen how many there are? It's gone viral, sir. That's why I'm calling, sir. You'll need a new Head of Security.'

Strindberg was astonished. 'You're quitting?'

'Quit, sir.'

'But we're in meltdown – Radspan, the hotel, the chaos . . .'

'Yes, sir. I think you'll need a new PR company, sir, as well.'

Strindberg could hear a flight being called. The man was already at the airport!

'You bastard, you—'

But he was talking to himself.

He disconnected and his phone immediately rang again. He answered, irritated beyond belief now.

'Yes – and this better be good news.'

All he heard was mocking laughter on the other end. Sounded a lot like some kid.

He stood there, in his mansion, beside his log fire and everything he knew was going up in flames with it, the laughter pierced by the sound of Dr Milan's voice on YouTube speaking. 'Test three thousand five – a healthy three-year-old Labrador called Max.'

34

School for Thought

They had to get off the highway a mile out of Squamish. Fire engines, cops, ambulances were racing at top speed in convoy towards Whistler. They watched them go by, Genie feeling a tad guilty. It was all her fault. People in Whistler would suffer.

'We need to get off this road,' Marshall told her. 'Take the next right. Keep it slow. There's the hotel overlooking the water.'

'Hotel?' Renée queried. Marshall didn't answer. He was coughing again; the smoke was still in his lungs. Genie set off again, there were way too many cops on this road for her liking; it was way too risky to be driving. She took the first right. They passed some people sitting outside their homes lit by camper lights. Each one of them with a shotgun ready in case, carefully eyeballing them as they drove by. No one said anything, but each of them in the truck realized that this was not the best night to be looking for somewhere to crash for free.

'Here?' Genie asked, confused, as they pulled up

outside a hotel.

'It's abandoned. Went belly up in the crash. Guy who owned it was a friend of my son's. It's going to be auctioned off.'

'We just break in?'

'The power's out so I doubt alarms are going to work and, even if they did, no one is going to respond tonight. I'm not saying there's warm beds to go to, but it's empty and they won't look for you guys here.'

'I'll get us in,' Rian said. 'Drive round the back, Genie. No need for anyone to see the truck.'

Genie had thought of this already. She backed up and drove around.

'We need sleep and a plan. Sleep first,' Marshall told them. 'Strindberg will work things out eventually and he'll make it his business to hunt you down. So we need to be clever. But right now, with everything in chaos, we can afford to sleep.'

The kids looked at him and agreed. They were exhausted.

Genie parked up and Rian got out. Genie grabbed Mouch, who was ready to follow him. 'Wait.'

He approached the five-storey building, a small budget hotel by the look of it. He looked for something to break a window with. He didn't like to do this, but they had broken enough laws already, what the hell was one more?

The sliding door to the ground-floor swimming pool was unlocked. It was stiff but he slid it open and entered. The smell wasn't good; he felt his eyes water from the fumes. The pool water had been drained, but someone had been using it to dump their waste. It stank. Not a good sign.

The door to the hotel lobby was likewise unlocked. He just hoped the rest of the hotel hadn't been trashed. If kids knew this was open, they'd get in to party and trash it for sure. He wondered how much looting was going on across B.C. Everyone always said how civilized Canada was but there would always be someone who'd take advantage. It was very dark now and he was wary; he had to feel his way along.

He found a flashlight behind the reception desk. Remarkably, it still worked.

Keys to the rooms were all in a slide-out drawer. Everything was surprisingly neat and tidy.

He took keys for the ground-floor suites. He checked the first room. There were beds, mattresses still wrapped in plastic. Bedding likewise. This was all brand new. Untouched. The hotel didn't look like it ever even opened.

He went back to the guys in the truck.

'Don't even think of looking in the swimming pool,' he told them. 'Grab your things. We have rooms.'

They cheered.

Genie took a room with Rian but, although exhausted, neither of them could sleep they were so tense. He opened the sliding door to air the room and they stood close together outside under the brilliant stars.

'It's so beautiful. Everything is so much prettier without streetlights. Reminds me of the farm. Look, see a shooting star.'

Rian nuzzled her ear. 'My wish already came true.'

She smiled, enjoying his hot breath on her neck.

'What are we going to do, Ri?'

'Think about that tomorrow.'

Genie frowned. 'We going to run for ever? You think Marshall's right? Strindberg is going to want revenge?'

Rian sighed. 'I guess. I don't know. I just want to make sure we stay together and you don't keep having to go places. I worry every time you disappear. Makes me ill, Gen. That time you nearly froze. I felt so bad. There was nothing I could do. Nothing.'

Genie turned and hugged him, kissing his shoulder. She wanted to promise never to disappear again, but how could she keep a promise that would always be broken?

'Just always be there when I come back to you, Ri. Just be there.'

She could see the canopy of stars reflected in the glass window. She felt comforted by them. This was all she had ever wanted. A boy who loved her and a carpet of stars to sleep under.

Rian felt her fall asleep in his arms then scooped her up and took her back to the bed. He closed the door and locked it. He looked back up at the stars. Genie was right. They had to think about what they were going to do. It definitely wasn't over.

He lay beside her and held her tight. He felt fear, love and not a little anger. All he wanted to do was protect her. It was hard.

It was a sunny morning. Genie stared at herself in the mirror. She'd slept fitfully, scared someone would discover them, and uncomfortable on the plastic-covered mattress. She would have dearly loved a shower but they just had to be happy that the toilets flushed. Rian slept on. She noticed on rising that he had burns on his face and arms. He'd never complained but they had to hurt.

Julia was sitting on the edge of the bath, watching her. She had a headache and she had come looking for

Genie hoping that one of them, at least, had some pills to take it away.

Genie glanced at her face again. Was she still Genie Magee? Her hair was growing but so was the white streak. She just knew she'd be for ever called skunk head when people saw her. It was clear across her head now and shockingly white.

'Can you dye white hair? I mean, I read somewhere that it doesn't take. I'm sixteen, Julia. I can't possibly have white hair, for God's sake.'

Julia said nothing. She felt Genie's hair and pointed to her own shaved head and signalled that she was worried about what would happen to her when it grew back – if indeed it grew back.

Genie put an arm around her and rubbed her bald head.

'Come on, we have to go through.'

Julia looked reluctant to leave the bathroom.

Genie took her hand. 'They're your friends, OK. It won't matter, really. And talk to Marshall. He lost his leg, remember. I mean, that must have been a shock. He'll tell you about who to talk to . . .' Genie blushed, suddenly realizing that was a mean thing to say. Poor Julia wasn't going to be talking to anyone.

'Sorry . . .'

But Julia shook her head. This was something she was going to have to live with in future.

Genie opened the bathroom door. Rian had gone, probably to find another bathroom, she'd been in there so long.

Cary had gone out with Renée earlier to Mac's convenience store, which was selling everything previously chilled at half price before it went off, and attracting a local crowd. They'd come away with milk, coffee, cereal, eggs, cookies and a choice of breads. Way too much. They'd even built a little fire outside to boil the water and fry some eggs. Now everyone was in the hotel kitchen eating breakfast, except Miho. Renée was in charge and making sure everyone ate.

Genie arrived with Julia. They could all tell Julia had been crying. She'd had been so slow to recover and everyone knew about the ninety-nine per cent transmission problem. Rian waved at Genie. She waved back, relieved he wasn't mad at her or anything. She felt robbed of her morning kiss.

Marshall coughed and clutched his head. He was unwell, badly affected by the smoke from the night before.

'Where's Mouch?' Genie asked. 'Has he eaten?'

Renée frowned. 'Haven't seen him since we came back

from the store. But he had some biscuits; nearly ate my hand off he was so hungry.'

Genie was relieved. He'd be close; he didn't like to wander far. Cary was pouring coffee or tea for everyone and seemed fine, which was a miracle. Considering what they all had been through, it was astonishing they weren't all traumatized for all time.

'We've worked it out,' Genie told them as they took places at the table.

'What?'

'Larynx. The bit that makes her speak hasn't come through. She can swallow and everything. It all seems normal, but she can't speak.'

Julia looked upset and Renée immediately went to comfort her.

'Can anything be done?' Cary asked. 'God, I'm sorry, Julia. I didn't know what to do. You were like all there one hundred per cent, then suddenly just one server dropped out and . . .'

Julie shook her head and blew him a kiss to say it was all right.

Genie looked at them all. 'She wants you all to know that she is happy to be alive and knows how lucky she is. She's upset but maybe something can be done. They can do all kinds of things now with electronics.'

Renée nodded enthusiastically. 'Absolutely. Get them to install something really cool so you can blow them away on *The Voice*.'

Marshall coughed again. 'I don't think that is quite feasible, Renée, but I'm really sorry, Julia. We will try to connect you with people who can help, OK? There's all kinds of people, specialists.'

Julia nodded, embarrassed to be the centre of attention.

Miho appeared in the doorway, Moucher in tow. She sported bandages on her forehead and left arm and was still dressed in her underwear; she looked deathly pale and a little frightened.

'Breakfast? Moucher says I have to eat.'

Genie smiled as the dog found her and looked up at her with his sad, hungry eyes.

'Moucher is correct. And, Mouch, you have had some biscuits, I know this. So don't look at me with those cute little eyes. If you want more we've only got cereal, but it's crunchy.'

Moucher wasn't keen but he did his best to wag his very sore tail, now bandaged to stop him from licking and nipping it.

'I never heard a dog speak before,' Miho said mysteriously as she sat down. 'He is so worried about all of us. It gives him a headache.'

Genie and Rian looked at each other but decided to ignore it. Clearly Miho was still disorientated.

'What's the great plan? What did you kids decide?' Marshall asked them as Cary handed round mugs of coffee.

'First of all, say thanks to your friend for letting us use his hotel,' Genie said, being sarcastic. 'Did you see what they put in the swimming pool? It stinks.'

'Someone didn't want to pay to have something toxic taken away, most likely and snuck it in,' Marshall said. 'Not our problem and as long as we clean up after us no one has to know we were here.'

Renée smiled. 'I can't believe it's just been left empty.'

Marshall shook his head. 'Built it just as the recession took hold. There's a lot of empty places like this now. Just glad I didn't have the money to get into real estate.'

'How's your leg?' Genie asked him. She knew he hated not being mobile.

'Sore. Think I must have bruised it when I fell. Or when I was on fire. Being around you kids is dangerous. But at least I haven't had a fit lately. Small mercies.'

Julia looked at Marshall and suddenly cried again. She was beginning to realize that she was like him now, for ever missing something.

'We need to make a plan,' Rian said. 'We can't go

home. It's never going to be safe there and I for one trust no one in Spurlake. Except your son, Marshall.'

There were some murmurs of agreement. They'd tried that before.

'Max quit. He didn't like what they did to you guys any more than you did,' Marshall told them. 'Shame, because he was a good cop.'

'It's Spurlake,' Renée said. 'It's a town without shame.'

'That's true enough,' Genie agreed. She looked at Cary. 'Nice coffee, Cary. Maybe we could open a coffee shop? That would be cool. We could all do shifts. Be a co-op. We could call it "Bean There – Done That".'

She could tell Renée was up for it, at least. She gave her the thumbs up.

'Our plan was going to be a surprise, but I have to reveal it now, I guess,' Cary said. 'It was Denis' idea actually.'

'Denis?' they all asked.

Genie suddenly remembered how Denis had gotten her out of the control room and then been left all alone. She felt so sorry she never got to say goodbye.

'I can't believe he stayed,' Genie said wistfully.

'He's OK, I promise. He wanted to stay.'

'So what's the surprise?' Miho asked.

Cary looked at them all. 'This excludes Miho, 'cause

she's already got a place at Emily Carr to study art.'

'They won't want me now.'

Cary smiled. 'Not true. We already fixed that. They're expecting you. You'll have to catch up but—'

'How will I pay? The scholarship was supposed to be for a year ago,' Miho said gloomily.

'Believe me, they're waiting for you to turn up. We made sure of it. Denis fixed it, I promise, Miho.'

Miho looked astonished. 'For real?'

Cary nodded. 'For real.'

'So what's our surprise?' Renée and Genie asked simultaneously.

Cary looked pensive. He wasn't sure they'd go for it.

'We're all going to school.'

'School?' Rian queried.

'The International Academy at Cobble Hill, actually.'

Rian laughed. It was the most expensive private school on Vancouver Island. Rumour was that only the brightest and best need apply. No way were they going there.

'School?' Renée protested. She'd hoped like maybe spending the next few years on a beach in Cabo. She glanced at Genie and could see the disappointment on her face too. Neither one of them had thought of this. They'd both hoped they were finished with school. The coffee shop idea was cool. They could easily do that. Not school.

Marshall leaned forward. He realized that this was probably not what they had in mind. 'Guys, you have to stay in hiding. Think about it. You just caused a major corporation to meltdown, help burn down a multi-million dollar hotel. You think Strindberg is going to forget it? No matter what problems he's got, he's not going to let that go without trying to find you and punish you.'

'But if we're in school, it would be easy to find us,' Rian protested. 'They'd never let us in anyway. You any idea what it would cost? Besides, term's already begun.'

Cary smiled and sipped his coffee as he watched their faces and bewilderment.

'At first Denis wanted us to win the lottery, and he's figured out a way to do it, he thinks. But then we got to talking and we realized that the one thing we all need to do is finish school.'

'I've been out of school so long, I don't think—' Renée began.

'And you are real smart, Renée. We all passed Grade Ten. The certificates are already on their way to Marshall's post office box.'

'Grade Ten!' Renée laughed and the others smiled too. They had skipped a whole grade. Only Miho was ahead of them; she had already matriculated.

'We're all going into Year Eleven and we'll all do well

and we're going to graduate together. That's the plan.'

Genie was smiled. It was absurd. She was only . . . actually she remembered she was sixteen now. Grade Eleven wasn't impossible at all.

'But we don't know stuff. They'll find out really fast.'

Cary shook his head. 'We know more than we think and we are all fast learners. Renée can speak French and Spanish. She learned it inside the Fortress.'

Renée shrugged. 'I was bored, had to do something.'

'So I'm the dumb one,' Genie complained. 'I can't go. I'll be laughed at. I don't want to be laughed at.'

'And it's a liberal arts school, Genie. You want to draw, I know you do. I've seen those secret sketches of Rian and Moucher. They're amazing.'

'I *thought* those were yours,' Marshall said with a big smile. 'I found one of Moucher in a bin. It was beautiful. Hell, I framed it for my bedroom. You have real talent, Genie.'

Genie didn't know what to say; they were just doodles.

'We're going. We're all changing our names,' Cary continued. 'That's the secret. We've already ceased to exist back in Spurlake. All the school grades are in our new names. Sorry, but we had to do this without telling you. Strindberg can look for us all he likes but we have officially disappeared. Better yet, Denis arranged for Strindberg to pay.' He grinned. 'He won't even know it came from his Cayman Island bank account. But we're paid up for two years. Got a house we can share, rent paid and . . .'

Genie looked at Marshall, feeling tears welling up. She'd wanted to go back to the farm. She'd felt so safe there, despite everything. She didn't want this. But then again, they could hardly keep running and she couldn't go home. Even if she had a coffee shop you could never be sure that Strindberg or Reverend Schneider wouldn't one day stroll in.

Marshall smiled back at her; he could sense her disappointment. 'The farm will be still be there when you graduate, so will Moucher, and you can come back any time in the vacations,' he told her. 'Any time. It's your home now.'

Genie took a deep breath and looked at Rian. Did he want school too? One glance and she knew he did. He had never really wanted to quit. He'd just wanted to save her – and that he had done.

Suddenly all eyes were on Julia. They remembered she couldn't speak. Would she want to go to school?

'I already talked to Julia,' Cary told them. 'I'm sorry about you losing your voice but it won't stop you going to dance school in the city. She can live there and everything. Jazz, tap, ballet – we think everything's covered.'

'Dance school?' Genie protested. If there were going to be choices, why couldn't she go to art school? She immediately felt guilty for thinking that. Julia had lost so much. Her family *and* her voice. She deserved dance school, if that's what she wanted.

Julia smiled and nodded her head. It would be hard for her, but there was absolutely nothing wrong with her brain.

Genie looked at Moucher, who was sitting by his half-eaten bowl of cereal. He wasn't happy. She went over to cuddle him.

'You have to go back to the farm,' she told him. 'I'm sorry. And I promise your fur will grow back. Shame, he looks so sad.' Mouch looked into her face and licked it, resting his chin on her shoulder. He sighed.

'He knows you love him,' Miho said quietly. 'But he misses chasing the rabbits.'

Genie laughed and cuddled him harder until Mouch squeaked.

'Mouch told me he doesn't want to go to school, as well,' Marshall said, making them laugh. 'I hope you learn something about pigs there, because I can't look after that thing for ever, you know.'

Genie smiled. 'You know you're going to eat it the moment my back is turned.'

'No way. I'm going to breed her. Good pig like that, she'll produce a great litter. I'll call them all after you guys.'

'You're mean.'

He grinned, then looked at the clock. 'OK, let's clean up, tidy beds. I don't want anyone to know we've even been here.'

He rose and Cary grabbed him under the arm. 'Going to need a new leg,' he remarked. He looked at them all staring at him. 'You should all get used to your names now, start using them. Make sure you're familiar with them. At least this way they can never find you again.'

'Who chose the names?' Genie asked, worried now.

'Denis,' Cary warned them all.

'God, it's going to be porn-star names. Cary, why didn't you stop him?' Renée complained

He grinned. 'Too late, Astra.'

'Astra?' she exploded.

'Oh God, what am I?' Genie asked.

'Rhiannon,' he answered. 'Julia is Rachel and Rian is Henry.'

'Henry!' Rian exploded. 'I am not a Henry.'

They all looked at each other, amazed.

'Who are you, Cary? Bet you have a nice normal boring name.'

'Christopher Gerald Madden. Denis found the names

in government files. We've got ID cards coming, everything. He's amazing on computers now.'

A radio suddenly came on. An alarm began to ring.

'They got the power back on fast,' Marshall commented. 'Come on, let's get busy. We have to get out of here.'

Marshall had found a broomstick to help him walk, held it with the brush under his arm. Genie helped him towards the truck.

'I saw your face when he told you about school,' he began. 'I know you don't want this, Genie. But think of Rian. He's bright. I'm not saying you're not bright, but if you didn't want to go, he'd follow you to the end of the earth. You know he would.'

Genie nodded. She looked at him with affection. Marshall was the closest she'd ever got to having a father. She knew he was right.

'I guess I never thought about what we'd do after. I was only thinking of running away.'

'And your instincts are right. Self-preservation is important. But so is getting an education. Finishing what you started. You've got a real chance here. You're just sixteen. It's too early to stop learning. Max didn't go to college. Became a cop. I wanted him to go to university. He could have gone far.'

'He's a good man, Marshall. Isn't that enough?'

Marshall reached the truck and twisted around to heave himself in. It was a strain and the bruising didn't help.

'Maybe. He's back at the farm now. His wife wants "space", whatever that means. He's going to help me get the farm back into shape. Maybe that's enough. But give school a chance. I want you and Rian to graduate. You'll be happy you did. Believe me, it is something you both need to do.'

Genie felt he hadn't understood. 'I'm not afraid of school. I want Ri to be happy and successful. I'm just scared someone will find me when I'm not looking and I'll be back at the Fortress.'

'The Fortress will have enough problems without hunting for you right now. Believe me, they won't be able to fix this problem and make it vanish. My guess is a lot of people are going to lose their jobs today.'

Marshall took the broomstick and tossed it in the back of the truck.

'Meanwhile, you'll have a new name, new life, new hair.' He ran his hands through her stubbly hair. 'You also have good friends who love you and owe you a great deal. They'll keep you safe.'

Moucher bounded out of the hotel with the rest of them.

'There's two alarms going now,' Renée told them. 'We need to be gone.'

'Who's driving?' Marshall asked.

'Me,' Rian answered swinging behind the wheel, looking back at Genie with a smile. 'Nice and slow and safe into the city.'

'Boring,' Genie told him and jumped into the back with Mouch. The rest piled in after.

She thought on Marshall's words. She still hated the idea of school, but he was right, she had to finish what she'd started, for Ri, if nothing else.

Miho squashed herself next to Genie. 'I want to see your sketches. Maybe you can come visit me at art school?'

Genie smiled and leaned against her. 'I'd really like to do that.'

Miho smiled, for the first time in a long time. Mouch lay across them, his ears pricked. This is what he liked. Everyone together and happy.

35

Winter of Discontent

I am certain of only one thing – uncertainty. Why do things fall apart? Why does it hurt my heart so? Grandma Munby told me when I was small that happiness was only ever found in brief moments – the rest is just getting through life. Only now do I realize she was telling the truth.

The small forest behind the old cedar cabin they had rented had quickly become a magical refuge for Genie. A place she could hide and breathe, away from the pressures of school and living with her friends. Her mother would have scolded her, of course, for being an ungrateful wretch and not appreciating just how good she had it. But then again, at least memories of her evil mother were fading and she, of all people, couldn't reach her here. No one could. The forest kept her sane, that was all and whereas Rian seemed to spend all hours in the gym – Cary in the science lab and Renée with her new friends, the forest, with its strange noises and animal activity, seemed to welcome her and keep her safe.

The first few weeks at the International Academy at Cobble Hill had been a frenetic blur of trying to fit in, catch up, and keep their necessary lies down to a minimum so they wouldn't be caught out. It was quickly apparent that the people here were different. Way different. Budding geniuses mostly, extremely competitive – especially with a rival school by Shawnigan Lake – and Genie just couldn't get used to it. She cursed Denis often. He could have at least found out what kind of place he was sending them to. If you misbehaved or had an attitude problem their idea of punishment was forbid you from going to the library for a week or making you do fifty laps around the sports field. She'd had to do laps for a whole morning for forgetting to bring in her homework the previous week. It was like a prison camp – and miles from anywhere. No one even watched TV. Beta-testing new computer games was actually on the curriculum and she seemed to be the only person who didn't get it. It was bad enough she had been considered a freak back in Spurlake for not spending five hours a day on Facebook, but here – they were obsessed. The others had adapted quickly to the situation. She seemed to be the only one who hadn't taken to the place.

Getting used to their stupid new names had been particularly hard. Rhiannon, for example. Why of all names had Denis picked Rhiannon for her? Learning to spell it the same way twice was even harder than saying it. Renée loathed being Astra – and Rian was no Henry, that was for sure. Your pet dog might be Henry, but not Ri. It was easier for Cary, who only had to remember Christopher, and he'd quickly become Chris.

It was weird how serious it all was in Cobble Hill. Kids in Spurlake would do anything to avoid hard work or join stuff, but here, in this private college hidden away atop of a hill in the middle of nowhere, everyone was super ambitious, future leaders of the world – as the Principal, Hollis, told them ad nauseum.

Most of the kids lived at the academy; only a few were like them, residing in the student cabins because all the dorms were full. Some really rich kids commuted from Victoria every day, coming in chauffeur-driven limos. Living outside the school made them outsiders right away, adding another barrier to fitting in. Genie said a small prayer of thanks every night that they were lodging out of school. The kids who lived and breathed school twenty-four/seven were way too intense. They might as well have been aliens compared to kids she'd known before. Serious and bright, everyone studied hard, aiming to get into the world's best universities. They played sports like they were professionals; no one seem to slack at all. She'd heard rumours of drinking sessions on weekends someplace, but they weren't 'cool' enough to be invited yet and Genie didn't care for drinking anyway. Chandra, her self-appointed 'buddy', lived in Cowichan Bay, her father owned fishing boats, and Chandra was 'too bright – a true genius' to go to the local high school so her pa sent her to the academy, where her mind could be sharpened. It was true that Chandra was most likely a genius, but she knew zilch about little things like combing her hair or taking care of her clothes, or anything normal like watching TV or movies. She, like many others at this weird school, was obsessed by learning and reading, and you could test her on anything Plato or Copernicus had for supper a few thousand years ago and she'd even know which plate they used.

She had to admit that Cobble Hill was a good hideout from the Fortress and the twin evils of Reverend Schneider and Carson Strindberg. Their cover story was simple. Their previous school had been flooded – which was true enough; everyone knew about the Spurlake floods the previous summer – and because this mythical private school had been washed away with huge loss of life, there was no one to check the facts with. If anyone asked, they would roll their eyes and say stuff like 'Can't deal with it yet, please don't ask . . .' It generally worked. No one liked to talk about death. Not here, anyway, in perky, squeaky-clean, 'I'm a genius' academy.

Ri and Cary seemed to love it though. Renée had adapted well too, but it just didn't suit Genie. Too serious, too remote and, she felt – and this was the crux of her feelings – that day by day Rian was withdrawing from her. The others too, but Rian in particular. He took school seriously. He'd always been more interested in study than her, but he took sports seriously too and being on the basketball team meant he practically lived in the gym.

Cary was on a science team and he and some geeky others were working on a 'secret' project that had him so obsessed he sometimes slept in the lab. Renée came home, kept her company in the evenings, but she'd suddenly developed a passion for design and talked so much about textiles and chairs it nearly drove Genie mad. She didn't know one Eames chair from another and couldn't care less; she found that her thoughts wandered when Renée talked about them and she got mightily offended. Who would have thought Renée could be passionate about chairs? She'd planned a whole career with *Elle Décor* already.

Chandra didn't think Genie should be at the academy at all. In tests Genie pretty much came last, even with coaching from Chandra. She just didn't have any interest in science or maths and the only area she was good in, art, no one had any respect for apparently, even though it was boasted about in the brochure. Anyway, it was more about art history and writing essays about artists than sketching and drawing. She was sure Rosetti was terrific, and she could just about tell the difference between Monet and Manet now, but none of this fitted in with Genie Magee – aged sixteen, fugitive teleporter. She was at Cobble Hill for Rian and that was all. And yes he loved it there – a little too much. She felt neglected. He'd saved her life, but now she was beginning to think he didn't care so much about her any more. They were all so absorbed by Cobble Hill and all it had to offer; it was like they were students in a cult. You had to do what everyone else was doing or what – leave? (She had seriously thought about it.) She was down for volunteering on the literacy programme at the K-5 elementary school nearby but so far hadn't quite made it there.

Which left the forest behind the house. You can tell a forest anything and it won't talk back. The forest was important for her sanity, sure, but it had taken a special place in all their lives when they had got their first power utility bill.

Denis, never once heard from again since they had fled

Whistler, had set up the fund that paid the school and rent, but he'd clearly not noticed they had to pay for the utilities – and it had been pretty much freezing ever since they had got there. They'd switched the boiler off the day they got the first bill. Now they showered at the gym in school instead. Genie had discovered the forest was more than just a refuge, but also a source of firewood. Now she had a good excuse to go every day with her basket and little saw to pick up logs and haul them back. It was never a chore. She loved being in the woods and it restored some equilibrium in the cabin as she kept it clean and warm and welcoming from when they all came home from school. At least, she hoped they appreciate her efforts. But no one ever said anything. Maybe they thought house elves lit the fire each evening and kept it going.

Though December had been mild, by late January it had begun to freeze hard and seemed stuck there behind a wall of high pressure, so cold the trees were reluctant to bud and nature seemed to stand still. Unseasonable, they said it was; the island was supposed to be warmer than the mainland.

Genie was out gathering logs, as usual, missing Moucher – which she did all the time – and wondering what Marshall and Max were doing back on the farm. Her life there had only been brief and sometimes filled with terror, but she'd found herself there and always wished she'd had longer. Now she was lost again.

She wanted to write to Marshall but she knew she couldn't risk it. It still wasn't safe. She sent one letter only when they arrived but had never given her address. It was ridiculous to miss a dog so much, but she did, and a sense of trust – Marshall had been the only adult she'd ever had faith in.

She exhaled and a cloud of steam spread out before her. It was getting colder. Pine needles felt crunchy underfoot and she stooped to pick up some large cones when she spotted a good length of branch that had fallen. She smiled. Score. She withdrew her saw from where it hung inside her coat and set to cutting the branch up into manageable sections. She was getting practised at this now and enjoyed the effort. Working up a sweat in the forest was good for her and this would be enough to keep them warm for two days. She truly was 'Guardian of the Fire' as Cary had christened her the first day she had hauled home logs.

She stood up, proud of her handiwork, and stashed the logs in her basket, leaving some aside for the next day. The last of the evening light filtered through the trees and she had a sudden urge to capture the moment. She dragged her sketchbook out from under her coat and leaned up against a tree to sketch the bulging basket, the golden light on the ground and tightening of the air, as it grew ever colder.

Her pencil worked quickly – she knew she had just moments to capture this before it faded to grey. She felt a keen satisfaction as it took shape. Mr Duckworth, the art tutor, had told her that she'd make a very good illustrator and it was the first inkling she had ever had of a career – a job she'd very much like to have. She'd known quite quickly that she didn't want to be an 'artist', but an illustrator, someone who could bring a kids' book to life maybe, that was serious, right? A living? Something worthwhile, something Ri could respect, perhaps? She hadn't mentioned it to him; she didn't think he was very interested in her sketchbook, didn't really think he thought much about her future. His maybe, but never hers.

She suddenly felt she wasn't alone. A small breath cloud on the periphery of her vision caught her eye. Her eyes left the page. A grey wolf was staring at her, sitting on his haunches in the golden light, his beautiful golden-yellow eyes staring at her with intensity. He was sitting absolutely still and quickly Genie began to add him to her picture. He was young, his fur was thick in differing blends of pure white to grey and brown, the sunlight catching the tips of the fur and giving it a kind of halo effect. Either way he was immaculate, and breathing short breaths but clearly not afraid of her. (She did think perhaps *she* should be afraid but he didn't look at all threatening.) Perhaps he lived nearby or was out seeking a mate; it would soon be that time of year to find one. It didn't look lost, just curious. This was the first time she'd ever seen a wolf up so close. It looked quite healthy and had an impressive long muzzle.

'You make a good model,' she told the animal. 'Moucher could never sit still for a second.'

The wolf continued to stare at her, his nose twitching, subtly sniffing her out. It showed no aggression, probably surprised to find her in its domain.

'Want to see?'

Genie turned the sketchbook round for the animal to look. His eyes barely shifted. She had no idea as to whether it could distinguish between her and the sketchbook but she smiled encouragingly anyway.

'It's cold,' she told him. 'I guess one of us has to make a move.'

It was at that exact moment she felt a flake of snow land and dissolve on her bottom lip. She looked across the forest and saw a wave of snow falling between the trees. It stole the sun with it. Silently, snow was falling all around her now. She had a sudden feeling of elation.

She looked back, but the wolf had gone. But there he was, captured in her sketchbook. She smiled to herself, quickly folding the book away from the snowflakes. Her first wolf and in the woods, no less. She smiled to herself that she'd been lucky not to be wearing anything red.

'Stay safe,' she called out in case it was still nearby. She buttoned up her coat again, just slightly regretting that she'd only had a pencil to capture the scene; the golden light had been so beautiful and the fur so luminous.

She bent down to pick up the basket and saw the snow was settling fast. She liked snow. At least the first fall. Not if it lingered for weeks and grew ugly, but the first day of a snowfall she loved the total transformation of everything.

She hefted the heavy basket, heaving it up on to her shoulder, the way Marshall had taught her to carry it. She imagined herself as an old-fashioned Christmas card. The peasant women bringing home the firewood in the deep snow in winter. It put a happy smile on her face.

That's when she saw the blood. A body lying impaled on a sharp tree stump. She stood absolutely still and blinked. It looked a lot like Cary. She inhaled sharply, took a step towards him and it was gone. She blinked again, breathing heavily, her heart thumping loudly in her chest. There was nothing. Just the forest. No blood.

Nothing. Just silent snow falling on cedar. A vision. She carried on walking. She'd had no visions since she had arrived. She didn't know whether to be scared or relieved that her gift hadn't completely abandoned her. Nevertheless – why now? Why had it returned now? Her heart began to beat nervously.

She emerged from the forest on to the narrow path that ran behind the small settlement – remnants of a holiday resort that had long ago gone broke in the sixties. Her boots were crunching crisp fresh snow underfoot. It was settling well – this snow was here to stay. She was thinking that everyone would be real pleased to see the fire tonight.

She frowned as she considered the bloody vision. The body impaled on a tree stump. A warning, clearly. She'd have to ask Cary what he was doing. He'd been so secretive of late. Ever since he'd joined the science club. Their tutor, Mr Briskin, looked like a spy. He walked on his toes and seemed suspicious of everything. He'd be a joke if he weren't so revered by the science geeks, who sang his praises all the time. He'd had no time for Genie at all. She was 'scientifically illiterate' apparently. She didn't care.

If what Cary was doing was dangerous, she had to stop him. He would have to listen. He knew her gifts. Surely he would listen.

She heard a dog bark in someone's backyard and the

hairs on her neck rose just a little. It sounded so like Moucher and tugged at her heart. She looked back – had a bad feeling now. Something was about to happen. She needed to be inside.

Her cabin fence was just fifty metres ahead now. There was nothing to fear. Just spooked herself with the vision, that's all.

Renée was suddenly standing at the gate looking for her – no coat. She seemed to be anxious, waiting for her. She was staring up at the snow in wonder.

'Hi. You're home early. I haven't got the fire going yet,' Genie called out.

Renée looked pale, definitely worried.

'What? Something's happened, hasn't it?'

'It's Cary. He's been hurt. He's been taken to Nanaimo General.'

Genie set down the basket and Renée took the other side.

'How? When?'

'He was flying. Don't ask me. A kid told me and said it was a secret. He was injured flying.'

'Flying? And you believed that?' It sounded preposterous, but then again, hadn't she just seen him lying in a pool of blood?

'Why would anyone make it up? He's hurt, Genie. I

tried calling the hospital but they wouldn't tell me anything. They didn't seem to have heard of him even. I know he went there.'

Genie lifted the basket with Renée and they carried it into the house together. She was thinking about her vision again. Cary impaled upon a tree.

'Where was he hurt?'

'Back of the school, in the woods. The kid said there was a lot of blood. Rian's gone to find out more. Said we have to stay here. He'll phone.'

Genie nodded. She set the basket down, nearly slipping as she was off balance. She felt annoyed with herself. That vision had come late. What use a vision that comes after the event? Absolutely pointless if you can't warn someone.

'I'm sorry, Renée. You must be really upset.'

Renée shrugged. 'It's not like before, y'know, but I'm worried for him, not knowing, right? You OK? You look pale.'

'Help me make the fire, all right?'

Renée nodded. 'You do look really spooked, though.'

'Just cold, that's all. Hadn't realized how long I'd been out there. Flying, huh?' Genie asked. 'You didn't know anything about it?'

Renée shrugged. 'Well, he hasn't grown wings. I think we might have noticed.'

Later with still no news from Rian, Genie sat by her log fire warming her toes. Renée had prepared something for supper, now slowly baking under the fire grate. They hadn't really talked much about Cary at all, which Genie found strange. They still didn't know anything and she knew Renée cared for Cary, or at least used to. Cary, like Rian with herself, had neglected Renée for weeks, but . . . maybe she was just worried. Renée sometimes liked to share, sometimes liked to be quiet.

Genie took out her sketchbook and appraised her afternoon's work. The wolf looked so real, so intense, and so curious. The background still needed filling in; however, she felt she'd captured it just right as it stared at her. It made her feel she had at least accomplished something with her day.

She wanted to send it to Marshall. He'd like it. She hated not being able to communicate with the one person she could trust. It was frustrating.

It was ridiculous to feel so alone when she had Rian lying beside her every night. It had been her dream for a whole year to be able to do just that. Now she was living with him. She had everything she wanted.

But.

There should be no buts.

But – sometimes, quite often now, she wondered if he still loved her.

'Your cell's ringing,' Genie called out to Renée.

'I left it in the bathroom,' she yelled, dashing out of the kitchen. 'Are the potatoes ready?' she called back.

Genie poked at the potatoes wrapped in tin foil under the fire grate with the veggie casserole. Another cost saving. They baked potatoes and just about anything they could under the fire grate now. That first utility bill had been painful and taken most of their money.

Renée came back with the phone and handed it to her. 'For you.'

'Another half-hour for the potatoes, I think,' Genie said. 'Ri?'

'Chandra. Who's Ri?'

'Oh hi.' Her buddy, her mentor, her pain in the butt.

'You still don't have your own phone?' Chandra asked.

'Just trying to save the environment one phone at a time, Chandra. You hear anything about . . . er . . . Chris?' (She nearly said 'Cary' and bit on her lip; when was she going to remember their fake names?)

'That the kid who got injured today?'

'Yeah.'

'No. I heard he flew right through the science-lab window.'

408

Genie's eyebrows almost flipped. 'Flew through a window?'

'Principal is mad as hell. It's Governor's Day next month and that stupid window is like an antique or something.'

'It is? Uh – what exactly is Governor's Day?'

'Oh yeah, you don't know. Well, every year they invite the school governor into the school to give prizes and scholarships for university and stuff. I'm giving a speech. Dad said I have to make sure they notice me.'

Genie had already noted that Chandra did everything her father told her to do.

'What's the speech about?'

'The importance of observation.'

'Huh?'

'In science.'

'Oh yeah, science.'

'So, like, who was the most important – I mean, the most famous person who used observation? I just don't know who to—'

'Chandra, you're not thinking. Darwin. You can't go wrong.'

Chandra squealed with delight. 'Darwin, you're right, you're right, natural selection. Thank you, Rhiannon, thank you. You're the best.' She rang off.

It was at that precise moment that Genie realized that Chandra had no friends. If she was willing to call *her* for advice, she couldn't have any friends at all.

'What?' Renée asked.

'Cary flew out of a window. The science-lab window.'

Renée stared at her with astonishment. 'Ouch. That was stained glass, right?'

Genie nodded. 'Not any more.'

Renée felt dizzy. Cary was not going to be OK. She'd almost dismissed this flying story as nonsense, but it was now looking true.

'What was he working on, Renée? Is it such a secret?'

'He didn't want anyone to know. But he and the team were working on—'

The front door slammed open and Rian was standing there, covered from head to foot in snow.

'Anti-gravity,' Rian said, letting a flurry of snow in with him. 'He was working on anti-gravity.'

36

Escape Route

Rian sat opposite her in front of the log fire, his wet socks steaming as they hung from a peg from the mantelpiece. She looked at him, wishing she could read his thoughts. He'd had a haircut, really short now – all the basketball team had the same cut with a V cut into the back: their tag. She missed his messy blond hair, she missed almost everything about him now. Cobble Hill seemed to have changed him so much in such a short time. He'd grown so serious. She massaged his ice-cold feet; he'd walked miles from the highway to get back home – his ride wouldn't risk driving on the snow-covered side road in case they got stuck.

They'd eaten in silence. He'd been too cold to say anything until he thawed out, and Renée had been upset that no one had thought to call her the moment Cary had the accident. She would like to have gone to the hospital too.

'I don't understand what happened, Ri, but I'm glad you went with him to the hospital. He must

411

have been scared.'

Rian shrugged. 'It was the teaching staff who were scared stiff – you just knew they were thinking about how much his father would be suing the academy for.'

Genie nodded. 'He probably would, if he even knew Cary was alive.'

'And that complicated things too,' Rian explained. 'They want to write to his parents. I don't know what address they have. I think we said his parents were missionaries in Africa and couldn't be reached, but I'm not sure. Denis handled that stuff. But they were relieved. It gives them time to think up a good story to give them.'

Genie frowned. 'But what *is* that story, Ri?'

Renée came to join them, kneeling beside Genie and putting out her hands to warm them. It was cold in all the other rooms without heating. 'Yeah, what is that story, Rian?'

Rian looked at her with surprise. 'You're his girlfriend – didn't he tell you?'

Renée snorted. 'I know you don't pay much attention around here, but in case you haven't noticed I sleep in my own room. Cary only used to come back to shower and he does that at school now. I haven't seen him for over a week, at least. He was obsessed with winning the Governor's Prize.'

Genie turned her head. 'What is it with this Governor's Day stuff? Why is everyone so worked up about it? I can't believe how competitive this place is – it's scary.'

Rian shrugged again, looking at her with an unfriendly gaze. 'Maybe *you* should start taking things more seriously, Genie. It's about scholarships, not prizes. Winning team gets a four-year scholarship to university – it's worth thousands. Even the runners-up get a year paid.' He looked at Genie directly. 'I can't believe you aren't even in a team already. We're at one of the best schools in B.C. It makes a difference – and you act like you don't care.'

Genie poked at a log, watching a shower of sparks rise up the chimney.

'We don't need scholarships, do we? I thought we were just hiding out – playing safe. You said we mustn't draw attention to ourselves. But – anti-gravity? You don't think *that* will get someone's attention?'

Rian pursed his lips. He didn't like it when he had his own words quoted back at him.

'Cary badly wanted a scholarship,' Renée stated. 'He wants a career in science. I thought he'd been superglued to the science lab. They're all as obsessed as each other. I met them, all dysfunctional geeks who looked at me like I was an alien.'

'You really think high-school kids can invent anti-gravity?' Genie asked. 'I mean – Cary's smart but . . .'

Rian looked at her with a puzzled expression. 'Cary's probably a genius – so are the other kids. It's not like Spurlake any more. We're with the brightest kids in the country, Genie. If Cary says he did it, he did it.'

'He did it?' Renée queried. 'You're saying he did it?'

'Two seconds. But it's just a start.'

'Wait? He spoke to you? When? I thought he was in a coma. You said a tree had punctured his chest and—'

Rian withdrew his feet from Genie and sat hunched over his knees. 'He's broken one arm and his left leg and he's got serious puncture wounds from his chest down to his groin. You try falling from the top of a giant spruce and see what it feels like.'

It corresponded to her vision. Almost exactly. She'd seen where he'd fallen. So weird and so stupidly late, but then again how would she warn someone who no longer even talked to her.

'He actually told you he'd done it?' Genie asked.

'In the ambulance – when they stabilized him. He said he was going to surprise everyone with the one thing every kid had ever wanted.'

'What was that?' Renée asked.

'A hover board.'

414

Renée blinked, not understanding, but Genie got it – she laughed. '*Back to the Future Part Two*. Oh my God – a hover board? Anti-gravity. Now it makes sense.'

Rian nodded. 'The team would make billions. Every kid in the world would want one.'

Renée couldn't believe it. 'Cary was obsessed by that film. I thought he wanted to invent a time-machine. It was the hover board he was interested in? What year was that supposed to be anyway?'

'2015 – I saw all three films back to back when I was like ten and still can't figure out how you run a car on old bananas,' Genie said smiling. 'But I *really* wanted a hover board.'

'So you *did* know what he was working on,' Rian pointed out to Renée. 'You just didn't ask the right questions.'

'Yeah, well, I knew he wasn't going to invent a time-machine. I mean, that would be crazy, right? Some things are just impossible.'

Rian shook his head. 'Nothing is impossible. You were teleported, remember. You tried telling anyone? You think anyone would actually believe you? Ever?'

Renée shook her head. They never talked about it to anyone. It was their secret and their pain. As long as the Fortress still existed, they could never talk about it – to anyone.

'What's your team working on?' Rian asked Renée.

Renée looked annoyed. 'You know you aren't supposed to ask.'

Genie shook her head. 'That's what I'm talking about. *We're* supposed to be a team. We shouldn't have secrets between us.'

'Academy rules. Each team has to keep it secret to prevent plagiarism. You'd know that if you were in a team,' Rian told her, his tone harsh to Genie's ears.

'I'm in *this* team. At least, I was,' Genie muttered. She was sensing it was a lost cause though.

Renée sighed. 'Well, we can't compete with a hover board. We're designing a multi-function chair. You know. One you could take anywhere.'

Rian pretended to look interested. 'A chair.'

'Ultimate chair,' Renée said, somewhat defensively. 'I didn't tell you that.'

Genie sighed. It made no sense to her at all. 'You guys take this stuff way too seriously.'

Rian shook his head. 'No, we don't. But *you* have to. You need to belong to a team, Genie. We have to belong here, fit in. I think you should make more of an effort. People notice if you aren't in a team.'

Genie said nothing. He was being openly hostile to her now. It was true then – all her instincts were right on this – he was officially falling out of love with her. She looked back down the corridor. Pity they didn't have another spare room.

'Yeah, you should be in a team before they force you into one. Governor's Day is like just over a month away and it's all about teams,' Renée told her. 'I'm serious, you don't want to be stuck with the lemon heads.'

'Lemon heads?'

'They suck.'

'Oh.'

Genie took her hot chocolate and drank it down, not looking at either of them. Her stomach was doing butterflies. She couldn't believe it. Rian didn't love her any more. It hit her like a tidal wave.

Did that mean he'd met someone else? One of the bitches that were always hanging out watching the basketball team? Well, if so, she wasn't going to humiliate herself. If he didn't love her any more she wasn't going to fight with any dumb blonde over his stinking sneakers.

'And you need to pull your grades up,' Rian was telling her. 'If you flunk out it will be your own fault. You can't just waste your time in the woods being a hippy. Life is tough, Genie.'

Genie bit her bottom lip. That clinched it. It was official. The one thing she loved, the woods, he hated. He

417

had never once wanted to see her sketches. Well, let him gather firewood and keep the fire burning, see how long he liked being cold. Even if she had to sleep on the sofa she wasn't going to sleep in their room ever again. It was over. She didn't mind underachieving; she knew she wasn't ever going to be brilliant at academic studies – it just wasn't her. She'd do the minimum to pass, but it seemed that everything they had been through together meant nothing. That's what made her mad. How swiftly romance dies.

She left them to it, walking down the unlit corridor towards the bathroom.

In the dark she turned too early and wandered into Cary's room by mistake. Annoyed, she turned to leave but her eye caught sight of a flashing light under the bed. She went to investigate.

It was a cellphone. Didn't even know he had one. A video message had arrived. She was trying to figure out how to turn it off when the message launched. Cary laughing towards the camera in the science lab. She stared as it played the scene. He was standing on a skateboard, pretending to surf, and the geeks were laughing in the background somewhere. Someone else was counting down.

'Five, four, three, two, one, ignition.'

The skateboard glowed and rose up almost fifteen centimetres. There were shouts of joy as Cary tried to balance.

'It's peaking!' some other kid yelled suddenly. 'Get off, get off . . .'

Suddenly Cary was pitched straight up, went right out of view it was so fast and the guy with the camera phone tried to keep up, catching the falling glass as Cary had already smashed through the stained-glass window.

Kids were yelling, screaming – glass was falling.

It ended.

Genie switched the phone off and put it back under his bed, then groped her way back out of the room towards the bathroom.

The hover board had worked. For two whole seconds. Way to go, Cary. Then it had damn nearly killed him. She wondered how he had done it. Rian was right. Those kids could make millions from it – if they figured it out.

And of course that's what this team stuff was all about. She got it. Competition. Bright kids loved a challenge. But what kind of team did a girl with a sketchbook join? Where were the big bucks in that? She was going to be put with the lemon heads, for sure. She realized that she really didn't want that.

* * *

Genie slept on the sofa that night, watching the dying embers of the fire, listening to the wind outside piling the snow up again the doors and windows. Her heart felt like ice now. She'd been so safe in the bubble Rian had put around her. She didn't know what she'd done wrong. She hadn't changed. Her hair had almost grown back. OK, she had tried to dye it black because she didn't want people to see the huge white streak she'd got from the teleport, but that wasn't enough of a reason not to love her, was it? She didn't get this competitive stuff, she didn't want to invent anything and make a million, or even go to university, although she would have helped Rian get through it and work jobs to help pay for it. Art school would have been nice. There was a lot to learn, new techniques and learning to draw with software, that would be useful, but what had she done to make him stop loving her? Why? When did it happen? Who was she? What had this other girl got that she didn't? She barely slept. And two rugs weren't enough; she had to get up and put on her coat to stay warm.

The worst of it was, he didn't even notice. He didn't come looking for her and make her come back to bed; he hadn't even noticed she wasn't there. Was probably relieved. He went for a run in the snow the moment he woke up and didn't even say hi. Just how had this happened so suddenly?

Genie barely touched her breakfast and then trudged up the hill in the snow. It was no longer magical white stuff. All the magic had been taken away. Her heart was like lead and she was kind of glad it was so cold because she couldn't feel anything.

Chandra met her on the way to class and told her all about her Darwin research.

She was all excited and Genie noticed she was wearing odd boots. How could she not notice one was black and the other brown? Chandra had tied her hair in bunches today and talked so loud and without interruption, Genie just let it all wash over her. She had a sudden thought that if she disappeared no one would care, or notice. It wasn't a good thought.

She got the bad news at eleven in break. 'You're on the lemon-head team,' Chandra told her, trying to be sympathetic. 'I saw it on the notice board. Bad luck.'

Genie made her way to the big-screen TV monitor in the rec room and sure enough saw her name, Rhiannon, on the notice of Governor's Teams. Six girls and a guy. Lemon heads – the kids no one wanted to pick for their team. First meeting fixed at two p.m. in the reading room. Genie's heart sank.

After class she went looking for Rian. She knew he

would be playing basketball at lunch. He was a creature of habit. She looked in at the court from the viewing gallery and sure enough there were three girls in non-regulation short skirts watching and giggling. She didn't know who they were but all three were hot. It kind of confirmed her worse fears. She ducked out in case Ri saw her. Even that was stupid. Just weeks ago he would have been upset if she hadn't looked in on him. What had she done so wrong?

She ate her lunch alone. Renée didn't appear. She was probably with her team discussing furniture. How do you even begin to get interested in chairs? she mused. As she nibbled her veggie sandwich she realized that she should have seen all this coming. She'd been eating lunch by herself since the start of term now and never even thought about it.

The snow had stopped, but it was bitterly cold outside. Wouldn't last, she was told. Spring comes early on Vancouver Island; this was just a weather freak show.

She wished she was outside making a snowman or on a toboggan herself, but she noticed no one was having fun. Everyone was in his or her teams, making plans, discussing things – these kids weren't kids any more. They didn't know what they were missing.

Genie went outside and stood admiring the way the

snow had formed a pattern on the arbutus trees. It was beautiful. She wanted to sketch them but it was just too cold to make her fingers work. She committed it to memory instead. She'd sketch it later; try to get the light just right. She was just about to turn and head on back in for the dreaded team meet when she saw the wolf again.

It was watching her from the edge of the playing field. It had to be the same animal. She waved. Stupid. Who waves to a wolf? It turned and left, ducking between the trees. Had it been waiting for her? Why was it there?

'You coming?'

Genie looked up and there was Mrs Finney – Head of the English department and her team monitor. It would have been her that put Genie (Rhiannon) on the list.

'I liked your story about the woods, Rhiannon. It was full of really well-observed texture and quite sad. Good writing.'

Genie smiled. She didn't know that she had marked them yet, let alone knew who she was. She never said anything in class and Mrs Finney never called on her to answer.

'I kind of feel for trees, I guess,' Genie said, trying to force a smile.

'You certainly do. I wish there were more like you.

Come on, let's see if we have any more passionate souls in our team.'

Inside the wood-panelled reading room Genie's heart sank. This was exactly a group of perfect rejects. The angry, the mumblers, the Little Miss Attitude and the 'I'd rather die than ever speak to anyone' group.

Joy. Rian was right. She should have tried to join a team before this happened. She doodled whilst the tension grew in the room.

Miss Finney was going to try her best to get them to talk. They sat in a semi-circle around the huge conference table and you could feel her heart sink. This was going to be tough.

'Governor's Day is all about teams coming up with ideas that can benefit the school, yourselves and of course your futures. You all know this. Each one of you I just know has a special talent or skill – so first, let's try to get to know each other a little.'

She turned to Zara, the one with attitude and cropped hair.

'Zara, what special skill do you have?' Miss Finney asked breezily.

Zara scowled at her and leaned forward, speaking particularly slowly. 'I make people feel *very* uncomfortable.'

Miss Finney laughed with embarrassment, then

shivered slightly. It was as if someone had opened a window to let the snow inside.

'Well, Zara, I happen to know you have a very high IQ – it should help us all come up with a theme for our research.'

'Yeah, manic depression. There's a theme for you. Wrap it up and sell it to the masses,' Zara said with a sly smile, which died immediately, as she went back to sulking.

Miss Finney began to clutch her head. Genie could feel it, Zara really could make people feel uncomfortable. It was truly a special talent.

'And your skills, Sophia?'

Sophia was hiding behind her mousey hair, hoping no one could see her. Genie looked across the room at her and sensed she had a talent – a gift even. She could feel it.

'Sophia,' Zara stated with an icy voice, 'would rather not share her special skills. I make people uncomfortable, she—'

'Don't say it,' Sophia shouted, still hiding behind her hair.

'Knows why,' Zara finished, letting a cruel chuckle escape.

Genie really hoped Mrs Finney didn't ask her anything.

'And you, Mr Ackroyd.' She turned to the boy,

quickly giving up on Sophia. 'Pierre, what can you bring to this party?'

Genie had only briefly glimpsed this boy before. Pierre Ackroyd. His father was rich. At Christmas he'd come to the island to fetch him in a Maserati, which all the boys swarmed around. For a nanosecond Pierre was popular, but it soon passed. This was only the second time she'd seen him, even though he was supposed to be in her history class.

Pierre mumbled something but none of them could hear it.

'What? Speak up. We have to build a team around something. You have something for us? A special skill for—'

'For projectile vomiting,' someone said. 'I've seen him throw up. No one could beat it, Miss Finney. Nine metres, someone said. Honest. A record.'

Everyone laughed. Pierre turned bright red and fled the room.

Miss Finney wasn't amused and rubbed her head.

'I can draw a little,' Genie said, to make things easier. 'I can't see us build a team around that.'

Miss Finney was annoyed. She snatched Genie's sketchbook from her, not appreciating that Genie was doodling, then stared at the page. She looked surprised.

426

'You drew this just now?'

Genie frowned. 'It's a just a doodle, I didn't mean . . .'

Mrs Finney was clearly astonished. Genie had drawn the entire group and Mrs Finney clutching her head, all with uncanny accuracy. She looked up at Genie with a mixture of annoyance and pride.

'Come and see me in my office after this, Rhiannon. I'll hold on to this meanwhile.'

'But . . .'

Genie seethed. That was *her* sketchbook, *her* lifeline. It had everything in there – a whole month of sketches – she couldn't confiscate that, she couldn't. She hadn't done anything wrong.

'Rhiannon's in t-r-o-u-b-l-e,' Zara trilled, pleased that no progress was being made.

'Is there no one here with a single idea?' Mrs Finney sighed. 'Your loving parents are paying God knows how many thousands a year to send you here. Do you not feel you owe them something, a little effort?'

'My father would pay double if you'd keep me here in the vacations too,' Zara stated. 'Apparently I make him uncomfortable too.'

Genie could believe it. She was annoyed about her sketchbook. Everything had gone wrong now. Rian didn't love her, Renée didn't seem to care, Cary was like broken

427

in pieces and now her sketchbook was confiscated. She looked out of the window and saw a smashed car on the road. Which was impossible – they only had a view of the top of trees. A bright-blue Mini smashed and a dead horse or deer . . .

'You've gone very white, Rhiannon. Are you OK?' Mrs Finney asked.

'Seen a ghost?' Zara asked, then laughed.

Genie turned her head. She didn't know if this was the future or it had already happened. Last thing Genie remembered was Sophia screaming.

'You're awake?'

Genie blinked. She was lying on a chaise longue in Mrs Finney's office.

Mrs Finney was thumbing through her sketchbook. She was smiling at her. Snow was falling again outside and it was curiously quiet.

'You are quite an artist, Rhiannon. Mr Duckworth tells me that he thinks you should be an illustrator.'

Genie said nothing. She felt quite light-headed.

'I should thank you. You fainting like that, got me out of that hell. That Zara makes my head pound and as for the others—'

Genie struggled to speak. 'I don't want to be

428

in that team,' she rasped.

Mrs Finney laughed. 'God, I wouldn't permit it even if you begged me to let you in. Every year there's always a group just like them.'

'But . . . I have to be in a team,' Genie protested, but very quietly.

'You're in a team of one. There's no one to touch your artistic skills. I am entering you in the special criteria category. That sketch of Sophia, with her little pixie ears poking up between her hair – priceless. I envy you, girl. I always wanted to draw. Never wanted to teach. Just be an artist.'

Genie felt herself relaxing. She wasn't in trouble.

She suddenly remembered her vision.

'Mrs Finney. Can I ask if you drive a Mini? A blue one?'

'That's Mr Calvino's car. Drives too fast, if you ask me.'

Genie nodded. She didn't know him but guessed he was a teacher.

'Why?'

'Do you . . . I had a premonition.' Genie closed her eyes. She didn't want to do this but it would be on her conscience if she said nothing.

'So Sophia said.'

Genie opened her eyes with surprise and sat up. 'What did she say, exactly?'

Mrs Finney stared at Genie a while.

'You're quite special aren't you, Rhiannon. Not at all surprised with a name like that. Was my favourite song, you know – 'Rhiannon'. Stevie Nicks. I was about ten and sang it all the time until my mother used to beat me to stop. That's another thing, of course; I wished I could sing. Never wanted to be a teacher at all, I suppose.'

'What did Sophia say, Mrs Finney?' Genie insisted.

'You saw something terrible. She said you could see the future.'

Genie laughed. It sounded fake even to herself.

'I know Sophia is strange and for that matter Zara too, but I know you saw something and I happen to believe very strongly in premonitions.'

'You do?'

'I do. I go to see a fortune teller in Victoria once a year for "check-ups". Don't tell anyone and I won't tell what you saw. OK?'

Genie nodded. 'Then I won't tell you Mr Calvino crashes his car into a horse or deer. That's what I saw.'

Mrs Finney sat back in her chair and thought about that. 'Of course, there is the matter of telling him. Making him believe it.'

'Hide his keys, Mrs Finney. Don't let him drive home in the snow.'

'Can one truly intervene in fate? What do you know about fate?'

'I know that you can change it. My grandmother said "forewarned is forearmed".'

'Did she now.'

Mrs Finney seemed to contemplate that a moment. She looked at her watch.

'If I took you with me to the staff room and perhaps distracted Mr Calvino for a moment, do you think you could find his keys?'

Genie stood up. 'I will try.'

'And I will send him home in a cab. You didn't see any cabs in your vision?'

'No. It was very quick. Just an instant.'

Mrs Finney made her decision and pushed her chair back. 'The first part of madness is believing what you hear. The second is acting on it. Consider me mad, my dear, and, please, upon your honour, this is between us.'

'On my honour,' Genie replied.

Mr Calvino was ridiculously tall. Why was it that tall men bought small cars and small fat ones bought big cars? This was what Genie was thinking as she stole the keys. He didn't even seem to notice she was there. A common trait in teachers, she'd noticed.

431

She'd arranged to meet Mrs Finney back in her office. The door was locked. She had to stay outside in the corridor, she desperately wanted her sketchbook back.

'Still here? She must really hate you,' Zara said as she walked on by. She was dressed in a huge fake-fur coat with hood. Genie was almost envious; her own coat was useless in the snow.

'Do you know where I can find Sophia?' Genie asked.

Zara stopped suddenly and spun around. 'Don't. She's scared of you.'

'I . . .' Genie didn't know what to say to that.

'But I think you're OK. You should know that your boyfriend is bewitched by Louise Hunterson. I mean, you're cute, but she's a killer. Gets anything she wants. You don't look like a killer.'

Zara turned around again and walked away. This was truly her skill – sucking the life out of people and moving on.

Genie stood quite still. She had a name. Her instincts were correct. Rian had found someone else.

'We saved a life today, I hope,' Mrs Finney was saying as she approached from the other way. 'I already called a cab.'

She opened her door. Genie walked in behind her and gave her the keys. Mrs Finney gave her back her sketchbook in return. She was looking at Genie more carefully.

'The boy – the one you keep drawing. Is he your boyfriend?'

Genie could barely speak. 'Was.'

'Oh.'

'Mrs Finney?'

'Yes?'

'Shouldn't it be enough to love someone? I mean, why would he look at someone else?'

'And let you escape?'

'Yes.'

'Boys break hearts – they don't even think about it. And yes, my heart was broken once – twice actually. I have a husband now. There is a Mr Finney – a nice, generous, nine-handicap Mr Finney – who couldn't break my heart if he tried it with a crowbar. It remains broken. If yours is breaking now, I'm sorry. I have no magic words to make you feel better.'

Genie clutched her sketchbook close to her and kept back her tears.

'Thank you, Mrs Finney. Thank you for not lying to me.'

'Come and talk to me anytime. This is just between us.'

Genie shuffled towards the door. She just wanted to curl up and die but she had to go home, where *he* would be coming home to.

'And Rhiannon?'

'Yes, Mrs Finney?'

'Any boy who could break your heart doesn't ever deserve you. Remember that. Get home safe and we will discuss what you will draw for Governor's Day on Friday. OK? Go home and eat something before you disappear.'

Genie got out of the room, left the building, reached the outside and then cried. It was so cold her tears froze to her cheeks.

The wolf was waiting for her at the gates. She barely acknowledged it as it walked beside her all the way home, staying near, just occasionally checking that she was close by. Both were covered in snow now, alone with their thoughts.

Genie paused outside her cabin. It was dark. No one home. No one would have lit the fire. She went down on her knees and tentatively put a hand out towards the wolf. It turned away in fright and bolted towards the trees.

'Thank you,' Genie called out after it, wondering where it went, how it lived. Why it had waited for her? She had a wolf for protection now. How strange was that?

She headed towards the cabin. There were no lights on. It would be cold. She resolved not to make a fire. Let them feel as cold as her heart.

At some point Rian would be coming home, smelling of Louise, and she didn't know what to do about that at all. She had some honey toast, curled up on the sofa with the duvet around her and much to her surprise fell fast asleep.

Genie ate breakfast alone in the freezing cold cabin. Renée didn't appear to have come home; Rian certainly not. This was ridiculous. They had come here as friends for ever and now what was left? Absolutely nothing. Rian knew, more than anyone else on earth, all the terrible things that had happened to her in her life and he'd sworn to love her for ever. She had relied on that, took comfort in that, built her future around that.

Now it was nothing.

There was no cereal or oatmeal or milk. It had been Renée's turn to shop and she had forgotten, again. She had to make do with black tea. She hated black tea. It was still cold outside but not snowing at least.

She contemplated her French class that began at eight thirty followed by double physics and then world geography. She knew she was going to flunk all three. Geography could have been interesting – if only the teacher had some enthusiasm or talked about something that would grab her interest. Earthquakes maybe or ice ages but no, it was all about climate change and pollution and soil erosion and it was just too depressing. Some days she didn't even want to save the planet.

She resolved to go see Cary instead. He'd need a visitor.

She didn't think about how hard it would be to get there. She'd walk to the highway and hitch. Seemed like a good idea. Someone had to visit him; it could get very lonely in hospital.

She looked out for the wolf as she trudged down the road, the impacted snow easier to walk on where the cars and trucks had been driving, although slippery in parts. No wolf, no cars and no people. It was uncannily quiet save for the distant sound of a buzz saw, something that no rural area could be without, apparently. Always someone got to kill a tree. It was a long slow walk in the snow. Four or five miles at least and she wished she had warmer boots and a warmer coat. She thought of her snug blue ski jacket back home and then remembered that that too would be gone when the house was swept away in the flood. Everything was gone. Her entire existence. She was Rhiannon now – with two 'n's for some stupid reason.

She was glad the wolf wasn't around. She didn't want to lead it to the highway where people would try to shoot it. She wondered how rare it was for a lone wolf to be living in her patch of the woods or even attach itself to someone. That had to be really strange. She should Google it. Marshall would know. She briefly thought that she should keep going. Catch the ferry at Nanaimo, hitch all the way back to Spurlake and the farm and see Moucher. Stupid, idiotic idea, right? Who would hitch hundreds of kilometres just to hug a dog? No one. Nevertheless, she really wanted to. She needed that sense of security back. She wanted to belong to something, someone. Rian had snatched it all away and she felt sick to the stomach with uncertainty.

It was a milk truck on the way to Nanaimo that stopped for her. Hen Bay Farm – *purified twice to make it nice* it said on the truck. She recognized the driver and his funny scruffy goatee. He delivered the milk to the school twice a week and he was always anxious about the turn around in the school parking lot. How on earth he recognized her, she had no idea.

'Knew it was you right away. No one walks like you.'

He'd stopped about thirty metres ahead of her. She hadn't even had her thumb out, it was so cold. He had chains on the tyres and wore tinted specs over a very sad moustache. She guessed he was about fifty but could be ten years out. He was always smiley at least.

'You ain't running away, are you?' he asked as she climbed in and practically hugged the hot-air vents.

'Going to Nanaimo General. Friend had an accident.'

'Heard about that. Principal mad as hell about the window.'

Genie nodded turning her head a little; her ears were burning they were so cold. 'My friend flew right through it. His folks can't visit. Not fair to be alone in hospital when something like that happens.'

The man nodded. 'Name's Ben. Been in hospital when I broke my legs back in ninety-six. No fun when no one visits, that's for sure. That's what persuaded me to get me a wife on the interweb. She takes care of me good. Doesn't like me being home much but takes care of me good.'

A case of way too much information, but she had a ride and that was fine by her. He wouldn't try anything either since she was an Academy girl.

They slowed at the Koksilah turn off. There was an accident ahead.

The traffic was light, but there were enough cops and ambulances there that it had to be a major incident.

'We got to stop in Duncan to offload some, but then we'll be on our way again,' Ben told her as he sucked on a peppermint.

They had to take a wide berth to get round the smash.

Genie stared at the carnage with astonishment. A blue Mini was wrecked, a dead horse lay in a heap on the highway and some First Nation men were looking glum as they argued with the cops. The driver of the Mini was clearly badly injured, but looked as though she'd live. Genie felt sorry for the horse.

'They let the horses run free. They can't see the road in the snow. Can't blame the horse,' Ben remarked. 'Waste of a good horse.'

Not Mr Calvino's turn to die then. Also, obviously there was more than one blue Mini out there.

'You all right? It's a nasty accident, but she didn't die.'

'Need a hot chocolate, I think. I feel a bit faint.'

'I'll get you something in Duncan. Always stop at the Pancake House. They buy our milk.'

Genie looked at him with sudden appreciation. 'I'd really like to have pancakes. I can't remember the last time I had pancakes.'

He smiled broadly. 'Then you shall have them. You need feeding up. You're not one of those girls who starves themselves, are you? I never understood why anyone would voluntarily starve themselves. Wife's always on a diet.'

'I can't pay,' Genie told him. She had less than four dollars on her. That was pretty stupid on her part. She hadn't been thinking straight at all.

'My pleasure. But you'll have to eat 'em. I ain't buying pancakes if you're just going to stare at them.'

Genie was looking back at the accident as they finally pulled away. The horse had died, but who could warn a horse? She didn't especially know why her visions had come back to her but she was getting used to them again now. It was like meeting up with an old friend. She looked at Ben again and nodded. Food would be good. 'I'll eat them, Ben. I'll eat them all.'

37

A Last Gasp

'I'm telling you, miss, there's no boy called Christopher admitted yesterday.'

Genie wasn't accepting this, or the hard-faced woman staring at the computer screen in hospital reception.

'He had a broken arm, leg and puncture wounds. It would have been a big deal. I know he was brought here. He's an Academy student at Cobble Hill.'

The woman stared at Genie with unspoken hostility.

'I can only tell you what the screen says. You want me to call security? You're beginning to be a nuisance.'

Genie couldn't believe this. Rian had brought him. Had told her he was with him all the way to the ER. There was no other hospital.

'What about the name of the boy who brought him?' she countered.

'We don't keep that on file unless it's a gunshot wound.'

Genie looked away a moment, refusing to admit defeat.

'What if someone got it mixed up? Mistakes happen. It would have been an emergency. Look up his name anyway.' It was a long shot, but what if Cary had been semi-conscious or something and given them his real name. She was sure if she was knocked down and left for dead she'd never remember 'Rhiannon'. 'Please. One last look, then I'll give up. Check for Cary Harrison.'

The women puckered her lips into a nasty cat's bottom and entered the name, getting ready her 'I told you so' when: 'E Ward. But they won't let you in – that's severe trauma.'

Genie was already on her way to the elevator.

'Thank you,' she called back. The receptionist glared, almost hating being defeated like that.

On the way up Genie suddenly thought of what just happened. If Cary was registered under his own name, Rian must have known this. He was with him when he was admitted. What did he think he was doing? It put them all at risk. Cary was under eighteen. It meant they'd automatically call his parents and they didn't even know he was alive, probably even got his body back from the Fortress and . . . it was devastating.

She found her way on to the ward, checked all the rooms one by one and no one took a blind bit of notice of her. Nursing staff were drinking coffee at the workstation and someone was serving tea to the patients.

His name was on a piece of card on the door. He had

his own room, which surprised her until she saw he was hooked up to all kinds of machines and something that helped him breathe. It was pretty scary. His face was swollen, his right arm and left leg in plaster and she could only imagine how bad his torso was after being impaled on a tree.

Genie took off her coat and washed her face in the sink. She needed that. Drank a glass of water too. She realized that she was exhausted. Didn't know how; all she'd done was ride in a truck and walk a little.

'You look awful,' Cary rasped from his bed.

Genie turned with surprise and then laughed, so happy to hear his voice.

'You can speak?'

'A little. Punctured a lung, but I think they fixed it already. Can't move though. They want to replace my liver or something, damaged it beyond repair. Machine keeping me alive right now.'

'Serious? I guess it's too late to order a new liver from the Fortress huh,' Genie said, moving to the side of the bed and taking his good hand.

Cary squeezed it a little. His hand was warm, his temperature very high. She could see his eyes looked really spaced. He was on painkillers, she guessed. She could see now that he was very lucky to be alive, even if he did look a weird shade of yellow.

'I'm sorry, Genie.'

'Hey, I'm not the one in hospital.'

'I didn't mean that. They got my name.'

Genie nodded. 'It's on the door. How did that happen?'

'The DNA database. You, me, we're all on it. Chris is dead. Denis stole his name from a database of dead teens. Yours too. The moment they took my blood it told them everything about me. They already . . .' He coughed a little, spittle dribbling down his mouth. Genie got a tissue and dabbed his chin.

'They already called my parents. My mother will be in shock. It's going to cause problems for you at school too. Sorry.'

Genie looked at him and nodded. She understood. 'It's all going to unravel, right? They can find us now. I can't believe Rian didn't mention this.'

'My fault.'

Genie smiled shaking her head. 'No one's fault. Hey, you invented the hover board, Mr Genius. Can't take that away from you. I saw the video of your crash through the window. It's probably on YouTube already.'

Cary's face clouded. 'Get the flash drive out of the shoebox back at the cabin, Genie. Protect it with your life. All my calculations are on there.'

444

'You'll be back soon,' she countered, not quite following him.

Cary grew agitated. 'No, I won't. It's all going to turn to crap. Get the memory stick out of the shoebox and hide it good, right? Promise me.'

'I promise. Now sleep, you've set the machines off. Cary . . .'

An alarm began to ring and he blacked out. Genie knew nurses and doctors would pile in at any moment. She grabbed her coat and backed away from the room.

Sure enough, hospital staff came running.

Genie hovered nearby, pretending she'd just arrived.

'Is this Cary Harrison?'

'Not now. Wait,' a nurse shouted at her as she ran into the room.

Genie drifted towards some chairs in the corridor.

A doctor came running and someone with a crash cart.

Genie wished she hadn't upset him. He looked really bad. She shouldn't have come. Rian hadn't said he was this bad. Rian didn't seem to notice *anything* any more.

She walked over to a patient sitting in a dressing gown reading a magazine. 'Is there a phone I can use?'

'Far end of the corridor, one floor down. The one on this floor is out.'

Genie nodded and looked down the corridor. She had to phone Renée and warn her. But surely Rian knew. Why hadn't he said anything? Made no sense at all.

She couldn't help Cary now, but she had to protect herself and the others.

The elevator took her down one floor and sure enough there was a phone, only there was an angry woman in dreadlocks shouting at someone about money she was owed. She'd have to wait.

The view was of the car park. A gusting wind had got up and snow was blowing across the cars. She saw nothing. She realized now that their secret had always been incredibly vulnerable to this. Whether Cary, or Ri, or whomever; the moment one of them had an accident, the DNA database would have thrown up their identity. And who had access? Strindberg and the Fortress, that's who. They would have no choice now. They would have to leave Cobble Hill or face being discovered.

Poor Cary. How was he going to face his parents? How would they face him? What would he tell them? How would they cope with the idea of him being a replica? They would have buried him once already – or at least come to terms with his death. How could they face losing him twice? Would they even believe he was their son? And worse, her own mother would hear about it and then she would wonder where she was. God, it was all going to unravel fast.

At last the woman stopped screaming and slammed the phone down. Genie approached it with caution, wiping it with tissues and anti-germ gel from the corridor dispenser. Who knew what germs lurked in hospitals? She couldn't risk getting sick, that was for sure.

Renée didn't answer. It went straight to voicemail. Genie wasn't sure what to say; she hated leaving messages.

'They know Cary's name. Tell Ri. We have to leave Cobble Hill. A day's gone by already, Ren. Someone's going to come for us, I know it. Cary looks bad. Going to be here a long time. They called his folks in Spurlake already. I'm at the hospital.'

She put the phone down, paid two bucks for the pleasure of the call to a cell. Now she had nothing. She shivered. She resolved to go back up, check Cary one last time and hitch back. She realized now that she shouldn't have come. Renée should be here shedding tears, not her.

Upstairs in the ward it was quiet. She spotted the nurse who'd gone in to see to Cary and walked up to her. She looked up from writing her notes and sighed.

'You know Cary Harrison?' the nurse asked.

'At school with him. He's my best friend.'

'You know he's in bad shape, right?'

Genie nodded. 'His liver . . .'

'Yeah. And the rest. We need to know. Was he a suicide risk? I mean, how did he get like this?'

'Cary? Are you kidding? Didn't anyone tell you? He's a genius. It was an accident in the lab, sent him right through the window.'

'Through a window?'

'He didn't tell you? He fell like thirty metres or something.'

'He hasn't spoken to anyone. He can't speak with the tubes in his mouth.'

'But . . .' That made no sense. She'd just been talking to him.

'Look, he's not allowed visitors. In a week maybe, but he's in very bad shape, you understand? Critical. What's your name?'

'Rhiannon. Can I just see him before I go?'

'You can look. I need to know for his notes. Any allergies? Anything you know about his medical history? We left a message on his parents' phone, but they haven't got back to us yet.'

'He's pretty well, was . . . always well. Never known him sick. You sure he can't speak? I mean . . .'

'Certain.'

Suddenly the alarms went off again.

'That's him now. You really shouldn't be here, y'know.'

The nurse began to stand up, and down the corridor someone shot out of Cary's room.

'Excuse me, sir? Sir?'

The man kept on walking away from them. They both looked at each other. they knew something bad had just happened.

'Sir!' She pressed a button and alarms went off everywhere.

Genie stared in horror. She knew that back, that shape, that walk. She knew it very well. Her legs began to shake.

'Stop him,' Genie yelled. 'Stop him.'

The man broke into a run, heading for the emergency exit.

The nurse and Genie arrived at Cary's room. He was awkwardly collapsed on the bed, all the tubes ripped out of his body, all the monitors disconnected. Alarms were screaming all over. Genie couldn't bear to look and began to give chase.

'Call security,' she yelled back. 'Call for help.'

The emergency doors slammed open and the man raced through as yet more alarms were set off. The door slammed in Genie's face and she had to kick them open again.

She emerged into a dark landing with the lights on the

449

fritz. She could hear heavy footsteps running down the stairs and looked over the balustrade.

She only the saw the top of his head in the gloom, but she knew him, knew him well. Reverend Schneider had struck again. She felt sick and her legs almost gave way.

She heard his voice, that booming evil voice echoing back up the stairs.

'One down, three to go,' he was saying into a phone to someone.

Genie froze. *One down, three to go.* She was one of the three.

She couldn't get back on to the ward; the doors were shut fast. She was nervous about going down the stairs, scared to death in fact. She went down the stairs a little way but none of the lights were working and she just couldn't take a single step further. She knew she had to give chase but fear stayed her legs. She felt paralysed. Reverend Schneider had been here. He had found Cary quickly. Must have had a tag on the DNA database. Had he killed him? He'd said 'one down'.

Genie heard a door slam from down below. Schneider had left the building.

The emergency exit doors opened behind her, the nurse and a security guard were standing there looking down at her.

'He got away,' Genie told them in a small, scared voice.

'Did you get a look at him?' the security guard asked.

Genie shook her head. 'Just the top of his head. He's big. At least six foot and heavy-set. He's wearing a black ski jacket.' She didn't want to give his name. She didn't want to explain how and why she knew him.

The security guard got on to his radio; he looked at her. 'Stay here. I may need a better description. Anything will help.'

The nurse gave her an encouraging smile. 'Come on back up.'

'Cary?'

The nurse shook her head. 'I'm very sorry about your friend. I'm afraid he's gone. The shock, his liver . . .'

It was if someone had dropped a heavy curtain on her. She heard it fall, felt it crash on her shoulders and she went down.

Genie didn't remember fainting. Had no recollection of being placed on a bed and she had a throbbing pain on the side of her head that had no business being there.

Someone was holding her hand and wiping her forehead.

'She's coming round,' a voice said. One voice she sensed was familiar.

451

Genie opened her eyes.

Mrs Finney was sat beside her, looking very concerned.

She was still in the hospital. She could smell disinfectant.

Mrs Finney sighed, withdrawing her hand. Someone else walked away but Genie found it tough to turn her head to see. 'Ow.'

'You fainted on the stairs. In future, take a tip from me – faint when close to a sofa or bed. That's quite a bruise you have.'

Genie nodded – even that hurt. 'I guess there's stuff to explain, huh?'

Mrs Finney just offered her a tight smile. 'At least I can take you home now. They wouldn't let me take you whilst you were unconscious.'

'How long?'

'An hour or so. I came just after young Chris, I mean whoever he was . . .'

'Cary was murdered, Mrs Finney.'

'So it would seem. The nurse was shocked. The police were here but they are as confused as anyone else. Your friend was already dead. So is Christopher. It might be that one set of records could be wrong – but two, I hardly think so!'

Genie struggled up. 'Can you take me home?'

'That's why I'm here. But you're going to have to tell me what's going on, girl. There's *something* going on. That poor boy. Dying twice. His parents wouldn't come. They say they have buried him. The academy is confused – and then there is the matter of the blue Mini and a horse.'

Genie sipped some water left by her bed.

'I saw it.'

'I heard about it on the news. That's why I went looking for you. Quite remarkable, quite.'

Genie lay back on the bed a moment, a tad dizzy. 'I don't understand why I can see things and not be able to warn them. I saw Cary lying on the tree stump, Mrs Finney. I saw the blood, but it had already happened. There was nothing I could do to help him.'

'But you saw the crashed car before it happened.'

Genie closed her eyes. The image of Cary lying on his hospital bed with all the tubes ripped out came back to her with an extraordinary vividness.

'I couldn't save Cary. I didn't see that they would try to kill him.'

'*They?*'

Genie opened her eyes again. Mrs Finney was standing. A nurse approached.

'Hello, Rhiannon. You feeling better? Can I just run

some tests? Can you see my fingers? How many am I holding?'

'Two.'

She opened up her hand. 'Now?'

'Five. And your wedding ring is pale gold.'

The nurse smiled at Mrs Finney.

'She's OK. Take her home. If the police want to talk to her they have your number.' She looked at Genie again. 'It's a nasty bump. If you even feel slightly dizzy, lie down. Don't go to school tomorrow and don't read anything. Understand?'

'Don't tell me, tell her,' Genie said with a faint smile.

Mrs Finney smiled and the nurse helped Genie up off the bed.

Genie looked at the nurse again. 'Are you sure he never talked?'

She shook her head. 'He couldn't have. He saw you, I think. At least you came. At least you were here.'

Genie felt numb. She let Mrs Finney guide her towards the doors and the elevator beyond. Cary was dead. Schneider had killed him. He must know the rest of them were on the island. How long had she got before he came for them?

'I know a nice little place for coffee,' Mrs Finney was saying. 'I think we have a lot to talk about.'

'Mrs Finney?'

'Yes, Rhiannon?'

'Sometimes things are too fantastical. I think you should know that.'

Mrs Finney looked at Genie with a curious expression as they went down in the elevator. She didn't speak again until they were in her car – something quite old and battered and quite suited to her. Genie felt quite reassured by it and the dents in the doors.

'I've been driving this old thing for thirteen years and I think I can get at least two more out of it,' she said, as Genie appraised the scuffed upholstery and the faded plastic.

Genie smiled, relaxing a little. 'I like old cars. Old Volkswagens are cool.'

She noticed it wasn't so cold any more. All the snow had gone. How had that happened?

'Glad the snow has gone. That's what I like about the island. Short winters,' Mrs Finney declared. 'Right. Coffee it is. I hope there's some cake left. They do a wonderful banana loaf.'

Genie took deep breaths. She was going to get through this. Whether Mrs Finney would, she didn't know, but she was right, an explanation was probably owed.

38

Coffee and Tears

'This is my secret place,' Mrs Finney said as she held the hot latté mug in her hands.

'I thought it was quite special, a hideaway from the school and my husband. Met a wonderful man here once. Of course, he turned out to be married. Wonderful men are always married, it seems.'

Genie had just told her everything. From being locked up by her mother and Reverend Schneider to the flood, to the Fortress and the bodies in the forest. She'd left nothing out. Not Marshall, nor Moucher, even the wolf. And all Mrs Finney had done so far is order another round of lattés. Genie must have talked for two, three hours. Her voice felt hoarse. Nothing. No reaction from her at all. The lattés were good though and she appreciated the place being warm as the wind battered the windows outside. They were the only customers and the barista was busy cleaning the far end, steering well clear.

'Of course, you know there are absolutely no wolves around Cobble Hill. Mr Finney and his pals would be out there with guns every night if they thought there were. And you are well aware of the Freudian interpretation of wolves.'

'The wolf isn't a dream and he's not even part of the story really,' Genie protested. 'He only just appeared.'

Mrs Finney looked at Genie with big round eyes over her coffee mug and pulled a face.

'And then again, we both know teleportation is utterly impossible, so I shall discount that part of the story, but the flood was real. I was in Chilliwack in January and it rained two hundred millimetres in a day, flooding homes and businesses and . . . well, I felt for Spurlake. I know it must have been devastating.'

'So you don't believe *anything* I said?' Genie asked, disappointed.

'What I believe is that you are one hell of a good storyteller, Rhiannon – or is it Genie? – and you are at completely the wrong school for you. Of course, what kind of school actually exists for storytellers, I don't know. It's the curse of modern education. They want facts, tests, aptitude monitors, almost anything but imagination and you, my dear, have a brilliant imagination.'

'But what about the visions? You know I saw a Mini crash before—'

'Precognition. That's an interesting area. I grant you

that, but you said yourself, it's something you can't control. But appearing . . . disappearing . . . that Mosquito attack, excellent, a very good detail. And I simply loved the bad guy. He's pure evil. Stringbird?'

'Strindberg. Carson Strindberg,' Genie corrected her, feeling very downcast. She should never have said anything. She'd exposed Ri and Renée for nothing. Mrs Finney didn't believe a single word.

'And that,' Mrs Finney added with shining eyes, 'that was the perfect *coup de grâce*. Making the school governor the evil genius behind it is just a perfect touch. I almost believed you until his name came up . . .'

'Carson Strindberg is the governor of Cobble Hill?' Genie exploded, nearly spilling her coffee.

'Why yes, dear. He owns most of the school. It was his project from the beginning. The best and the brightest all together. *Permissum indoles vigeo* – let genius bloom. His own words.'

Genie felt dizzy again. She had walked into a trap. *Denis, how could you have done this to us?* Strindberg *owned* Cobble Hill. No wonder Reverend Schneider had found Cary so quickly. The worry was, where was Reverend Schneider now? On his way to kill Ri and Renée? But then, why hadn't he killed them earlier?

'Are you all right?'

Genie shook her head. 'We have to go back to the school. I need to warn my friends.' She drank her coffee quickly and stood up.

'It doesn't matter that you don't believe me, Mrs Finney. Nothing matters. It may be too late. Reverend Schneider is probably already at the school.'

'The man who steals souls.'

'It was him in the hospital today. He pulled the plug on Cary. He hates us. We survived. He won't want witnesses.'

'But you didn't say you recognized him at the hospital.'

'I can't. They can access the police radio, all emails, they can intercept everything. You have no idea of how quickly they can find people, Mrs Finney. If I told them who it was, they would know it was one of us who IDd him and they would go through all the CCTV data at the hospital – I'll be on it.' She looked at Mrs Finney. 'I'm not kidding, Mrs Finney. We have to go now.'

Mrs Finney shrugged. 'You do know that it's one thing believing a fantasy, Rhiannon, but living it can only end up one way – and that's in a straitjacket.'

'I'd never have that luxury, Mrs Finney.'

Reluctantly, Mrs Finney picked up her car keys and headed towards the door.

She paused momentarily. 'If I called this Marshall person, do you think he would corroborate your story in any way, Rhiannon?'

Genie smiled and shook her head. 'I'd be disappointed if he did. He knows no one believes us. We tried before. Not going down that road again.'

Mrs Finney opened the door and the bell trilled. She stepped back a moment, surprised to find someone there. Reverend Schneider was standing outside, about to enter. Genie let escape a short, sharp scream. She couldn't help herself, then coughed, quickly looking down, in the vain hope he wouldn't recognize her.

Mrs Finney was all smiles though.

'Padre, you're a long way from home.'

'Mrs Finney?'

Genie was stunned. They knew each other? How was this possible?

'Just having a heart to heart with Rhiannon,' she said in her most earnest, confidential tone. 'Sometimes it's good to listen.'

'Much in favour of talking things over myself. Well done, Mrs Finney.'

Reverend Schneider raised his hat and let them pass. He looked at Genie with a penetrating stare, but didn't say anything.

'*Padre?*' Genie asked Mrs Finney. She dare not talk to him directly.

'Oh you don't know. Padre McGrath has been sent to us for a semester. Padre Ronan was taken ill suddenly last week. But still –' she turned back to face Reverend Schneider '– I don't know how you know this particular coffee shop, Padre.'

'I was asked to go to the hospital tonight and say a prayer for that poor unfortunate boy who died. And they recommended this place. Only coffee shop still open this late and I'm very partial to strawberry cheesecake.'

'Oh it's the best. Enjoy, Padre. Safe journey home.'

Genie despaired. Now Mrs Finney knew him as Padre McGrath. How could she prove he was Reverend Schneider? How soon would he strike? He must have recognized her. Must have wanted to strangle her on the spot. She would keep an eye out for his car on the road in case he tried anything.

'You both get home safely now. I'll see you in assembly tomorrow.'

Mrs Finney smiled. 'You too, Padre. Come on, Rhiannon. We have a long way to go and my cat will be hungry.'

Genie followed her to the car closely, her legs shaking again. Why was she so afraid of him? She'd stood up to

461

him before. She braced herself for attack, expecting a knife to be thrown in her back or something. She glanced back quickly and discovered he was inside the coffee shop ordering cake. Perhaps she'd been lucky. She looked so different now and had hair. So lucky she'd dyed it black. She could hope at least.

'That was quite a scream,' Mrs Finney said as she got into the car.

'I . . .' Genie felt a sudden urge to throw up and raced to the grassy area beyond and let it go.

Mrs Finney watched her in amazement as Genie heaved at least three times. Then shrugged. 'Better out than in,' she told herself and turned the ignition key.

The explosion threw the car high up into the air before it crashed down again burning fiercely. Genie saw nothing. She'd been blown five metres or more into the bushes. She'd stopped vomiting with the shock of the blast.

She looked up. Reverend Schneider had disappeared. The windows of the coffee shop had blown in, the barista was staggering around, bloodied, but alive.

A car suddenly started up down the road; she heard tyres squeal. Genie glimpsed a Mercedes speed off, leap high into the air over a speed hump and disappear down the road.

Mrs Finney was no more. Genie backed further into the bushes and began to walk away in the other direction. Let Reverend Schneider believe she was dead. Had he seen her at the hospital? How was it possible he'd even known she was at the coffee shop with Mrs Finney? Mrs Finney hadn't believed her. Not a single word. Lesson learned. No one ever would.

She had to get home to the others before Reverend Schneider got there.

She noticed lights coming on in buildings everywhere. They all must have heard the blast. Sirens were coming towards her in the far distance. She discovered she was standing by an old Chevy truck, much like Marshall's.

She looked up to the sky and thought of God. If she ever needed proof he existed, this had to be something right? It was a miracle she hadn't died.

'Hi, God. You do know I'm a lost cause, right? You should know I haven't got long to live. Find someone else to protect. I'm not going to be around much longer.'

The truck door was unlocked. She flipped down the sun visor and the ignition key fell into her lap. Just like Marshall's. She looked around. She was alone for the moment. With luck everyone would be looking at the burning car by the coffee shop, not her, not at the old truck. It was theft. She was going to break the law and

God would be angry with her, but she *had* to get to Rian and Renée before Reverend Schneider. Break the law or let them be killed. No contest in her mind.

She got it started on the second try. Backed out of there and was on her way.

Maybe she was crazy, just as Mrs Finney had said. But right now, she figured, crazy wins. She thought of poor Julia and Miho. Had he already found them? Or were they safe? With luck they probably didn't know they were alive again. She hoped so.

39

Stay or Go?

She cut the engine and waited a moment. She had parked one block away from the cabin after cruising up and down the narrow track that fed the few homes nearby. No Mercedes was hidden that she could see. But that didn't mean Reverend Schneider hadn't walked down from the school. If he knew her name was Rhiannon, which he did, then he could check the admin computer and it would give the cabin's address. Simple. What she didn't know was whether she was here before him or whether it was too late.

It was good the snow had melted. The clock on the truck was broken, but she knew it was about eleven p.m. Renée would be in bed, Rian most likely studying. She wondered if they had made a fire. Wondered if they had missed her, or even cared, or checked the message she'd left. Or were their bodies lying on the floor, their blood spilling down between the cracks? She wished the wolf were here now. She definitely needed protection.

She had waited long enough. No one was around

465

and it was very dark on a night without a moon. No streetlights out in this part of the world either. Starlight would be her guide.

She got out, closed the door quietly and went round the back to the forest side. She felt safer here than out on the road. She approached the cabin cautiously in case Reverend Schneider was there watching, waiting. She had the element of surprise, of course; he'd think she was dead in Mrs Finney's car. He hadn't waited to verify it; he was so sure she'd got in with her.

She entered by the back gate. Stealthy, cautious, holding her breath, watching, being as soundless as possible. Rian was slumped over the table inside. At first she feared the worst, but quickly realized he was asleep, the remnants of a fire burning in the grate. Renée she guessed was asleep in her bed.

There was no one around.

She tapped lightly on the window. Rian didn't stir. She tapped louder. Rian still didn't stir. It was Renée she woke. She came stumbling out of her room in her underwear, rubbing her eyes. She could see Genie waving to her from outside and stopped, surprised.

Genie tapped again and Renée came over and unlocked the door.

'What? Why? What's wrong with the front door?'

Genie entered. 'Didn't you check the phone?'

Renée looked at her blankly. 'Shit. No. I put it on charge yesterday and—'

'Pack. Wake Ri. We have to go.'

'What?'

Rian began to stir. 'Genie? What's up? Where you been?'

'We're busted. You have to pack. We have to leave. Now!'

Rian looked at her uncomprehending. Renée sat on the floor like she was going back to sleep.

'Guys, wake the hell up! Cary is dead. Reverend Schneider killed him. He's tried to kill me tonight. He's coming here. We're busted. *We have to go.*'

That sort of got their attention.

'Dead?' Renée began to cry.

'Schneider?' Rian queried, disbelieving.

'Yes. Now, get your stuff and we have to go. He knows who we are, where we live and he's coming for us. Tonight. I'm not kidding.'

Rian looked at her and noticed the bruise on her head for the first time.

'What happened to your head?'

'Fell in the hospital. Look, take this seriously. Schneider's coming. Something else too – Strindberg's the

467

school governor. If we ever meet up with Denis I'd like to punch him hard. How could he have not known about that?'

Rian blinked. 'Strindberg? No way.'

'This is his little genius laboratory. You think Cary would have been able to hold on to anti-gravity if Strindberg knew about it? Or any other crazy idea these kids get? I know you like it here but it's over. We can't pretend to be anyone else any more. They know. You can stay or go, Ri, but I'm going.'

Rian at last took it seriously. He didn't have to think about it, he knew Genie was speaking the truth. 'I'll get my stuff. Renée, get dressed. Pack light.'

'I don't want to . . .' Renée began. '*Cary is dead?*'

'Schneider pulled all the tubes out of Cary. He died quickly. He bombed Mrs Finney's car,' Genie told her. 'This is deadly serious now. We have minutes before he gets here, Renée. You'll have to cry later.'

'Mrs Finney – the English teacher? She's dead?' Renée protested.

'He thought I was in her car. It went boom. She's toast.'

Rian came out of the room looking at Genie. 'You pack too. What do you need?'

'Got nothing I want – sweater maybe. My sketchbook and pens. Toothbrush.'

'I'll get them. Map. We need a map.' He dived back into the room again.

She remembered something though.

'Shoebox. Where's the shoebox?'

'Cary's?' Renée asked, tears running down her cheeks.

'Yes.'

'In the cupboard, by the boiler.'

Genie made her way across the room. She slid the door across and there it was. Just as Cary had said. A shoebox. The memory stick was hidden inside a dirty sock. She slipped it into her jeans. He *had* talked to her then. She hadn't hallucinated that, at least. She probably wouldn't be able to do anything with it, but at least no one else would either. The hover board would have to stay in the future.

She quickly changed T-shirt, grabbed her favourite sweater and scarf. She wasn't going to carry anything else. She went into Cary's room and pocketed his phone. No need to leave evidence around.

'I'm not kidding. We have to go now,' she told Renée, who was staring at her overnight case and not able to make a decision. 'Schneider would have got here before me. He just has to access the school records and he'll know where we live by now.'

'I hate running.'

'Not as much as you hate dying. We're going, Renée. With or without you.'

She looked at Genie with hate. 'You never liked it here. I like it here.'

'Then stay. Make the best of the next hour of your life. It's the last hour you've got.'

Genie headed for the back door again. She'd come with nothing, she'd leave with nothing.

Rian was behind her, had a bag with all kinds of stuff in it.

'Blankets,' he said, putting one round her shoulders. 'No need to freeze to death.' He handed over her sketchbook and she quickly pocketed it into her coat.

'I got us a truck,' Genie told him. 'It's good until someone misses it. You ready? Or you want to say goodbye to Louise?'

Rian looked at her with astonishment, then flushed red.

'It doesn't matter, Ri. I'm over it. Let's go.'

Renée arrived. Peeved, silent, had a bag stuffed with anything, but she was ready.

'Don't look back,' Genie said as she slid open the door. 'It's going to get tough from here on.'

Genie started the truck and her heart sank as she stared at the fuel gauge. They were practically on empty.

'I don't believe it,'

Rian saw it too. 'There's a twenty-four/seven gas station on the highway.'

'We're broke. You got any cash?'

Renée suddenly remembered something. 'Wait, guys. I know where Cary kept his stash.'

She leaped out of the truck before they could stop her and ran back to the cabin, went straight to the front, just what Genie didn't want her to do.

'Damn. She isn't thinking.'

'She's upset about Cary.'

'We're all upset about Cary.' Genie stared straight ahead; she didn't want to look at him. 'You don't have to come. You didn't teleport. You aren't on the database. He won't be looking for you. Besides you wouldn't want to disappoint Louise.'

Rian sighed. 'I'm not doing anything with Louise.'

Genie snatched a glance at Rian. 'Don't lie to me, Ri. You should stay. You don't need to come. It's just me and Renée he's after.'

'I go where you go, you know that.'

'I don't know that.'

'I made a promise.'

'I'm releasing you from that promise. I'm not what you want. I don't even like basketball. I'm not cute,

471

I'm not hot like her.'

'Will you shut up, Genie! I haven't done anything with Louise. She kissed me, that's all. She likes me; I never said I liked her.'

Genie shook her head. 'Doesn't matter. I know when something has died. I'm not stupid – well, not as stupid as you think I am.'

'I never said you were stupid.'

'I believe you did. "You can't just waste your time in the woods being a hippy. Life is tough, Genie".' She looked out towards the cabin. 'Where the hell is Renée?'

'Look I—' Rian began.

They both saw the silver Mercedes creep into view and park at the opposite end of the road, its lights off. No one got out. It was just waiting.

'It's him,' Genie whispered.

'Keep the engine running, but no lights, OK,' Rian told her calmly.

'I hope Renée has the sense to come out the back way,' Genie said, but knew she was wasting her breath. 'She'll lead him right to this truck. What do we do, Ri?'

'Run or fight. But we can't outrun him in this, especially without gas.'

'Fight him with what?'

'We're smarter than him, remember?'

'You're smarter than him. Not me.'

'You're alive. He won't be expecting that, right? Get out. Get into the trees. Stay close but out of sight.'

'What are you going to do?'

'I don't know but I want you out of here – now. Go!'

Genie leaped out and ran to the trees. She turned when she heard a door slam. Renée, bird-brained Renée, had left by the front door. She was walking down the centre of the road towards the truck. She held up something in her hands and waved to Rian. So much for being discreet.

Behind her the Mercedes began to creep along the road. Renée didn't even notice. She was smiling, happy she had found the stash.

The Mercedes suddenly began to speed up, lights off. He was going to mow her down.

Rian rammed the truck into gear, flipped the full beams on and drove straight at Renée. For a second there she had no idea what was happening – turned, saw the car coming straight for her and only just leaped out of the way. Rian swung the truck headfirst into the Mercedes. There was an almighty crunch and a spray of hot liquids.

It was old solid Chevy versus German crumple technology. No contest. The Mercedes folded, just like it was supposed to, and inside the vehicle the air-bags popped, trapping Reverend Schneider from all directions.

Renée was shouting, confused at what just happened.

'Get off the damn road, Renée!' Genie shouted from the woods. She couldn't believe how dumb she was being.

As Renée ran into the trees, Genie could see Schneider begin to move. She had to get Rian out of the truck fast.

She ran for the truck, tore open the door, which crashed to the ground, and saw that Rian was dazed and bleeding. The windshield was cracked and there was a terrible smell of gasoline.

She grabbed him, pulled him out of there and dragged him to the bushes.

He didn't say a word so she knew he was hurt.

Renée had gathered her wits at last and was there beside her, and together they dragged him further away from the truck.

'Take care of him,' Genie told her. 'I need my sketchbook.'

'No, Genie, smell the gasoline . . .'

But Genie was gone and she'd jumped back up into the truck. She tossed all their hurriedly packed possessions out towards the bushes.

'Don't you ever die?'

Schneider was standing just outside the truck, holding a handkerchief to his bleeding forehead. 'Your luck just ran out, Genie – or is it Rhiannon?' He smirked.

Genie noticed he had a tyre iron in his hands. She furtively looked round the cabin for something to fight with, but what exactly? He was heavy. It would be like a flea fighting an elephant.

'What makes you sure I want to live, Schneider?'

Reverend Schneider raised the tyre iron and approached the cabin. 'No time for philosophy, I'm afraid. You first, then Renée and the boy.'

He raised his hand, reached in with his other hand to pull Genie out. She tried to back up but the gearstick was caught in her coat.

Suddenly there was a blur of snarling grey. The wolf came out of nowhere and big sharp teeth clamped down on Schneider's arm. He was spun around and caught off balance and fell between the two vehicles, the wolf holding on, his jaw getting ever tighter as Schneider screamed in pain.

Genie heard her coat rip as she tried to break free and then everything seemed to happen in slow motion. The stench of gasoline was suddenly overwhelming; she saw the spark from broken wiring ignite a rush of blue flames, which ran under both vehicles. Seconds later the fuel tanks suddenly erupted.

Renée was blown over by the blast. The Mercedes seemed to lift off the ground a moment as the glass blew out and a moment later the truck exploded likewise.

Genie for one complete second recalled Cary's video of him flying through the window as she too was propelled out of the truck across the road.

She landed hard, her coat on fire. As she rolled to put it out, someone was screaming – it might have been her.

Strong hands pulled her up. She saw Reverend Schneider rolling on the ground roaring with pain, his clothes on fire. Someone threw a blanket over her, but not before she saw the wolf running down the road with a severed hand in its mouth. She realized that it was the safety of the wolf she was most worried about.

'Can you hear me?' The blanket was pulled off her. She was staring at a man with poppy eyes wearing pyjamas, standing on the cold road in his bare feet. He looked as scared as she felt. The neighbour. They had never met.

Suddenly Rian was there, picking her up, carrying her away. Renée at their side, crying. And then she realized she was going to pass out. Someone had filled her head with gasoline and she most certainly, absolutely had to . . .

Rian was watching the video of Cary on the hover board. Seemed to be playing it over and over. Renée was fixing her hair and somewhere in the background there was a deep drumming noise that Genie couldn't quite place.

She opened her eyes.

'Thirsty,' she croaked. 'Where are we?'

Renée immediately gave her some water to drink. She looked very relieved to hear Genie's voice.

'Where are we?' Genie croaked.

'Ferry,' Rian told her, turning to look at her. 'How do you feel?'

Genie thought about it for a moment.

'Hungry.'

Rian nodded. 'Us too. We had only just enough money for the ferry.'

'Where . . . ?'

'We'll be there soon.'

Genie sat up, suddenly aware she was in pain and her midriff was bandaged.

'Oh yeah, we had to pay for the bandages too. You might be a bit sore but the burns aren't too bad. You'll live,' Rian added, patting her legs.

'I had to take masses of glass out of your back and shoulder,' Renée told her. 'Bet it's real sore now.'

'Uh huh,' Genie said, beginning to sense she was pretty sore all over. She checked her hair. Amazingly, she still had some. She had pictures of exploding cars in her head and Reverend Schneider burning. That was going to stick in her mind for a very long time.

'What I don't get is where that wolf came from and how it knew who to attack. It was like it knew what to do,' Renée was saying. 'I mean, it bit his whole hand off and ran off with it. How weird was that?'

Genie smiled. She *loved* that wolf. He really was her guardian angel. Who would it protect now? she wondered. Would it know she had gone?

'It was young,' Rian said.

Genie turned her head. 'What was?' She realized that Rian was looking at her sketchbook. 'Hey, that's my stuff.'

'The wolf. You actually sketched it. It was in the woods with you?'

Genie nodded.

'Pretty amazing stuff in here, Genie Magee. How come you never showed me any of this?'

'Like you never noticed me sketching?'

Rian looked at her blankly. 'When? I swear I never saw you sketch.'

Genie looked at him, anger rising again, but she didn't feel like fighting.

'I like the one of Cary and Renée sleeping. Oh yeah and the basketball sketch of me dunking – you got the movement and everything.'

'I liked the ones of Zara and Sophia. It's like totally their zombie expressions,' Renée said with a sigh. 'God, I wish I had talent.'

'You have chairs,' Genie reminded her.

Renée pulled a face, then laughed. 'Yeah, chairs. I have chairs.'

'What now?' Genie asked, feeling sad suddenly. She should have thanked that wolf. It saved her life. 'What happened to Schneider?'

'Someone wrapped him in a blanket, staunched the blood, but when the ambulance arrived he'd disappeared. We got out of there just before the cops arrived. Got a ride with a neighbour.'

'He should have died. It's not right he lived,' Renée stated.

Genie sipped some more water. She sensed the ferry was slowing or turning. 'What about Strindberg?'

Rian looked at her and took her free hand. 'We have to come up with a plan. Clearly he's not going to forget us.'

Renée stretched and yawned. 'We need to negotiate a truce.'

'How do you make a truce with the devil?' Genie asked.

Rian shrugged. 'Make him an offer, I guess. Promise him something he wants.'

'You may not have noticed, Rian, that we have

absolutely nothing – except our lives.'

'Which might be a negotiating point.'

'Huh? You think I'm ever going back to the Fortress?'

'None of us are.'

'Then what?'

'I don't know, but we have to find something he wants enough to leave us alone.'

'Like what?'

'I don't know, but enough.'

'You seriously think that could happen?'

'It has to happen. We can't run for ever.'

Genie thought about it for a moment. 'Show him Cary's video. The one you keep looking at on the phone.'

Rian looked at her a moment and frowned. 'Why?'

''Cause we can make him feel bad about having him killed, for starters. Make him realize he killed a one hundred per cent genius.'

'I don't get it,' Renée queried. 'What does that achieve? Showing him a video of Cary crashing through a window.'

'Hover board.'

Renée and Rian exchanged glances.

'Cary's dead, remember. The secret died with him. The kids in his team were just his assistants. I know this,' Renée stated with a certain amount of passion. 'Cary really was clever and I know I didn't know exactly what he was doing, but I know only he knew what he was doing, if that makes sense.'

Genie felt in her jeans pocket. The twenty-four-gig memory stick was still there.

'Not exactly true, Renée. He wrote it all down.'

Renée eyes began to mist. 'You spoke to him in the hospital?'

'He knew he was going to die. I'm just glad I got there before Schneider.'

'So – we do have something to trade,' Rian said. He pulled Genie towards him and gave her hug. For a moment she felt goosepimples, then suddenly remembered Louise and it didn't feel so good any more. And as for trading Cary's work? No way. Had Ri learned nothing?

'I think we're docking,' Renée was saying.

They finally got off the ferry. Renée was holding her hand as she walked beside her.

'You look happy,' Genie remarked.

Renée laughed. 'I guess you don't see what I see.' She was turning her head to look towards the drop-off point.

Genie followed her gaze. There was an old Chevy truck and a very patient dog sitting beside it.

'Moucher!' Genie screamed.

She ran. Mouch must have seen her at the same time and they collided somewhere in the middle in a tumble of yelps and screams and both rolled over and over as Mouch practically had a heart attack, he was so happy to see her. Huge trucks rolled off the ferry just centimetres away but neither noticed.

Genie climbed to her knees, aware that her back hurt more than ever, but she didn't care, it was so good to see this dog.

Marshall pulled her up as Moucher began greeting Renée and Rian all over again, wetting the tarmac, he was so excited.

'Never gets that excited when I get home, little traitor,' Marshall said with a grin.

Genie sneaked a look at Rian. 'You called him.'

He smiled. The one he used to give her before he broke her heart.

Marshall wrapped his arms round her and hugged her tight. She inhaled his scent. Apples he always seemed to smell of apples.

'Missed you, girl. And you have hair!'

Genie couldn't speak, her vision clouded by tears.

'Hungry? I know a good place for breakfast,' Marshall asked, stroking her head.

Genie laughed and took his hand. 'Starving. I can't believe you're here, Marshall. Best surprise of my life, for sure.'

Marshall squeezed her hand. 'Seems you guys have a lot to tell me. Get in. One has to sit in the back with Mouch. There's a rug.'

'That'll be me. I have a lot to say to that dog.'

Marshall nodded, a little surprised, but he knew how fond of Mouch she was.

He looked back towards the water. 'No one coming after you? No men with guns, I hope?'

Rian shook his head. 'We're good – for now.'

Marshall nodded his head and walked towards the truck. 'Glad to hear it. There was something on the news about Reverend Schneider. Police found his burned-out car. He's wanted in connection with two murders in Nanaimo. All they have of him so far is his hand. Can you believe that? It was bitten clean off. Cops are still looking for him.'

'He should be in hell, Marshall,' Genie told him as she jumped up into the back of his truck. 'Where he belongs.' She still felt cheated that he'd survived.

Rian handed Mouch over to her. 'Don't worry. Schneider's got too many problems now to worry about us.'

Marshall paused by the driver's door. 'By the by, there's an expectant mother out by my place who might be happy to see you.'

Genie frowned for a moment before she twigged.

'The pig. I don't believe it.'

Marshall laughed. 'I reckon she found herself a friend in the woods, so God knows what will come out, but I reckon they'll be pretty special.'

Genie grinned, feeling happy the pig had survived. She settled down with Moucher and spread the rug over them both.

'You sure you're OK back here?' Renée asked, hovering by the door.

'Get in. Let's get going. I'm hungry.'

Renée smiled and swung into the cabin.

Genie looked up at the big grey sky as they drove off. A huge weight had been lifted from her soul. No more school. No more hiding. No more Louise.

'We're going home, Mouch.'

He licked her face, resting a paw on her shoulder.

Genie felt the memory stick in her back pocket. Thought of Cary in the hospital dying with all his life-support ripped out. No way Strindberg was getting anything. You don't trade with the devil and keep your soul. This much she had learned.

THE
HUNTING

Sam Hawksmoor answers our questions!

Who would be your dream cast if *The Repossession* and *The Hunting* were made into a film?
It would have to be unknowns. Kids grow up so fast I'd hate to have to choose. Getting Genie right would be tough and Renée would have to be a mouthy redhead. Even finding the right dog would be hard, never mind a moody handsome Rian.

The casting of evil Rev Schneider would be interesting. It would have to be someone you completely trust playing against type.

Which songs would be on the soundtrack?
Listening to lots of Spanish guitars at the moment. My guess is some retro stuff like 'Cool for Cats' by the Cure or 'Bright as Yellow' by The Innocence and some C&W which is big up in the back country of the Okanagan.

Are your characters based on anyone in particular?
Genie is Roxanne – a tough but really beautiful TA girl (Territorial Army). Renée is based on a very sassy funny/actress waitress in Vancouver. Rian on a boy who stopped to help dig me out of snowdrift in winter and he'd been caring for his sick Ma since he was about six. There are always remarkable people out there – all you have to do is see them.

What is your favourite scene in these books?
When Genie is left alone in Radspan for the first time and getting colder and colder …

What was the hardest scene to write?

When Genie has begun to realize that something is going wrong with her and Ri. She's out there in the woods gathering firewood, it's starting to snow and everything has changed and she has no idea why ...

What books do you like to read yourself?

YA fiction of course. I am a big fan of Paulo Bacigalupi and Carrie Mac who should be world famous.

When did you realize you were destined to be a writer?

Well, initially I wanted to act when I was quite young (my father dead against it) and then began to write plays at school. Took just one rehearsal to realize I was never ever going to remember any lines. So I stuck to writing. I think my father wanted me to be an architect. If you have ever seen me try to assemble an IKEA bookshelf or sofa you'd know I made the right choice.

Were you surprised by anything in particular while doing research?

I like to remind myself about the laws of unintended consequences in science and there is this conflict in both books between what Reverend Schneider wants (saving souls) and Strindberg (instant DNA cosmetic restructuring) that has come out of the Teleportation experiments. We start with one goal but arrive at something unexpected.

Where do you write and any particular rituals?

Coffee shops, preferably sitting in a sunbeam. Much of this book was written in three different coffee shops: one in Vancouver (Epicurian) out on the narrow terrace with Koko (the dog) at my side, one in Biarritz (Miremont – like writing in the First Class lounge on the Titanic with a view of the ocean), one in Portsmouth (Café P) where I was teaching and doing tutorials at the time. Rituals? Yes. Always read back what you wrote before. Keeps you in line and in voice.

What advice do you have for aspiring young writers?

Get a day job. Writing is a hard choice. There are no guarantees about anything, especially money. I've sent a lot of my ex-students towards copywriting. It's well paid and sometimes creative and often advertising companies are fun places to work.

I guess writing a blog can help too, but then again – the best advice is get that book written and share it as you go along with people who will tell you the truth. If people like it they will want to see more. That's the best test. I was very lucky. I had people reading (like Freya and Roxanne) as I went along and it spurred me on as they were all keen to know what would happen to Genie and Rian.